ALL THE *little* THINGS

USA TODAY BESTSELLING AUTHOR
RACHEL LEIGH

Copyright © 2022 Rachel Leigh

All rights reserved. No portion of this book may be reproduced in any form without permission from the copyright owner. This is a work of fiction. Names, characters, businesses, places, events, locales, and incidents are either the products of the author's imagination or used in a fictitious manner. Any resemblance to actual persons, living or dead, or actual events is purely coincidental.

For permissions contact: rachelleighauthor@gmail.com

ISBN: 978-1-956764-13-0

Cover Design by Opulent Swag & Designs

Editing by Fairest Reviews and Editing Services

Proofreading by Rumi Khan

www.rachelleighauthor.com

"You need to let the little things that would ordinarily bore you suddenly thrill you."
— **Andy Warhol**

*For my Shameless Sisters.
I love you, all!*

NOTE TO READERS

I'd like to thank you for taking a chance on my story. I'd also like to remind you that this is a work of fiction and all facts may not be entirely accurate. Even with extensive research, there is a possibility that some technical terms and protocols slip through the cracks. If you notice such, please forgive me. With that said, I hope you enjoy Kit and Ryker's story. I can't wait to hear what you think.

xoxo Rachel

INTRODUCTION

You know those people who can put their head down on a pillow and fall right to sleep? The ones who don't have a million thoughts running rampant through their minds, or anxieties that rear their ugly heads as soon as they close their eyes—only to return once they open?

I wish I had that ability.

I'm too young to have the weight of the world on my shoulders—but I do. Some days it's so heavy, I feel like I'm getting pushed into the ground. Other days, I wish I'd get pushed further, so I could hide away and escape the worries of the world. I'm not a quitter, though. In fact, I'm anything but.

This is a story about a girl who overcame every obstacle life threw at her and a guy who never gave up even when life kicked him down.

It's a story about redemption and learning to love yourself so that others can love you back. A story about savoring every second of the day and embracing all the little things life has to offer.

This is our story.

PLAYLIST

Jessie Murph, Always Been you
Dare You to Move, Switchfoot
From Where You Are, Lifehouse
Chances, Five For Fighting
Still Falling For You, Ellie Goulding
Come On Get Higher, Matt Nathanson
You And Me, Lifehouse
Ruin My Life, Zara Lawson
She Is Love Parachute
Nothing Left to Lose, Mat Kearny
Meant to Live, Switchfoot
Somewhere Out There, Our Lady Peace
Learning to Breathe, Switchfoot
Whatever It Takes, Lifehouse
Over My Head, The Fray
100 Years Five For Fighting
Crazy for This Girl, Evan and Jaron
Bright Lights, Matchbox Twenty
Wait, Seven Mary Three
My December, Linkin Park
Secrets, One Republic
Broken, Seether
Listen Now: https://spoti.fi/37J3uUJ

CHAPTER ONE

KIT

Fourteen Years Old

It's Friday night, so I shouldn't be surprised at the knock on my bedroom door. Or that it opens only seconds later, without me even granting entrance.

My sixteen-year-old brother, Carter, has a curfew of midnight. He comes in through the door at twelve on the dot, only to leave again out my window, then returns before sunrise. Different weekend. Same song and dance.

"You know Dad's gonna catch you one of these days," I say to Carter as he swipes open my curtains and pushes my windowsill up.

He flings one leg over, straddling the sill. "Nah. He won't catch me because my favorite little sis has my back."

I'm on my side, blanket wrapped snug around my shoulders and tucked under my feet. "I'm your only sis so your point is moot."

He tosses his other leg out and drops to solid ground, eyes peering over the sill as he grips it with both hands. "Still my favorite. Be home in a couple hours. Don't wait up." He pulls the window down gently, not making a sound, and disappears into the night, leaving my curtains open. I could get up and close them, but what's the point? They'll open again when he comes back.

Kicking the covers off my legs, I pull my phone out from underneath me. I must have rolled on it while I was sleeping. *As suspected, it's midnight.* I roll from my side to my back, staring at the neon glow of the plastic stars stuck to my ceiling.

If Carter and I could just switch rooms, I wouldn't have boys constantly climbing in and out of my window. Dad doesn't trust Carter, though. Well, not completely. So I'll be woken up again in a few hours when he returns, likely with Ryker, his best friend.

My eyes close and I beg for sleep before that time comes.

Eventually, I doze off, and the next thing I know, I'm waking up to pounding on my window. A glance at the clock proves it's only been a couple hours since Carter left.

More pounding has me clenching my teeth. *You have got to be kidding me!*

I angrily fling the blanket completely off my legs, stomp over to the window, ready to push Carter back out, when I notice it isn't him.

With two hands, I shove the window up as far as it will go. "Ryker. What are you doing here?"

His eyes travel from my chest to my face, and it's a humiliating reminder that I don't have a bra on. I clap my arms over myself to hide my breasts. A couple years ago, when we'd have these encounters, it wasn't a worry. Since then, I've blossomed—more so than I'd like.

Ryker's bloodshot eyes gloss over and the stench of beer rolls off his tongue. "Can I come in?"

"You know Carter's not here, right?"

"Yeah, I know. I just need to crash. Can't go home. You know how my old man is."

I sigh heavily and step to the side. "Yeah. I guess." I wave him in.

I can't turn him away in this state, not that I would. Ryker is like another big brother to me. We all grew up together. Played

ALL THE LITTLE THINGS 3

baseball in the backyard with the neighbor kids, ate Popsicles while floating in the pool in the summer. He might be Carter's best friend, but he's become a good friend to me, too.

Well, he was. The older we get, the more I feel the distance between the three of us widening. I get it, though. What sophomore boys want to hang out with an eighth-grade girl?

Ryker's hands press to the windowsill, and he pushes himself up, using all his upper body strength. I watch intently as the veins in his arms protrude and his muscles flex. It was nothing for him to hurl his entire body inside. However, landing seems to be a problem. He stumbles to the left, then right, before crashing into my nightstand, knocking over my table lamp, and spilling a full glass of water on my beige carpet.

"Oh shit," he mumbles. "My bad, Kit-Kat."

Ugh. That nickname. I've been plagued with it since I was seven years old. Ryker would bribe me with candy bars when he and Carter were up to no good and they wanted to ensure my silence.

"It's fine." Picking up the now empty glass, I push the nightstand back to the wall then grab his arm, trying to lift him, but he's dead weight. "Okay. You're going to have to put in some effort here, Ry." I pull again, and this time, he staggers onto his feet. That is, until he trips, and we both go flying backward onto my bed. Him on top of me.

Ryker laughs, but it isn't funny at all. I have to wake up early tomorrow for a doctor's appointment in Harbor City, which is a three-hour drive. Dad will want to talk the entire trip, because we barely see each other anymore, so sleep isn't an option on the ride.

I look into Ryker's emerald eyes, noticing the way he's staring back at me. I can't tell if he's looking through me or trying to read my thoughts. Either way, it's uncomfortable.

"You can get off me now."

Still looking at me, he pushes his hands down on either side of me and gets up. "Sorry, Kit-Kat." He holds up his hands in a Boy Scout salute. "Never drinking again. I solemnly swear."

"Yeah. Sure." We've all heard that more than once. I take hold of his arm again, this time with enough strength to lead him, but not enough to fall with him if he goes down. "Let's get you to Carter's room before my dad wakes up. He'll call your parents and you really will be in deep poo."

He laughs. "You said poo."

My cheeks flush with heat, but I chuckle along with him. "And now you just did."

Ryker nudges me, a little too hard, and my hip hits the side of my dresser. "Say shit, I dare ya."

Okay. I might only be fourteen, but I *am* fourteen. He acts like I've never said a cuss word. I know what he's doing, though. It's our thing. Dare is one of the games I'd play with him and Carter often when we were younger. Granted, it was innocent stuff like drinking a concoction of mixed garbage or prank calling someone. Not that saying *shit* is immoral.

"Shit," I finally say, just to appease him. "You will be in deep *shit*."

Teasing, he claps a hand over his mouth and hee-haws. "Damn, girl. Didn't think you had it in ya."

I pull open my bedroom door, practically dragging him out, and I'm ready to dump him in the hallway. "Here's another one for you. You're a pain in the ass, Ry."

He releases a drawn-out exhale, eyes locked on mine. "You're right, Kit. I am a pain in the ass." His free fingers rake through his messy brown hair. "Shit!" he bellows a little too loudly, causing me to slap my hand over his mouth before he wakes my dad, though it doesn't shut him up. "I'm such a screw-up."

Here we go. The emotional side of drunk Ryker is coming out. I hate this side of him. Not because I don't want to hear what he has to say, but because I hate hearing him beat himself up all the time.

Leading the way, we walk up the stairs, which are a struggle. I let him use the banister for support, instead of my shoulder, because there's a good chance we'd both go flying back down if I let him brace himself on me.

We somehow manage to make it up without falling. We reach Carter's bedroom, and I quickly open the door while Ryker rambles on about his grades and how he'll never get into college. Once we're inside, I close the door so Dad can't hear us from down the hall. Ryker's still mumbling nonsense, so I cut him off. "You're not a screw-up, Ry. You're just…trying to find your way."

A smile spreads across his face as if his emotions have suddenly shifted. "You're too good to me, Kit-Kat."

"And you're drunk. Go to bed, Ry."

I turn to leave Carter's room, but Ryker stops me with a hand on my shoulder. "Why are you so mature for your age? You know it's okay to not be perfect *all* the time?"

His words take me by surprise, but I laugh them off, unsure how to react to that statement. Sure, I'm more mature than most girls my age, but I also have responsibilities that most people my age don't have. As for being perfect, I'm far from it. Ryker might be the drunk one, ready to spill his feelings, but I keep mine bottled up inside. When you don't share your problems with the world, they have every reason to believe that everything is okay.

Instead of responding with words, I spin around to face him and do what I always do. I hold out my hand with a cheeky grin on my face.

I'm not seven years old anymore, but you're never too old for chocolate.

Ryker looks down at my hand, then back to me. He pats the chest of his leather jacket and tips a frown. "Sorry, Kit. Fresh out."

Pouting, I tilt my head to the side. "Since when?"

He laughs. "Since you were like eleven and I no longer bribed you with candy. Not to mention, you shouldn't have chocolate anymore, Kit-Kat."

My eyes roll. "Not you too? I thought you were on my side."

Ryker sweeps my hair from my shoulder, grinning. "Always on your side, baby girl."

My arms cross over my chest, a reminder I don't have a bra on. "Ya know, without paying the fee, you'll have to exit back out my window."

Ryker scoffs. "Well, I don't have a candy bar." He pauses for a beat. "Maybe this'll make up for it." He leans forward, taking me by complete surprise. His lips press to my cheek—imprinting me, though he doesn't know it yet. Hot breath spills down my body while my thoughts escape me.

He pulls back, a smirk on his face that sends butterflies fluttering through my stomach, while the scent of booze lingers around me.

I'm speechless. Stunned. Shocked. I look down. *Are my feet still on the ground?* I look back at him, knowing I'm blushing as I pull at my ear nervously, but I don't even care.

Why did he kiss me? It was just the cheek, but still. He's never done that. Forget the candy bars. I want him to do *that* again.

His green eyes glisten as the corner of his lip tugs up. "Night, Kit-Kat."

"G...g'night...Ry."

I turn to leave him in Carter's room, but when he clears his throat, as if he has something to say, I turn around and question him with my eyes.

There's a brief moment of silence before he says, "Good luck with your surgery tomorrow."

He remembered. It's no big deal, just a minor procedure. But the fact that he remembered tugs at my heartstrings.

Grinning from ear to ear, I walk back to my room with my hand on my cheek and a foreign feeling in the pit of my stomach. My fingers graze the damp spot where his lips were seconds ago.

He kissed me.

And that's the night I fell in love with my brother's best friend.

CHAPTER TWO

RYKER

SIXTEEN YEARS OLD

"Slow down, man. We've got all night," Carter, my best friend, says as I down another beer.

He's got all night. I'm about two minutes away from getting the hell outta here and crashing in his bed. That last drink really did me in.

I burp, feeling the beer ride back up my esophagus.

Yep. Time to go before I hurl in front of everyone here.

I don't even say anything before turning away from the fire and the crowd on the beach.

No one told me Ava would be here. I should've known, considering she's Stacy's best friend. It seems no matter what I do, I can't escape her.

I can't escape the past eight months we were together, or the month we've been apart.

Fuck it and fuck her.

I toss the beer can over my shoulder, not even sure where it lands, and make my way up the sand dune. Just over the top is my exit outta this place. Unfortunately, I'm leaving on foot.

Not because I'm drunk, but because I don't have a car. I don't have the luxuries all these rich kids do. Not that I judge them.

Hell, if my parents were loaded, I'd gladly accept a Benz or a Bugatti. They're not, though. In fact, we're lucky our electricity was turned back on this morning after being off for three days straight.

Most would bitch and moan about my living situation—I'm just grateful we live in Oakley Shores, where heat isn't needed. Well, technically, I'm outside of O.S. in Alcove, but I still attend the public school because it beats the slums of Alcove High. Apparently, my parents were thinking of my future when I was starting out. Wish they'd think of it now.

"Ryker! Wait up."

That voice. Fuck. That voice.

Go away! I internally beg her.

"Please. Just wait a damn minute so we can talk."

I don't look at her once she joins my side. I just keep walking, my eyes focused on the dune in front of me. "Nothing left to say, Ava."

She grabs my shoulder, trying to stop me, but I shake her hand off.

Blowing out an exaggerated breath, she stops walking while I continue. "Why are you doing this, Ryker?"

"Because I want to."

Or because I have to. If I listen to what she has to say, I'll get sucked back in. It's happened twice since our relationship began. Twice that she cheated on me with the same member of *my* football team. Twice that I took her back. Never again.

"Fine," she shouts from behind me. "Have it your way."

I flip my middle finger over my shoulder, and it's like life really wants to beat me down because I trip and face-plant into the front of the dune. I'm eating sand as I push myself back up on my feet. Sweeping my hands off on my pants, I spit the gritty shit out of my mouth.

Well-played, karma. Well-played.

I'm kicking rocks and trying to keep my body upright as I walk through the parking lot and down the one-way drive that leads to our private spot on the beach. I'm not even sure who owns this chunk of oceanfront property, but we've basically claimed it as our own since no one ever comes and breaks up our weekend parties. Not that it would matter. The students of OSH get away with whatever they want. I might be a nobody, but my friends are somebodies. At least, their parents are, and one day, they'll take their rightful place. I've known since grade school I don't fit in, but for some reason, I've been accepted with open arms. After seeing me at my worst these past couple years, they still keep me around. It has to be my stellar skills on the football field because that's all I've got going for me.

The more I walk, the more my overindulgence of alcohol kicks in. I find myself swaggering up Carter's driveway. I stop midway and look up at the place. My best friend has it made—and I don't mean the big-ass house and expensive things inside. I mean the family inside.

I make it to Kit's window and tap the glass. We started sneaking in and out her window last summer because it's on the lower level of the two-story house, and we've done it ever since. She's a cool kid, and Carter and I trust her not to rat us out—probably because I bribed her with candy when she was younger.

Kit finally emerges behind the glass, pushing it up until it's settled in place. "Ryker. What are you doing here?"

My dry and tired eyes travel down her body, and for the first time, I realize Kit is not a kid anymore. I wanna tell her to grab a blanket and cover herself up before someone sees her, but then I remember no one is around and she's in the privacy of her bedroom.

As if she sensed my awareness of her braless state, she covers her chest, and I chuckle. It's funny that she thinks she has to hide from me. The girl is like my little sister and I'd murder any guy who even thought about looking at her inappropriately.

My head tilts to the side as I try to gain entrance. "Can I come in?"

She looks back at me with puzzlement. "You know Carter's not here, right?"

It's not the first time I've come here without him. Carter is always the life of the party, without even drinking, while I tend to venture off on my own after a few drinks because I'm not exactly a people person. "Yeah, I know. I just need to crash. Can't go home. You know how my old man is."

Kit blows out an annoyed breath. "Yeah. I guess."

I push myself up and fling my legs over the sill. Instead of getting to my feet, the alcohol takes hold and sends me crashing into Kit's bedside table. Her lamp falls to the floor, along with a glass of water that spills all over her carpet. "Oh, shit. My bad, Kit-Kat."

Kit-Kat is a nickname I gave Carter's little sis when she was just a kid. Well, we were all kids. Carter and I are only two years older than her, and while it seemed like a big gap when we were young, it's not a huge difference as we get older.

Kit picks up the glass, then grabs my arm, trying to pull me up, but I can't stop laughing and I don't know why. Maybe it's because my strength is depleted and this girl is trying her best to get me off her bedroom floor, and at this point, she probably wants to throw me back out the window.

"Okay. You're going to have to put in some effort here, Ry."

I finally get to my feet, but I stumble, and we both collapse onto the bed—me on top of her. If it were any other girl, this would be awkward. But this is Kit.

Still, I don't move. I'm not sure if it's because I'm intoxicated and lazy, or if it's because of the way she's staring back at me.

Looking into her blue eyes, I wonder how she grew up so fast. This is the girl who trailed behind me and Carter for years. She's in every single one of my childhood memories, and here we are, teenagers, and she's still here. The entire Levine family is still here and hasn't turned their backs on me.

"You can get off me now," she finally says through a clipped breath. Probably because I'm putting my full weight on her fragile chest.

I roll off her and steady myself on my feet. Feeling like a real ass, I throw my hands up in surrender. "Sorry, Kit-Kat. Never drinking again. I solemnly swear."

"Yeah. Sure." She grabs my wrist and begins leading me across her room. "Let's get you to Carter's room before my dad wakes up. He'll call your parents and you really will be in deep poo."

I can't help the laugh that slips between my lips. "You said poo."

"And now you just did."

I playfully nudge her side with mine. "Say shit, I dare ya."

She won't do it. Not sweet little Kit. And if she does, there is no doubt in my mind she'll blush.

"Shit," she sighs, "you will be in deep *shit*."

"Damn, girl. Didn't think you had it in ya."

As suspected, her cheeks flush, and she rubs the bottom of her earlobe. It's so easy to know when Kit is embarrassed or angry—she always rubs her ear.

She pulls open the door, practically shoving me out, and joins my side as we walk down the hall to go upstairs. "Here's another one for you. You're a pain in the ass, Ry."

A heavy breath escapes me when her words hit more than just my ears. They sting a little because Kit is exactly right. I'm not sure why this family even puts up with me anymore.

"You're right, Kit. I am a pain in the ass." I rake my fingers through my hair, hating myself more and more with each passing second. I shouldn't have come here. This innocent girl, who has no business seeing me like this, is now bearing witness to my meltdown. If only I could tell her to stay far away from me because she doesn't need this kind of behavior in her life. She's a good girl.

"Shit!" I bellow. As soon as the word flies out of my mouth, Kit shuts me up by slapping her hand over my mouth. I continue to talk, though my voice is muffled. "I'm such a screw-up."

I am a screw-up. I'm stellar on the stairs, though. Not even a missed step. I'm actually feeling pretty level-headed right now. Then again, it could be because Kit is using all her strength to help me.

"You shouldn't be helping a lowlife like me. I'm doing terrible in school. Probably won't get into any colleges. I'll end up working my life away at my granddad's shop. A grease monkey for life." I'm pretty sure she's ignoring everything I say, but I keep going because, for some reason, it helps to say it all out loud and I'd never admit this to anyone else. Not even sure why I'm admitting it to her. "Lately, all my free time is spent wallowing in self-pity. I'm a mess, Kit. A mess you need to stay far away from."

Once we're inside Carter's room, Kit closes the door. "You're not a screw-up, Ry. You're just…trying to find your way."

And this is exactly why she's the one person I can be myself around. "You're too good to me, Kit-Kat."

"You're drunk. Go to bed, Ry."

When she turns to leave, I stop her. I'm not ready for her to go. I wanna stay awake and talk for hours about absolutely nothing while I have someone who's willing to listen. I know Kit would. It's what she does—helps everyone else, while forgetting to help herself. "Why are you so mature for your age?" I ask. "You do know it's okay to not be perfect *all* the time?"

She's silent for a good minute while I brace myself by pressing a hand to the wall, head tilted toward my shoulder.

Suddenly, a smile tugs at her lips, and she holds her hand out. No words, just a cheesy grin on her face and those soft, innocent eyes looking back at me.

My hands pat at my chest, showing her that I don't have what she's asking for. "Sorry, Kit. Fresh out."

She pouts, as if she was really expecting me to have a candy bar for her. "Since when?"

A breathy chuckle climbs up my throat. "Since you were like eleven and I no longer bribed you with candy. Not to mention, you shouldn't have chocolate anymore, Kit-Kat."

I'm pretty sure that chocolate is one thing she's supposed to avoid. If I remember right, Carter said she had to change her diet and exercise. She doesn't even cheer anymore, just assists the coach, so she can still be part of the team. It's sad because cheer was always her favorite pastime.

When she rolls her eyes, I sense her frustration.

"Not you, too? I thought you were on my side."

A stray strand of hair is stuck to her cheek, so I sweep it away. "Always on your side, baby girl." Even if there was a divide and the entire world stood on one side with Kit and Carter on the other, I'd be right there with them.

"Ya know, without paying your dues, you'll have to exit back out my window."

I scoff, observing the sincerity in her eyes. "Well, I don't have a candy bar, so," I shrug casually before leaning into her, "maybe this'll make up for it." My lips press softly to her cheek.

When I retreat, I look at her, and it's obvious I surprised her. It was just a kiss on the cheek. Same way I'd kiss my mom. I laugh at her nervousness. "Night, Kit-Kat."

"G...g'night...Ry."

"Oh," I say, catching her before she leaves the room, "good luck with your surgery tomorrow."

Her head tips the slightest, and she smiles. "Thanks."

Looking at her in the dim of the light, she seems different. The same girl, but older and more beautiful than I've ever seen her before.

That night I lie in my best friend's bed for hours...thinking about his younger sister.

CHAPTER
THREE

KIT

Fifteen Years Old

"Can you believe it?" Kaylee scurries to my side, books hugged to her chest. "We're in fucking high school now."

"Shhh," I hush her, looking around to make sure none of the teachers heard her.

Keeping in step down the hall, I make every attempt not to bump into someone while Kaylee practically forces people out of her way.

"Aren't you even the slightest bit intimidated?" I ask her while I take in her clothing choice. A pair of black jeans with more holes than fabric, a white tank top that shows a sheen of her stomach, including her belly button ring, topped off with a pair of black heels. She definitely doesn't look like a freshman in high school. More like a freshman in college. "Better yet, how did your mom let you out of the house wearing that?"

"To answer your first question, no, I'm not intimidated at all, and you shouldn't be either. They're just high schoolers like us. Second, she didn't." Kaylee opens her arms wide, showing off the upper half of her body. "I had a flannel on."

I laugh. Gotta love her.

On the other hand, I'm definitely not dressed to impress in my black leggings, white slip-on Vans, and a white tee shirt that says, *Wake me up when it's Friday.*

Kaylee stops walking abruptly, her eyes glued in front of her. "Whoa. Who in God's green earth is that and was he put here just for me?"

I follow her line of sight and see a new face. It's not the new kid that catches my eye, though. It's who's standing next to him. Asher Collins, aka perfection, and my second biggest crush.

I shrug my shoulders. "Must be new."

Kaylee grabs my wrist and begins pulling me in their direction. "Then we *must* say hello."

"No. No. No," I beg her the entire way over, but she ignores me completely. "I need to find my locker, Kay." But the next thing I know, we're there in front of them.

I shouldn't be so nervous. After all, we spent much of our summer with Asher and his friends. After years of being invisible, Kaylee and I have finally come out of our shells. Well, she has, anyway. I'm just the loser friend that lives in her shadow. Over the summer, Kaylee really grew up. She's drop-dead gorgeous, and I knew it was only a matter of time before every guy in Oakley Shores noticed her. She's no longer the awkward teenager that I still am. It's just my luck that I'm her best friend and I was forced to go to every social gathering with her. I'm not sure if it's a curse or a blessing, and I have yet to decide.

"What's up, boys?" Kaylee says, biting her bottom lip while looking the new kid up and down.

There are four of them. The most popular guys in our class—Asher, Logan, and Micah—and, of course, the new guy.

Logan pats the newbie on the back. "I was just telling Damon here about the big game coming up against Alcove." Logan returns his attention to Damon, I presume. "They're good, man. But not as good as us."

"Football, of course." Kaylee blows out a breath before extending her hand to Damon. "I'm Kaylee, junior varsity cheerleader, and this is my best friend, Kit."

"Hi." I smile, showing off the full set of metal on my teeth with an awkward wave.

I hear a muffled laugh and look over to see the corner of Asher's mouth tug up while his head shakes subtly. I know it's in response to my weirdness.

Asher doesn't talk much, or smile much, or do much of anything that involves human interaction—unless it's football. He's sort of mysterious, which I've always liked.

Micah is joined by his girlfriend, Carly, and her best friend, Liza. He places a hand on Carly's waist, and my stomach does a little flip. I hope to have that one day: a guy who looks at me like that—touches me like that.

"Kit, huh?" Damon says, breaking the silence between us. "That's an interesting name."

"It's actually Katherine, but no one calls me that." Not anymore, anyways. From what I've heard, my mom did before she left us when I was only two years old.

"I like Katherine. It suits you," Damon says, causing my cheeks to flush with heat.

"Do you cheer, too?" Damon asks, and I'm unsure why his attention is on me. It's obvious he's new or he wouldn't even bother.

"Yes," Kaylee chimes in, making her presence known. "Well, sort of." She looks at me sympathetically, and I hate it. "Kit sort of…assists the team now."

Damon tips his chin. "Oh, like a captain?"

The next thing I know, I'm getting lifted off my feet and twirled around by Logan, the class clown. "Kitty, the captain," he singsongs, loud enough to grab the attention of half the student body in the halls.

"Put me down." I squeal a laugh, hitting his shoulders repeatedly as he spins in circles so fast, I get light-headed. "And I'm not the captain."

"No, she's just a maimed teammate," Asher says as he brushes past us. My heart drops into my stomach as I watch him leave.

Logan stops spinning and sets me down, steadying me with his hands on my hips.

Kaylee leans in and whispers, "Ignore him."

I swallow down the hard ball forming in my throat, not allowing myself to show how deep his words cut. The truth is, I am maimed—broken beyond repair.

"Grady," a familiar voice comes from behind, "hands to yourself unless you never wanna throw a ball again."

Logan quickly drops his hands that were still resting innocently on my hips. I look over my shoulder and see Ryker. His eyes wide and fixed on me. "Get to class, Kit."

Not far behind is my brother, Carter. When he spots me, he picks up his pace, joining our little circle. "What's going on?" he asks Ryker. "Someone bothering you, Kit?"

Heat consumes my entire body. A mixture of humiliation and anger. "No, but someone is now." I walk toward Carter and grab his arm, pulling him away while Ryker follows. "Please don't ruin my freshman year. I'm begging you. If you see me, turn away. Both of you."

"He practically touched her ass," Ryker says, fueling the fire.

"He did not!" I spit out, getting furious with the entire situation.

Carter's eyes shoot over my shoulder. "Who touched her ass?"

"Logan Grady."

"Ryker! Stop it." I smack his arm. "He did not touch my ass!"

They continue to talk as if I'm not even standing here. "The one in the Cougars jersey?"

"Yeah. He's the new running back for the JV team."

I wave both of my hands. "Umm, hello. Why are we still talking about this?"

"Rumor has it, he and Asher Collins are pretty damn good."

"Carter!" I shout, much louder than I intended. I point to my left. "Junior hall is that way." I finally get their attention. "You can go now."

"All right. I hear ya," Carter says. "But you come find me if any of these idiots gives you trouble."

I nod repeatedly, feeling a little calmer now. "I will. Thanks." I know he's got my best interest at heart. Carter and Ryker have always been super protective, and I don't expect that to change now.

"Me too, Kit-Kat. We're only two halls away." Ryker pulls me in for a hug and I squeeze him back, suddenly feeling like we're the only two people in the hall. He smells so good. Feels so warm. I wish I could just stay here forever.

In a swift motion, I push him back, remembering that we're not the only ones here and that Ryker is my brother's best friend, who still looks at me like a little girl. I've been trying really hard to get over this crush by focusing my attention elsewhere. So far, it's not working, but I have every intention of changing that sooner rather than later.

"See you guys after school."

I don't even tell Kaylee I'm going to find my locker. I just walk away with an abundance of mixed feelings. We haven't even had our first class, and it's already been a day from hell.

Welcome to high school.

◆

"THANKS FOR RUINING my first day of school, guys. How was your first day?" Sarcasm drips from my tone as I climb into the back seat of Carter's car.

"Oh, don't be so dramatic, sis. Those guys are lame-os anyway. Can't you hang out with someone more…nerdy?"

Ryker, being the instigator that he is, laughs at Carter's choice of words while I wanna smack them both in the back of the head.

"And why would I do that? Because I'm nerdy?"

"No, because guys like Logan, Micah, and Asher only have two things on their minds—football and sex."

My face drops in my hands, and I can feel myself blush. "Oh

my God, Carter. I can promise you that none of those guys have that on their mind, at least not with me."

Ryker shifts in his seat, turning around to face me with a hard expression. "If you really believe that, then I think it's time for you to be homeschooled."

"Why in the world would guys like that ever want…" I can't even say the word. This conversation with Ryker and Carter is too weird. "They don't, okay?"

"You're more than what your self-esteem tells you, Kit-Kat. You're probably the prettiest girl in that school, so if you believe what you're saying is true, then we've got bigger problems than we thought."

I slap my hands to my legs. "We have no problems! No one did anything wrong and no one has an agenda with me." I laugh, not because it's funny, but because this entire conversation is absolutely ridiculous. Right now, being homeschooled sounds more appealing than dealing with these two, day in and day out at school.

Wait. Did Ryker just say that I'm probably the prettiest girl in school?

My head tilts slightly, eyes squinting as I look at him watching me. His eyes are soft and welcoming, and I wish I could hear his thoughts right now. Every muscle in my body tightens, and I can literally feel the blood pumping through my veins.

Does he really think I'm pretty or is he just being nice?

"Our last two years of high school have officially gone to shit," Carter says as he flips the blinker to turn down our road.

Ryker finally drops back in his seat, and I resume breathing.

One step forward, two steps back.

Instead of moving forward, I literally fell backward. In my defense, someone did push me.

CHAPTER
FOUR
RYKER

Seventeen Years Old

The minute I spot her, my feet don't stop moving. Shoving people left and right as I walk steadfastly down the hall.

I don't even know whose hands are on her waist, but it's all I can focus on. Fingers gently moving around as if they're trying to worm their way up her shirt.

Back up, Kit. Get the hell away from him.

For Christ's sake, it's the first day of school. How the hell are Carter and I supposed to get through an entire year of this shit? Watching guys gawk at Kit? She's only fifteen, no one should be gawking at her. But I know how the minds of these teenage boys work—I am one. And I'll be damned if any guy looks at her like she's anything but someone's little sister.

"Grady," I holler from six feet away, still walking toward them. When his eyes peer up, I know he heard me. "Hands to yourself unless you never wanna throw a ball again."

When he removes his hold on Kit, I look at her to assess the situation. I swear to God, if he made her feel uncomfortable, I will destroy his freshman year.

She doesn't seem to be too concerned with him, though, but

more so with me. Her eyes widen, and when she doesn't back away from the hormonal teenage boy, I say, "Get to class, Kit."

Ignoring me completely, she stands there as if she's trying to prove a point to me that she can do what she wants.

Carter joins us and I'd love nothing more than to watch him pummel this guy's ass. If I did it, it might seem a little weird. Carter, on the other hand, has every right to make sure Kit isn't getting taken advantage of.

"What's going on?" Carter asks me before looking at his sister. "Someone bothering you, Kit?"

"No, but someone is now." She grabs Carter and pulls him away, and I follow behind as she continues to give him hell, even if I'm the one who drew attention to the situation. A perk of not being the actual brother, I guess.

Kit won't tell him the complete story, so I do the honors. "He practically touched her ass."

"He did not!" I can tell Kit's getting fired up, but I don't care. She's too trusting.

Carter sees red as he looks past Kit to the group of guys. "Who touched her ass?"

"Logan Grady."

Kit smacks my shoulder, and I fake a shriek while rubbing the spot. "Ryker! Stop it. He did not touch my ass!"

"The one in the Cougars jersey?"

"Yeah," I tell Carter. "He's the new running back for the JV team."

Kit tries to get our attention, and while I see her, I'm more concerned with making sure Carter handles this the right way by putting this guy in his place.

"Umm, hello. Why are we still talking about this?" she asks, angered by our mere presence.

"Rumor has it, he and Ava's brother, Asher, are pretty damn good."

"Carter!" she shouts, grabbing our attention and pointing her finger down the hall. "Junior hall is that way." I'm not sure about Carter, but I'm a little offended that she's trying to get rid of us. "You can go now."

With a hefty sigh, Carter gives her a hug and says something along the lines of, "*Find me if you need anything."*

When they break up their little sibling moment, I pull Kit in for a hug. "Me too, Kit-Kat. We're only two halls away." I hold her a little longer than planned, and I'm not sure if it's because I want her to know I've got her back, or because I want the boys in her class to wonder if I'm the reason she's off-limits. Regardless, she is.

Kit quickly breaks away and avoids eye contact with me. *What's up with that?*

"See you guys after school," she says before walking in the opposite direction.

Once she's gone, I nudge Carter. "You're really gonna let those guys get away with touching her like that?"

He doesn't even look at me, just stares straight ahead at Logan Grady. "Hell no. I've got my eyes on these boys, and if they step out of line, we'll put 'em back in place."

◆

"Throw me one of those bottled waters," I tell Carter, who's behind me in the kitchen. Before I know it, I'm getting smacked in the back of the head.

"Dude, what the hell?" I rub at the sore spot and grab the bottle that fell beside me.

"What?" he asks, shoving a handful of chips in his mouth. "You said throw it."

He drops down beside me, bag of chips in hand. "You staying for dinner?"

"If that's an invite, then yes. Yes, I am."

"Since when do you wait for an invite?"

"True." I reach over and dig my hand into the chip bag, grabbing a fistful of them.

"They're all yours. I gotta shower. I smell like ass from practice. Coach really put us through the wringer today."

He's not lying. He reeks. Which means I do, too. "Yeah, I should probably do the same. I'll take one when you're out. Ya know, since I'm staying for dinner." I smirk, popping a chip into my mouth.

"Just use Kit's shower. She's out with her friends."

"All right." Closing the bag of chips, I stand up and grab my water. I twist the top off and take down half the bottle, then leave it on the center island in the kitchen.

Walking down the hall, I pull my sweaty shirt over my head. Carter was right, Coach did put us through the wringer. I'm not sure if it's because we're playing our rival school this weekend, or just because he enjoys being an ass. Whatever the reason, I'll be feeling it tomorrow.

Kit's door is cracked open, so I push it open farther. It's been a while since I've been here—a month, at least. The only time I'm ever in this room is to sneak in and out her window with Carter.

I walk slowly to her bathroom, stopping to look at the board on her wall full of pictures. There's one of her with a big, cheesy grin that really shows off her braces. Beside her is Kaylee. Those two are always together. Much like me and Carter.

When I look down, I notice an old notebook with pictures and colorful sticky notes stuck to it, full of reminders and quotes.

My fingers run over the hardcover. *Looks like a scrapbook, or a journal.*

Temptation draws me in. Her deepest, innermost thoughts are probably written in this book. Part of me wonders if there could be something about me inside.

It's a total invasion of Kit's privacy, but I can't see myself walking out of this room without a peek inside. I'm not sure why I even care, but I do.

I pick it up, tap it a couple times in the palm of my hand, telling myself to drop it and forget it even exists. She's a fifteen-year-old girl. There's nothing of interest inside here.

Or is there?

I give the room a sweep, checking the door to make sure no one's coming.

Against my better judgment, I flip it open, and all it takes is the first page for me to wish I'd never opened the damn thing in the first place.

In all caps are the words, "I love Asher Collins," with a heart around it.

Asher Collins? Ava's asshole brother? Since when does she *love* that fucker?

I wanna laugh because it's cute that Kit has her first crush, but it's not funny. It's not funny at all.

It irks me. I'd rather claw my eyes out than see that Kit is in love with Asher. I've known the kid for a while, and he's a fucking prick.

She might only be a fifteen-year-old girl, but he's a fifteen-year-old boy. I was a fifteen-year-old boy only two years ago, and it's the age I lost my virginity—to a fifteen-year-old girl.

The thought infuriates me to no end. If she's got a crush on this guy, that means she'd allow him to do whatever he wanted to her. Kiss her, touch her, maybe even more.

Fuck that.

I'm about to flip to the next page when I hear the front door open and close. In a fleeting motion, I drop the book back down on her vanity and haul ass to Kit's en-suite bathroom.

Once the door is closed and locked, I press my back to it, wishing I'd never found out that sweet little Kit thinks she's in love with some asshole jock.

I get undressed and get in the shower, letting the hot water run over me while I try to clear my head. I don't wanna think. Not about school, football, my fucked-up home life, not even Kit and how there's this insatiable need to protect her from guys like Asher Collins—guys like me.

Why do I even care? It's not like she's my sister. Sure feels like it sometimes. Other times, I'm glad she's not.

Once I've washed off the sweat and grime from practice, I step out onto the bath mat and grab a towel that's hanging from a hook. I'm not sure if it's clean or dirty, but it's the only one I see, so I use it.

"Umm, hello," I hear someone, or rather Kit, say.

I holler back, "Hey, it's me." I rub the top of my head with the towel, hoping she doesn't notice I looked at her journal. "Carter said it was cool if I used your shower."

"Oh. Yeah. It's fine. Just wanted to make sure there wasn't some crazy person in my bathroom." She laughs and I find myself smiling in response.

I reach into the pocket of my jeans and pull out my cigarette pack. Flipping it open, I grab one and stick it behind my ear. "No one said I wasn't crazy."

More laughter and sounds of her opening and closing a drawer to her dresser that's right outside the bathroom door.

"Stay in there for a sec, 'kay? I need to change real quick."

While she's changing, I get dressed and stand at the door, waiting for the okay to come out. "You leaving again?" I ask, curious if she'll be here for dinner.

"Yeah. Margo just got her license so me, her, and Kaylee are meeting some friends at the mall."

"What friends?" I blurt out, digging deeper than I usually do.

"Just some friends."

"Same guys you were hanging out with this morning?" I bite my bottom lip, waiting for her to reply, but the long pause gives me the answer I was looking for.

More silence then has me pressing my forehead to the door. "Kit?"

"I'm here," she pauses for a beat before saying, "you can come out now."

When I pull open the door, I'm not prepared for what's standing in front of me—or who is standing in front of me. It's not Carter's little sister. The one who sticks her gum under the dining room table. No. I'm looking at a teenage girl who is dressed like a high schooler. Because that's what she is now. Kit's in high school, and there isn't a damn thing Carter or me can do about it.

Doesn't mean I won't try, though.

"You really think Carter's gonna let you go out in that?"

Her forehead creases as she looks down at her formfitting jeans and tee shirt that reveals the outline of her black bra. Her sapphire eyes slide up to mine, wide and quizzical. "What's wrong with what I'm wearing?"

I wanna tell her she should put on something a little less revealing. I also wanna tell her she's beautiful, but I don't say either of those things. "Nothing. Nothing's wrong with it."

"Ryker." Kit winces, reaching toward me. I take a step back, unsure why she's coming at me. "Why are you still smoking?" She plucks the cigarette from behind my ear and holds it up. "Don't you know these things will kill you?"

"Something's gonna. Might as well enjoy life while I can." I go to grab it back, but she retreats and holds it up.

She laughs in a mocking tone. "And these things aid in your quest to *enjoy life?*"

"Maybe they do. Or maybe I just like the taste."

Kit fakes a gag and looks at the cigarette in her hand like it's some sort of mysterious object. "You're better than this." Her eyes slide up, and she hands the cigarette back to me. I'm actually surprised she didn't break it in half.

I don't take the cigarette from her. I'm not sure if it's fear of judgment or because I want her to always believe I am better than my mistakes. Even if it's the furthest thing from the truth. "No, I'm not."

Tilting her head toward her shoulder, she gives me those sympathetic eyes. The ones that tell me, once again, she's ready to defend me against myself. "Yes, you are. You just need to believe it."

I look down at my bare feet, draw in a heavy breath, and say, "Hard to believe you're worthy of anything when you've constantly got someone in your ear telling you you're not."

"I believe in you." Her voice is soft, tranquil even. It catches me by surprise, though I'm not sure why. Kit is always kind. She has the sweetest voice and her words are always uplifting.

My heart jumps in my chest when I look at her and it's an odd feeling. "You shouldn't. I'm almost positive I'm as good as I'm gonna get."

Kit takes my hand into her soft, warm one and lays the cigarette in my palm. "I dare you to do better, Ry."

I chuckle, closing my hand around the cigarette. "You dare me?"

"Yeah. I do. Are you afraid of a little dare?"

"Ryker Dawson isn't afraid of anything," I tease, knowing it's a lie. I'm scared of a lot of things—failure being my biggest fear—losing the people I care about being the second.

"You always say you're gonna do better. Prove it." She pokes a hard finger in my chest. "I dare you to try."

"All right," I drawl. "I'll take your dare and I'll raise you a promise."

Kit smirks, crossing her arms over her chest and pushing up the bit of cleavage she has. I fight not to look, though temptation, once again, is tugging like a motherfucker. "A promise?"

"Yep. Promise me you'll be careful."

She blows out an airy chuckle, shoulders waggling. "Okay. Done."

"I'm serious, Kit-Kat. High school is brutal, and boys…well, they're boys. Don't be so trusting."

It seems I've lost her attention when she walks over to her vanity and picks up a tube of lip gloss. "I'm always careful, Ry. You know this." Pulling the applicator from the tube, she rubs some over her lips then smacks them together. "But aren't you the one who told me not too long ago that I'm too mature for my age."

I nod, because she's exactly right. "You can have fun and be careful at the same time. I just don't wanna see you get hurt."

Kit runs her fingers over her journal and my heart stops for a minute, hoping she doesn't notice anything out of place. "I'll be fine."

I breathe a sigh of relief when she turns back to me, oblivious to the fact that I looked inside her journal before she got here.

A horn beeps out front, grabbing Kit's attention. "My ride's here. I gotta go."

She goes to leave, but I grab her arm. "What about that promise?" Our eyes catch and something unsettles inside me. I find my gaze shifting down to her clear, glossy lips. The tip of her tongue darts out and I swear, for a moment, my heart stops beating.

Something pulls at me, or us, rather. Drawing us closer, like a magnetic force that cannot be denied. Her eyes widen in surprise. Mine do the same. I lean in, invading her space, unsure what the hell I'm doing. We meet halfway, our mouths ghosting, pulses pounding—or at least, mine is.

Beeeep.

Kit's ride lays on the horn.

I instantly drop my hold on her arm as reality slaps me in the face. This is Kit. My Kit-Kat. Carter's little sister.

What the fuck am I even doing?

Better yet, why is she still standing here looking at me like I'm some broken boy in need of a hug?

She swallows hard, rubbing her ear timidly. "I really should go."

Yet, she doesn't. Not yet. It isn't until I nod, giving her the approval she seeks. "See ya later, Kit-Kat."

Then she's gone. Taking the promise she never gave me with her.

I drop down on her bed, staring at her ceiling and feeling the weight of regret on my chest.

That can never happen again. I'll lose my best friend. I'll lose her. I'll have nothing left.

Kit never gave me the promise I wanted, but I stood true to my word and took her dare. For some reason, she saw something in me no one else did and because of that—because of her—I wanted to do better.

I almost did.

CHAPTER
FIVE
KIT

Sixteen Years Old

Knock. Knock. Knock.

You have got to be kidding me.

"Go away!" I growl, my eyes still tightly closed.

Pound. Bang. Crash.

I'll strangle him. That'll stop this.

That's it! I'm going to kill him.

One eye opens, while the other is lazy and still praying for sleep.

My window flies up, hitting the top of the sill with a thud. Carter pokes his head in, and I curse under my breath.

"Oh, hey, sis." Carter smirks as he rolls onto his side on my bedroom floor. He pushes himself off the floor, staggers a bit, then trips and falls onto my bed.

"Carter!" I hiss, shoving him off me. "You're drunk!"

Why am I surprised? Well, because Carter hardly ever drinks. He's usually the more responsible one of his crew and I've only seen him like this one other time...

"She dumped you again, didn't she?"

Dammit. I sit up, rubbing my eyes and wiping the sleep from them. "What was the excuse this time?"

On the bed with his feet on the floor, Carter drops his face in his hands.

Forget killing him; I'm going to kill her.

I hate when he's like this. Carter is the sweetest guy in the entire world, and I hate when his heart is hurting.

"Yeah, it's over. She says we're going in separate directions."

"Oh, Carter," I say, wrapping an arm around him and resting my head on his back. "It's her loss…again."

Carter and Stacy have been together on and off for the past two years—more off than on. I don't like her. In fact, I downright hate her—along with her bestie, Ava. Ava treats Ryker just as bad as Stacy does Carter. Maybe worse.

Stacy is the head cheerleader, who thinks she's better than everyone else. I'm a cheerleader, too, but I would never treat anyone like they're beneath me.

Not to mention, she's so awful to Carter. Two weeks ago, she keyed his car that was parked in front of Ryker's garage while he and some of his friends worked on Ryker's old Chevelle. All because he was hanging with his friends and not with her.

"It is what it is." Carter lifts his head and smacks his hands against his legs. "I need water."

He climbs to his feet and weaves across the floor with wobbly legs as he tries to get to the door. Hiccups climb his throat and he hangs his head, moping, as he turns the handle.

Before the door closes behind him, I say, "Go to bed before you wake Dad. I'll bring you some water, Carter. It'll be okay."

Hiccup. The door closes, and my heart breaks for him.

Carter and I have always been really close. It's just me, him, and our dad. My mom left us when I was only two years old, so I don't even have memories of her, but Carter does. As for our dad, he's great, but he works a lot. Somehow, he's always managed to make it to all the important events in mine and Carter's lives, but as for the day-to-day stuff, he's absent a lot. It's okay, though. I know he does it for us. Besides, Carter and I have always managed to make it work.

After staring at the door for a solid minute, I drag myself out of bed to get Carter some water.

I walk over to the window to close it, but something catches my eye. Or someone, rather.

"Ryker," I mutter, not loud enough for him to hear me.

Why is he running?

I push the window back up, and when I notice he's not slowing down, I take a step back. He comes barreling into my room. Tucked in a ball, he crashes on my bedroom floor.

Grunting and groaning, he rolls onto his back.

I grab his hand and attempt to pull him up. "What the hell are you doing?"

He's no help as he lies there stiff as a board. He's out of breath and panic-stricken. "Close the curtains."

I do as I'm told, suddenly panicking right along with him. With two hands, I snap the curtains shut and return my attention to, yet another, drunk in my room.

"You better tell me what's going on right now or I'll…" I stutter, grabbing the full glass of water off my nightstand. "I'll dump this water on you."

Ryker laughs, though it's not funny at all.

"What did you do this time, Ryker?"

He rolls onto his stomach, and it's like déjà vu. People always ask me why I'm so tired and this is why.

Once he's steady on his feet, I realize he's actually not as bad off as Carter is. He might not even be drunk at all.

"It's best if you don't know, Kit-Kat."

"Not helpful. Explain. Now." I raise the glass and give him a look of warning, threatening to chuck it at him.

Ryker throws his hands up in surrender. "All right, all right. Put the weapon down."

Watching him out of the corner of my eye, I slowly lower it to the nightstand.

"Got myself in a little trouble tonight."

I exhale a pent-up breath, finally setting the glass down. "Dammit, Ry. You've been doing so good this school year."

Ryker sits down on the edge of my bed, running his fingers through his hair. "In my defense, it wasn't my fault. And if the sheriff wasn't such a douchebag, I wouldn't even be here right now."

"Please tell me this doesn't involve the sheriff." Stacy's dad is the sheriff of Oakley Shores and he's a real jerk to those he thinks are beneath him. He's always given Ryker a hard time.

He winces, biting the corner of his lip. "I guess I won't tell you then."

I wish he wouldn't do that lip-biting thing. I wish he wasn't even in here right now. Every time I think I've moved on from my schoolgirl crush, Ryker pops up out of nowhere, reminding me I'm still very much in love with him.

"All right," I throw my hands up in defeat, "keep your secret. I just hope it doesn't come back to bite you in the ass. Carter's in his room, hopefully sleeping off whatever he drank."

Ryker stands up, his eyes burning into mine. There's a sheen of sympathy that has my chest tightening. "Sorry, Kit. I'm gonna do better."

He's so gorgeous. Just being in his presence has my heart pounding out a million beats a minute. A six-foot-two Adonis. Muscular build, messy, dark brown hair and the brightest green eyes I've ever seen. A leather jacket that I don't think he ever takes off. He wears the grunge vibe, and he wears it well. Even more so than his good looks, he has such a big heart, even though he doesn't show it to many.

I don't like to pry, so I drop the conversation and let him have the privacy of his own mistakes. I nod, lips pressed together tightly. "I know you will." Ryker doesn't have an easy life, so sometimes, I think his actions are justifiable. This past year, he's really been trying to get his life together, and I hope whatever happened tonight doesn't set him back.

When he leaves and goes to Carter's room, I remember that I

was supposed to bring Carter water. I'm hopeful he's asleep, but on the off chance he's awake, I better fetch it for him so he's not dehydrated when he wakes up.

As I'm walking down the long stretch of hallway to the kitchen, I think about what Ryker always says to me—that I'm too mature for my age.

It is true. Most days I feel like I have to be. Mom isn't here; Dad is always working. Even if I am two years younger than Carter, I look out for him—and he does the same for me.

I'm not rebellious at all. Don't take chances—mostly because I can't.

Okay. Laying it all out there…I was born with a heart defect. I didn't even know I had it until I was twelve. It was the beginning of cheer season, and I was doing a running back handspring when my heart started beating fast. Like really fast. No matter what I did, it wouldn't slow down.

After that, it started happening daily. Sometimes, I can get it back on track myself; other times, I need medical intervention to reset the rhythm.

When I was fourteen, I had surgery to try and correct an extra pathway in my heart. It was unsuccessful and it left me with some scar tissue that actually worsened my condition. And while it's okay, and I'm okay, I still have to avoid super stressful situations and overexertion. I also have to take a handful of medications daily and see my cardiologist all the time now. It's not the condition itself that has me so on edge—I'm not dying or anything, at least, not from this—it's the anxiety that comes with it. I never know when my heart is going to jump into a tachy it won't come out of without medical intervention.

So, that's my reasoning, and while some days I wish I could still be immature, I just can't. I'm also only sixteen. I remind myself often that I have the rest of my life to misbehave and let my guard down a bit. One day, I hope to be fixed.

I open the cupboard and reach for a glass. Just as I grab one, I hear heavy footsteps coming from upstairs. My hand freezes around the glass that's still sitting in the cupboard while I listen.

A door opens. There's shouting. Lots of shouting and it's coming from Dad.

A door slams shut, and my body jolts.

Heavy footsteps begin thumping down the stairs, so I grab the glass and shut the cupboard.

"You've got some nerve running here after the stunt you pulled tonight," Dad says, and he's livid. I can almost feel the heat rolling off him, and he's not even in view yet. "I thought you were beyond this. You were on the right track, Ryker."

My stomach twists into knots. Whatever Ryker did, he's been found out.

They both come into view in the open space of the living room, and I watch as Ryker hangs his head low. It looks as though the disappointment from my dad is slicing through him. "I've got no excuse. I was impulsive and I screwed up."

"Damn straight you screwed up. Everything you worked hard for, both on and off the field, is out the window because of your *impulsive mistake*. You better hope charges aren't pressed."

I freeze, glass in hand, when Dad escorts Ryker to the door.

"Dad," I blurt out, not even sure what I want to say, but I have to say something. He can't just kick Ryker out. If he goes home after getting in some kind of trouble, there's no telling what his dad will do to him.

All eyes shoot to me—Dad's and Ryker's, and seconds later, Carter appears—drunk and disorderly, rambling on and bumping into furniture with his hand shoved down his boxers. *Gross.*

I set the glass down on the counter and pin him with a hard glare. *Should have stayed in bed, Carter.*

Carter shakes a lazy finger at my dad with his eyes half-closed. "He's fine. Let him stay."

"No!" Dad shouts. "He's not fine and neither are you. I'd expect this from Ryker, but you, Carter." The disappointment in his tone is formidable. "This kid is back to dragging you down and you're allowing it."

No. It's not Ryker's fault. And he's not the same person he was before. He wants to do better—he wants to *be* better. I want to scream it at the top of my lungs, but I don't. I stand here, still and quiet, and let them hash it out without my interference.

Carter raises his hands and rubs his fists to his eyes, then scratches his bare side. "Can we deal with this in the morning? I've got a—"

"We'll deal with this now!" Dad points a stern finger at Carter, then to Ryker. "Your mom is on her way."

My heart sinks deep into the pit of my stomach.

My worry is no match for Ry's, though. I can see it in his eyes. Yet, he hides it in his voice. With a nod, he tips his head and gives my dad a respectful, "Yes, sir."

Ryker's mom will take him home to where his monster of a dad is. While I've never personally talked to Ryker about his dad, rumors have circulated this town for years. Mr. Dawson is a drug addict, who emotionally and physically beats his wife and sons. Last year, Ryker was out of school for an entire week, and Carter told me it was because he had an "accident." I later learned that the accident was a couple broken ribs from his dad.

Carter's offered to let him stay here and finish out high school, but Ryker refuses because he wants to be home to protect his mom and Ezra, his thirteen-year-old brother.

"Can't he just stay here?" I spit out the words without a second thought.

While everyone assumes I mean for the night, I actually mean…forever. Or at least until Ryker can find a safe place to live.

Dad doesn't say anything, just looks to Ryker as if he's expecting him to handle the question. Ryker immediately shakes his head no. "Can't, Kit-Kat. I've gotta go home." He turns the handle on the door and looks at my dad. "Sorry for the trouble I've caused." His eyes shoot to Carter. "I'll call ya tomorrow."

"Actually," Dad says with a firm hand on Ryker's shoulder, "I think it's best if you stay away for the time being. Let Carter get back on the right path. You two could use a break from each other."

Stay away? No!

"What the hell?" Carter scoffs. "Ryker's practically family. What are you doing, Dad?"

Dad takes it upon himself to open the front door for Ryker before saying, "I'm doing what I think is best."

Carter curses under his breath, then drops down in a chair in the living room.

I look at Ryker and our eyes catch. I can see the pain he's feeling. It's like it burns into me with his gaze, and I'm able to feel it, too. I walk over to him quickly, Dad watching intently, though I ignore his unwanted stare.

Ryker tenses when I close in on his personal space. It's an awkward moment of clarity, for me, anyway. He stands there so vulnerable, like he's awaiting conviction the minute he walks out the door. Facing the judgment of his father and getting punished for a crime I don't even know if he committed.

"Be safe," I tell him, before wrapping my arms around him in a tight hug.

He whispers into the shell of my ear, "Don't worry about me, Kit."

Tears threaten to fall and I can't help but feel like this goodbye will be the last one for a long time.

We disengage, and Ryker reaches into the front pocket of his jacket and hands me something. I look down at his hand and instantly smile. Before I take it from him, I look him in the eyes. "Thought you didn't carry those anymore."

"Stocked back up. This one's overdue. Just promise me something before you take it."

"Okay?" I drawl.

"Act your age, Kit. Don't grow up so fast. Take time to enjoy all the little things in life while you still can. One day, they'll be the big things."

He takes my hand, unfolds my fingers, and lays the mini candy bar in my palm—this time, a Kit Kat.

Then he's gone. Out the door and disappearing into the night. Part of me hopes he runs and avoids his dad altogether, but it's doubtful. He'll face him head-on and take whatever is coming to him. Because that's what Ryker does. He might make a lot of mistakes, but he owns up to them.

"Back to bed, Kit," Dad says sternly as he crosses the room to Carter, who is now lying sideways across the beige lounge chair.

I don't say anything. I just head down the hall to my room. Stopping halfway down, I listen to the conversation being had.

"I'm eighteen years old, Dad. You can't exactly tell me who I can't hang out with."

"You're eighteen years old and living under my roof. If you don't want to follow my rules, you're welcome to leave any time."

This isn't like the two of them. Dad and Carter have always been close. He sees Carter as he is right now, but I don't think he understands that this isn't normal behavior for him, or even Ryker. Carter excels at everything he does. Shoot, he's graduating at the top of his class. Ryker isn't a bad influence. If anything, he helps Carter let loose a little. We all need to do that from time to time.

"What's the big deal, Dad? So we drank. I'm sure you drank a time or ten when you were underage."

"This isn't about drinking, son. While I don't condone it, I'm not naive enough to think it doesn't happen. This is about Ryker slashing tires at the motel parking lot, then running from the sheriff all through town and coming to our house as his hideout. It's proof that this facade he's been putting on is all for show. The boy hasn't changed, and I worry he never will. He's a bad influence on you, and he's a bad influence on your sister. We need to protect her from boys like that. Not drag them into her life."

Ryker was slashing tires at the motel? That doesn't make any sense. Ryker doesn't vandalize property, or at least, not that I've ever heard of.

"What? Slashing tires? No. Ryker wouldn't do that," Carter says, as stunned as I am.

"Well, he did…"

I can't listen to this anymore. I go to my room and sit down on the edge of my bed, still clutching the candy bar. I wish there was something I could do to help Ryker. But I don't think there is anything anyone can do.

My hand opens slowly, and I look down at it, remembering the words Ryker said before he left. "Take time to enjoy all the little things in life while you still can. One day, they'll be the big things."

That was the last time I saw Ryker before he moved to Colorado, without even saying goodbye.

CHAPTER SIX

RYKER

Eighteen Years old

"Epic game, man," Leon, our wide receiver, says as I pass him on the field.

I turn around, walking backward as I peel off my helmet. "Couldn't have done it without ya."

The last game of the season just ended, the crowd is parting, and in about ten minutes, the field lights will go out. The next time they come on, it'll be someone else's game.

Cloud nine doesn't even describe where I am. If heaven was built on a football field, I'd say I'm there.

Scouts from two of the top schools in the country were here today, and they saw the sixty-yard pass that won the game in the final six seconds.

My grades are up. They're not great, but I've been busting my ass this year to keep my GPA in good standing.

For the first time in a while, I've got hope. I could potentially get the hell out of this place and be the first in my family to attend college. If I do happen to fail, I'll do what every Dawson man before me has done—I'll work as a mechanic at the family garage. I'll live out the dream of my great-great-grandfather, instead of my own.

"You comin', man?" Carter hollers from the track. He's already changed out of his uniform and has his equipment bag hanging from his shoulder.

My eyes wander, and I notice everyone is gone except him and Coach.

I look at the scoreboard one last time before it shuts off, and it hits me. It really is over.

There's an ache in my chest. A reality I'm not prepared for. It's over and I've got no fucking idea what's next. I started out as a bobblehead in a helmet when I was only eight years old. Never missed a practice, never missed a game. Even when my body ached because of a beating from my dad—I still showed up and put forth my best effort. Can't say the same about school, but you live and you learn. I'll do better in college; I'll be better.

Coach puts a hand on my shoulder, snapping me out of the memories of my last game. "Game's over, son."

I nod, eyes still on the blank scoreboard.

I should say something to him. Thank him for saving me from myself and for stepping in when my dad stepped out. He's been so much more than a coach. He's a mentor, a hero, and dare I say, a friend?

I turn to look at him, my mouth opens to speak, but the words get lodged in my throat. My helmet is clutched in one hand, jersey in the other, as sweat slides down my forehead. "Yeah. It's over."

"You did good tonight. Be proud of that." He pats my shoulder again. "Ya know, in all my years of coaching, I've never witnessed so much growth. You're going places, Dawson."

A smile tugs at my lips. Those words coming from such a noble man mean more than he'll ever know. A thank-you seems so insufficient. Instead, I drop my helmet and throw my arms around him. "If at first you don't succeed…"

"…do what your damn coach told ya to do in the first place."

A moment of seriousness takes hold as he steps back, looking at me with stern eyes as he says, "Now don't go and screw this up, Dawson. Good things are coming from those scouts." He places two hands on my shoulders and gives me a subtle shake. "I can feel it in my bones. Go home. Get some rest and keep your wits about ya."

I nod in response, but as I do, I look past him at Carter, who has since been joined by a few other teammates. They're all waiting for me to go to the after-party at the beach.

"Don't worry, Coach. I won't let you down."

He shakes his head, clicking his tongue on the roof of his mouth. "Not me, boy. *Yourself.* Don't let yourself down."

I'M ON THE BEACH, ass in the sand, watching the waves crash in front of me while everyone else is gathered around the fire thirty feet behind me.

My wrists dangle over my knees, and I stare out into the abyss, thinking about life and my purpose in it. I mean, there has to be one or I wouldn't be here, right?

Obviously, football isn't the reason I was put on this earth, but it's still my ride to a decent school. Lord knows my parents aren't funding my education. After a few years of rebellion, someone dared me to do better because she believed in me. I've been trying to win that dare and not disappoint her ever since. Now, I just have to hope all I've fought for is enough—not just for her, but for my future.

I'm taken away from my thoughts about the future when an arm rests on my shoulder and a hand holding a cup of keg beer is in my face. All it takes is seeing the charm bracelet on her wrist to know it's Ava. I bought her all the charms on it, never once telling her they were from the dollar store.

I scoff, ignoring her peace offering, or friendship. Whatever the hell it is that she thinks she has and I want.

She takes a seat beside me, double-fisting the cups. "Thought we were good, Ryker."

I don't say anything, because the truth is, we're supposed to be. We haven't been together for a couple years, but I've had a few moments of weakness. Drunk and lonely nights will do that to ya.

Regardless, it doesn't mean she's a friend. I'll never trust her again. Not with my friendship, and certainly not with my heart.

Looking over at her, I can see the contempt in her eyes. "Really?" She snaps her body around to face me, her toes digging into the sand beside my leg. "This again."

"It's not you—"

"It's not you, it's me? Is that what you're gonna say? Save it, Ryker, because we both know that, with time, you'll come crawling on your hands and knees, begging for me to take you back. Probably tonight when you're drunk and bored."

I shake my head, looking back at the ocean. "Those nights should've never happened."

She laughs, mockingly. "You're fucking pathetic. You know that?" After a big gulp of her beer, she continues to beat me down, much like she always does. "You think that because you won a stupid game and some scouts saw you that you're going places? I can promise you, Ryker Dawson, the only place you're going is back to your dump of a house and working at a garage with outdated equipment. When you wanna meet up tonight and recreate one of those nights that *should've never happene*d," she chucks her empty cup in front of her and gets up, "don't bother."

When I don't respond like she wants me to, she hisses, "Fucking loser," before walking back to the party.

I smirk, nodding in response while keeping my mouth closed. I've heard it all before. So much that, some days, I actually believe everything that's been said. One day I'll thank the bitch, because she's given me the motivation to be more than what everyone thinks of me.

Once I've determined Ava is far enough away from me, I get up from where I'm sitting on the beach. Without even brushing the sand off my jeans, I go back to the fire.

That conversation needed to happen. So many days were

spent fighting with that girl while trying to live up to her expectations of me being the perfect guy. I'm not even sure she ever really liked me. Everything is about attention when it comes to Ava.

To my left, I spot a small group gathered around Stacy, who is sobbing into her friend, Dana's, shoulder. In a normal situation, I'd feel bad seeing a girl cry, but that whole clique is full of dramatics.

I scan the party, looking for Carter. The crowd is on the smaller side—only about a dozen of us—but he's nowhere in sight.

Knowing I'm going to regret it, I approach Stacy, who's now only sniffling as she talks to her girls. Tipping my chin, I ask, "Where's Carter?"

She sniffles again, choking on her words. "He left."

I blow out a heavy breath. Carter was my fucking ride tonight. He better not have taken off. "Left where?"

Stacy shrugs, rolls her eyes, and looks away. "Hell if I know. We broke up."

My eyes show my surprise as my brows hit my forehead. "You what?"

"It needed to be done. I'm going to New York in the summer and he's staying here so he can be a second father," she air quotes, "to his sister. It would've never worked."

She dumped him, yet she's crying. Typical.

I run my fingers through my hair, looking up at the sky. "Fuck," I mutter into the air. For some reason, Carter loved Stacy, so wherever he is, he's probably emotionally fucked up.

With a shake of my head, I look down at the sand, stuff my hands in the front pockets of my jeans, and begin my walk out of here to go find his ass. With any luck, he's sitting in his car waiting for me.

"Dawson!" Leon hollers from behind me. I pivot around to face him. He holds up an unopened bottle of beer. "Have a drink with me. Let's celebrate that kick-ass win."

"Nah. Maybe next time, man." I wave with two fingers. "I'm out."

Two minutes later, I'm over the dune and breathing a sigh of relief when I see Carter's car. But the closer I get, the more my hope diminishes because it looks empty.

I lift the driver's side handle, and of course, it's locked. Cupping my hands around my eyes, I look inside the window and notice the beer we brought is no longer on the floor of the passenger side.

"Dammit!" I smack the top of the car, spinning around and searching the parking lot again.

Nothing.

I pull my cell phone out of the pocket of my leather jacket and shoot him a text.

Me: Where the fuck are you?

As I wait for a response, I kick my foot up on his door and lean against it. I tilt my head back and stare up at the empty sky. Not a star in sight, which means rain is coming.

My phone buzzes in my hand, and I hold it up in front of my face, reading the message from Carter.

Carter: Left. Drunk. Stacy dumped me. Going home to bed.
Me: How far out are ya? I'm leaving, too.
Carter: Just hit Coswell Blvd.
Me: Walk slow. I'm coming.

This is just great. Carter's walking down the street, drunk, and likely carrying a twelve-pack of beer. It's not like him at all. In fact, he wasn't even planning to drink tonight. It was for me, not that I even feel like drinking myself.

I'm over this shit. The parties. The relationships. The breakups. The drama. Unfortunately, it'll continue regardless.

As of right now, I'm stuck, but with any luck, I'll be getting some good news soon. News that will ensure a full ride and a career in my future.

I make it to Coswell Boulevard and glance at the motel to the right. It's a dumpy place for being in such a ritzy town, and rumor has it, it's getting shut down soon. Nothing but druggies and high-end prostitutes at that place—including my own father.

I spot his truck immediately. I shouldn't be surprised that he's inside. Likely shooting up like he's been doing more and more of lately. He'll get high, then he'll go home and take his aggression out on my mom. I'm just glad Ezra, my thirteen-year-old brother, is with a friend tonight.

I've tried to get my mom to leave. Talked until my throat felt like it was bleeding, but she didn't hear me. Never does when it comes to him. For some fucked-up reason, she loves the man and thinks she can save him. All I want to do is save her—save us.

Maybe I can't save her life, but I can save her for tonight.

Glancing around, I make sure the coast is clear before I jog over to the parking lot. Donny's old, rusted-out pickup truck sits right under the blinking motel sign. I reach my hand into the inside pocket of my jacket and pull out my pocketknife.

Gripping the end of the knife, I draw my hand back, sweep my eyes around the lot one last time, before I drive the blade into the front passenger tire. Squeezing and pushing with a great deal of pressure, I drag the blade through the black rubber. Once it's got a nice gash, I pull, but the blade sticks. I pull harder and harder, finally freeing it.

Wasting no time, I hurry over to the driver's side and repeat my actions, feeling pretty pleased with myself. I might have that man's DNA, but he's no father to me.

I go to pull the blade out, knowing it'll take some effort, but before I can get it out, I notice the flash of red-and-blue lights and then a quick siren sounds.

My chin drops to my chest. "Fuck."

In a swift motion, I yank the knife out of the tire and look up slowly, noticing that the officer is still in his car.

I take one step back, then another, before his door swings open, and Sheriff Meyers appears. "Drop the knife, boy."

A glance down at my hand has me staring at the knife. In a knee-jerk reaction, I drop it to the ground, and it hits the concrete with a clank. Both of my hands go up, showing him that I don't have it anymore.

Sheriff Meyers takes a step toward me. He's holding a flashlight with the beam pointed right at me. I squint at the light and notice his left hand resting on the holster holding his gun. "Don't you run, boy."

Each step he takes forward has me taking one backward. In a split-second decision, I turn around and haul ass across the parking lot. I can hear the rattle of his keys as he chases after me, shouting and trying to get me to stop—but I don't stop. I'm no stranger to Sherriff Meyers. In fact, he's at my house more times than I care to admit. Mostly because of domestic shit between my parents, but a couple times because of me—petty theft, vandalism. That was my past, though. He doesn't see the changes I've made. Not that it matters now.

Once I'm out of the parking lot, I keep going. Past houses, through lawns. I trample over a flower garden, jump a chain-link fence, and fall into a large bush, planted right in the middle of someone's yard.

Smacking away the branches and leaves, I look over my shoulder and see the beam from his flashlight pointed at me. He's still pretty far back, but he's closing the distance, more and more, with each passing second.

I push myself up from the ground and my feet keep moving.

After turning a few corners and jumping a couple fences, I'm certain I've lost him. Hugging my knees to my chest, I hide out behind someone's house while listening to the sound of a dog barking from the window above me.

"Shut up. Shut up. Shut up," I grumble under my breath. That damn dog is about to give me up.

When he doesn't stop, I get to my feet. Now that I'm in the dog's sight, he's clawing at the window and growling like I'm his midnight snack. A light in the house comes on and I'm back to running.

Once I'm out of the yard, I slow my steps. My hands hit my knees and I curl over for a second, taking a breather.

I'm only two blocks from Carter's house and part of me would rather go home and face what's waiting for me than risk disappointing Carter's dad. It's closer than my house, though, and I need to get somewhere safe before more officers begin searching for me.

Sheriff Meyers saw my face. He knows damn well it was me. Not to mention, my fingerprints are all over that knife. My family is quite familiar with the Oakley Shores Police Department, and they're not too fond of the Dawson family, not in the least.

Hopefully, I can at least hide out at Carter's until morning. One way or another, I know my punishment will be carried out at some point.

By the time I make it to Kit's window, I'm out of breath. It's completely dark inside her room, but the window is open, which is odd.

I'm such an ass for what I'm about to do, but I've got no choice.

My feet don't stop as I run up to the window. Kit's there, and just as she begins to close the window, she sees me and shoves it back open.

"Watch out, Kit." I'm not sure if she hears me, but then she moves to the side, out of my way.

I bend my knees, then jump and tuck myself into a ball as I fly through the window and crash onto her floor.

"Ugh," I groan, feeling the knocking of my knees on the floor from my hard landing.

"Ryker! What the hell are you doing?" She tries to pull me up, but I need a minute.

"Close the curtains," I tell her.

Kit drops my hand, hurries over to the window and snaps the curtains closed. I just lie there, staring up at her ceiling in a breathless state.

She keeps talking, but I don't hear her. All I can do is replay the events of tonight. In a matter of minutes, I fucked up my entire life. There's no changing what I did, and now I have to face the consequences of my actions.

That night, I lost everything. But my mom was safe.

CHAPTER
SEVEN
KIT

Seventeen Years old

"Move over, bitches."' Kaylee slides her ass in between me and Margo on the floor of my living room. Once she's settled, beer bottle in hand, she looks around the circle, taking in each and every person.

There's around eight of us at the moment. People get up and leave while newcomers join in. We were in the middle of an innocent game of truth or dare, but with Kaylee and Liza both here now, playfulness is out the door.

Kaylee tries to burn her death glare into Liza, who sits directly across from her. Beside Liza is her boyfriend, Damon—also known as Kaylee's crush since he moved here freshman year.

"How about a new game?" Kaylee says before she tips her half-full beer back and chugs the rest of it, leaving nothing but a drop of foam in the bottle. She's still staring down at a nervous Liza, who is trying to avoid eye contact.

I nudge my best friend, who has obviously had a little too much to drink. "What are you doing?"

She doesn't even look at me, just crawls into the middle of the circle and sets the bottle in the center. "Just having a little fun."

Our ideas of fun are drastically different. While Kaylee is outspoken and loud, I'm more reserved and…well, nice.

When she fills the space next to me again, her knee hitting mine as we sit cross-legged, I say, "Okay. Let's keep it fun." She smirks, so I pin her with a hard glare. "No drama. I mean it, Kay."

Her hands go up in surrender. "Wouldn't dream of it."

She's lying. Sitting next to me is the queen of drama. Ever since Liza and Damon started dating, Kaylee's been waiting for the chance to stick it to Liza.

Kaylee pushes herself up on her knees, making herself the center of attention. "All right, my party pals, the game is spin the bottle. You're familiar, right, Liza?"

Our friend, Margo, laughs at Kaylee's antics, egging her on while my face meets my palm.

"Fuck off, Kaylee," Liza says as she reaches over and takes Damon's hand in hers. Bad move, Liza. Very bad move.

I curse under my breath as Kaylee says, "I'll start."

She stretches her entire body out, cleavage peeking out of her skin-tight, black tank top, and directs it right at Damon. Then her ass shifts upward, giving everyone behind her a show.

The bottle spins and she drops back down next to me. To her dismay, it does not land on Damon. In fact, it doesn't land on a guy at all.

"Come here, bestie." Before I can react, she grabs my face and kisses me.

My head tilts slightly to the side, and our noses brush. The bitter taste of booze rims my lips and when her tongue slithers in my mouth, so does the tang of the beer. There are hoots and hollers from the group, mainly the guys, and when my eyes open, I see that we've drawn a crowd around us.

Giving them a show, Kaylee pulls my face closer to hers, kissing me hard. Her fingers press into the skin of my cheeks while mine rest lazily on her shoulders.

I'm not usually one to draw attention to myself, but with a best friend like Kaylee, it's hard not to.

Kaylee pulls back, smirking, and I trace my fingers around my mouth.

"Holy shit. That was sexy as hell. More. More. More," a trio of guys chant.

Kaylee and I burst out laughing, and when I follow her gaze to Damon and Liza, I'm certain she's pleased with herself. Damon sits, his mouth gaping, while Liza smacks his leg, but he doesn't stop staring at Kaylee.

"Okay then," I finally say, hoping to remove some of the unwanted attention, "looks like I'm next."

I reach out and touch the bottle, but freeze when I see a newcomer in the circle. My eyes travel from his white high-top sneakers to his black skinny jeans, all the way up to his solid white tee shirt. I swallow hard, observing the way it hugs his muscular chest so tightly that I can see the outline of his six-pack through the thin fabric. His chestnut-colored hair is flipped over to one side, showing off the clean shave beneath the disheveled layers. Asher Collins is what wet dreams are made of.

"Don't stop on my account." He smirks, his dark eyes locked on my blue ones.

My cheeks flush. Bringing me down from the cloud he unknowingly swept me away on, I give the bottle a spin and sit back down. My heart is beating so fast that I'm worried everyone can see it threatening to break free from beneath my baby blue cami.

I'm still reeling from his entrance when Kaylee bumps me. "Earth to Kit."

I look at her. "Huh?"

She points a finger and I follow its angle to the bottle on the floor. A bottle with its mouth pointed right at Asher.

Stunned, I just sit there wide-eyed and awkward.

Kaylee bumps me again. "Kit!" she grumbles under her breath, "do something."

My eyes skate from the bottle to Asher, who is not sitting but crouching down between Damon and another guy from our junior class. His empty hands are folded into fists and pressed against the floor between his wide spread legs. He's completely void of any emotion, which makes it hard to read him. Does he want me to kiss him? Will he shoot me down?

His head tilts slightly to his right shoulder, watching me. Waiting for me to *do something.*

Fuck it.

I grab the drink from Kaylee's hand that some sophomore just fetched her. Not even knowing what it is, I tip back the red plastic cup and swallow down all the fruity liquid. It tastes good—before it begins burning my esophagus. I don't drink often, or at all, really. And if my dad or Carter found out, I'd be in a world of trouble. But this liquid courage is a necessity, and fortunately, Dad's on a business trip and Carter is out with his own friends.

Once the burn subsides, I shove the cup into Kaylee's chest, not even looking at her.

I stand up, knowing Asher wouldn't dare come to me. Asher does not accommodate others. He prefers that they gratify him.

Everyone is watching me as I take slow steps through the ring of fire, passing the bottle until I'm standing in front of a still kneeling Asher.

My head is spinning and I'm not sure if it's from whatever was in that cup, or the spell I'm under every time I'm in this guy's presence.

"Are we gonna do this or what, Levine? I ain't got all night."

I squat down in front of him. My hands tremble, so I rub them together, trying to calm my nerves.

I've kissed guys before. More than I can count. Hell, I've kissed girls—one, only minutes ago. But Asher is different. He's this untouchable hero at Oakley Shores High. One that has done absolutely nothing to claim that title, aside from being the star quarterback and a walking sex symbol.

Asher blows out a breath, getting bored with this lag in his time.

Do I make the first move?

I have to. He won't.
Shit. I can't do this.

What if he pulls back and laughs at me, causing everyone else to follow suit and laugh along with him.

"Kiss already, damn," Damon grumbles from beside us.

The silence is broken as people go back to what they were doing before the bottle spun. Chatter resumes, along with game of beer pong being played in the dining room. Most of them are likely thinking I won't go through with it and that I just wasted three minutes of their precious time.

Oh my God, Kit. Quit thinking and just fucking do it.

I lift my hands, setting them on his knees to brace myself as I lean in, closing the space between our mouths.

And I do it.

Softly, my lips brush his. His nostrils flare and his warm breath hits my face. I inhale it, filling my lungs and holding it in. Asher doesn't move at all; his lips are only slightly parted, so I take the initiative to press harder. My tongue darts out, sweeping against his bottom lip, and to my surprise, he invites it in. I tilt my head, while he does the same.

My heart jumps into a frenzy, and I curse internally. *Don't you dare betray me, you stupid heart.* I talk to the organ inside me as if she's a traitorous friend. *We need this.*

Deep inhale through my nose. Forced exhale into his mouth. I lift one hand, bringing it to the back of Asher's head, and I pull him deeper into the kiss. His tongue invades my mouth as our lips move leisurely and in sync.

A small moan escapes him, and it has me smiling against his mouth.

Is Asher actually enjoying this?

Everyone around us disappears, and it's just us. Us and this kiss that ignites something inside me. A feeling I've been searching for since I was fourteen years old—the night I fell in love with a boy I can never have. After three years of being stuck in this headspace of depression over never having that love reciprocated, I finally gave up on him.

Once I did, I spent years seeking out a thrill. Anything that would compare to the way I felt that night and the days that followed. I craved the high. The ecstasy. The heart-squeezing, pulse-pounding, can't eat, can't sleep rush.

"What the fuck is going on here?" The words come from the left and hit me like a tidal wave.

Asher and I break the kiss and my eyes snap to the offender. The person who ruined it for me. I was almost there; I almost felt it again.

"You've got ten seconds to get your ass up and get the hell away from my sister before I break every goddamn bone in your face."

"Carter!" I gasp. "Stop!"

I jump up and hurry over to him to stop him from embarrassing me further. With a tight grip on his arm, I pull him away from the circle and toward a new crowd of guests, who are oblivious to the situation. "What are you doing?" I grit out, feeling like I could potentially break his bones for doing that to me.

Carter's paying me little to no attention. His gaze is laser-focused on Asher, who is now flirting with some junior. "Is that the asshole QB who flipped your skirt up at the game two weeks ago?"

I forcibly swallow the lump lodged in my throat. "Thanks a lot, Carter." I drop my hold on his arm and push through the crowd.

"Kit," he shouts. "Kit!" His voice becomes more and more strained the farther I get away from him. I walk past the keg sitting in the center of the kitchen and head steadfast for my bedroom down the hall.

Tears sting the corners of my eyes, but I ward them off, already feeling humiliated enough for one night. The last thing I need is the pity from my peers.

I open my door and slam it shut, then drop my back to my bed. Grabbing my scruffy teddy bear, I've had since I was a year old, I rest it over my face and try to steady my breaths as I breathe into it.

My door flies open, and my body shoots up. "Go away!"

Disregarding my demand, Carter shuts the door with him inside my room.

"I'm sorry, Kit. Seeing him touch you. Kiss you." He fakes a gag. "I just…you can do better than that pompous asshole."

I sniffle and swipe away the tears from my cheeks. "Oh yeah? Can I, Carter? Who? Where is this person who is better?"

"He's out there. Somewhere. But I can guarantee, that guy is not him." Carter rests his hand over mine, stopping me from plucking the fur from Teddy. "You're seventeen, Kit. Stop searching so hard for something you don't need."

"You don't know what I need."

"You're right. I don't. But I do know that I miss my little sister. The one who—"

"The one who took care of everyone else and ignored her own needs. I don't, Carter. In fact, I don't miss her one bit."

"Kit," he says softly in an attempt to pacify me.

I jerk my hand away, hating myself for behaving like a child and taking life's frustrations out on the one person who is always there for me. "I just want to live. Is it too much to ask?"

"So live. But do so with caution."

I threw caution to the wind a long time ago, when a certain someone handed me a candy bar and told me to embrace all the little things in life. Only to leave me seconds later and disappear forever. He took all the little things with him, and no matter how hard I try to just be happy with what's right in front of me, it's never enough.

"How is he?" I blurt out, instantly regretting it, because I'm not so sure I want to know. Carter just returned from a three-day trip to visit his old bestie.

"Ryker? He's good. Really good, actually."

It hurts.

"He's preparing for his mechanics test and working with his uncle at his shop. I think leaving Oakley Shores was a good move for him."

A good move. How is any of this good?

My chest feels heavy. The weight is almost unbearable. How can I hate Ryker for leaving, yet love him so much at the same time?

Will I ever pick one or the other? Love or hate?

I cut him off as he goes on about his visit to Colorado to see Ryker. "I…I've gotta get back to the party, Carter."

Looking straight past him, I get off the bed, feeling the weight of the world on my shoulders.

I have to get out of this house.

I DON'T GO BACK to the party; I end up sneaking out the back door and leaving approximately seventy high school students at my house. Valuable items are likely getting broken. The front and back lawns are more than likely covered in trash. Sex is probably being had in my dad's bed right now.

And I don't even care.

With a fifth of vodka in my hand, I trail down the streets of Oakley Shores with no destination in mind.

That's a lie.

I know exactly where I'm going.

Two miles later and half of the bottle gone, I'm standing in front of Dawson Auto Repair.

I look straight ahead at the weathered building. It's one of the originals from back when Oakley Shores began populating. Ryker's great-great-grandfather started up the business, and it's been in the family ever since. Much of his youth was spent here, as well as Carter's.

Ryker loves cars. He loves fixing shit—he also seems to enjoy breaking things. Such as my heart.

I still don't know why he left town. Couldn't even stick around for his own father's funeral. Not that I blame him there. That man was never a dad to him.

I'll never understand unless Ryker gives me a reason to. He's never even given Carter any inclination as to what he was running from, or at least, not that I've heard of. But I know it was something. To just up and leave his mom and Ezra behind the way he did, it had to be profound.

I tip back the bottle, knowing I'm breaking all the rules. Rules from my doctor, rules from my dad and Carter. Even rules I've made for myself. But some days, you just have to say, "Fuck it."

Fuck all of it. High school, boys, even life.

"Do you hear me, Ryker Dawson?" My words come out a whisper under my breath, but something snaps inside me. "Fuck it all!" I scream, "And fuck you!"

My adrenaline is pumping, heart racing, but instead of hiding from it or trying to correct it, I embrace it. I laugh at myself, probably sounding like a maniac. "This is what you wanted, right? For me to embrace life? Well, here I am doing just that."

I take another drink, relishing the burn, before raising my hand and throwing the bottle at the garage door. It shatters on impact. "I hate you!" I scream so loud that the words bounce off the building, echoing in my ears as my heart beats at an unhealthy rate.

"Wow, someone really pissed you off." The voice comes from behind me, and for a moment, I feel a rush of hope. *Ryker?*

That is, until I turn around and see who's standing there.

It's not him.

"Asher? What are you... How'd you find me?" My body sways as my head begins to feel like an inflated balloon.

He looks over my shoulder and I turn around to see the broken bottle before looking back at him. "Saw you leave and wanted to make sure you were okay."

"Since when do you care if I'm okay? I'm maimed, remember?"

I really don't feel good. I feel like I'm gonna…

"Whoa, girl." He swoops in, wrapping an arm around my waist. "Let's get you back to your house."

I'm breathless. Light-headed. Something is very wrong.

I don't know what happened after that. Three days later, I woke up in the hospital surrounded by doctors. I was told I went into sudden cardiac arrest. Fortunately, I survived long enough to finish telling my story.

CHAPTER EIGHT
RYKER

Nineteen Years Old

"Turn the fucking music down!" I scream at the top of my lungs for the umpteenth time. I can't even hear myself think, let alone study for this damn test. It's almost midnight and the asshole kid should be in bed. Okay, he's not a kid, but he sure as hell acts like one.

Biting down on the pencil, I tap my fingers against the stainless-steel desk. It's not technically a desk. It's an old tool bench that was once mint green. Uncle Greg pulled the thing from his shop and stuck it at the end of the road with a piece of paper that said *free*. After we closed up that day, I tossed it in the bed of my pickup truck and brought it home—or to his house, rather. I guess it's home. Has been for a year now. I sure as hell don't have any other place to call home. Not anymore.

When the music only grows louder, I fling my legs over the bed and get to my feet in a fit of rage. I don't have one of those swivel chairs, so I've got the makeshift desk pulled up to my bed.

Tearing the door open, I shout louder, "I'm gonna kick your ass, Denny!"

There's not a chance in hell he hears me. The paper-thin walls are vibrating from the bass, rattling an already crooked family photo hanging on the wall. I guess you'd call them a family. More so than the one I got.

I moved in with my uncle Greg and his fiancée last year when everything went to hell. His son, Denny, also known as my cousin, is a fifteen-year-old know-it-all, who's about two seconds away from getting his head shoved in the box of his speaker that's blasting this heavy metal music.

Without knocking, I throw his bedroom door open. He's sitting at his *actual* desk, headphones on and face in his phone.

"You're kidding me, right?"

He doesn't hear me. Just like he didn't hear all the shouting to turn this shit down. Why? Because the idiot has headphones on while also blasting his music so loud, you'd think we're standing in the mosh pit of a concert.

I cross the room, rip his headphones off, and toss them on his bed that sits three feet away from us.

Denny spins around in his chair and shoves me back a few steps. "What the fuck, dude!"

"What the fuck is right. The entire neighborhood doesn't need to hear your shitty music. Turn it down or I will."

With a growl, I go to leave the room, but as soon as I reach the door, I'm shoved from behind. I only stumble a couple steps before spinning on my heel and shoving Denny back. "You got a fucking problem, kid?"

"Yeah. I do. You. If you don't wanna hear my music, go back to where you came from."

My teeth grind as I stare back at the five-foot-seven punk. "Fuck you."

He shoves me again, warranting a bout of laughter, because if this douchebag really thinks he's gonna kick my ass, he's dumber than I thought.

"You think it's funny?" He shoves me again, and again, while I continue to laugh. My back hits the door, and while I could easily end this by grabbing his face and headbutting him, or just punching him square in the nose, I don't. He's got a bad attitude, but he's practically a child. I was once him. Thought I was untouchable. Thought I could get away with anything I wanted. Not to mention, as much as I hate it here, I've got no place else to go and Uncle Greg would boot my ass if I knocked out his precious offspring.

We're nose to nose, well, more like nose to chin because the kid is only fifteen and hasn't hit a growth spurt yet. Then again, he might have. His dad, my mom's brother, is on the shorter side, too. I hope for his sake he puts on a few inches because he's gonna need the height and the muscle to back up that mouth of his.

"Word of advice, cuz, swipe the razor down, not up. Lesser chance of razor burn." I pat him on the cheek with a smirk before sliding out of the space between him and the door. I turn the handle and pull it open, hitting him with the corner of the door. He steps aside as it opens farther.

"I hate you," he screams. "You've ruined my life."

Cue the dramatics. Walking down the short hall of the three-bedroom trailer, I run my fingers through my greasy hair. As I do, I sniff my left pit and the stench reminds me I need to shower. I've had my nose in these textbooks, studying for my ASE certification test that's in two weeks.

That's right. I'm following in the footsteps of every man in my family and becoming a mechanic. Something I swore I'd never do. Unfortunately, every choice has a consequence, and I had to learn that the hard way.

In a matter of minutes, all my dreams disappeared before my eyes. One split-second decision, and my life was forever changed. Not only did I quit high school and settle on a GED, I threw away a college education. I had no choice but to leave. Left my mom, my little brother, Carter and his family…her.

When I'm inside my room, I drop down onto my back on my twin-size bed. Staring at the chipped paint on the ceiling, I think of her—Kit Levine. Carter said she misses me, and I've never said the words, but I miss her, too. How could I not? Carter may have been my best friend, but Kit and I were close, too. She was like this miniature therapist, who I could talk to like an adult. Far too wise for her age and much too mature. I swear the only smiles that girl wore were forced ones. With the exception of the time I kissed her on the cheek. Before my lips even left her delicate skin, I could feel the heat rise. One look and I was certain, she was blushing.

I did that. I made her smile. Part of me worried she'd develop some sort of crush on me after that and things would be awkward, but if she did, she never showed it.

I didn't either. As time passed and I started cleaning up my act, I began to notice her more. She wasn't a little girl anymore. Growing up before my eyes was a girl who would one day fall for a guy. My only hope is that she chooses him wisely.

"Fuck," I grumble, shooting up on the bed. My fingers dig into my eyes as I rub them aggressively.

Why am I thinking like this?

Reaching over my head, I grab my pack of smokes sitting on the ledge of my headboard. I pull the lighter out of the front cellophane and retrieve a cigarette from the pack, sticking the butt between my lips and lighting it up. I've been trying to cut back, but every once in a while, I need a fix.

As I draw in a long drag, feeling the smoke hit my lungs and already settling me from my trip down memory lane, my cell phone rings from the makeshift desk behind me.

I reach over and pick it up and see that it's Carter.

Scooching myself up, I take another hit off my cigarette. "What's up, man?"

"Something bad happened, Ryker."

I can tell by his fear-stricken voice this isn't good. My stomach twists in knots and I fling my legs over the bed. "Is it Kit?" There's a beat of silence that has me heading toward full-fledged panic mode. "Dammit, Carter. Is it Kit?"

"Yeah. Her, umm…her heart stopped all of a sudden today. We're not really sure what happened. She was drinking and—"

"Kit was drinking?" I spit out on impulse. "Kit doesn't drink."

At least, she never used to. She's just a kid. I guess she's not really a kid anymore. She's seventeen, so she's passed the age that most kids begin indulging. But this is Kit, she's not like most kids.

"There's a lot Kit does these days that she never used to."

"She's gonna be okay, though…right?"

"She's stable, but she's in a medically-induced coma to regulate her body temperature. They're talking about doing surgery and implanting some device in her chest, once her body is strong enough. They're also putting her on a transplant list, but the chances of getting a donor are rare unless she's critical."

I run my fingers through my hair, blowing out a heavy breath before drawing in a drag of my cigarette. "I'm here for you, man. All of you. Tell me what you need me to do." I dab the other half of my cigarette out in an aluminum skull ashtray sitting on my dresser, perching the butt on the dip of the tray so I can smoke it later.

"Nothing," Carter says in a placid tone. "There's nothing anyone can do. We just need to hope they can implant this device and get her on the transplant list. Her heart is getting weaker and without it…"

"Don't go there. She's in good hands. Kit's young, she takes good care of herself."

Carter sighs. "She did. Over the past year and a half, she's gotten more and more carefree. It's like she completely ignores the fact that she's even sick. She's hanging with a new crowd and doing things she's never done. It's like she just doesn't give a damn anymore."

"She's a teenager. It's normal. Look at us, we're still teenagers, and we still do dumb shit."

"True. But we don't have a life-threatening condition. I'm just worried about her. Ya know?"

"I get what you're saying." I look over at my stack of books, knowing my test is coming up but willing to leave it all behind. "Maybe I should come back."

"No," he blurts out, "you know you can't do that. Besides, you're doing good in Colorado. Don't risk losing all you've gained on my account."

I wanna tell him that it's not on his account and that Kit's like a sister to me, too. He's right, though. Going back is a bad idea. "Keep me updated, okay? And if you need me, I'll be there. I don't give a shit what it costs me."

"You know I will."

We end the call, and suddenly, I'm not in the mood for studying. There's a weight on my chest that won't let up. Something is telling me to go back to the place I swore I'd never return.

I decide to take a shower to clear my head, only to flood it even more with an abundance of worries. Not just Kit and Carter, but issues that go beyond them. Oakley Shores is my home. It's where my family is. I haven't seen Ezra or my mom since I left last year. I couldn't go back and they couldn't afford to come here. Some days, I just wanna say, *fuck it*, and return to face whatever is waiting for me.

Maybe I will.

CHAPTER NINE
KIT

Eighteen Years Old
Present Day

"Good morning, my beautiful daughter," Dad says as he presses a chaste kiss to my forehead.

My head twists to look at him as he shuffles to the refrigerator and pulls out his chocolate coffee creamer. My eyebrows cave, and I force a smile. I know that tone. He's leaving again.

As he mixes his creamer and coffee, I press my elbows to the center island, leaning forward. "Where to this time?"

He looks at me with sorrow in his eyes. "How'd you guess?"

"Oh, I don't know. Could be the buttering up." I angle my head toward the papers on the counter. "Or the trip itinerary."

Dad drops a spoon in the sink then fists his coffee cup with one hand. "It's only a week."

"And the catch?" I know there is one. Dad goes on business trips all the time. Ever since he got promoted to CEO of Elton Pipelines, he's gone at least once a month. This time is different; I can feel it in my bones.

"Carter's going with me."

"Okay," I shrug, not understanding the big deal here, "I knew he was doing an internship. So what's the real catch, Dad?"

He delays his response with a long sip of his coffee before finally saying, "I've thought long and hard about it and I'd prefer for you to not stay here alone."

Here we go again. It's nothing new, but it is getting old. I'm so tired of Carter and my dad treating me like I'm this fragile girl who is on the verge of breaking.

"Fine," I say, giving up the fight, "I'll stay with Kaylee. Problem solved."

Not the first time. Won't be the last. In fact, Kaylee's house is like a second home to me.

I grab a banana out of the fruit basket and peel back the layers as Dad talks.

"That's the thing. I talked to Rhonda yesterday and they'll be heading out of town the same day we leave."

He's not lying. Kaylee's parents are dragging her to Alabama to visit family.

"When are you going?"

He takes another sip of his coffee and peers at me over the rim. "We leave late Saturday morning?"

"This Saturday?" I spit out. "Wow, thanks for the heads-up."

"It was a last-minute decision."

"So, what?" I laugh. "You're hiring a babysitter? I'm eighteen years old, Dad." I bite into my banana as Carter walks into the kitchen.

He must've just got done working out because he's only wearing gym shorts, and he's a sweaty mess. "Babysitter for what?" Carter cuts in. Using the towel from his hand, he wipes the bead of sweat from his hairline then wraps it around his neck.

"Me!" I laugh. "Eighteen-year-old me." I stomp on the lever of the trash can and drop my banana peel inside.

Dad takes a sip of his coffee, then sets the mug on the counter, still gripping it. "Don't look at it like that. Look at it as…a houseguest."

"Okay. Well, I can think of some people I'd like to have as houseguests. I do have other friends, ya know?" I snap my fingers, pointing at Dad. "Margo. She can come stay with me while you're gone."

"Margo Javis? Hard no," Dad says.

Carter grabs the milk from the refrigerator, twists the top off, and drinks straight from the jug. He licks his milk-stache, jug still in hand. "Wasn't she one of the girls who was just busted for vaping in the girls' bathroom?"

I snarl. "Eww. Get a glass. And how do you even know that?"

"Don't you know by now that I'm resourceful? I pay attention to the people my kid sister hangs out with."

"First of all, I'm not a kid. Second, Margo was part of that group, but that's beside the point. Practically every senior and some juniors vape, aside from me." I clap my hands to my chest and grin sheepishly. "Because I'm an angel, of course."

Carter finishes off the milk and twists the top back on before setting it on the counter. "Ha. An angel, my ass."

"Not helping, bro."

"Look," Dad interrupts, "I'll figure something out but just keep an open mind, okay? It's only a few days." He picks his mug back up and kisses my forehead.

Frowning, I nod in agreement. "I'll keep an open mind but you also need to understand that it won't be long and I'll be living in the college dorms, and while it's only thirty minutes away, you two can't baby me forever."

Dad chuckles. "I, too, am very resourceful. We'll see about that."

I swat at him playfully. "Byyyye, Dad."

"I'll be late tonight. Gail made stir fry for dinner. Just warm it up."

Gail is our housekeeper/former nanny. She's been with us for years, but she now has her own family and only comes twice a week, often prepping meals for us while she's here.

When Dad's out the door and it closes, I catch Carter looking at me as if he has something to say. "What?" I ask.

Stepping on the lever to the garbage, he opens it up and drops the milk carton inside. "Anyone asked you to the homecoming dance yet?"

Ugh. The homecoming dance. A subject I'd rather not discuss because the truth is, no one has asked me, and it kinda sucks…a lot. "Nope. No date, therefore I'm not going."

"What about Kaylee? Why don't you two just go together?"

"We decided we're only going if we have dates. And so far, no dates. Not looking good, considering it's just over a week away."

Kaylee and I made a deal at the start of football season that if one of us gets asked and the other doesn't, we sulk like losers at home then go to the after-party together. The thing is, Kaylee will never say yes to anyone except Damon. Therefore, we're likely not going.

"You should consider going. It's your senior year."

I shrug my shoulders, not caring to continue this conversion because it's miserable knowing not a single guy asked me. "We'll see."

"All right," he pats my shoulder as he passes behind me to the coffee pot, "let's get you to school."

"Would you mind putting a shirt on? Really don't need the entire female student body gawking when you drop me off."

"Why?" He smirks. "Doesn't bother me one bit."

I just shake my head, and he leaves to go get a shirt. When he returns, I grab my backpack off the barstool and fling it over my shoulder. "You don't agree with him, do you? That I need someone here with me?"

I'm not sure why I'm asking him that question. Carter is more overprotective than my dad is. Of course he agrees.

Carter's hand lingers over the cupboard, then drops to his side. "You're not gonna like what I have to say, Kit. But yeah. I do agree with him. And I think it's high time you start taking your condition more seriously."

There's a pang in my chest I wasn't prepared for. I hate when he does this, and the last thing I want is to argue, so I forget he said anything. "All right. I'll keep an open mind about someone staying, but please, do not let him bring home some Debbie Downer or Watchful Willy."

Pulling the towel from around his neck, his grin turns mischievous. "A Debbie Downer, I can put a stop to. A Watchful Willy might be necessary." Carter twirls the towel around until it's balled tight at the end.

"Don't you dare," I warn, half-serious, half-humoring him.

I walk backward until I turn around and I'm full-on running through the house to get away from him. He chases after me, laughing, as I run into the living room. "Carter! Drop the damn towel."

I'm cornered by the front door when he snaps the towel at my leg. I let out a high-pitched squeal. "Stop!"

He lets the towel fall to the side. "Maybe if you'd put on some longer shorts, it wouldn't hurt so bad."

I look down. "What's wrong with my shorts?"

"Uhh, they're too short. Are you trying to give the entire class of Oakley Shores High a show?"

This is so typical of Carter. Always trying to get me to cover every inch of skin on my body. Some call it brotherly love; I call it insanity.

"Maybe I am." I flip my hair over my shoulder as I spin around and open the front door.

"Better not be," Carter shouts as I close the door, cutting off anything else he has to say.

I love my family more than life itself, but damn, sometimes I wish they'd just let a girl live.

CHAPTER
TEN
KIT

Ahh. Oakley Shores High. Home of the Cougars: a melting pot of testosterone and hormones for all.

Kaylee, my best friend, comes skipping down the hall, her long, brunette pigtail braids flapping against her chest. She slides up to me, presses her back to my neighboring locker, and whispers, "You are not going to believe what just happened!"

I twist the combination, pull my locker open, and humor her. "You're right, I probably won't, but let's hear it."

She pouts, as if I just ruined her entire vibe. "Wow, someone's a sourpuss today."

I drop my bag to the floor and kneel down, pulling out all my textbooks and my laptop then drop the ones I don't need in the bottom of my locker. "Sorry, Kay. I'm just in a funk today. Can't you skip this trip with your family? I need you here." I shake my head, shutting myself up while looking up at her. "Sorry. We can talk about that later. What's this unbelievable news?"

Kaylee is the queen of gossip at OSH, practically running the rumor mill. It's one of the many perks of being her friend—my name stays out of it. Among other things, like her bubbly personality and her ability to always cheer me up when I'm down.

"Well," she drags out, her shoulders dancing, "someone officially has a date for the homecoming dance."

My eyes shoot to her, wide and full of the same excitement she has. "He asked you?"

"Mmhmm." She nods with tightly pressed lips as she bites back a smile. Her cheeks flush with the smallest hue of pink.

I jump up, dropping and scattering books and papers all over, and pull her in for a hug. "Wait," I look at her with my hands on her shoulders, "we are talking about—"

"Damon! Yes!"

"Ahhh," I squeal, vise-gripping her body and jumping up and down with her. "I'm so freaking happy for you, Kay."

I really am. Kaylee has had the biggest crush on Damon Walters. So many diary entries, doodled hearts, and MASH games revolved around her feelings for this guy.

We pull out of the embrace, Kaylee all smiles as she says, "All I have to say is, it's about damn time."

"Your persistence has paid off." I laugh, because we both know it's true.

"Damn straight it did."

After all this time, Kaylee never once gave up fighting for this guy. And it's not like he didn't see her, because he did. Once he transferred here, he became part of our group. He jumped right into a relationship with Liza, though, and it wasn't until this past summer that they finally called it quits. Rumor has it, Liza is now dating a sophomore at Oakley Shores University.

Once I've got my papers and books shoved back in my locker and the ones I need in hand, Kaylee hooks an arm around my neck as we walk to class.

I look over at her, noticing she's empty-handed. "Where are your books?"

"In class already. Got here bright and early today."

I stop walking, eyebrows pinched together. "You what?"

"I...got here early."

"Okay. Who are you and what happened to my best friend?"

"Damon sent me a text last night. Asked me to meet him in the library before first period. So I got here an hour early. Ya know, just to play it safe in case I missed him."

"Girl. You've got it bad."

Her hip bumps mine. "I wish you'd set your sights on someone so I could get excited for you."

"I'm not sure that's possible in this town."

"Still hate Asher?"

"Uh, yeah. Need I remind you that the guy also hates me?"

Taking a more serious note, Kaylee peers over at me with sympathetic eyes. "Asher hates everyone, babe. He just needs to get to know you."

"Pass. I know all I need to know about that asshole. Big ego, small brain."

"Well, if you're sizing him up. Maybe there are other parts of his body you need to explore." She waggles her brows, and I just laugh it off.

I may have been head over heels for Asher at one time, but that changed the minute my entire life did.

After I collapsed in his arms last year—which I have no recollection of—Asher apparently called an ambulance and even rode with me to the hospital. Once I was released, I went to his house to thank him, and I saw him for who he really is.

I'm making my way down the stairs when the chatter of the occupants in the basement hits my ears. It's all the proof I need to know Asher isn't alone. My nerves climb as I descend the staircase. I'll just thank him and leave. Like a Band-Aid.

Before I reach the bottom, I'm able to see who his guests are—Liza, Carly, Micah, Logan, and Damon. This is just perfect. I can feel my pulse quicken as I rub my hands together, trying to settle the anxiety brewing inside me.

Logan is the first to notice me, and he wastes no time making my presence known to everyone else. "Well, look who we've got here."

Asher's head snaps around from where he's sitting on the couch, and following his actions is Liza. All she sees is an opportunity to belittle me in front of her friends. I can feel it already.

She chokes on a laugh, and I'd love nothing more than for her to continue choking on it until she's unconscious on the floor.

"What are you doing here?" Asher asks.

"Your mom let me in. Can we talk for a minute?" I ask, looking right at him.

He turns back around, stretches his arm out over the back of the couch. "I'm busy."

Liza is glaring at me, though she's scrunched under Damon's armpit now. "Are you deaf, Kitty Cat?" *she seethes.* "He said he's busy."

I'm just gonna say what I came to say, clear my conscience and leave these assholes to do whatever they were doing before I got here.

"Oh, come on," *Logan says.* "Let her stay and hang out." *He pats his lap.* "Saved a seat just for you, Kit."

Logan is the more humane of the bunch, with Micah and Damon not far behind. It's Asher that gives everyone shit, and right now, I'm on the receiving end.

"Thanks, Logan, but I'm not staying. I just stopped by to thank Asher for his help. If it weren't for—"

"You said your thanks." *Asher completely cuts me off.* "You can go now. Ya know, before you pass out again."

Liza busts out in laughter, while a couple others choke back a laugh. My cheeks flush, only it's not with humiliation, but anger. "You know what, fuck you," *I spit out in one breath.*

In a swift motion, Asher gets up. "What did you just say?"

"I said, fuck you." *I point a finger at Liza.* "And you."

Then I'm back up the stairs and hurrying out the front door, hoping I never have to talk to these insensitive pricks ever again.

If only that were the case. I never would have guessed Kaylee would slowly become part of that group over the summer, or that I'd be right there by her side. When we're all together, I do my best to avoid Liza and Asher, but I actually like the others. I suppose that's why I keep hanging out with them.

"First of all," Kaylee says as we walk into our first class

together, "you're too good for Asher. Second, the entire student body gave him that big ego. They worship him and he eats it up." Her arm drops from around my neck before she shuffles to her seat on the other side of the room.

At the beginning of the year, Kaylee and I sat right next to each other—we always do at the start of every school year—and like every class, every year, we get separated for talking too much. If you aren't forced away from your best friend in class because you have so much to share, are you truly best friends?

I'm settled in my seat when my phone buzzes from inside the front pocket of my hoodie. I pull it out, see Kaylee's name on the screen, then look across the room and give her a questioning look before reading the text message.

Kaylee: I'm such a bitch. You had a rough morning and I never gave you a chance to tell me why.

I type back quickly as Mr. Banks takes his place in front of the class.

Me: Doesn't matter. Today we celebrate your sexy ass snagging the boy of your dreams for HOCO. The Soap Box after school?

The Soap Box is our hangout spot. Technically, everyone from OSH hangs out there but, considering Kaylee's family owns the place, it was ours first.

We share another look through the fifteen feet of space between us, then our eyes both drop to our phones in our laps.

Kaylee: Hells yeah! I'll drive ;)

Me: Unless I'm walking, you have no choice but to drive me…

"Ms. Levine," Mr. Banks says, grabbing my attention before I can finish typing out my sentence. "Is there something more important in your lap that you care to share with the entire class?"

My cheeks fill with heat as I slowly slide my phone back in the pocket of my hoodie and look at Mr. Banks with a grin. "No, sir."

This isn't the first time I've been called out in class, but I still hate the attention. I can't even count the amount of times I've been pulled aside by teachers who have told me that Kaylee is dragging me down. Those exact words were never used, but it was presumed.

She's always been the wild one, while I sort of hid in her shadow—until now.

I'm not a teacher's pet, per se. But I have always been a favorite. I know that sounds a little egotistical, but it's the truth. I'm a good student, and I've always been a good kid.

Or, at least, I was.

Up until sophomore year, I maintained a 4.0 GPA. I put school first and my social life second. There was a time when I was downright scared of life. I was scared to fail, to disappoint, and most of all, scared to die. Then one day, everything changed. I began to live and with it came sacrifices. I have no regrets. I'm not graduating at the top of my class, my GPA dropped an entire point, but the weight of the world is no longer on my shoulders.

I chose myself, and it's the best decision I've ever made.

For years, I took life too seriously. I said no when I wanted to say yes. I said yes when I wanted to say no. Always planning for my future, while forgetting to live in the moment. I've taken my medication at the exact minute of the exact hour every single day for as long as I can remember—nine a.m., three p.m., nine p.m.

Four years ago when Ryker kissed my cheek, everything changed. It's crazy, I know. But I woke up to this new feeling inside and I've been searching for it ever since. A year later, when he told me to take time to enjoy life, I did just that. Through all the little things life has to offer, I've found myself. Whether it's doing one cheer with the team because it makes me feel alive. Eating a candy bar. Dancing to music. Drinking a beer. Or, going out with friends and letting time pass without acknowledging it, all the while missing my nine p.m. medication.

I survived those things. I didn't die because I danced, or took a pill two hours late. Instead of killing me, those nights made me stronger. I refuse to be that person who looks back and says *I wish I would have*. I'm going to look back and say, *I'm glad I did*.

With all that said, I know my limits. This device in my chest may save me, but my heart is still weak. I've learned what my body can and can't handle. I'm not a complete idiot who thinks that she can defy science or beat death.

But, we'll all die someday, right?

Today is not that day for me. In fact, today is a gift and another day to live. Which is exactly what I plan to do as soon as the final bell rings.

Mr. Banks wraps up his lecture on dissecting frogs, which has me cringing. Next week we start digging in, literally, and my stomach is already arguing the matter.

"I hope you got some good notes today. Pop quiz tomorrow morning. Study the material and be prepared. If you fail the quiz, you won't be in the first dissection group."

I swallow hard and look over at Kaylee, whose smile doesn't falter. I can't tell if it's because she wants to laugh at my distaste of the subject, or because I know she loves this shit. The girl probably can't wait to slice into a nice fatty frog.

With a heavy sigh, I snatch my belongings off the desk and meet Kaylee at the front of the class. "Well, there's one way to get out of gutting a frog," she whispers.

"It's tempting, but my sliding GPA tells me to take my chances."

Kaylee and I go to our lockers together, then part ways for the rest of our classes. We've only got first and last period together, which sucks, but at least we have lunch to catch up.

When lunch rolls around, the rumble in my stomach has me walking briskly down the hall, in hopes of getting in line before the entire senior class rolls in.

"Hi, Ezra." I wave to Ryker's little brother in passing.

He responds with a smile and keeps on his way. It'll never get easier seeing him. He's a constant reminder of Ryker and his spitting image. Fortunately, he's only a freshman, so I don't see him often.

Kaylee hooks an arm around mine. "Damn, girl, slow down. I'm gonna break my ankle in these shoes."

"Maybe it'll teach you not to wear four-inch wedges to school."

Kicking a leg out, she shows off her cheetah print shoes. "Even a broken ankle wouldn't trash these babies."

"You're insane."

Kaylee lays a slobbery kiss on my cheek. "But you love me."

"Yes, I do. Even if I question your sanity most days."

"Oh! Speaking of sanity. What's this news that had you looking as if your goldfish drowned?"

A burst of laughter climbs up my throat. "I don't even have a goldfish." I shift to a more serious tone. "So, Carter and my dad are both leaving town for a week, and you know how they are. They think I need someone to stay with me. It's ridiculous, but there's really no way out of it."

Kaylee tips a frown. "Shit. Let me guess, they're leaving while I'm out of town, visiting my distant relatives I've never met before?"

"Bingo."

"Trust me, I don't wanna go on this little family vacay any more than you want a babysitter. If I could get out of it, I would."

"Ugh. Babysitter." I shake my head. "It's so stupid. Why can't my dad and my brother be normal and let me live like I'm eighteen?"

"Because they love you."

We walk into the cafeteria, and the line is already massive. We spot Damon immediately, and he waves us over. I shake my head no, not wanting to cut in front of two dozen people and risk pissing them off.

"Come on," Kaylee says, pulling me toward the front of the line.

"It's okay. Let's just wait like everyone else."

"Um. No," Kaylee says, "we get a chance to cut this line, we cut."

"Fiiine," I drag out the word as I follow Kaylee, like I always do.

A few students throw shade our way as we pass them because they know we're cutting, but Kaylee being oblivious, like she always is, only has her sights set on one thing—or person, rather.

It isn't until we're at Damon's side that I notice who he's with. I shouldn't be surprised, though. Damon, Asher, Logan, and Micah are always together.

"Aren't you two looking mighty fine today?" Logan says, being the charmer he is.

I put my hands on my cheeks like I'm blushing and say, "Aww, thanks."

He throws an arm around my shoulder and pulls me close. "Glad to see this fucker hasn't scared you away from us yet." He slaps Asher on the shoulder. "He tends to do that."

Asher huffs, turns around, and completely avoids everyone. It's no secret that Asher is cruel to most people, but I'll never understand why I get the worst of it. I've hung out with him and his friends for the past four months, and he still pretends I don't exist.

"Isn't this cute," Liza says, stirring to our side with her bestie, Carly. "The bitch finally got what she wanted."

She's referring to Kaylee and Damon, no doubt.

Liza nudges Damon's shoulder as she passes by him. "Go away, Liza. You're not wanted here," Damon says in a low voice.

"Well, neither is the stray kitty, but she's always at Kaylee's side." She looks at me, then back to Damon. "Our friends are dating so get used to me, babe." She bops Damon's nose then steers to Carly's side.

Kaylee lunges toward Liza, but Damon quickly pulls her back. "She's not worth it."

"Fuck off, Liza," I say, not regretting my word choice one bit.

Liza puts a hand over her mouth. "Ooh, someone's realized she has a voice."

"I've always had a voice; I just choose my battles. But if you want to make an enemy out of me," I raise both hands curling my fingers toward my chest, "bring it on."

Everyone laughs, including Asher. Carly being the only exception, since her loyalty lies with Liza.

"Why are you even here?" Liza spits, fuming from humiliation.

"Why the fuck are you here, Liza?" Asher asks in a monotone voice, taking everyone by surprise. He doesn't even turn around to look at her.

A pin could drop, and we'd all hear it. That's how quiet the entire line goes. Liza has a reputation for putting people in their places—much like Asher. Not to mention, she's the most popular girl in school. It has to be because people are intimidated. She's a bitch, and Asher's a dick.

Liza doesn't respond, just blows out a heavy breath, crosses her arms over her chest, and waits her turn in line.

Once we've got our food, we go to the same table we've sat at since senior year started. All the people who were in line, including Liza and Carly. My and Kaylee's friend, Margo, also sits with us occasionally, but it looks like today she's sitting with our old group of friends. That's the table where I actually belong. I don't belong here with these people. I keep coming back for Kaylee, though.

"You boys ready for the big game tomorrow night?" Kaylee asks.

"Hell yeah, we are. Alcove isn't gonna know what hit them," Logan responds, before shoving a fork of salad in his mouth. He speaks, mouth full, ranch dressing smeared on his lips. "They don't stand a chance against our boy, Asher."

I'm wiping gravy off my hand when I drop my napkin on the floor. I lean down and grab it, and when I come back up, I notice Asher staring back at me. I expect him to look away; instead, he tips back his milk carton that has the top completely open and drinks the entire thing down while watching me.

My head tilts to the side as I challenge him to look away. Asher doesn't usually acknowledge me, unless he has something rude to say, but so far today, he's defended me against Liza—well, sort of—and now he's looking me straight in the eyes.

Kaylee bumps my arm, and I peel my eyes off Asher's. "Kit?"

"Huh?"

"Logan asked if you were going to Asher's party after the game tomorrow night. Since you were off in la-la land, I answered for you. Yes, Logan. Kit will be there."

"Awesome-sauce," Logan says, nodding his head in delight with her response. Logan is the class clown, and also the class flirt. He's also the sweetest guy in the world, aside from my brother.

We finish up lunch, and I'm at my locker, getting my books for my next class, when Logan pops up out of nowhere. "Hey, sexy." He throws an arm around my shoulder. "Rumor has it, you don't have a date to HOCO. It just so happens, I don't either. How about you and I go together and make it a thing? Not like you and me as a thing, but a thing where we go together. That sort of thing."

I chuckle at his completely screwed-up offer, but I also think it's really thoughtful. The truth is, I don't have a date, and without him, I probably wouldn't have one, so he's saving me from flying solo or ditching the dance altogether.

We begin down the hall and I say, "That's, umm…sweet, Logan. I'd—"

"Actually, she's going with me," Asher cuts in, catching me off guard.

Logan and I both stop walking. Asher does the same.

"What did you just say?" I'm pretty sure I heard him incorrectly. First of all, Asher can't stand me. Second, he doesn't date or even acknowledge any of the girls in this school.

"Yeah," Logan repeats my question, "what *did* you just say?"

"I said she's going with me."

Logan chuckles. "Since when do you want a date for a dance?"

"Since now," Asher deadpans.

Logan gives me a look, seeking confirmation, while his arm is still draped over my shoulder.

"I guess I just don't remember you asking me?" It's a question, not a statement, because we both know Asher never once asked me or even hinted he was going to ask me.

Asher raises his shoulders. "I'm asking you now. What do you say?"

My eyebrows pinch together tightly, and I bite down on my bottom lip. "How about…no." I look from Asher to Logan, still unsure what the hell is going on.

Asher laughs, as if me turning him down is some sort of joke. "You can't be serious?"

"Oh, I'm dead serious." I pull Logan's arm and lock mine around it. "I already have a date."

Asher glares at Logan, as if he's putting some sort of unspoken spell on him. His teeth grind, and he nods his head slightly to the right, gesturing for him to get lost.

I look at Logan, hoping he's not seriously intimated by this guy—his friend.

"Hey," Logan says, "there are plenty of fish in the sea. Go with my boy, Asher. Just promise you'll save a dance for me?" His arm drops, and he gives Asher a bro tap, awaiting my response. He goes to pull away, but I tighten my hold.

"Logan, wait."

"Don't worry about it. You two will have a," he glares back at Asher, *"amazing fucking time."* Logan begins walking backward slowly, eyes still locked on Asher, before he turns and picks up his pace down the hall.

I feel like I'm in the twilight zone. This is too weird, and I'm going to need a minute or twenty to wrap my head around what just happened.

"So, it's settled. I'll pick you up around seven for the dance?" Asher goes to leave, but I stop him.

"Wait a minute." The words fly out of my mouth before I even know what I'm going to say. Spinning around, he quirks a brow. "Just because Logan rescinded his offer, doesn't mean I'm going with you."

This guy is something else. It's a little presumptuous of him to assume that no date means I'll automatically go with him.

Asher chuckles, looks left then right, before blinking back to me. "Why wouldn't you say yes? There isn't a girl in this school who'd say no."

My eyes widen and I'm pretty sure the device in my chest just shocked me back to life. "Wow." I shake my head, unsure how to respond to such a pompous statement.

"Come on, Kit," he steps closer, "we both know you've had a crush on me since freshman year."

"Umm. No. I *did* have a crush on you, but that died the minute my heart did. You've proven to be everything I despise in a guy, so I suggest you pick out one of your grovelers and take them to the dance."

I leave him standing there silently, dumbfounded.

Un-fucking-believable.

CHAPTER
ELEVEN
KIT

"Carter," I holler, swinging my backpack off my shoulder and dropping it on the dining room table. "You home?"

His car is here but that doesn't say much. He could be out with friends or studying at the library. I laugh at the thought. Carter at the library. That'd be a sight.

Growing up, I always pictured Carter doing great things. He's intelligent and goal-driven, but lately, it seems like he's settling. I didn't expect him to follow in our dad's footsteps and work for Elton Pipelines, yet that's exactly what he's doing—for now, anyways. With two more years of college to go, I'm hoping he decides to live out his own dreams instead of our dad's.

Footsteps padding down the stairs give me my answer: he is home.

I pull open the refrigerator and grab a tub of strawberry yogurt and a spoon. I peel the aluminum top off and take a spoonful when Carter comes in.

"Hey. You didn't need a ride home, right?"

I shake my head, speaking with a dollop of yogurt sitting on my tongue. "It's Thursday. Rode with Kay and we went to The Soap Box."

Carter and Kaylee alternate bringing me home, while Carter is usually the one to bring me to school.

"Whew." He wipes his hand across his forehead, heading to the fridge himself. "For a second, I thought I forgot ya."

"Wouldn't be the first time."

Carter sticks his tongue out at me and makes the worst cringe face.

"Don't worry," I tell him. "Won't be long until I can drive myself."

"'Bout time. That fancy car sitting in the garage needs its pistons opened. How much longer ya got?"

"About a month. I see Dr. Shaw next week, and I'm already planning to beg him to release me from my restrictions sooner."

Carter grabs a bottle of water and shuts the fridge, then leans over the counter beside me. "No point in rushing it. You've got the rest of your life."

I sigh. "Easy for you to say."

One of the downfalls of having a heart condition is restricted driving. Well, I guess it's not restricted when you can't do it at all. I've had my license since I was sixteen—even got a brand-new car for my birthday—but haven't driven it since I was seventeen. When the device in my chest was implanted, I was put on a six-month driving restriction, and thankfully, that time is finally coming to an end.

Watch out world, Kit Levine is almost free.

"So," Carter begins, "remember the talk this morning about finding someone to stay with you while Dad and I are gone?"

I grumble, "How could I forget?"

"I've found a solution that will make us all happy. Or a person, rather."

My eyes shoot to him, wide, yet cautious, because if he's planning on having one of his ex-girlfriends or one of his crazy friends stay here, I'll punch him for even considering it. "Go on," I say, giving him the benefit of the doubt.

Carter grins, taking a long sip of his water as if he's purposely building up the anticipation.

I grab the top to the water and shove it into his chest, causing him to spill water down his chin. "Out with it already!"

He laughs, wiping the excess dribble with the back of his hand, then finally pulls the bottle away from his mouth.

"I'm already prepared to argue this because if it's taking you this long to tell me who it is, it can't be good."

"Let's just say a friend of mine—"

"Nope," I pop my lips. "Not happening. Your friends are slimy."

He laughs before grabbing my spoon from the empty tub of yogurt. When I least expect it, he taps it on my nose. "Dude!" I slap his hand away, before wiping the yogurt from my nose and smearing it down his white tee shirt. Then, when his guard is down, I snatch the spoon from his hand, ready to give him a yogurt facial.

"All right, all right." He holds his hands up in surrender. "I come in peace."

"Peace, my ass." I drop the spoon on the counter. "Who is it?"

The sound of someone coming down the steps has me on high alert. "Is someone here?"

Carter doesn't respond, just stands there with a mischievous look on his face.

The footsteps come closer and closer, until...

He's here.

"What's up, Kit-Kat?"

No way.

It's him.

Stunned doesn't even begin to describe what I'm feeling. I open my mouth to speak, but the words get lodged in my throat.

He's changed. Wow, has he changed. I'm pretty sure he's the same height, but he's definitely packed on some muscle, not that he was scrawny before. His dark hair is a little longer, but the same style he always wore it—close shave on the sides, messy on the top and flipped over to the right. His eyes are softer now, which leads me to believe he's found some sort of peace with himself.

"What the hell is he doing here?" My words come out much harsher than I planned, but it was almost necessary to show my disdain. I'm almost positive I know why he's back in town. His granddad passed away last week, and he and Carter were always pretty close.

"Surprise," Carter says, unsure whether it's a good surprise or a bad one. Carter joins Ryker's side, hooking an arm around his neck. "Found this guy walking down Coswell Boulevard with his thumb in the air. Figured I'd give him a ride before some cougar snatched him up—no pun intended."

"Always the jokester." Ryker fakes a few punches to Carter's gut, and we all laugh.

Carter knows, to an extent, how angry I was with Ryker when he left, so he should know better than to catch me off guard like this. To Carter, it was just a phase of being left without a goodbye. But that's not the case and it was never something I got past.

My emotions prick at my skin and I have the urge to claw at them. So many things hit me at once—all the pain I felt those days after he left. Pain that never really subsided, I just learned to ignore it as it slowly morphed into anger.

Ryker opens his arms as if he expects me to just bury myself into his chest. "Come on, Kit. It's been almost two years. Aren't you happy to see me?"

I swipe my yogurt container off the counter and turn around to drop my spoon in the sink. "Two years too late," I mumble.

I'd love nothing more than to throw myself in his arms. Bury my face in his chest, and inhale the scent of the leather jacket he's still wearing. I wish I could cry happy tears for his arrival. That first year after he left, I would have. Not anymore.

"He's gonna stay with you while Dad and I are gone."

My eyes snap to Carter's. "He's what?" I shake my head. "That's not happening. Besides, Dad would never allow it."

"Dad and I talked, and he knows Ryker's changed a lot since then. He said it was fine. Made a few small threats, but he's cool with it."

"I highly doubt he's *cool with it*."

I'm having a really hard time believing this. My dad always pegged Ryker as an instigator and was worried he'd drag Carter down a dark path. To leave him alone in a house with his daughter for an entire week? Not a chance in hell.

Carter leans close and whispers, "Let go of the past. Give him a chance, Kit."

"A chance to what? Be my friend and leave again?" This time, I don't mask my words. I say them loud and clear as I turn around to face the boy who left us behind. "Because that's what he'll do. That's what Ryker always does."

Dad walks in the kitchen and the tension in the room thickens to the point of suffocation. His expression is stern as he sets his briefcase in the corner of the room, where it always sits. He undoes the button on the sleeve of his baby blue dress shirt and rolls it up slowly, assessing the situation. I look from him, to Carter, to Ryker.

My thoughts overpower the voices outside of it, while I try to steady my jelly legs. He's really here. He came back, but for how long?

I snap out of my own head when Dad tips his chin to Ryker. "How've you been?"

"Not bad. Working a lot, ya know?"

Carter and I watch intently as the two struggle to hold a conversation.

Dad clears his throat. "Glad to hear you're doing something proactive with your time."

"Okay then," I interrupt, with my eyebrows dancing across my forehead. "I'm going to study for a little bit. Got a quiz in bio tomorrow. You all enjoy this…conversation." I grab my bag off the table, spin on my heel, and leave.

That was brutal, but I'm happy I was able to dip out. Poor Carter is stuck.

My dad isn't a total browbeat; he's actually an amazing dad with a huge heart. He loves Carter and me more than anything. Which is exactly why he's always been a little over-the-top protective. Not so much Carter as me. I get the constant supervision, questions, and curfews while Carter gets endless talks about his future. Regardless, I love him for it, and I know he's just trying to do the best he can as a single parent.

My shallow breaths make me feel dizzy as I travel down the hall. I wanna peek back in the kitchen to make sure I'm not dreaming, but right now, I just need to get away from there before I pass out from shock.

He's really here.

Once I'm in my room, I close the door and drop down on my bed with my phone, seeing that Kaylee has left me a chain of text messages and missed calls.

Kaylee: Call me.

Kaylee: KIT! Call me.

Kaylee: Ok, what are you doing that's got you this preoccupied?

Kaylee: I have news. Double news! Call me, dammit!

Kaylee: Forget it. I'm coming over.

Kaylee always has news. As the editor for the school paper and the class gossip, she always has something to tell me. I love the excitement she gets when she fills me in on all this random drama, but I don't listen because I care about everyone else's problems—I listen because she likes having someone to tell.

Instead of texting her right back, I lean over the side of my bed, and slap my hand around underneath the frame until I've got my shoebox full of memories. Sliding it out, I lift it and set it on the bed.

I sit there and stare at it for at least a minute before flipping the top off. Inside are all my favorite memories and sitting right on top is my favorite of all.

Picking up the fun-sized Kit Kat, I run my thumb over the red wrapper. It's the last candy bar Ryker gave me. My fingers teeter with the small tear in the side, where I almost opened it and ate it. For some reason, I never finished.

I'm still holding the candy bar with the lid to my box off when my bedroom door flies open. Kaylee barges in and slams the door shut behind her.

"Girrrrl," she drags out as she crosses the room to my bed. "Did Ryker Dawson really just answer your door?"

"Good to see you, too, Kay. And yes." I chuckle. "Ryker is back in town. Temporarily," I add.

Her eyes shoot to the candy bar in my hand. "No." She sits down, holding her hand out for the candy bar. "No. No. No. We are not doing this again, Kit."

I smile because I love that she cares so much. "It's not like that. I promise."

"Then give me the candy bar." She rubs her fingers on her palm, practically begging for me to hand it over. "Come on. Give it to me. I'll eat that bitch right now."

I drop the candy bar back in the box and place the lid on where it's out of Kaylee's reach, because she totally would eat it. "It's two years old. Trust me, you don't want to." I laugh.

"I don't care. If that's what it takes to stop you from falling for this guy all over again, I'll eat two-year-old sushi."

"Now that's just gross."

"What's gross is all the snot I wiped from your nose while you were crying over this guy."

She did do that. My head tilts to the side, and I look at her adoringly. "You're a good friend, Kay."

"I won't be. If we have to replay sophomore year all over again, I'll go batshit, psycho friend on your ass."

I laugh again before taking a serious note. "Look at me," I cup her cheeks in my hands, "I promise you, I'll never fall for him again. Not after he left the way he did."

If anything, his unannounced visit makes me even more furious with him. He left us without even saying goodbye. Years of friendship forgotten, like it meant nothing to him. Sure, Carter and him kept in touch, but he didn't just leave Carter, he left me, too.

"Promise promise?"

"Promise promise promise. Forget all this Ryker nonsense. I've got news, too."

"Oooh." Her shoulders do a little dance as she gets comfy on the bed. "Let's hear it."

I nod in response. "You're not going to believe this," I pause for a beat, adding to the anticipation, "Logan asked me to HOCO."

"Damn you. I thought you were gonna say Asher asked you." She swats my hands away from her face.

Kaylee has this fantasy of her and Damon dating at the same time as me and Asher. She also ignores the fact that I can't stand the guy.

I tsk. "Seems Oakley Shores High's queen of gossip is out of the loop more than I thought."

Kaylee sweeps her hand through the air like my news is mundane to her. "Yeah. Well, Logan doesn't count as gossip. He's too…Logan."

"You never let me finish. Logan asked me, and before I could answer, Asher interrupted."

"Okay. I'm listening." Folding her hands together, she rests her chin on her fists, eyes twinkling with excitement. Kaylee loves a good story.

"So Logan asked me. As friends, of course."

"Yeah. Of course." She blinks rapidly, hurrying me along to the good stuff.

"Then out of nowhere comes Asher with his chest all puffed out and says," I put on my best man's voice, "she's already got a date."

"No, he didn't."

"Oh, he did. Basically, it was his way of asking me without eating his pride and actually asking me."

"Well, bitch…what did you say?" The anticipation is eating her alive, and it's comical.

"I told him no."

As if all her hopes and dreams just shattered into pieces on the bed, Kaylee drops her chin to her chest. "Nooooo!" she cries out, falling onto her back on the bed. Her head lifts. "Any chance you'll change your mind?"

Dramatic much?

"Do I look desperate?"

Her head falls back down while she curses under her breath. "Can't you at least try to remember the Asher you once fell for? He's not all that bad."

"Not all that bad?" I huff. "He basically mocked me for months for having a heart condition. He refers to me as broken and uses me as the butt of his jokes."

"He stuck up for you today."

It's like she didn't hear anything I said.

"Haven't you heard that guys bully the girls they like because they don't want them to know?"

"Kay," I drawl, "this isn't middle school. Asher had every opportunity over the summer to be nice to me and he chose the alternate route. I'm not going with him. Besides, this whole HOCO offer seems a little sketchy."

"Okay. Let's weigh your options." She holds both hands up like they're scales. "We've got Logan: semi-attractive and funny but flirts with anyone with a vagina. Not to mention, a guy who is more like a brother than boyfriend material." She lowers her hand, raising the other. "And we have Asher: all-star athlete, drop-dead gorgeous, and most sought-after guy in school—"

"Who treats everyone like they're beneath him."

"It's his character. I thought you wanted to be the one who got to see a different side of him. That side you saw the night you had your health scare."

"That was until I went to thank him and he all but kicked me out of his house."

"This is about Ryker, isn't it?"

"What? No! Ryker literally just got here."

"How long is he back?"

I shrug my shoulders, unsure myself. "Don't know. Apparently, Carter wants him to stay with me while he and my dad are out of town, since *someone* has to go on a family trip." That someone being her.

"Oh God, no. Kit, this is bad. Very bad. You cannot be stuck in a house alone with him for a week. You're sure to fall."

"Would you stop it? I'm over Ryker. I'm not sure I could ever look at him the way I used to."

Ryker knows my mom left when I was a kid. He knows from me, and from Carter, that I struggle with abandonment issues. I always thought he cared, but him leaving proved he didn't give a damn how I felt.

"Okay. I'm giving you the benefit of the doubt, but due to this new information, I'm going to get on my hands and knees and beg my mom to let me stay home from the trip. For your own good."

A knock at the door has us both looking at it.

"Come in," I holler.

"Hey," Carter says, poking his head in the door, "Ryker and I are heading down to Tasty Dip for ice cream. Wanna come? For old times' sake?"

I shake my head, disappointed in him for even mentioning old times. "You're really going to keep pretending? Aren't you?"

"Please, Kit. I know you're still angry, but do this for me. He's only back for a little bit."

And that's exactly my point.

"Fine. I'll be right down."

"Thanks, sis."

Carter leaves and I look at Kaylee. "Come with us. Please."

She rolls off the bed and gets to her feet. "Can't. I've gotta babysit for the Millers at five."

I growl and throw a little hissy fit before finally acknowledging it's not her fault. "All right. Tell me this news first that you were blowing my phone up over.

"Oh! Get this. Carly dumped Micah."

"No fucking way!"

She nods. "Yep. Rumor has it, Liza talked her into it, just so she could go to all the college parties with her and hang with the college boys."

"They've been together for like, ever."

"Not anymore." Kaylee drags herself to the door. "Call me later when you're ready to admit you're still in love with your brother's best friend." She blows me a kiss before leaving.

I hope she isn't holding her breath for that phone call.

❖

Ryker and I are sitting at a picnic table in front of Tasty Dip while Carter goes back up for napkins.

I run my tongue up the side of my peanut butter ice cream that sits high on a sugar cone.

"How is it?" Ryker asks.

"It's fine." I lick it again, catching him in my peripheral. The corner of his lip is tucked up and I grin. "What?"

"Nothing. Just remembering how much you love sweets."

"Surprised you remember anything after all this time." My voice is a low rumble.

"What's that?"

I shake my head. "Nothing."

"Look, Kit-Kat—"

"Don't call me that," I deadpan. He has no right to use my nickname. We aren't *us* anymore.

His entire body turns toward me, and he straddles the bench.

There's only about a foot of space between us, so I inch over a bit to get away from him.

"I know you're angry with me." I keep licking my ice cream while he talks, stroking it with my tongue faster and faster, hoping to give myself brain freeze, so I can focus on that instead of the sound of his voice. "But there's a lot you don't know."

"Save it," I tell him as I stand up. "Nothing you say is going to make me feel any better." I take a few steps but stop walking. Turning around, I glower at him. "You never even said goodbye." My own words prick at my chest. I swallow hard, pushing down the lump in my throat, while warding off tears.

I don't even notice Carter walking in my direction when our shoulders brush. "Hey, what's wrong?" he asks, but I keep walking.

I have to get away from here.

My feet don't stop moving as I walk down Main Street, passing by the row of buildings that are all connected. Ryker's words replay in my head like a beating drum. *There's a lot you don't know.*

Is that his excuse? If so, it's a shitty one. If there's a lot I don't know then he should have told me. I may have only been sixteen years old when he left, but it never stopped him from spilling his innermost thoughts to me before. He could have called. He *should* have called.

I know the saying goes, "the phone rings both ways," but I wasn't the one who left. He is. And now he's going to do it again. I can't let him back in. It'll hurt too bad when he deserts us.

Passing by a trash can on the sidewalk, I drop my ice cream cone inside.

"I see you still don't eat the cone." His voice hits me like a train wreck, sending warmth that mimics the feeling of oozing blood spilling down my spine. I hate that he has this effect on me.

I don't turn around, and when he's at my side, I don't look at him. "Stop pretending you know me. I'm not the same girl I was when you left."

"I can see that."

In my head, he's grinning. A big cheesy grin that bares his perfect white teeth. I don't look to find out, though.

"Kit-Kat, please—" He grabs my arm, but I jerk away.

I stop walking and shout, "I said stop calling me that." A few looks from passersby have me moving my feet again. "Stop calling me that." This time, my words come out in a whisper.

"Would you just give me a damn minute?" He raises his voice, taking me by surprise. "Please?"

Something doesn't allow me to keep moving. I stop, look down at my feet, and give him the minute he so desperately wants.

"I had to go. There was no time to say goodbye. I wish I could tell you more, but you have to believe me when I say it's best if I don't."

My eyes slowly lift until I'm looking back at him. His green orbs are soft and welcoming. Just like they always were. My entire body feels like goo and I should turn away before I forget I'm mad at him.

"Okay." That's all I can say because I know he won't stop if I argue it. I also know that if he had any intention of telling me why he left, he would have done it by now.

"We're going to be in your house together for an entire week. I'll be driving you to school, picking you up. I really want us to be good, Kit."

I nod, still looking deep into his eyes. There is so much I want to scream in his face, but I know it will end with me in tears and I'd rather not relive the last two years. It was unbearably painful. Not just grieving the loss of him as a friend, but also the trauma my body endured. I want to tell him I really have changed. I also want him to know it's all his fault.

Instead, I just nod in agreement, knowing there is no way he'll be the one staying with me while Carter and my dad are gone. I can't do that to myself.

"Good," he says, throwing an arm around my neck and

turning me around to walk back the way I came. "Let's go find Carter before he sends out a search party for his missing sister."

We make it a few feet before I feel like a total ass for not offering my condolences. "Hey, Ry. I'm sorry about your granddad. I know how close you two were."

"I appreciate it. He was one of the few people who ever believed I'd amount to anything." He laughs, as if it's funny to think anyone would have faith in him. "Must've really seen something in me because he left me everything."

"Oh, wow. The shop and all?"

"Yup. The entire building is mine. Apartment, shop. Now I just have to decide what I plan to do with it?"

"Wait," I stop walking. "Are you planning to sell? That building has been in your family for generations."

He shrugs his shoulders and keeps walking ahead of me. I jog to catch up, and he says, "Not really sure yet."

It's a crazy notion, but Ryker could keep it and work there, but that would mean staying in town, and it's obvious that's not his plan.

The rest of the walk to Tasty Dip is silent, but my internal thoughts are screaming as I draw in a deep breath, inhaling the scent I've missed so much.

Just because I'm angry with him, doesn't mean I don't still miss him. Even as he's standing right beside me.

CHAPTER
TWELVE
RYKER

Twenty Years Old
Present Day
Get your hands off her!
I said, get your fucking hands off her!

My eyes shoot open, and my body springs up. I take in a deep breath and wipe the bead of sweat from my forehead.

It was just a dream, Ryker. It was just a dream.

Gasping for air, I drop my head back down on the pillow, placing my hand over my stampeding heart. I slow my pulse by focusing on the beam of light on the ceiling from the street lights outside the window. It's a distraction, nothing more, nothing less.

Once I'm fully awake and calmed down, I turn to look at the clock on the nightstand beside me. *Six a.m.* Better than most nights, and I thought for sure being back in Oakley Shores would wake me sooner.

Not that it matters. The fucking darkness follows me everywhere I go, rearing its ugly head every night. Every. Single. Goddamn. Night.

I rip the sheet off me and sit up, then pull my drenched tee shirt over my head and toss it to the floor.

Doubt I'll be able to fall back asleep, so I get up, ready to start my day. I've got a lot to do in my short time here and my productivity is shortened even more now that I'll be staying with Kit while Carter and his dad are out of town.

I haven't gone to my mom's yet. Haven't even told her I'm back. I know I need to go see her and Ezra. My absence has nothing to do with them. I've missed them both. It's just that house. Those memories. Leaving was supposed to erase them, but it's obvious at this point that there is no escape. The demons live in my head. My hand doesn't ever stop shaking. And the image is fresh in my mind as if it all just happened yesterday.

There's a good chance she'll scold me for returning. It was our deal, after all. But what does it matter now? The old man died two months after I left. My permanent stay with Uncle Greg has nothing to do with them and everything to do with my own emotional detachment. Living here would be a burden to everyone I care about.

After I take a quick shower and the sun has started to rise, I head out of the apartment that was once my granddad's. He's lived above the garage ever since he took ownership when his own father passed away. It's nothing fancy. Just a small one-bedroom place with running water and heat. The floors are old hardwood and the walls that were once white have a yellowish film from his chain-smoking habit. While I'm here, I plan to fix the place up a bit, so I can rent it out until I decide if I'm closing up shop or not.

I wish there was another way. A way I could keep it running while also keeping it in the family. I'm just not sure that's feasible. My granddad could barely afford to keep the place open. He lived on whiskey and stale bread and spent every waking hour working, just so it could stay afloat.

Doesn't matter right now. Buck, his lifelong friend and employee, is doing all the work right now, and he's talked about bringing someone in to help him with smaller tasks until I make a decision.

I walk down the old rickety staircase from the apartment and open the door that leads to the garage. I'm not surprised in the least when I see that Buck's already started work for the day.

"Well, I'll be damned," Buck says, tossing his cigarette on the cement floor and stubbing it out with the toe of his boot. He pulls me in for a hug and I give him a subtle pat on the back. "How ya been, kid?"

"Good to see ya, Buck. I'm hanging in there. How about you?"

Buck runs his fingers through his lengthy gray beard. "Doing the best I can. Sure do miss the old bastard, though."

"Yeah, we all do. He'd be glad you're still here working your ass off, even though he's gone."

"That old man probably wants me to work myself to death, just so I can join him up there and raise hell by his side."

We both laugh because we both know it's true.

Buck slaps a hand to my shoulder. "He'd be proud of you, too, kid. Heard you finished school and plan to follow in his footsteps working in automotive."

I nod. "Just a GED but yeah, I finished. As for working in automotive, it was never plan A, but it's better than plan C."

"Oh yeah? What's that?"

"Not doing jack shit."

Buck blows out an airy breath of laughter. "Sounds pretty damn nice to me."

"You know how it goes. Bills gotta be paid and they sure as shit don't pay themselves."

He nods slowly, stroking his beard. "That is true. That is true. Oh, hey. How's that friend of yours doing—Carter? I hear he's going corporate with his dad."

"Yeah. Carter's doing great. In fact, he's leaving for a business trip tomorrow, and I'll be house-sitting for the Levines."

I leave out the part that I'm staying there solely to keep an extra eye on Kit, but I know these old men are hornballs and he's sure to make the situation into something it's not.

"Living the life of luxury. Nice."

The shop bell rings, signaling that someone came in through

the office door. Buck pulls out his pack of smokes from the front pocket of his shirt and grabs one with his teeth. "Well, duty calls. I'll see ya around, kid. Might need a hand if you're in town for a bit."

"For sure. I'll be around."

Buck leaves the shop, and I take a moment to look around. Absolutely nothing about this place has changed. Still got the Rotary lift Granddad had installed in the early '80s. I don't even know how long he's had the bubble balancer, but there was never a time it wasn't here, so I'm guessing that's from the '80s, too. Everything in this place is outdated, but the loyal customers keep coming back. That's the thing about Dawson Auto Repair—it's not just the owners who make this place a family business, it's the customers and their families, too.

I let that sink in before climbing into my rusted-out, single-cab pickup truck. One I couldn't even afford to buy, but Carter lent me the money for it. I've been paying him back in small increments, and he's never once bitched about me owing him. That is until he used the favor to ask for his own favor—me staying with Kit.

Driving down Coswell Boulevard, I can feel my anxiety creeping in like an unwanted visitor. I reach over and grab my cigarettes from the passenger seat and light one up. Drawing in a deep breath, I inhale and hold it, then exhale slowly, letting the smoke roll from my mouth to the open window.

Five.

Four.

Three.

Two.

One.

And that damn motel is in my rearview mirror. I knew one day I'd have to drive past the place where I thought I made the biggest mistake of my life. What makes it harder is that I've come to realize, it was never a mistake. My future might've gone up in flames, but I created a better one for Ezra and Mom.

Flipping my blinker, I turn into the trailer park, and I'm hit with a rush of emotions. It's all the same. I'm starting to wonder if anything in this town ever changes. The road that runs through it is still covered in potholes. The cement sidewalks are still cracked. Mr. Barber is still out watering his dead flowers. I wonder if he'll ever realize he's killing them with all that water, instead of bringing them back to life.

I look to my left to where he stands, and I can hear him shout, "Slow your ass down."

Smiling, I take it all in because it's been a while since I've heard that grouchy motherfucker's voice.

Yep. Nothing's changed.

When I come up to 23C, I slow down, until I'm trolling over the speed bump in front of my old place.

Same baby blue box trailer with a cracked shutter next to the aluminum screen door. The small porch is weathered and one of the steps is missing a board.

There's a rusted-out minivan parked in front that I take to be Mom's new vehicle. Glad she sold Dad's piece-of-shit car when he died.

It takes me a minute to get out. I contemplate leaving, while convincing myself they're better off with me gone. But before I can make a choice, Ezra comes walking out the front door and his eyes immediately land on my truck.

There's a pang in my chest when I see how much he's grown. He's fifteen now, and the man of the house. A role I've heard he takes seriously. It's proven true when I see the 2x10 piece of wood in his hand.

Ezra sets the wood up against the trailer, a smile growing on his face. "Ma," he yells while jumping down the steps and walking toward me. "Ma, get out here."

I fling the door open and Ezra crashes into my chest before my feet even hit the ground. Sobs of happiness escape him and I find myself doing the same. My arm stretches out, holding my lit cigarette out the door while my other hand rests on his back.

"Are ya back for good?" It's the first question he asks, and I don't wanna answer him at the risk of letting him down.

"Good to see you, brother." I pat his back and let him hold on as long as he needs to.

Once the moment has passed, Ezra takes a step back and looks me up and down. "You're still as ugly as you were when ya left."

I chuckle, rubbing the top of his head. "Look who's talking. What the hell is up with the purple hair?" I take a drag of my cigarette as I get out of the truck.

"Trends, man."

I don't bother telling him that he obviously doesn't know shit about trends because purple ain't his thing.

I tip my chin toward the trailer, as I drop my cigarette on the paved slab of the driveway and step on it. "How's she doing?"

"Good and bad days. She's been working long hours at the restaurant, so I've been trying to help out as much as I can, but with school and football, it's hard, ya know?"

"Yeah. I remember those days. Glad you're helping out, though." Seems like just yesterday I was holding that same weight he's holding now. I wish I could tell him it gets lighter, but the truth is, it only gets heavier.

"Have you seen Carter? I see his sister, Kit, at school sometimes. She's pretty hot." His brows waggle, and it's funny because I'm not used to seeing Ezra express interest in girls. Let alone one I've secretly been pining over. Guess he's at that age now.

Before I can respond, the trailer door swings open, and Mom comes rushing out. Wiping her hands on her floral apron, she shuffles toward us in a pair of house slippers. "Oh my Lord, it is you." Tears stream down her cheeks, and I choke on my own. Her curly brunette hair is shorter, shoulder-length now. She's still as tiny as I remember, though, which leads me to believe she's still not eating the best. Her skin is free of the cuts and bruises my dad used to leave on her, though, and I'm thankful for that.

"Hey, Mama." I meet her halfway, pulling her in for a hug. She smells like cinnamon rolls and cheap perfume, and right now, it's the best smell in the world.

Squeezing me tight, she doesn't let go. "Oh, Ryker. I've missed you so much."

"Missed you, too, Mama."

Her breath hits my ear as she whispers, "You shouldn't be here. But I'm glad you are."

"Yeah. Me too." The truth is, I'm not feeling very courageous right now. Standing here in front of the trailer that built me is one thing, but entering is a whole different story.

"Come on inside. I've just made a fresh batch of cinnamon rolls. Ezra's planning to throw some dogs on the grill after he fixes that old step."

I swallow hard, wishing I could accept the invite, hating myself because I can't. "Actually, I've got somewhere to be. I'll be in town for a while, though. Rain check?" I look at Ezra, who wears a face of disappointment.

"Oh. Okay. Well, how about dinner Tuesday night? I'll cook your favorite, homemade lasagna." Her eyes light up with wonder and hope that I'll accept this time.

I fight hard against the voices in my head telling me no, that I can't do it. It's for her and Ezra. I've gotta let this shit go. In one breath, I spit out, "I'll be here."

"Wonderful." Mom claps her hands together. "It'll be so nice to have my boys together again." She pulls me in for another hug and while it's nice and warm and feels like home, the urge to leave is strong.

Mom takes a step back, still smiling from ear to ear. I slide onto the seat of my truck through the open door. My hand rests on the window as Ezra and Mom stand a foot away from the bumper. He throws an arm around her shoulder, and they watch as I shift into reverse. Once I'm headed down the road and out of sight, I slap my hand to the steering wheel. "Motherfucker."

There was a time I felt like part of that circle. Now I feel like a stranger to my own family. And it's all because of *him*.

CHAPTER
THIRTEEN
RYKER

I walk into the Levines' house without knocking, much like I've always done. Carter is sitting at the kitchen table buried in work and doesn't even lift his head when I sit down in the chair across from him.

"Must be porn in that folder for you to be that into it."

He takes off his glasses and sets them beside the folder and lifts a smile. "Hey, man. Didn't even hear you come in. And for the record, there's no porn here, unless crunching numbers turns you on."

"I'll pass on the numbers but give me a picture of a nice round ass with some big titties and you can slide that thing my way."

Carter closes the folder with a laugh. "I see you've still got your crude sense of humor."

"It ain't going nowhere. I'm the me I'll always be. How 'bout you? You got a stick up your ass yet, now that you're a suit and tie kinda guy?"

He snorts. "Fuck that shit. This is only temporary while I finish out college. It's worth credits, and I get paid." Leaning back in his seat, he loosens the tie around his neck. "To be honest, I'm not sure what my plans are once I get my degree. I'm starting to realize I'm not a businessman."

"Well, you got time." I find myself looking around the room, as if I'm expecting Kit to walk out at any second.

"She's in her room," Carter says, reading my mind. "She's still pretty pissed, though, so I'd tread lightly."

My laughter drips with sarcasm as I say, "Yeah. Now you tell me after I agreed to stay here with her for a week." It's mostly a joke, but partially true. Carter told me she'd be cool with it. After yesterday, I'd say she's anything *but* cool with it.

"Well, that's sort of the reason I asked you to stay. You're my best friend, and she's my sister. I'd really like you two to get along like you used to."

"Tell her that."

"I have. She's just been stubborn lately. The last couple years she's started spiraling. Her grades have dropped, she misses appointments, she's been going to parties with her friends every weekend."

Kit goes to parties? I wanna laugh because I never thought I'd see the day, but it's not funny at all.

I stand up and push my chair back in, while gripping the back of it. "I'm gonna go talk to her. Try to ease into this staying-here situation."

"Well, we leave tomorrow, so ease into it quickly."

"Is that even possible?"

"Probably not," he laughs, "so good luck."

It's Friday night and I know there's a big game tonight against Oakley Shores's rival, Alcove. Kit is likely getting ready, since she still assists with the cheer team, at least, last I knew she did. If what Carter says is true about her going to parties on the weekends, she'll likely be going to one tonight.

My knuckles knock softly on her door, but it's enough for it to pop open. "Kit?"

When she doesn't respond, I push it open farther. "Can I come in?"

I wait a few seconds, and when she still doesn't respond, I poke my head in the door. It's like a blast to the past when I look inside her room. Only, the girl sitting on the bed wearing ear buds, bopping her head to the music while writing in her journal is not little Kit from my past. Her dark blonde hair is piled in a messy bun on the top of her head. She's wearing a pair of black yoga pants and a black sports bra. Out of the corner of the left strap is a bulging scar where her defibrillator was implanted, and my gut wretches at the sight.

One thing's for sure, she wasn't kidding when she said she's not the same person I remember.

No. Kit is not that same person. She's not a kid anymore at all. In fact, she's all grown up. Perfection personified. Even more beautiful than I remember. I watch her as she sits there in a state of vulnerability, and when she mouths the words to whatever song she's listening to, I crack a smile, wondering what she's writing about.

Stepping into the room, I move slowly, taking care not to startle her. "Kit," I say, my voice slightly higher than when I was outside the door. Her room is different. Instead of everything being pink and girly, it's now neutral colors of off-white and mint green. There are new pictures on her memory board, live plants on a stand in front of the window, and ivy vines with little white lights strung around her headboard.

Wide eyes shoot to mine and she rips one of the earbuds from her ear. "Jesus, Ryker," she slaps a hand over her chest, "you scared the shit out of me."

"Sorry. I knocked, but you didn't hear me."

She pulls out the other earbud and clutches them both tightly in her hand, while flipping her journal shut. Staring at me for a second, I do the same to her as I try to scramble together some words. "Can we talk?" I finally say.

Her legs fling over the side of the bed, and she stands up. Crossing the room, she goes to a pile of clothes lying on the floor and grabs a white tee shirt that says Oakley Shores Cougars. "I thought we already did that?" She pulls the shirt over her head.

"We did. But I don't like this divide between us. Don't you feel it?"

Looking out the window of her room, she gives me her back when she says, "I don't feel anything toward you, Ryker. Nothing at all."

"That's a lie," I spit out. I know damn well she's lying. How can she not feel anything toward me? After all we've been through.

I eat up the space between us until I'm standing directly behind her. "Look at me." She doesn't even budge. "Look at me, please."

With a heavy sigh, she turns around. Her hand plants on her raised hip while the other rubs her earlobe nervously. "What?"

"This. The way you're acting. It's like…you hate me or something."

Her bright blue eyes burn into mine, and I can feel the heat of indignation spilling from her pores. "I told you, I feel nothing toward you."

I shake my head, not believing her. "Sure, you do. Even if it's anger. At least it's something. Talk to me, Kit-Kat."

My gaze travels down to her lips and slowly back to her eyes. It's still there. That magnetic pull. The temptation. She might not feel it, but I certainly do.

"Okay, I'll bite. I'm angry, Ryker." She pushes past me but continues to talk. I spin around and watch while she starts laying her blue-and-white cheer uniform out on her bed. "One day you were here, and then you were just…gone. No goodbye. No excuse. You just left."

"I told you—"

Her head lifts and she looks at me momentarily before returning to her task at hand. "I know. You told me you had to leave and I said it was enough but the truth is, I lied. It's not enough. Carter might have been the reason you were part of my life, but you were part of it."

She's right. Kit was a big part of my life. She was more of a friend than most of the ones I hung out with on a daily basis. "Okay," I nod. "You deserve more than a lame, *I had to leave.*"

"It's not even you leaving or the reason why you did." She lays a pair of white socks on her navy blue uniform. "It's the two years in between where I never heard from you. You don't even have any social media accounts. I mean, who doesn't have at least one in this day and age?"

The corner of my lip tugs up in a smile. "So you searched for me?"

She scoffs and rolls her eyes as she walks to her closet. "Yeah. I did." She stops in front of the closet door and turns around. "Did you ever search for me?"

Pain sweeps over her expression when I don't respond. I can't, because I never did.

"My point exactly." Kit disappears into her walk-in closet, but I follow her inside.

"I fucked up. I am fucked-up, Kit."

Acting as if she doesn't even hear me, she shuffles quickly through the clothes hanging on the back wall of the closet. "I'm sorry," I say with sincerity. "Dammit, Kit." I grab her shoulder and spin her around. "I'm sorry."

Her chest heaves and her lips part slightly. She stares back at me and the air shifts. "I'm sorry I let you down," I whisper, watching her as her gaze trickles to my mouth.

My chest tightens, breathing labored, and I find myself gasping for breath.

Her body trembles beneath my hands, goosebumps climbing up her arms.

I lean in. She does the same. Our lips brush—

"Kit, you in there?"

Oh, fuck.

There's some knocking on the door before Carter says her name again, "Kit?"

Alarmed eyes shoot to mine, but I'm not sure who seems more stunned—me or her. "Shh," she says quietly.

We could both walk out of this closet right now and Carter would be none the wiser. Or, he sees us walking out together and wonders why the hell we were in there in the first place. Nothing happened, but is it worth the risk of assumption on his part?

"Go," I mouth, nodding my head to the door.

Her hand presses to my chest, pushing me back a few steps, so I'm out of view. "Stay here and be quiet," she whispers.

"What's up, bro?" she says chipperly. In my head, she sounds obvious, but that could just be my own guilt chewing on my insides.

"Did Ryker come talk to you?"

"Uhh, yeah. He just left my room."

"Weird. I can't find him anywhere. I've gotta run to Dad's office. If you see him, tell him I'll be at the game later if he wants to come watch."

"Will do. Drive safe."

"Good luck tonight." There's a brief pause before he continues, "Oh, and if you plan on going to Asher's party, be responsible. No driving and absolutely no drinking."

"Yes, Father." Her words have a snarky bite to them. "I'll be on my best behavior…as always."

So Asher is having a party? And Kit's going?

I can't help but wonder if something blossomed between those two in the time I was gone. Wouldn't surprise me. After all, she apparently *loved* him. Though I doubt she even knew what love was at the age of fifteen. I sure as fuck didn't. I thought I loved Macie McGreggor because she milked my cock within twenty-seconds. Turns out, I didn't love her. I just loved the way she sucked cock.

Once I hear the door latch shut, I give it a couple seconds before stepping out of the closet.

I poke my head around the open door, making sure the coast is clear.

Kit presses her back to the door and her eyes travel to mine. "You can come out."

"I'm so sorry," I blurt out, knowing it needs to be said. My fingers trace around my mouth where her lips almost were, had Carter not come knocking. Thank fuck he did or else we'd both be swimming in a mountain of regret.

Kit's shoulders rise and fall. "Why are you sorry? Nothing happened." She takes baby steps to her bed and brushes her fingers over her uniform.

I run my hand over my head, looking down at the white rug I'm standing on. "Yeah and nothing ever can."

"Glad we can agree on that." There's a bitterness to her tone and I get the feeling that nothing has changed.

"You still mad at me?"

"Just because we almost kissed—"

"Don't say that," I grind out. "Please don't ever say that again."

Tilting her head, she cracks a sinister smile. "Why? Would kissing me really be all that bad?"

"Yes," I spit out, feeling the creases in my forehead. "It would. We both know that can never happen. You're—"

"Carter's little sister." She bobs her head, returning her attention to her uniform before her mood shifts and she doesn't give me a chance to speak. "That's all I've ever been to you, isn't it? Carter's little sister? I was never your friend. You were his friend and I was just the third wheel you were nice to."

"No, Kit. Where the hell is this coming from?"

She turns around, grabs a duffel bag off the floor and begins stuffing her uniform inside. "You can go now."

I've never seen her like this. So angry and aggressive. Kit was always so soft-spoken and kind.

"Look. I'm sorry. Again. I want us to be good, Kit-Kat. I don't know what more I can do to show you that you're more to me than Carter's little sister. You're my friend, too."

She doesn't even look at me. "Please just go."

I start toward the door but stop midway. "This stays between us, right?"

Nothing happened, but we both know the mistake that almost did.

Her head lifts, and this time, she looks sad. I want to console her and make her understand everything, but I can't. At least, not yet.

"Yeah, Ryker. This stays between us."

I leave the room with a plan. This next week is going to be focused solely on rebuilding our friendship. Nothing more, nothing less. And when I leave Oakley Shores again, I plan on making an extra effort in keeping that friendship alive because I can't lose her again.

CHAPTER
FOURTEEN
KIT

"Up or down?" Kaylee asks, regarding her hair. She's bunching up her curly brunette locks with her hands, making a duck face and posing like she's a model for a shampoo ad.

"Up." I flip the page in the yearbook on my lap. "You'll wanna show off some shoulder skin at the party."

"I like the way you think." I smirk as she grabs a blue scrunchie off her vanity and ties it around the ponytail.

I turn the page again. Class of 2020. Carter and Ryker's senior year. I gag internally when I see a picture of Ryker's and Carter's exes, Ava and Stacy, at the senior prom. Beside them are Carter and Ryker with their tongues out in a 'party-on' pose. I'm almost positive they were broken up then, but for some reason, Carter and Ryker still took them as dates. I guess old feelings really do die hard.

Ever since my *almost* kiss with Ryker, my heads been in a fog. My legs feel weak, and I have this weird feeling in my stomach I haven't felt in a while. We can't put ourselves in that position again. He said so himself.

Once Kaylee is dressed in her uniform—sleeveless OSH Cougars top and matching mini skirt with white tennis shoes—

she sits down at the vanity, facing me on the bed. "Well, are you ready for my news?"

"Of course you have news," I gush, teasingly, as I close the yearbook.

Kaylee's eyes light up and she does a little dance with her shoulders. "My parents said I could skip the family vacation and stay with my aunt. And," she perks up, "you can stay with us."

"Oh," is the only thing that comes out of my mouth.

"Oh?" She laughs.

"I mean, that's great." I crack a smile. "Why the sudden change of heart?"

Kaylee's parents have very little trust in her, so I'm not surprised they'd have her stay with her aunt. It's not that I don't want Kaylee to stay, because I do. A week without her, especially at school, sounds tortuous. It's just that, I've sort of warmed up to the idea of Ryker staying at the house. Deep down, I think I was always glad it would be him staying with me, even if I didn't show it. What can I say? I'm stubborn, and I wanted Ryker to see how upset with him I am. Maybe so he'd think twice when it comes time for him to leave again.

"It is great because this means you can stay with me." Excitement drips from her pores. She jumps up, joins me on the bed, and grabs both of my hands. "Let's throw a party at your house one night. We can sneak away from my aunt's. It'll be fun."

I'm trying really hard to wrap my head around this sudden news. Better yet, I'm searching for the right words to let her down gently. "Whoa. Slow down, girl."

Kaylee's shoulders go slack, and she pouts. "No party?"

I chuckle. "Yes. I mean, no. Kay, listen." I turn my body toward her, bending my leg at the knee on the bed. My hands squeeze hers. "Plans have already been made. Don't miss your family trip for me."

She pulls the scrunchie out of her hair and pouts. "It's him. Isn't it?"

"Ryker? God, no." I look away because if she looks into my

eyes, she'll know I'm lying. If anyone can read me like a book, it's her.

"Then why won't you look at me?"

See what I mean?

I turn my head, tilting it toward my shoulder. "This has nothing to do with my feelings, or lack of feelings, for Ryker."

"Liar," she spits out, jerking her hands away and slapping me in the knee before falling onto her back on the bed. "I knew this would happen. The minute I saw his face when he opened your front door, I knew you'd fall right back down that rabbit hole."

Dropping down beside her, I stare at the ceiling the same way she is. "I didn't fall down a rabbit hole."

Kaylee sticks her finger in her mouth, faking a gag. "He's an asshole, Kit."

I turn my head to face her, cheek resting on the bed. "Ryker is a lot of things, but an asshole is not one of them."

"What happened to our motto that we started at the end of sophomore year, once you finally let your feelings shift from hurt to pissed? Fuck Ryker Dawson."

"I mean, if it's an option…" I giggle, permitting another swat from my bestie. "Too soon?"

"Uh, yeah. Too soon." She swats my back. "So, tell me. What's the plan here?" Kaylee rolls onto her side, propping her head up with her hand. "What happens when he leaves and goes back to being a mountain man at a mechanic shop in Colorado?"

"There is no plan because nothing is going to happen. But even if those feelings did return, which they won't," I add, "I wouldn't put you through that misery again. I'd deal with my heartbreak on my own."

"Don't you dare." Kaylee wraps an arm around my stomach and rests her head on my shoulder. "Don't you dare cut me out. If you're hurting, I'm there, babe. You wanna light his truck on fire, count me in. And if you wanna spend a week alone with him in your house and risk the heartbreak, I want details."

I rest my hand on her arm, feeling the warmth of her hug, of her friendship. "I'm so lucky to have you. It won't come to that, though. I'll be cautious this time around."

"Good. That means we can double date to the dance." She springs up suddenly, not giving me a chance to respond.

"Whoa. Whoa. Whoa. We've been over this."

She bats her long black lashes. "The best way to get over one guy is to get under another."

I laugh, because how can I not? This girl is fire and the words that come out of her mouth never cease to surprise me.

"Now get your ass ready. Pregame practice starts in twenty minutes."

I slide off the bed and look at myself, hands draped at my sides, in her body-sized mirror on the wall. "What do you mean? I *am* ready."

Kaylee comes up behind me, resting her hands on my shoulders while looking at my reflection in the mirror. "Yes, you are. My smoking hot bestie. I wish I had your ability to wear a natural look." She taps my shoulder and skedaddles out of the room while hollering, "I'll grab snacks for the ride."

❖

"Five. Six. Seven. Eight."

Bent over, I stretch to touch my toes along with the team. Technically, I should be able to cheer with them. Normal, everyday activities as a teenager shouldn't be a problem. However, doing so requires written permission from my cardiologist and the guy is a royal pain in my ass. Has been for years. "Give it a year before we loosen restrictions," is what he said. Well, he better totally let go of the driving restrictions I'm on because I'm ready to get behind the wheel and go where I want to go, without feeling like a burden to everyone I care about.

"All right, ladies, out to the field," Coach Lynn says, carrying the folded banner we designed last night. Once we're on the field, half of us stand on one side while the other half stretches the banner down the other side, facing our home fans in the bleachers.

On the banner, it reads *KICK SOME ALCOVE A*** in big, bold letters with the players' names and numbers all around it.

The scoreboard comes up and the five-minute timer begins counting down to the start of the first quarter. When the guys come running out, helmets on and asses looking mighty nice in those pants, the crowd begins cheering and chanting while we do the same.

"Go Cougars," they all shout from the stands. "Let's get a win tonight!"

Like a pack of wild animals, the team runs toward us, crashing into the banner with growls and shouts, riling themselves up. Everyone but Asher. He slows to a jog and as he passes by me, he looks right into my eyes and winks before catching up with his team. Butterflies swarm my stomach and I hate it. I find myself questioning everything I thought I knew. Like, maybe he doesn't hate me, after all. If he can still give me those giddy feelings, maybe the flame he once lit inside me isn't completely out.

The players take their spots on the field and as we walk at a leisurely pace toward the track, we begin our opening chant, while shaking our pompoms. "Let's go Cougars. Let's go Cougars."

While the girls get in their starting positions, centered in front of the overstuffed bleachers, I join Coach Lynn near the bench directly in front of them.

Coach Lynn is taking a drink from her water bottle when I say, "One opening cheer?"

She looks over at me, grinning around her straw as it slides out of her mouth. "One."

"Yes!" I beam, skipping over to the team with my pompoms shaking in the air.

"I mean it, Kit. Only one."

I return her stern look with a smirk. "Yes, Coach."

I know it's a risk for her to allow this, but occasionally, she takes that risk for me.

I'm on the end in the front row, and we begin our first cheer of the night.

"It's time to get started, it's time to begin. We're the mighty Cougars and we're here to win."

We repeat the cheer three times, and I step away while the girls do their thirty-second cheer intermission.

"See. I survived it," I say with chipper sarcasm, joining Coach Lynn's side.

"Get that note from your doctor and I'd be happy to have you out there the entire game. You're an asset to the team, Kit. Don't ever doubt that."

Her words, while meant to be encouraging, stir something inside me that is anything but. I've tried to get released from restrictions. I've begged my dad to let me see a new doctor. No matter what I do, he doesn't budge and insists it's all for my own good.

Well, I call bullshit. I feel better right now than I ever have in my life.

The first half flies by, and I'm headed to the bathroom during half-time when I catch Carter and a group of his friends out of the corner of my eye. I jog over to where he stands, ready to just give him a tap on the shoulder in passing, but I'm dumbstruck when I notice who he's with—Ryker. Not just Ryker, but also Carter's ex, Stacy and her best friend, Ava. I don't see either of them often, since they attend college out of state, but they still carry the same confidence they always have.

"Hey, sis," Carter hollers over the shoulders of his friends while waving me over. "Get your butt over here and say hi." I force a smile and continue in their direction. "You remember Stacy, right?" Carter asks once I'm the center of attention in their small group.

"Yeah. Good to see you, Stacy." Lies. All lies.

"Aww. You've grown up so much," Stacy says in the voice one would use if they were speaking to a toddler.

Carter tosses an arm around my shoulder, pulling me close. "She's a senior now. Won't be long until she's heading to college herself."

"Well, I hope you have someone there to keep an eye on her. College boys swarm pretty girls like that."

I chuckle uncomfortably. Compliments and attention aren't really my thing. "I'm sure my wonderful big brother already has a plan in place."

"Hell yeah, I do. Those college boys don't stand a chance." He continues on, but I drown out everything he says when I catch Ryker looking at me with a blank expression. I'm not sure how long he's been staring, but I'd give just about anything to hear the thoughts in his head right about now.

"Well," Ava finally speaks for the first time since I've joined them, "show starts in an hour. Ya'll ready?"

I'm pretty sure Ava has lived on the West Coast her entire life, but she has this sweet southern accent that pops up from time to time, and I'm almost positive it's as fake as the *Gucci* sunglasses perched on top of her head.

"Yep. Let's do this," Ryker chimes in.

"Wait. You're not staying for the second half?" I'm speaking to Carter, even looking at him, but Ryker is the one who responds.

"Do you want me to?"

My eyes snap to him, eyebrows raised. "I mean you don't have to stay if you have plans."

"Oh, sorry," Ryker laughs, "Ava asked if I was driving. Glycerine is playing at the waterfront park tonight."

Okay then. I nod, feeling my cheeks flush with heat. "You all have fun." I turn around and head back to the field, since the third quarter is about to begin. Never even made it to the bathroom, but I'd rather piss my pants than pass by them again.

CHAPTER
FIFTEEN
KIT

The Cougars won the game, as I knew we would. Alcove is good, but they haven't beat the varsity team since our boys stepped up junior year.

Even though we packed a change of clothes, so we could go straight from the game to Asher's, Kaylee insisted we change plans and stop at my house on the way to get ready for the party. In my opinion, I'm already ready. She begs to differ.

"This one," she says, dropping a slinky black dress onto the bed. It's still got the tags on it because I've never worn it. In fact, I'm pretty sure she picked it out when we were shopping. "And I'm borrowing this." Holding up a solid white dress to herself, she looks at her reflection in the mirror.

"You do realize that's see-through, right?"

"Exactly the point." She begins stripping down to her bra and underwear then slips the dress on. It fits like it was made for her body. Kaylee has all the right curves and the cleavage to boot. I'm not unhappy with my body at all. I've got boobs and an ass, curves and a good complexion, but I don't carry myself like Kaylee does. Her confidence is admirable, and even if I do wear the dress she picked out, I'll end up throwing a hoodie over it before we even make it up Asher's driveway.

"Well, what are you waiting for? Get dressed, girl. There is fun that needs to be had."

So many different excuses run through my head as to how I can get out of this. My dad and Carter leave tomorrow, so it would be nice to spend time with them before they go. However, Carter is at the waterfront concert and my dad is stowed away in his study.

With a heavy grunt, I put on the dress and save an argument I'd likely lose. "Fine." I sigh. "I'm wearing the dress, but you're leaving me alone after this. No extra makeup. No curls to my perfect ponytail."

"Wouldn't dare suggest either."

Once we're dressed, we take turns looking in the mirror and I actually look pretty hot. My hair, being in a high ponytail, shows off my shoulders beneath the thin spaghetti straps. The dress is simple, yet I feel sexy in it.

"Holy fuck," Kaylee beams.

"What?" I gasp in response. "What's wrong?"

"You! You are going to give Asher a heart attack in that dress. My bestie is a hottie."

I laugh it off, once again feeling uncomfortable with the compliment.

"Let's go," I say, grabbing her hand and pulling her out of my bedroom.

As soon as we turn the corner, we both crash into abs of steel. I look up and see Ryker—shirtless.

"Sorry, ladies. Didn't know you were here."

"Uh, yeah," I respond, tripping on my words a bit. "I didn't know anyone was here either. I thought you and Carter were going to a concert?"

"We did. It was lame, so we came here to get something to eat before heading to a party."

"Oh?" I pause. "With the girls?" I'm not sure why I'm even asking, of course they're going out with the girls. Stacy and Ava are a big part of Ryker and Carter's pasts and it looks like the past is repeating itself. I still haven't figured out how I feel about it. I never liked the way either of those girls treated the guys.

"That's the plan. It's been a while since we've all hung out, so we thought it'd be nice to catch up."

I nod repeatedly, unsure what to say.

"All righty then." Kaylee pulls at my arm. "You boys have fun and we'll do the same."

We're walking away briskly when Ryker says, "Wait."

I glance over my shoulder and he's in the process of looking me up and down, as if he's inspecting my clothing choice. "It's a little chilly out tonight. Shouldn't you, like, put on a sweater or something?"

"She's got one in my car," Kaylee retorts, still tugging on my hand like we're about to miss a scheduled flight or something.

Ryker holds his stare, not accepting the answer. "Maybe we should ask Carter what he thinks?"

Why does he always do this? He drags Carter into it because he can't speak up for himself.

I jerk my hand away from Kaylee and turn to face him completely, hands pressed firmly to my hips. "Is there something wrong with what I'm wearing, Ryker?"

His eyes wear his surprise at my outburst. "No."

"Do I look hideous?"

"What? God, no. You look—"

"Okay then. Do I look like a prostitute?"

"You look great. I just don't want you to get cold."

"It's seventy-five degrees out, not to mention I've always done a pretty good job at keeping *my* body temperature at a comfortable level. But thanks for your concern." This time, I take Kaylee's hand and pull her out the door, then slam it shut behind me.

"Damn, girl, you sticking up for yourself like that sort of turns me on."

I blow out a breath of laughter as we walk hand in hand to her silver, sport BMW that's parked in front of our three-stall garage, parting ways when I get in the passenger seat.

By the time we get to Asher's house, the street is already lined with cars. Fortunately, he lives on a dead end, with the neighbors spread out pretty far. He's had more parties here than I can count—even if I haven't attended many—and rumor has it, they never get busted.

I'm tightening my ponytail when Kaylee reaches into the back seat and comes forward with an unopened bottle of tequila. My stomach turns at the sight. "You plan on drinking that straight?"

"Of course not." She hands me the bottle and I take it while she retrieves an entire fricken bag of lemons and a huge-ass container of salt from the back seat. I'm talking one of the ones with the flip-up metal lid.

"You're something else. But, I must ask, how the hell do you plan on getting us home?"

"Sober Squad…if it comes to that."

One of the perks in this town is a designated driving service offered by a group of very smart, very safe students. It's a no-questions-asked service that came to fruition when a fellow classmate was killed in a drunk driving accident. It's also a secret that's not so much a secret. The service is actually illegal, but none of the parents say anything because they prefer we make the right decision to call the Sober Squad versus driving drunk. I've never used it, but I'm grateful it exists.

"If it comes to that?" I hold up the bottle. "Or *when* it comes to that?"

Kaylee takes it from my hand and unscrews the top. The smell alone makes me feel like I'm going to hurl. Tipping the bottle back, she takes a small swig and cringes at the taste. "When," she says with a sour look on her face.

After a quick gag, she puts the top back on. "Highly recommend a chaser or the lemons and salt."

"Ya think?" I laugh.

We both get out, Kaylee holding her beverage for the night and the bag of lemons. Before we even make it to the driveway, we're joined by Damon and Micah. I'm not surprised to see that

Carly is not attached to Micah. I guess Kaylee was right when she said they broke up. If I didn't hear it from her mouth, I'd know it from the pitiful look on his face.

"There's my girl," Damon says, setting a hand on the small of Kaylee's back.

His girl? Since when?

I knew they were going to the dance together, but I guess I missed the part where they became an item. I'm positive Kaylee missed it, too, because she is grinning from ear to ear at the comment.

Damon nuzzles his face into Kaylee's neck. "You gonna let me drink that tequila off your sizzling body tonight?"

Great. I've officially become a third wheel. I look over at Micah, who appears to be on the verge of crying. "Hey," I nudge him, "you doing okay?"

"Eh." He shrugs his shoulders. A man of few words tonight, I see.

"For what it's worth, I hear she's not coming tonight, so hopefully you can let loose and have some fun."

His eyes widen in surprise. "She's not coming?"

Damon looks at me, then Micah. "Yeah. She's coming." He gives me a look, telling me to play along.

"She better. It's the only reason I'm here. We're gonna work this out. We have to."

Reaching my arm between Damon and Kaylee, I grab the bottle from her hand and pass it to Micah. "Here. This'll help."

He tips a smile and takes a shot—a very long shot that has me grabbing it out of his hand. "It's supposed to help you feel better, not put you over a toilet all night."

He licks his lips, taking in the excess liquor. "Already feeling better."

The bass from the music begins vibrating through my body and echoing in my ears as we reach the house. Kaylee and I shake our bodies to the beat, and I'm suddenly glad I didn't make an excuse not to come.

It looks like the entire junior and senior class is in attendance, along with a few graduates from prior years.

"Damn, Levine," a voice comes from my left. I look over and see Asher gawking with a bottle of beer in his hand. "You clean up nice." I'm not sure if it's meant to be a compliment to how I look tonight, or a jab to how I look on a normal day.

Without a response, I keep walking, Asher now at my side. "There's a keg and fire out back. More beer inside, along with some concoction of shit Logan mixed up. Help yourselves." He's talking to the others, then looks at me. "And I'm sure we can find you a glass of water."

Damon and Micah laugh, all expecting the joke to fly over my head, but it doesn't. This isn't the first time Asher has referred back to my night of intoxication, where he claims to have saved my life.

"I'm good. Actually…" I grab the bottle of tequila, this time from Damon, who has the mouth pressed to his lips.

Some of the liquid trickles down his chin, and he curses, "What the hell?"

Ignoring him, I bring the bottle to my mouth, already feeling like I'm going to vomit, and I take a small swig. The taste is horrid. So much that I instantly regret my desire to prove I can do what I want. "Salt," I say, letting some of the liquid pool in my mouth while I hold my hand out to Kaylee.

"You need a lemon first." Someone mouths back.

I stop walking. "Salt," I say again, on the verge of laughter that will send the rest of this sip flying out of my mouth.

Kaylee hands it to me, but Asher snatches it away from her. "Allow me." I watch him as he licks his wrist then sprinkles some of the salt on it.

Is he serious?

Asher brings his wrist close to my face, and I internally say, *fuck it*. My tongue darts out, trailing lightly across his wrist—eyes down to avoid looking at him—while taking up the small grains of salt. It doesn't taste much better but overpowers the tequila almost immediately.

I come back up, licking my lips, when he says, "My turn." Asher grabs my hand and turns it palm up. Raising my hand to his mouth, he takes it upon himself to wet my wrist with his tongue. Warmth spills down my spine and I'm not sure if it's the liquor or his touch. Probably a mixture of both.

Asher dashes some salt on it then shoves the container into Damon's chest. The others say something about heading up to the party, but I'm too focused on every move Asher makes to care that they are leaving.

It isn't until they're six feet away that I notice Kaylee has the bottle. "Wait. You don't have tequila."

Asher smirks, bringing my wrist to his mouth and licking the salt off for no reason at all, other than to stir something inside me. He's toying with me and he's so damn obvious.

Once my wrist is clean and all that's left is dampness from his saliva, I pull back and wipe it down the side of my dress. That was weird.

"Didn't need it. I make my own rules. Seems you do the same." He tips back his bottle of beer and finishes it off in one gulp, before tossing it to the ground.

"I guess sometimes we have to take matters into our own hands. Though, I don't see how that has anything to do with salt."

"It doesn't." He takes my hand in his, and we begin walking toward the house. In my attempt to pull away, Asher only squeezes my hand tighter. "It's my way of saying I don't give a fuck what we're supposed to do. I do what I want."

I bite back a smile. "And you wanted to lick my wrist?"

"You're something else, Kit. Always giving me a hard time."

"Me?" I clap a hand to my chest. "Seems you've got things a little backwards here. Need I remind you of all the jabs I've endured over the years?"

"Guess it's just my fucked-up way of showing you I notice

you." His shoulder brushes mine playfully, and I wanna scream at myself for falling under his spell again.

Asher is either a really good manipulator, or really bad at flirting. It's hard to believe girls get weak in the knees over this guy. It's hard to believe I was once one of those girls.

"So, it's safe to assume you're drinking tonight. This means I'm obligated to stick by your side. Ya know? Just in case."

We're submerged in the crowd at this point and Asher is still here. He hasn't blown me off for his friends that keep calling him over or passing by with bro taps to his shoulder. "Just in case I pass out on you again?"

The corner of his lip tugs up, exposing his prominent dimples. "Precisely."

"For the record, I'm not drinking, so you're safe to make an escape."

He shoots a thumb over his shoulder in the direction we came from. "But you just—"

"Took a small swig to calm some of my nerves. Yeah, I did. I have no interest in drinking more, though."

"But you can…drink, right?"

I pull the tie from my ponytail, letting my hair down. "Much like you, I can do whatever I want."

There's a bit of snark to my tone and it's exactly how I wanted my words to come out. Asher Collins might be the king of the school, but he needs to prove himself to me before I'll ever see him as more than a cute guy with a big ego. Even if he can still soak my panties with a mere smile.

Asher stops walking and steps forward until his chest is flush with mine. He's so close I can feel the heat of his breath rolling down my neck. His head tilts slightly to the left. "So, what do I gotta do to calm your nerves entirely?"

Wow. He's smooth. I'll give him that. "You can start by taking about two steps back."

His expression drops before he pulls his lips back up in a

smile. "Well, damn." He throws his hands up. "All right. I can take a hint." He laughs, and I catch myself doing the same.

"You look empty-handed, my friend." Logan appears out of nowhere, breaking up this tense moment. He's got two cups of something and hands one to Asher, offering me the other.

"No, thanks."

"Guess it's mine then." He takes a sip and shrieks at the taste. The look on his face makes me glad I passed it up, whatever it is.

"What the fuck is this?" Asher asks, making the exact same face.

Logan's head seesaws back and forth. "Little of this. Little of that." He takes another drink, this time not stopping until the cup is empty. I shudder just watching him.

But I also use this opportunity to excuse myself. "I'm going to see what kind of trouble Kaylee's getting herself into. I'll see you two around."

"If anyone gives you shit, you just let me know," Asher says, under the assumption that people other than him give me shit.

It's not like I'm a bug on the floor everyone steps on.

I bow out gracefully while we're on civil terms. So far, it's looking like it could potentially be a good night.

I'm halfway up the steps to the front porch when I feel the sweep of a hand on my lower back. I turn around, not sure who I was expecting, but it definitely isn't the person looking back at me.

"Ryker? What in the world are you doing here?"

"Same thing you're doing here. Hanging out. Having some fun." His brows dip low. "You *are* having fun, aren't you?"

"We just got here…but I guess I'm having fun." Someone comes hurling down the stairs, bumping me to the side.

"Watch it, asshole," Ryker huffs, giving him a shove until he's stumbling to catch his fall.

The guy, a junior I believe, holds his hands up in surrender. "Sorry, man. I don't want any trouble." The guy staggers off, and Ryker returns his attention to me.

Pressed against the stair rail, I cross my arms over my chest. "You do realize this is a high school party and you're bound to look like one of those loser graduates crashing it."

"Well, at least I'm not alone then. Loser party of four." He waggles his eyebrows.

"Oh, right." My eyes roll subtly as I search the crowd. "Carter and your dates for the night."

"Friends. Carter and our friends," he corrects me.

"I see you made a friend of your own." He glances over his shoulder to where Asher and Logan stand, who have since been joined by Liza and a couple of her groupies.

"Were you watching me?" I stammer, ready to jump into defensive mode. "Wait. Is that why you and Carter came here? To keep an eye on me?"

"Noooo," he drawls. "We came because Ava lives here, remember?"

Palm to face. I didn't even put two and two together. Ava is Asher's sister, which slipped my mind. I guess I'll let them off the hook this time.

"Well, you can see why I'd question it. You two are always lurking in my shadow. Telling me what not to wear, who not to hang out with. At least…you were before you left."

"Could you two, like, move off the steps, please?" some petite little girl with a big attitude says as she passes by with two overflowing cups of the same stuff Asher and Logan had. "People are trying to get through."

"Sure will," I bite back. "Enjoy that drink. Heard it's really good."

I walk up the rest of the stairs and step to the side, so we're out of the way. "I was just about to find Kaylee inside, so have fun with your *friends*." I air quote the word friends.

"Wait," he smirks, "are you jealous I'm hanging with Ava?"

"Wow," I drag out the word. "You really are delusional." I don't dare tell him that maybe I am. Or most definitely am, rather.

"Just a simple question."

"I'm most definitely not jealous. But I could ask you the same thing, after all, you're the one who was spying on me and Asher."

"Just think you can do better, that's all."

"I won't argue that." In my opinion, anyone could do better than Asher, and I pity the girl who ends up with him. She'll always be second seat to his ego.

We continue walking across the porch and Ryker places his hand on my back, leading me into the house. It's a strange feeling. It's like this forbidden touch that only feels wrong to me and being wrong makes it feel that much more right.

If anyone else were to see us, they'd think nothing of it. *Oh, it's just her big brother's friend being nice to her.* But those people didn't see what happened in my bedroom earlier today. They didn't feel what I felt—what I'm certain he felt, too.

"So, is it safe to assume you're not mad at me anymore?"

I look to my left where he stands, our shoulders bumping as we walk through the crowded house. "I'm not mad at you anymore, but I do have some stipulations if you leave Oakley Shores again."

"When," he points out.

"Huh?"

"*When* I leave Oakley Shores again. My stay here is temporary, Kit-Kat. Once I do what I need to do, I'm going back." He stops walking, so I do the same. "But, I'm assuming your stipulation is that we keep in touch." He flings an arm around my shoulder and steers me toward the door. "You bet your ass I'm not missing out on two more years of your life. That is, assuming you're not sick of me by the time I'm done being your babysitter." An airy chuckle escapes him, and I smack his chest.

I grab his hand that hangs freely over my shoulder and squeeze it tightly. "If you ever refer to yourself as my babysitter again, I might be the one kicking you out of my life." When I look up at him, his smile slices through me. A reminder that I can never stay mad at Ryker for long.

"Never gonna happen. You missed me too much. After all, you did attempt to stalk me on social media."

Pulling my hand away, I snap my fingers. "That's another thing. Get with the times, man. It's twenty-twenty-two. At least get yourself a Facebook account."

"Eh. I don't know a damn thing about that stuff."

"I'll help you. On one of our many nights of doing absolutely nothing this week."

Mesmerizing eyes meet mine, sending shivers down my spine. "It's a date."

A date with my so-called babysitter. This should be interesting.

I spot Kaylee across the room. She's dancing to her own tune, swaying her hips to a beat that is not "Ruin My Life" by Zara Larsson. Her back is pressed to Damon's chest as he sways back and forth with an almost empty bottle of tequila.

Damn. It's only been twenty minutes, tops, since we parted ways.

"Is she all right with that guy?" Ryker asks, assessing the situation.

"Yeah. Damon's harmless. I better go check on her, though."

Before Ryker can even drop his arm from around my shoulder, Asher walks up.

He looks at me, then Ryker. "Little old for this sort of thing, aren't ya?"

Ryker's eyes sweep the crowd, not once landing on Asher's. "Half your guests are out of high school. I don't see the problem. Besides, I'm here with your sister and our friends."

Asher brings the bottle of beer in his hand to his lips slowly, takes a small drink, still eyeing Ryker, then says, "My sister, huh? Then why is your arm around my homecoming date?"

If Asher's existence alone wasn't enough to annoy Ryker, that sure was. He looks down at me, brows pinched tightly together. "You're going to the dance with him?"

"No," I blurt out. "I mean, he asked me, but—"

"But we haven't finalized the plans." Asher wraps an arm around my waist, pulling me out of Ryker's hold. When I'm at his side, he doesn't drop his hand that's now squeezing my hip. "I've got her from here. Why don't you go find Ava? I think she's in her room."

"You've got her?" Ryker mocks him, strengthening his hold on me. "How about if you get lost?"

I tap my hand to Ryker's chest, hoping he doesn't make a big deal out of this. "It's okay, Ry. You can go hang with your friends."

With his hand still on my hip, Asher steers me away before I can say or do anything. I glance over my shoulder as we're walking through the crowded living room in the direction of Kaylee and Damon. Ryker is still watching us, intently at that. He doesn't move a muscle as his cold eyes burn into mine, his forehead still creased prominently from his distaste in this situation.

I can't tell if he's planning to charge Asher and take him down, or go fetch my brother, so he doesn't have to insert himself into my personal life.

Either way, neither of them are going to let this go. If they think for a second I'm planning to go to a dance with the biggest asshole in school, they'll certainly have something to say about it.

"Dance with me, babe," Kaylee says, now at my side, pulling me away from Asher. I feel like a toy getting passed around tonight, which is new, and also a little unsettling. I'm not used to attention and now that I'm getting it, I'm not sure I want it.

Kaylee and I begin dancing to "Good Ones" by Charli XCX. Her hands on my hips, my arms dangled over her shoulders. My head falls back, and I let the music take control. My body sways to the rhythm while others join us in the middle of the dim living room. Some sing along, some dance, some do both.

Asher comes up behind me, sandwiching me in between him and Kaylee. His hands rests above hers and he guides my motions, slowly pulling me into him and away from her. My head rolls back, eyes closed, when I feel the warmth of Asher's breath spilling down my neck. His lips press lightly to my exposed collarbone. I don't step away or stop him as he begins trailing his lips upward until they're ghosting the lobe of my ear. It feels nice. The attention from a guy, even if it's not the one I want.

Damon joins in, standing directly behind Kaylee, still holding the bottle.

I try to ignore the fact that Asher is supposed to be my enemy, but it's hard when he's crushing my ass with his pelvic bone. I'm here to have a good time, though, and that's exactly what I'm doing.

Damon passes Asher the bottle and his left hand leaves my waist while the other still grips me tightly, not allowing me to separate from him.

Asher takes a drink then holds the bottle to my lips. I shouldn't. But I do. Asher's free hand climbs up until it's around my throat. He tilts my head back slightly and assists me in taking a drink of the tequila. It slides down smooth, but when I've had enough, he keeps going, forcing me to drink more. I turn my head and a shot's worth of the clear liquid dribbles down my chin and into the V-neck of my dress.

"Shit. Sorry about that," Asher says. "Thought you wanted more."

I doubt he's actually sorry. Wouldn't surprise me if he was purposely trying to get me drunk. I don't trust the guy, but I'm not letting it ruin my night. He passes the bottle to Kaylee and resumes writhing against my backside.

It isn't until the next song begins—"Without You" by Kill the Noise, Seven Lions and Julia Ross—that I look to my right and see Ryker. He's standing in the middle of the upstairs staircase, squeezing the railing with so much tenacity that the color in his knuckles has drained. I swallow hard, still tasting the booze, feeling it ride down my esophagus and settling into a puddle of warmth in my stomach.

His eyes burn into mine and I can't look away.

Why is he watching me? Better yet, if he sees the way Asher is holding on to me, why is he allowing it?

Ryker and Carter have never let a guy touch me and get away with it. Whether it's one of them hollering across a crowded room, telling the perp to keep their hands to themselves, a cruel jab, or a loaded threat—they always have something to say.

Not this time, though. But why?

I keep moving while staring deep into his eyes. Each second that passes has him looking more and more tortured by the sight in front of him.

Asher's hand shimmies up my side, and I find myself placing my hand over his as he crosses his arm over my shoulder, his forearm pressed against my neck.

I dance us around slowly until I'm fully facing Ryker.

Maybe I'm trying to get a reaction out of him. This could be my chance to find out if he really did want to kiss me earlier today, or even all those years ago. Did he feel that magnetic pull? Does he feel it now? As he's watching me with another guy's hands all over my body.

Ryker shakes his head no, in a very slow and threatening manner. He wants me to stop.

But I won't. Not until he stops me himself.

"So," Asher whispers in my ear over the loud music, "we going to the dance together or what?"

Before I can respond, I see Ava walking up the stairs to Ryker. Beautiful, perfect Ava. Sleek, blonde hair that reaches her tailbone. Crystal blue eyes and tan skin. Perky breasts that peek out of her all-white tank top and cutoff jeans that fit her to perfection.

Her hand on his shoulder steals his attention from me, and when he leans forward and whispers something in her ear that has her giggling, it hits me—she's everything I'll never be.

"Yeah," I finally say, still watching Ryker with his ex-girlfriend, "I'll go to the dance with you."

CHAPTER SIXTEEN
KIT

I wake up the next morning with a homecoming date. One I didn't even want and regret agreeing to.

Lying in bed, I replay the look on Ryker's face while I was dancing with Asher. One minute he was there, and the next he was gone. I'm pretty sure he went up to Ava's room and spent the night with her. I can't be certain, but it's to be assumed since they disappeared together. Carter and I caught a ride from the Sober Squad, and Kaylee stayed at Damon's house.

There's a knock at the door, followed by, "You awake, Kit?"

"Yeah, Dad, I'm awake."

"Come down and have breakfast with us before Carter and I take off."

Somehow, I completely forgot today is the day they leave. My heart begins thudding in my chest as the realization hits me that Ryker is going to be staying in this house with me for the next week. A full week of temptation hovering over us like a dark cloud, ready to unleash a storm if we give in.

It'll be fine. One week and then we can both go back to our normal lives, this time, staying in touch—as friends.

I roll out of bed and go to my bathroom to brush my teeth. One look in the mirror has me pitying my own reflection. I look like hell, but it's just Carter and Dad. The two men who have seen me at my worst and love me anyways.

I'm walking down the hall, combing my fingers through the matted mess of my hair, when Ryker rounds the corner. He stops, and I do the same.

"Um. Hi," I say, feeling really vulnerable standing here in an oversized tee shirt and shorts that are hidden underneath it.

"Good morning." Ryker chuckles, continuing to walk in my direction.

Oh shit, what is he doing here? Carter and my dad are home. I hold up a hand. "What are you doing?"

He points a finger past me, a serious expression on his face. "Going to the bathroom. That okay?"

My lips press together, and I bite back a smile while nodding. "Yeah." I look down as he passes. I could slap myself for being so damn awkward.

What did I think he was doing? He sure as hell wasn't coming to ravish me in the hallway.

As I'm walking to the kitchen, the smell of bacon and pancakes fills my senses. I expected cold bagels and prepackaged muffins. Having breakfast as a family isn't a typical morning for us.

"Good morning, sweetie," Gail says as she flips a pancake on the griddle. There's a stack next to it of probably a dozen pancakes.

"Good morning," I retort with a yawn. "Smells delicious. But that's a lot of pancakes."

"I'll be freezing some for you to eat during the week while your dad and brother are away."

"You're so sweet, Gail. You didn't have to do that, though."

"Sure, I did. Go ahead and join everyone in the dining room. I'll bring breakfast out shortly."

Carter and Dad are sitting at the oblong table on opposite ends, like two kings on their respective thrones.

"Well, good morning, sunshine. Glad you could finally join us," Carter teases.

I snarl at him as I take a seat beside Dad, who's got his face buried in a newspaper. "What time are you two leaving?"

Dad folds the paper in half and sets it on the table. "Ten o'clock. Our plane leaves at noon."

I nod in response. "Did Ryker stay the night?" I'm surprised he's here, actually. I thought for sure he stayed with Ava.

"No," Dad says, "he got here this morning. I wanted to go over a few things before Carter and I leave."

I can tell he's still not happy with the situation and I'm shocked that he's allowing Ryker to stay with me while they're both gone.

Ryker returns from the bathroom and takes a seat beside Carter. A tense silence fills the room while Dad watches Ryker intently.

"I'm just going to get this over with. Ryker," Dad says, "you lay a finger on my daughter and you won't live to hear me tell you off."

"Dad!" I spit out. "What in the world?"

Dad continues, "If my daughter is hurt in any way, shape, or form, you will not live to hear me tell you off."

"Dad," Carter cuts in, "he's doing us a favor. Besides, it's Ryker," he laughs, "Kit's like a little sister to him, too. She's in good hands."

"Better be," Dad deadpans.

Gail brings in breakfast, and we all eat in what can only be described as a very awkward silence. Once we finish up, Dad goes over the lighter rules. Ryker is to bring me to school, drive me to my doctor's appointment, make sure I have my phone with me at all times for important calls, and help out with any practices I attend. Dad also offered to give him gas money, but Ryker politely declined.

Once I've finished and everyone says what needs to be said, I excuse myself to text Kaylee and see how she's faring this morning.

I'm on my back in my bed as I tap into my phone.

Me: Are you alive?

Kaylee: Barely. My head is pounding and my vagina hurts like a motherfucker.

I laugh out loud.

Me: Guess that answers my next question. So, how was it?

Kaylee: Painful. The guy is hung like a horse. If that says anything about the company he keeps, you better jelly up before you let Asher in.

Me: Oh my God, Kay! NOT HAPPENING! I can't stand the guy, like I'd ever invite him between my legs.

Kaylee knows damn well I'm a virgin and Asher is the last guy I'd give my first time to.

Kaylee: Just saying. You two were all over each other last night. Everyone was talking about it.

Well, that's just great.

Me: Everyone? As in…

Kaylee: As in EVERYONE. Someone took pics of the entire party and posted them on Insta. Liza and Carly are having a field day. Reshares and cruel comments.

I swipe out of our message screen and into my Instagram account. My notifications show multiple tags by various accounts, so I click on them one by one. Every single picture is Asher and me dancing. His hands on my hips, my chest, and my neck. There's also ones of me taking a shot.

This is just great. The last thing I need is more unwanted attention. Asher is the guy every girl wants at OSH and if they think for a second he's into me, I'll be on the most-hated list.

I go back to the screen to text Kaylee, and she's already sent three messages.

Kaylee: Looks like the king has found his queen.

Kaylee: Don't sweat it. You're untouchable now that you're under his arm. This is good, Kit.

Kaylee: This is good, right?

I type back a response.

Me: It is what it is. Asher has been extra nice, so I'm giving him the benefit of the doubt. I still don't trust the guy, but I also don't care what anyone has to say about me.

Kaylee: Good! On another note, I'm back to going on this stupid trip. We're leaving in an hour.

Me: I'm sorry, Kay. I feel like it's my fault.

Kaylee: Nah. My aunt's worse than my parents. I was only doing it for you. All good. Maybe I'll find out I have a hot cousin I never knew about.

Me: Now that's just gross.

Kaylee: Gotta pack. Check in later.

Me: Have fun!

I drop my phone to my side on the bed, wondering how I got myself into these sticky situations. The dance with Asher—Ryker staying at my house for a week. What has my boring, quiet life become? I decide to get all my feelings out in my journal. I used to write in it daily, but I've been so busy lately that I just do weekly updates.

After I finish spilling my guts onto the pages, I take a quick shower and put on some comfy clothes for a lazy day at home.

CHAPTER
SEVENTEEN
RYKER

I STAND BACK AND WATCH AS EVERYONE SAYS THEIR GOODBYES. Carter says he'll call and check in later, and when I think I'm in the clear and they're ready to head out the door, Gerald looks at me and tips his head to the side.

Following his lead, we venture away from Kit and Carter.

"I'm trusting you, Ryker. The past is in the past, but Kit's my little girl. Take care of her."

I nod. "Yes, sir. She's in good hands."

With that, he follows Carter out the door and they're gone, leaving just Kit and me standing in the entry way.

"Well," she says, "I guess I'll just go study for a while."

"Actually," I stop her from leaving, "I was thinking maybe we could hang out. Watch a movie. Order a pizza."

"Okay," she smiles, "we can do that."

Kit didn't even give me a choice in what movie to watch. We're sitting on a sectional, in the family room in the basement. Her sitting cross-legged on one side, me reclined on the other.

"Oooh," she stirs, getting into the movie. "This is my favorite part." She tosses a few pieces of popcorn in her mouth and I find myself watching her instead of *The Notebook*.

She's none the wiser that she has an audience as her lips part slightly during the kissing scene on the television. Her blue eyes light up, and she doesn't peel them away as she grabs another fistful of popcorn.

The thoughts in my head are terrible. The things I could do to that pretty mouth. What I wouldn't give to feel her soft skin pressed against mine.

"Ryker," Kit says, snapping me out of my reverie. I'm still looking at her and she's caught me.

"Yeah?"

"I asked if you want some." She holds the bowl out, offering me some of her microwaved popcorn.

"Sure." I push my legs down, closing the recliner, and walk over to where she's sitting on the couch.

I go to take the bowl, but she puts up a fight. "I still want some, too." She pats the space beside her. "Sit down." Her eyes return to the movie and her hand is back in the bowl at the same time mine is. Our fingers brush and she doesn't think anything of it. I do, though. I quickly grab some and pull my hand out, inching farther down the couch, away from her. I'm too close. Too close to saying *fuck the rules.* Too close to going against everything that is right and doing something wrong because I'm weak. Because I think with my dick and let my hormones get the better of me.

"I still can't believe you've never watched this movie," she says, interrupting my thoughts.

"Not really my thing."

"And what is your thing? Tell me about Ryker in 2022. Fill me in on all I've missed."

"Not really much to tell." I dump the entire handful of popcorn in my mouth and speak while I chew. "I'm still the same person, just freer from my past out there."

"There's nothing wrong with the person you were before, Ry. Don't be so hard on yourself."

"I fucked up back then. Hell," I throw my arm over the back of the couch, "I am fucked-up and I've come to realize that no matter what, I always will be." There's just so much she doesn't know. I hide skeletons in my closet, ones that would destroy my life and the lives of others if they fell out.

"No," she shakes her head, "you are not the awful things you think of yourself." She grabs the remote and pauses the movie. It's frozen on a scene where the guy and girl are standing in the rain.

"You've always tried to make me see the best in myself, Kit-Kat. Even after all I did to hurt you, you're still trying." I turn to look at her. She has her head angled toward her shoulder and a look of pity on her face. "Don't pity me, Kit. I'm doing all right."

"All right isn't good enough. I want you to be great. You're capable of big things, Ryker. You just have to believe it."

This is the Kit I remember. Always seeing the best in people, even when they're at their worst.

"I could say the same for you."

She pops one single piece of popcorn in her mouth. "What do you mean?"

"I see you, Kit. I see how you've changed. I saw you drinking last night. Watched you dance with Asher, while letting him rub his grubby hands all over you. You're better than that."

Flattening her lips, she snaps, "I'm eighteen years old. I was having fun."

"All I'm saying is, don't screw up your life over a boy or a drink. You can have fun and be careful at the same time."

She chews on her bottom lip, looking back at me. "You've said that before."

"Probably." I shrug my shoulders. "Sounds like something I'd say."

"I dared you to do better," she says point-blankly, staring off as if memories are replaying in her head. "And you asked me to make you a promise."

I remember that. The dare. The promise. Her room. Us. "That's right." I snap my fingers. "You never gave it to me. You left to go out with your friends and took that promise with you."

"You're right. I never did. But you're so concerned with the way I've lived my life all this time you've been away and what you fail to realize is that you're the reason for it."

"Me?" I blurt out defensively. "Because I left?"

"Isn't this what you told me to do?" She shoves the bowl of popcorn into my chest aggressively, causing a few pieces to fly out of the bowl. "You told me to enjoy all the little things in life and now that I am, I'm what...screwing up my life?"

Not even bothering to pick up the fallen popcorn, I set the bowl on the coffee table in front of the couch. "I did say that. But, damn, Kit. When I said it, I meant *the little things*." I air quote. "Ice cream for breakfast, eat a candy bar for dinner, or swim in the dark." The words drip from my mouth like hot lava. "I didn't mean go to parties and drink while letting guys like Asher Collins grind their fucking dicks on your ass." Now that I've said them, I wish I could take them back because the look in her eyes says I went too far.

"Wow," she scoffs, getting to her feet. Her hands fly up, mouth open to speak, but she doesn't say anything until she's halfway across the room. "You've got some nerve." She points a finger at me, eating up the space she just took. "Coming back to this town and treating me like I'm the one screwing up. At least I didn't run when things got hard."

This isn't how this conversation was supposed to go. Not at all. I get to my feet and go to put a hand on her shoulder to calm her down, but she swats it away. "No! You don't get to make me feel like shit then touch me."

"I'm just trying to help you."

"News flash, Ryker. I don't need your help. I've done just fine for myself while you've been away, so why don't you...just go back to Colorado and continue to live like I never existed."

"You don't mean that."

Her arms cross over her chest, and she blows out a heavy breath. "Maybe I do." She stomps off and heads up the stairs.

My fingers press firmly to my temples, massaging them as I try to wrap my head around what just happened. *Could I really be the reason Kit changed so drastically?* She was once this shy, sweet girl, and now, she's the eye of the storm I never saw coming.

CHAPTER
EIGHTEEN
KIT

It's been thirty-six hours since my dad and Carter left. It's also been twenty-four since I talked to Ryker. I've avoided him at all costs and spent all of last night and today in my room.

Some pretty harsh words were exchanged, mostly on my part, but how dare he accuse me of screwing up my life. He doesn't even know me anymore. Did he really expect me to just pause time and remain the same girl I was when he left?

I pull my tee shirt over my head and let it fall to the floor, followed by the rest of my clothes.

As I step into the shower, I notice I don't have a razor. Stepping back out, I grab my pink, silk robe hanging on the door hook and throw it on.

I'll just go take one of Carter's. He'll come home and tell me to quit stealing his shit, I'll laugh, then I'll do it again. I'm his little sister; I'm supposed to piss him off occasionally. God knows he does the same to me. Like asking his best friend to stay with me when he knows damn well I've been upset with the guy for two years. Therefore, my petty theft of a razor is completely justified.

Fortunately, Ryker is staying in the guest bedroom on the opposite end of the hall from my room. There's a good chance he's in either the kitchen or living room, both of which I have to pass by to go upstairs, so I decide I'll just pretend he's not there like I've done since last night.

I'm probably being too hard on him and I'll eventually get over it, but right now, I have so many mixed emotions in my head that I need to sort out.

Carter's bedroom door is cracked open, so I give it a push and walk inside. Everything is in place, like it always is. Carter is the most organized human being on the planet and sometimes it makes me sad for him. Let a dirty towel stay on the floor for a day or two, leave your clothes in a basket. What harm does it do?

It makes me think of what Ryker said about the little things I'm supposed to be enjoying. What the hell does he know? I enjoy life plenty. He's the one who's trying to grow up too fast. Maybe there was a time I was too mature for my age, but I lightened up. Now he's the one who needs to quit taking life so seriously. It's like our roles have reversed.

I open Carter's bathroom door and gasp at the sight in front of me. My hand flies over my mouth, and while I should turn around and run, something holds me in place.

"Fuck, Kit." Ryker shrieks as he grabs a towel off the sink and attempts to cover himself. I say attempt because it's a washcloth, not an actual towel, and his erect dick is no match for the squared cloth.

"I'm...I'm so sorry."

Walk away, Kit. Go.

Still standing here, I gawk at his mesmerizing form. He's completely naked from head to toe. My eyes trail down the flesh of chest to his taut abs.

Ryker in all his glory who, only seconds ago, had his hand wrapped around himself, masturbating in my brother's bathroom.

"I had no idea you were in here. I wouldn't have interrupted if I'd known you were...in here." My mouth draws back, tightening the cords of my neck.

Ryker bends over to grab his boxers off the floor, giving me a perfect view of his ass in the reflection of the mirror. I chuckle a little as he curses and slides them on. "You still didn't tell me why you're here."

"I came for a razor."

I'm not sure I'll ever get that image out of my head. I'm not sure I ever want to. Ryker is big. Like, scary big. I don't have much to compare it to, but I've watched porn, I've got a dildo, and it's nothing like that monstrous thing between his legs.

"Kit," Ryker snaps. My eyes trail back up his body to his face and my cheeks flush with embarrassment when I realize I was literally staring at his crotch. I wipe my hand across my mouth. No drool. Thank God. "You can grab a razor. I was just getting ready to take a shower."

"I can see that." I press my lips together firmly, choking on a laugh.

He snaps the waistband of his boxers and looks at me with a stern expression. "Are you laughing at me?"

"No," I shake my head, biting back more laughter, "I've just… never been in this position before, and I'm not really sure what to say."

"Yeah. Well, that makes two of us. How about if you start with, I'll never mention this to a single soul, especially my brother."

"Okay. I'll never mention this to a single soul, especially my brother."

There's a brief moment of silence before Ryker breaks it. "Well, this is awkward."

I'm not sure who's more embarrassed right now, him or me.

I spot a bag of razors behind him on the sink vanity, so I walk deeper into the bathroom. It's a small space, and I'm on the verge of suffocation as I reach behind him and grab the bag. "'Scuse me. Sorry."

He doesn't even attempt to move. Just squares his shoulders and remains in my way. I can feel my robe dipping down, and when I look in the mirror, I can see my breasts on full display. My arm brushes across the side of his stomach and when I've got the bag in hand, I look up at him, frozen in place.

His eyes, warm and seductive, peer down on me, and he cracks a smile.

I immediately adjust my robe and give him a quick smile of my own before hurrying my ass out of that room.

As soon as I hit the hall, my back collides with the wall. I take in a deep breath, exhaling slowly.

My God what a gorgeous sight.

I'm still mad at him, but I'd gladly stare at that body all day long.

CHAPTER
NINETEEN
RYKER

Well, that was unexpected. Little Kit just got quite the show. I should be more embarrassed than I am. After all, she did catch me jerking off. If she only knew that she's the one I was thinking of while I was doing it. It's a shame the image of her in that tight dress Friday night was interrupted, but it's since been replaced with something better.

Those perfect tits settled nicely in that silk robe. She knew it was opened, but she gave it enough time for me to see before she closed it. Maybe this is a game to her. And maybe I wanna play. Even though I shouldn't. For a lot of different reasons.

Stepping into the stream of water, I breathe out a calming breath. The hot water feels so refreshing on my bare skin.

Wasting no time, I grab a bottle of body wash and squirt a good amount in my hand. Rubbing up and down my neck, my chest, my pits, I lather my hand up more and settle it around my cock.

Coming back here, I knew Kit wouldn't be the same girl she was when I left. Even had a feeling it might be difficult, considering I've fought against feelings for her in the past, but we were kids then. Now, she's older and more beautiful than I ever imagined she'd be. A nice round ass, perky tits that are just the right size to fit in the palms of my hand.

My eyes close and I imagine what she'd look like naked. Long legs that ride up to a mound of hair coating her pussy. The smooth skin of her stomach and those perky breasts. And plump lips that would wrap nicely around my cock.

I keep stroking, my orgasm within reach. The picture of her is still painted perfectly in my mind. Lying on her bed, head tilted back, exposing her long neck. I'd smother it in kisses while working my way down until I'm rooted between her legs. Two fingers parting her lips while my tongue sweeps up the length of her pussy.

Stroking faster, warmth courses through my veins while my heart thunders in my chest. I'd give just about anything to look into her eyes while I suck on her clit.

The desire to touch her, to taste her, to watch her, is almost more than I can handle.

"Fuck," I grumble, picking up my pace. My mouth falls open, and I watch while I stroke myself, imagining it's her bringing me this pleasure. The thought alone sends me over the edge. I pump my hand a few more times, watching as cum shoots from my dick all over the shower wall.

It takes me a second to come down, and when I do, I'm slapped in the face with guilt. I shouldn't be thinking about her like this. She's Carter's little sister. This is Kit. Fuck! What the hell is the matter with me?

Not to mention, Kit's too good for me. I've made it a point to make sure she doesn't attach herself to asshole guys like me.

◆

IT'S BEEN a few hours since my awkward encounter with Kit. Now, I'm choking on guilt as I talk to Carter.

"How's she doing?" he asks on the other end of the phone. I

prop my arm under my head on the couch and stretch my legs out while the game is on TV.

"Doing good. She's been watered and fed and is playing in her room."

Carter laughs. "Well, I'm glad to hear she's not giving you shit for leaving anymore."

"Well," I drawl. "I wouldn't go that far. I almost forgot how scary the attitude of an eighteen-year-old girl can be, but she hasn't killed me yet, so we'll call that a win."

"Glad to hear." He chuckles. "All right, I've gotta get some sleep. We've got a meeting early in the morning."

"All right. Good luck, man."

"Later."

I end the call and set my phone on my chest.

"Who was that?" Kit asks, appearing out of nowhere.

My head shoots up and I see her standing behind the couch, wearing a button-up, baby blue pajama top and matching shorts. "Carter." I push into a sitting position, hoping that her coming down here means she's ready to talk about our fight last night.

"I made a pizza. Just thought I'd let you know in case you want some." She turns to leave the basement, but I stop her.

Pizza is a start.

"Kit, wait."

Her feet stop, but she doesn't bother to turn around. "Yeah?"

"Come here."

Of course, she doesn't. She just stands there, waiting for me to beg.

"Would you quit being so stubborn and get your ass in here?"

Her shoulders drop and she turns back around, dragging her feet as she joins me on the couch. Taking the spot farthest away from me, just to prove she's still upset.

"Why are you so mad?" I tip my chin, arms spread out and resting on the back of the couch.

After she breathes out audibly, she says, "I'm just tired of everyone treating me like I'm broken. I always thought you were on my side, but you're clearly not."

"Kit-Kat. Of course I'm on your side. Why would you think that?"

"Because you act like them. Watching my every move and judging me like I'm supposed to be perfect."

It's been a very long time since Kit and I have had an in-depth conversation, and I can see that it's overdue.

I slide down on the couch until I'm sitting directly beside her, my arm still hanging over the back. "Hey," I say, lifting her chin with my thumb. She resists but eventually turns to look at me. "You are not broken. You're just bruised." She blinks back a few tears and I sweep my thumb under her eye. "You're not perfect either."

She exhales a heavy breath. "Gee. Thanks."

"You're not supposed to be perfect, Kit. No one is. Besides, perfection is boring. I happen to like you just the way you are. Your temper, your scars, and all your imperfections."

She cracks a smile. "You have to say that. You're Carter's best friend."

"Actually," my eyes lift to hers, "I *shouldn't* say that because I *am* Carter's best friend."

There's a moment of clarity between us. As if the past has vanished and we're back in her bedroom closet the day I almost kissed her. All the bitterness, pain, and anguish that's strangled us both over the past two years has dissipated; only, this time, I don't think I can stop myself.

I grip her chin and pull her face to mine. Our lips collide like a train wreck because that's exactly what this is. I'll soon regret it. But right now, this is all I want. She doesn't push me away or fight me off. Instead, her lips slit open, and I use the opportunity to slide my tongue in her mouth, tangling it with hers in a messy web of desire.

Kit's hands rest on my shoulders, and when I inch away, she

pulls me back in. When I try to unlock our lips, she forces the suction.

I've wanted to do this for so long. And it feels just as wrong as I knew it would. For weeks, I dreamt of what she felt like, tasted like. I memorized her scent, and it's instilled in my mind.

But it's wrong. This is Kit. Carter's sister.

In an instant, I pull away. "I'm sorry, Kit. I shouldn't…I shouldn't have done that." My head keeps shaking no as guilt slices through me. I run my fingers through my hair, looking down at the space between us, because looking at her will only make it worse.

"You're right. You shouldn't have…and I shouldn't dare you to do it again."

"What did you say?"

Her tongue sweeps across her bottom lip. "Kiss me again, Ry. I dare ya."

She knows I'd never turn down a dare. She knows I'll kiss her. Fuck the dare. I'd do it anyway.

It only takes a second before my hands are cupping her cheeks, heart thudding in my chest.

I lean into her, emotions spilling into our kiss. Years of temptation freed while falling willfully into a pit of desire.

Sliding my hand down the side of her body, I grip her waist.

Her fingers tangle in my hair, and we kiss so hard our teeth clank together. My cock stiffens in my pants, and I'm going straight to hell.

"Fuck, Kit," I breathe into her mouth. "We shouldn't…" My words trail off when Kit slides her hand up my shirt, trailing her fingers over my abs while still gripping a fistful of my hair.

She tastes like sweet mint. Smells like roses and fresh rain.

Her back arches when my fingers toy with the band of her bra. My fingers dissolve into her milky skin, and my stomach twists into knots of hunger to feel more. To taste more. Do more.

Kit leans back slightly, pulling me along with her, and when I place the pressure of my body on hers, she rests her back against the arm of the couch, sliding down more and more with each exhale of breath between us.

I need to stop this, but I don't think I can.

"Ryker," she says in an audible breath against my lips.

My eyes open and I see hers are open, too. I pull back, but she keeps her hold on my head.

"Yeah?" I ask, wide-eyed and curious.

"I want you."

Fuck. "Don't say that, Kit. You don't mean it."

"But I do. I want you...I want you to be my first."

There's a pang in my chest. A feeling I wasn't expecting. Not one of want, need, or desire, but one of heavy sorrow.

The man in me says to take her, mark her, and claim her. The friend in me says...don't. Not Carter's friend, but hers. What would that do to us? To her?

I stare into her longing eyes as I battle the demons in my head. As I search for any excuse that would make this okay. But nothing trumps the fact that it's wrong and it's something that can never be undone. If I give her what she wants, while taking what I've craved for so long, our lives will be changed forever. Her heart will break more than it ever has and mine will never be whole again.

"I can't do that, Kit-Kat."

The corners of her eyes glisten with tears of shame and resentment. "Please don't call me that. Not now."

In just these few moments, I feel like I've already lost her. Like the friend I've had since I was a kid has disappeared before my eyes. I can feel the tension strengthening its hold and the space between us multiplying even as we lie here with no air between our pressed bodies.

After a few seconds of reflection and likely that same weight of guilt I'm feeling, Kit pushes her hands to my chest. "Please let me up."

I take her hand in mine, still holding it to my chest. "Don't do this. Don't be angry. You have to know how wrong this is."

Her head turns to the side, looking away from me. "I'm not a child, Ryker. I can make my own choices." She squirms again, yanking her wrist from my hold. "Get up."

A single tear falls down her cheek, and I sweep it away. "Maybe in another lifetime we could have been. But in this one… we just can't."

"Get up!" she howls through strained vocal chords.

There's nothing I can say, so I do as she asks. I use my hands to push the cushions on either side of her small body and get to my feet.

In a matter of seconds, Kit is walking briskly across the room, sniffling and wiping her tears. I want more than anything to chase after her and make this right, but how can I without fucking everything up further.

I drop down on the couch, elbows pressed to my knees. My face falls into my hands, fingertips digging into my temples.

God, I wanted her. So bad. Not just to be her first, but her second, her third, her last. I've felt her heart calling to mine for years. Even during the two years we were apart, I still felt it. I constantly fed the tension chord between us so I didn't do something stupid like I did just now. I gave in and now I'm not sure how long I can resist before I give in entirely.

No! I can't, and I won't. We'd both be hurt in the process, and I'd lose everything—including her. She'll get bored with me. I could never give her the things she deserves. There are so many reasons why we can never give in to temptation.

CHAPTER
TWENTY
KIT

"You have to talk to me at some point," Ryker says from the driver's seat of his truck. I insisted on calling someone else for a ride to school, but he wasn't having it, and I was tired of arguing. So here we are.

"Kit," he says my name with a softness that sends heat down my spine, "are we good?"

I laugh sarcastically, staring out the passenger window as we turn onto the main road that leads to the high school. "Yeah, Ryker. We're great." My words come out just as cutting as my laugh.

"All right then," he slams on the brakes, veering off to the side of the road, "you leave me no choice."

My eyes shoot to him. "Have you lost your damn mind?"

"Yeah, Kit," he raises his voice, "I think I have. You're making me crazy."

"Me?" I shout, matching his enthusiasm. "You're the one making me crazy."

We come to a complete stop as cars fly past us, including a school bus loaded with students. With my backpack in my lap, I fumble with the straps anxiously, ready to get out of this truck, because it feels like all the air has been sucked out of it.

Ryker shifts the gear into park and grips the steering wheel with both hands, squeezing tightly as he glares at me. "Quit shutting me out when you get mad. If you have something to say, say it. If you wanna scream at me, then for heaven's sake, fucking scream at me, Kit. But please do or say something because this silent treatment is getting old."

"Fine!" I stammer, pushing my backpack onto the floor at my feet while turning my whole body to face him. "You want me to say something? You want me to *express* my feelings? I am angry, Ryker." My voice rises to a near scream. "I am so angry with you." I swallow hard, forcing down the lump lodged in my throat. "You pushed me out of your life like I had no value in it. Then you come back and think we can pick up where we left off. You tempt me and almost kiss me, but say we can't. Then you do kiss me, only to push me away and treat it like a mistake. What the hell do you want from me, Ryker?"

He stares at me long and hard. Either processing my words, or plotting his own. Heavy moments pass.

"You told me to say something, so I did, and now you have nothing—"

Suddenly he's there. In my face, shutting me up. Hands clenching my cheeks as he pulls my lips roughly to his. Our mouths crash together and my stomach whirls with anticipation. A need for more. So much so that I'm not sure I can breathe without the air he's expelling into my mouth. I need him just as much. To fill my lungs, to consume my body, to destroy me and put me back together.

"I want you, too, Kit," he breathes into my mouth. His words are a whisper against my lips. "I've wanted you for so long."

This moment, those words—it's what I've always wanted.

His tongue slithers in, taking my own hostage, tangling in a messy web of desire laced with intent.

I climb over the center console and onto his lap. His hands plant firmly on my waist. "Then have me." More cars continue to pass us on the road, but I don't let up. I freeze in his lap and decide to stay there as long as he'll let me. "Stop thinking with your head and follow your heart."

And he does. Passion spills into my mouth. Years of anguish slackened, but still there, because more will never be enough with him. I want it all, every inch of his body. I want to consume his thoughts, the same way he does mine.

"I don't wanna lose you, Kit."

I open my eyes to see him looking back at me. "You won't."

"But I will. Eventually. If we do this, I'll lose you both."

I firmly shake my head no. "You'll never lose me unless you allow me to get lost."

"It's not that easy."

"But it is." I kiss him again. His body tenses up beneath mine, but he doesn't pull back. He doesn't stop me or tell me all the reasons why this is wrong. Instead, his hand snakes up my shirt. I put my hand over his, above the fabric of my shirt, and guide him upward. His fingers slip under my bra, and when I grind myself against his erection, he lets out an airy moan and cups my breast.

The little space between us still feels like too much. I roll my hips, grinding against him, and he bucks up.

"Fuck, Kit. You're killing me," he mutters into my mouth.

I smile against his lips and kiss him harder. Dropping my hand from his head, I reach down between us and pop the button on my jean shorts.

His eyes shoot wide open, lust-filled, yet cautious. "What are you doing?"

I'm not sure what's happening to me. Usually I'm more reserved, but I'm not letting this opportunity pass me by. I take his free hand from my waist and press his palm to my stomach, slowly moving it down. "Touch me."

Ryker stares back at me, questioning me with his eyes. "Not here."

I look around, remembering we're on the side of the road. He's right. This isn't where I want this to happen.

I nod in response, buttoning my shorts back up. "Okay."

Ryker tilts his head to the side with downcast eyes. "Don't do that."

"Do what?"

"Get all pissy again."

I chuckle. "I'm not pissy. I'm agreeing with you. Under one condition."

"Of course. Let's hear it."

"Promise me you'll keep an open mind about us."

"Oh," he smirks, "a promise instead of a dare?"

"Okay. I dare you to keep an open mind."

Somehow his hands find my cheeks again and he's pulling me back to him. My heart gallops in my chest, and I never want this moment to end. Ryker parts his lips slowly, head tilted to the side, and he kisses me so tenderly I can barely feel the contact. His mouth opens and closes against mine while jagged breaths escape him.

"Dare accepted."

CHAPTER
TWENTY-ONE
KIT

I'VE BEEN FLOATING ON A CLOUD ALL DAY, EVEN WITHOUT KAYLEE here. People pass by in the halls, noticing my smile that doesn't falter. Even at lunch, while Margo and a few of my and Kaylee's other friends pressed me about what daydream I was living in, I couldn't stop.

This morning, I got all the clarity I needed. All these years, Ryker has felt what I did—what I *do*. Now that I know, I'm ready to dive in headfirst. He's still hesitant, which is to be expected. He actually said, in his own words, *I've wanted you for so long.*

Chills shimmy down my entire body just thinking about it.

It's the end of the school day and Ryker should have been out here to pick me up.

"Hey, Kit," Asher hollers from the driver's side of his car.

"Hi, Asher."

"You need a ride or you just gonna stand here alone for another twenty minutes?"

I look down at my Apple Watch. *Holy shit.* School got out a half hour ago. Where the hell is Ryker?

"I have a ride coming…I think." I pull my phone out of the side pocket of my backpack. No missed calls.

I tap Ryker's name and hold up a finger, asking Asher to wait.

Straight to voicemail. "Hey, Ryker. Where are you? I'm out in front of the school waiting."

Before I can even end the call, Asher says, "If you're talking about Ryker Dawson, I don't think he's coming. He's a little… preoccupied right now."

I tap End on the call and stick my phone back in the pocket of my bag, walking closer to where Asher is parked beside the curb. "What's that supposed to mean?"

"He's actually at my house. With my sister."

My heart drops deep into the pit of my stomach. "He's with Ava?"

Asher nods. "I mean, I could take you to my place if you want. We could hang out, or whatever. Or, I can just bring you home."

Well, it seems I don't have many options, so I nod in response, lifting the door handle.

"Thanks. My house is fine."

Asher sweeps his hand across the passenger seat, pushing some papers and empty Gatorade bottles onto the floorboard.

Once I'm in, I close the door and put on my seatbelt. "How do you know Ryker is at your house?"

He shifts into park and burns out of the parking spot. "Cameras. I get an alert any time someone pulls in the driveway." He messes with his phone, while sitting at the stop sign, waiting to leave the parking lot, then hands it to me before pressing on the gas. "Don't think anyone else driving that piece of shit truck would be at my house."

I look down at the screen and, sure enough, it's Ryker's truck parked in the circle drive in front of Asher's ginormous house.

"You know what? I think I changed my mind. Do you have plans tonight?"

His head turns, and he's as stunned as I am. "Not really. Practice was canceled because of the storm coming in."

"Great." I sink down in the seat. "Let's hang out then, but how about my place instead?"

Asher reaches over and squeezes my leg. "Works for me."

It's not Asher I want to spend my time with. One year ago, this is exactly what I would have wanted. Now, his fingers feel more like spiders on my lap.

Inviting Asher over has nothing to do with him and everything to do with this sick need inside me to test the boundaries between Ryker and me.

He forgot to pick me up today because he's with Asher's sister, who is also his ex-girlfriend.

Fuck that.

I won't pretend I'm not bothered that he's spending time with that girl. So much time that I must have completely slipped his mind. I'm also curious about how bothered he'll be to see that I'm spending time with Asher. Time for him to get a taste of his own medicine.

Asher cranks up the volume. "Zombified" by Falling in Reverse plays so loud I can feel the bass drumming through my entire body. I'm actually grateful, because it means we don't have to try to engage in some awkward conversation.

We pull up to my house and I'm not surprised when the driveway is empty and my phone hasn't rung at all with an apology for Ryker's forgetfulness.

Asher wastes no time getting out, and when he rounds the car to my side, I think for a second that he might open the door for me. I'm proven wrong when he heads to the front door. Scrambling to grab my things, I get out and jog to catch up with him.

Once we're inside, I drop my bag on the couch. "This way." I take a sharp turn down the hall to my bedroom.

He stops, checking out some of the family pics on the wall. "He's a fucking legend," Asher says of Carter, pointing to a picture of him on the wall during the last game of his senior year. Beside it is one of Carter and Ryker. "This guy's all right, too. Sort of an asshole, if you ask me." He taps the frame over Ryker's face.

"They were *both* pretty epic on the field." I turn the handle to my room and push the door open. "You're not so bad yourself."

"Not so bad?" He laughs. "I'm an asset to the team and they know it."

Wow. If I thought for a second his ego shrunk, I was sadly mistaken. Some things never change.

"So, this is your room?" He looks around, taking it all in. "Cute."

Cute? Yeah, it's girly, but cute describes a child's room.

"Yep," I wave my arms around, "this is my room. Until I leave for college, that is."

Asher drops down on my bed, shoes still on. He kicks his feet up, crossing them at the ankles, and tucks his folded arms under his head. "Where ya headed?"

"Just Oakley Shores Community. I have no plans to go far. You?"

"Jackson U. Got a full ride on a football scholarship."

"That's awesome. Congrats." I'm not surprised. Even if he is an asshole, he's very smart and extremely athletic.

"So. Have you got your dress yet?" He pats the mattress beside him. "I'm thinking we should color-coordinate."

It completely slipped my mind that I agreed to go to the dance with him. I haven't even thought about a dress. It's hard to do that when Kaylee isn't here to advise. Maybe I'll wait until she gets back. I'll be cutting it close, but I can't shop for one without her.

Part of me wishes I'd never said yes to Asher. Agreeing to be his date almost feels like I'm betraying myself in some weird way. Any attraction I had to Asher disappeared after my health scare. He's shown me time and time again how little respect he has for me, or women in general.

Against my better judgment, I sit down beside him. "Not yet. I'll let you know when I get one."

"I'm glad you decided to go with me. I mean, if you hadn't, you might be dateless. Logan snatched himself up a junior bombshell."

God, he's such a condescending jerk.

"I think you mean we'd both be dateless. From what I hear,

you had a date and you dropped her. Why is that, by the way?" It's a totally justified question. He was going with Dana, and suddenly, he couldn't stand the girl.

Asher chuckles. "Trust me, I would have had no trouble filling your space."

Just as I'm about to call the whole thing off, because I can't handle any more of him, he pulls me on top of him.

I'm instantly drawn in by his gorgeous face. Maybe that's what holds me here because, for whatever reason, I don't get up.

Asher places a hand on my cheek, guiding my face toward his, but before our mouths connect, my bedroom door hits the wall with a thud. I spring up in panic. "Ryker?"

"What the fuck is going on in here?" He looks from me to Asher. "Get the hell off her bed."

"What's he doing here?" Asher asks, not even flinching at Ryker's demands.

"I said, get the fuck off her bed!" Ryker raises his voice, walking steadfast toward me. He grabs my hand and pulls me off the bed and away from Asher. "Now!"

I knew Ryker would come home eventually, and I knew he'd be bothered by Asher being here, but I didn't expect this.

"Calm down, Ryker. We're just hanging out."

"You can hang out at The Soap Box. He doesn't need to be on your fucking bed."

I'm stunned at his outburst, but I also think it's a little suspicious. "Is that where you and Ava were hanging out? At The Soap Box?" I know they weren't, but that's beside the point.

"How'd you know I was with Ava?"

"Asher showed me his home camera feed."

He points a finger at Asher, who is still comfortably lying on my bed without a care in the world. "Were you spying on us?"

Asher chuckles. "Yeah, I was spying on my sister and her boyfriend because I have nothing better to do." His legs fling over the side and he finally gets up with a heavy sigh. "Actually, I gave

Kit a ride home because you forgot her. Ya know, because you were so busy with my sister."

Ugh. Hearing it out loud makes it hurt even more. One step forward, two steps back.

Ryker looks at me, contempt in his eyes. "I'm sorry about that, Kit. Ava's car wouldn't start, so she called and asked me to take a look at it. Time just got away from me."

I hold up a hand stopping him. "Don't. I really don't care. Can you please leave my room? I have company."

"No," he says, a seriousness to his tone that unnerves me. "I'm not leaving. You two can hang out in the living room."

"Ugh," I growl, grabbing Asher by the hand and pulling him toward the door. "Come on. Let's go to your place." I pin Ryker with a hard glare. "It seems my father returned earlier than planned." Going to Asher's house is the last thing I want to do, but I'm all about proving my point to Ryker. I'm not a child and he needs to quit treating me like one.

In one heated breath, Ryker grabs my arm, pulls me away from Asher, and shoves him out of my room. The door slams shut, and he clicks the lock. With my back pressed against the door, he cages me in with both hands on either side of my head. "What the hell are you doing?" he grits out.

"Trying to leave, if you'd stop being so obnoxious." I reach behind me and grab the handle, but it's no use with the pressure Ryker is laying on the door.

His jaw tics furiously. "You're not going to his house."

"Watch me."

"Kit," Asher pounds on the door, rattling my brain, "open the damn door. Are you coming or what?"

"Tell him no," Ryker whispers with intent.

"Look, I've got shit I could be doing, so open the door or I'm out."

Ryker challenges me with his eyes deadlocked on mine. "Let him go."

My head is in a fog and I'm not in any position to make decisions right now, especially when they involve emotions. I couldn't care less about Asher, but Ryker means everything to me. All we've done since he got here is bicker, and I'm ready for some peace.

I don't even blink as Ryker watches me, waiting for me to do or say something. "Go ahead without me, Asher. I'll talk to you tomorrow at school."

A glint of a smile parts his lips.

"Are you all right in there? Do you want me to call my sister to come and handle this guy? She's tough. She'll put him in his place."

"No," I blurt out, crossing my arms over my chest. "I'm fine. Ryker's just a little protective. Ya know, being my brother's best friend and all." It's a statement we both know to be true.

"All right. I guess. We'll talk tomorrow and finalize plans for the dance," Asher says before we hear his feet trudging down the hall.

It isn't until the front door opens and closes that Ryker drops his overpowering stance. His hands fall to his sides and his shoulders go slack. "Are you going to the dance with him?"

"Yeah. I am."

I'm not sure why Ryker looks like he was slapped in the face with news he wasn't expecting. "You're changing plans, right?"

My shoulders rise and fall, back still against the door. "I already said yes. I can't back out now. Especially with the dance being less than two weeks away."

"Come on, Kit-Kat," he drawls. "Drop the guy. Tell him to fuck off."

"Hmm," I tap my chin with a devious grin on my face, "now who's jealous?"

He's silent for a minute before his hands fly up. "All right. Fuck it. Maybe I am."

I nibble at the corner of my lip, my stomach swirling with heat. A big part of me is relieved that Ryker's possessiveness has everything to do with his feelings toward me and not his protectiveness over me. I suppose it's also time to give him reassurance that Asher means absolutely nothing to me. Not anymore. "He's just a friend, Ry. In fact, I don't even think I'd go that far. He's a guy who's taken this sudden interest in me for reasons unknown."

"He wants to fuck you," he deadpans with a small shrug to his shoulders.

I wince. "He does not."

"I know men, Kit. The guy wants to fuck you, and it makes me wanna fucking kill him."

"Well, I can promise you that will never happen. I can barely stand the guy."

"That's encouraging." Ryker takes my hand in his, trailing his finger over my palm. "It's good to know you're not in love with the guy anymore."

Wait. What? I blow out an airy chuckle. "What makes you think I was ever in love with Asher?"

"I just…assumed. Aren't all the girls in your school?"

"You should know better than anyone that I'm not like all the girls in my school. So why would you say that?"

His eyes shoot over to my vanity, and I follow his gaze. He blinks a few times before looking at me like a guilty dog with his tail between his legs.

"You didn't!" I spit out, jerking my hand away. My cheeks flush with heat-infused rage as I walk over to my vanity and pick up my journal I've had since I was like thirteen years old. It's packed full of all the secrets, memories, and crushes I've ever had. I grab it, holding it up. "Did you read my journal?"

His lack of response is all the answer I need.

"Unbelievable, Ryker." I begin pacing my room, trying to remember everything I ever wrote in that thing. There was nothing too incriminating, but that doesn't even matter. He had no right.

"Kit. Stop it." He walks toward me, testing the waters.

"Don't." I point a finger, stepping back and bumping into my vanity. "How could you invade my privacy like that? Even after I didn't press you about your own personal stuff when you came back, you still came in here and read my innermost thoughts on paper."

"No. I didn't."

"Liar!"

"I swear, Kit. I didn't read your journal. I haven't even touched it since I've been back in town."

"Since you've been back in town? What's that mean? You read it before you left?"

"No." His chin drops to his chest, and he runs his fingers through his messy hair. "Fuck."

"Quit lying and just admit it."

He doesn't even look at me when he speaks. Just stares at his feet like a coward. "I never read it. A couple years ago, I was in here, and I wanted to. Fuck, I really wanted to, but I couldn't bring myself to do it."

"So how do you know if you didn't read it?"

Finally looking at me, he drops his arms to his sides. "I opened it. But all I saw was the first page, the one where you wrote that you love Asher, then I shut it again."

"First page? Where I wrote, *I love Asher*?" I know it's written on the entries inside, but… I grab my journal, covered in sticky notes, and it hits me when I flip the cover open. Tiny fragments of paper stick out of the spine where the page was. I tore it out that same night I went to thank Asher at his house. "That had to have been before you left Oakley Shores."

"Yeah. It was one of the days I used your shower after practice. Margo had just got her license and you were going out with her."

He's right. I remember like it was yesterday. I came home and he was in my bathroom. He must have opened it before I got here.

Ryker is a lot of things, but dishonest has never been one of them. At least, not yet. In this case, he does deserve the benefit of the doubt.

"Okay." My lips press together. "I believe you."

He raises an eyebrow. "You do?"

"I'm still pissed that you even opened it. But I believe you didn't read it any further." I hold up the open journal, showing him page two that's still intact. "If you'd flipped any further then you would have seen this."

His eyes lift from the page to me. The corner of his lip tugs up in a smile and I can't help but do the same. I have so many reasons to be angry with this guy, but what is love without a little madness?

"You love me more?" He laughs, eyes glistening with mischief as he steps closer.

"In my defense, I wrote that when I was fourteen years old."

"But it's still there. In big, bold letters, *I love Ryker more*." He grabs me by the waist, fingers tickling my sides.

I squirm under his touch, feeling the heat in my cheeks, and the way he's grinning at me only makes it worse. "I was a kid," I spit out defensively.

Ryker tries to grab the journal from my hand, but I grip it tighter. "I don't wanna read it," he says with a shift in his tone.

I loosen my hold on it and he takes it from my hand. Reaching behind me, he sets it on the vanity, his eyes never leaving mine.

In a fluid motion, he jerks my body to his. Peering down on me, he whispers, "I thought about you every day, Kit."

My heart jumps in my chest. A feeling I'm getting used to. I'm still trying to figure out what each skip, jump, and zap means, and right now, I can't tell if it's him or the device living inside me. I'd say a little of both.

"I thought about you, too." So much more than I'm willing to admit. It's easy to be both vulnerable and scared at the same time.

There's a long beat of silence between us that speaks volumes. His eyes drop to my mouth and I slide my tongue across my lower lip. *Kiss me, Ryker.*

His breaths become audible, and I can feel his heart beating against my chest.

I need him to kiss me.

A loud boom of thunder startles me, and I find myself completely enveloped in his arms.

Ryker chuckles. "Big storm is coming."

I nod, my chin brushing against his collarbone.

"I wanna take you somewhere."

I look up, questioning him with furrowed brows.

"Do you trust me?"

"I do."

I really do.

CHAPTER
TWENTY-TWO
RYKER

"It's practically a monsoon out there." Kit shivers on the porch when a gust of wind rips through. "You've lost your damn mind."

I wrap my leather jacket around her shoulders as we stand on the front porch, shielded from the rain by the veranda. "It sure feels that way when I'm with you."

An elbow in the gut, followed by laughter, tells me it's time to make a run for it. "Ready or not," I tell her, before grabbing her by the waist and flinging her over my shoulder.

"Ahhh," she squeals as I run through the downpour to my truck, her body flapping over my shoulder while I hold on tight. "You're insane!"

"I told you, you make me crazy," I shout back as rain hammers the tin bed of my truck.

Pulling open the driver's side door, I set her down on the seat, and she slides across to the passenger side.

I jump in and slam the door shut. "Wow! It's really coming down." I shake my head, dewdrops spraying from my soaked hair.

Kit tightens the ponytail on her head and wipes the sleeve of her hoodie across her eyes. "Tell me again why we're out here."

I turn the key, starting the ignition. It sputters a few times before the engine purrs to life. "You'll see," I tell her, knowing she'll poke me with a dozen questions before we get where we're going.

I glance over and see her pulling the drenched leather jacket from around her shoulders and folding it in her lap. "Hold on to that. You'll need it in a few minutes."

"Still not telling me where we're going?"

The windshield begins fogging over, so I crank up the defroster. "Nope. But I will say, the rain is only half the fun."

She chuckles. "Your idea of fun is much different from mine."

I look over at her, holding her stare for a moment as I drive slowly down the desolate road. "That's the whole point."

"I'm not following."

"Your idea of enjoying the little things in life is much different from mine. Now you get a chance to see what I had in mind when I said those words."

"Okay." She bobs her head, putting her feet on the seat and tucking her knees to her chest. "Show me what you got, Ryker Dawson."

I crack a smile as I flip my blinker to turn down Coswell Boulevard. It quickly fades when I see the motel. I grip the steering wheel, and I hold my breath as I cruise past it, not giving the place a second look.

Once it's in the rearview mirror, I drop one hand to my leg and rub my sweaty palm across my jeans.

"You okay?" Kit asks.

"Great. You?"

"What just happened back there? You got all weird."

"Nothing," I say, turning into the garage while hoping she doesn't drag this out. She's very perceptive.

It takes a second, but she eventually stops looking at me when she notices we've stopped. I'm relieved when she doesn't press about my strange behavior. Looking around the lot, she snickers. "Seriously? This is your idea of fun?"

"Just follow me and maybe I'll reward you with something you love more than Ryker Dawson." I'm teasing her and she knows it.

"You're gonna regret picking on me for that. I'm gonna make you eat your words. You just wait."

Hoping she's right, I swing open my door, wishing the rain would let up.

Thunder rolls while a strike of lightning dashes across the sky. I'm walking around the truck to help Kit, when her door opens and she puts her feet on the ground with nothing covering her from the rain.

"Well, well, well. Someone realized she isn't gonna melt."

Kit swats me on the shoulder and scowls. "Never said I'd melt. I just don't like getting wet."

There's a lot I could say to that statement, but I'll keep my mouth shut for now. Instead, I take my jacket from her and wrap it around her shoulders again.

With her hand in mine, we walk hurriedly to the garage entrance, while another roar of thunder ripples. A gust of wind rips through, rattling the tin, free estimate sign out front.

"Holy shit," Kit howls as we pick up our pace until we're full-on running.

Rain pelts my face, so I look down. Once we're at the door, I unlock it quickly, and let Kit inside first.

Bent over, she catches her breath, and it takes her a few seconds to straighten back up.

"You all right?" I ask her.

Nodding, she begins shaking like a wet dog, while I close the door behind us. "This way," I tell her, walking past a car on the hoist, toward the back of the garage.

"I don't mean to sound rude or anything, but I could have come up with some much better ideas than this if you were looking for a little fun tonight."

"Oh yeah," I say, "like what?"

"Frozen yogurt at The Soap Box, pizza and a movie."

I open another door that takes us back outside. Holding the handle, I tip my head, telling her to come out.

She looks at me like I've lost my mind. "Back outside?"

My lips press together, and I nod. "You do those things all the time. Quit being such a pain in the ass and get out the door."

"Oh, so now you're kicking me out?"

"Yeah, I am, and I'm coming with you."

With a heavy sigh, she walks out the door, only this time, we're protected by the tin overhang.

"Look at you standing there all wet and not bitching about it." My words warrant a smack to my shoulder and a glowering glare.

"So, where's this reward I'll apparently love?"

I nod toward my jacket around her shoulders. "Inside pocket."

Lips pressed together firmly, Kit watches me as she digs into the pocket. Before her hand even leaves the inside, her eyes widen and a smile stretches across her face. "Ry!" she beams, pulling her hand out with a candy bar in her palm. "Where did this come from?"

"Four years ago, someone gave me shit for not having them, so I've carried one around ever since."

"You've carried this in your pocket for four years?!"

"Well, I've replaced it quite a few times after long days at the shop. But yeah, I'm never without."

Kit peels back the wrapper and takes a bite, still grinning from ear to ear. "You're seriously the sweetest guy in the world, you know that, right?"

"Sweeter than that candy bar?"

"Eh," her head wavers back and forth as she takes another bite, "that's debatable, but it's definitely the nicest thing anyone has ever done for me."

I chuckle. "It's just a candy bar."

Her expression goes pensive, and she stops chewing. "No, Ry. It's so much more than that."

There's a long beat of silence before she looks over my shoulder, and her eye catches on something. "Whose car is that?"

"This old thing?" I walk over, trailing my fingers down the hood. "She's mine now. 1969 Chevelle SS. My granddad bought it when I was twelve years old. We spent so many nights working on this baby together. Once the shop picked up and he got busy, we ran out of time to get her running. He told me one day it would be mine, and now it is."

"Does it even run?"

I shake my head. "Not yet. One day she will. A few minor repairs, a couple major ones, and a fresh coat of paint, and she'll be good to go."

Kit walks over to where I stand beside the hood of the car, pushing her arms through the sleeves of my leather jacket. "So tell me, Ry. When do you plan to do all this? You're leaving Oakley Shores soon, aren't you?"

I look at her. Her hair is darkened from the rain, ends dripping with water. Droplets sprinkled across her long lashes. I sweep a stray strand stuck to her cheek. "Someday."

Her posture dampens and sorrow washes over her face. "Someday you might run out of time again?"

Those words are like a kick in the gut because she's right. "I guess *someday* is a better answer than the truth—which is, *I really don't know.*"

"Oh, Ryker," Kit drawls as she climbs onto the hood of the car. Lying flat on her back, she stares out at the storm. "So many empty promises and failed dares."

"What's that supposed to mean?" I lie down beside her, one leg spread in front of me, the other dangling off the side of the car. Our heads rest against the bottom of the windshield, and I'm really hoping the glass in this thing doesn't crack any more than it already has.

"It means, actions speak louder than words. Seems you haven't been holding up your end of the deal either."

"Sure, I have," I spit out defensively.

She turns her head to look at me while I do the same. "No, Ry. Neither of us have. I don't know about you, but lately, I feel like as long as I'm getting through each day, then it's enough."

"For someone who claims to be living her best life these days, it sure doesn't sound like you're very happy."

The rain picks up, turning to balls of hail that batter the tin roof above us, so Kit raises her voice. "I could say the same about you. If I remember right, you said you wanted to be better. So tell me, do you feel like you're living your best life?"

"Not a chance in hell." I don't even have to think about my response. "I'm right there with you on the *just getting by* bullshit."

"So what are you gonna do about it?"

I shrug my shoulders against the hood of the car. "Not much I can do."

"Oh, come on." Kit jolts up. "After years of talking about how I was too mature for my age and needed to embrace life, you're telling me you're going to just give up fighting for the life you want?"

"I don't know what you want me to say, Kit. I don't have the support system you do. Besides, everything I touch turns to ash."

"No." She purses her lips. "You don't get to do that. Beating yourself down is a thing of the past. What do you want, Ryker?"

I can't even look at her. The shame I feel inside for the years I've wasted on dreams that are not my own, it's downright pitiful. "I'm gonna finalize things here with the shop and return to my life in Colorado."

Darting her gaze to the falling rain, she shakes her head in disappointment, then whispers, "Coward."

"Whoa. Hold up. Did you just call me a coward?"

She nods. "Sure did."

"You don't understand. No one does." I sound fucking pitiful, but it's the truth.

"Then make me understand. Tell me why you left. Explain why you can't come back. You say I have a support system and you don't, yet you have a mom and a brother who love you very much. Have you forgotten about them, Ryker?"

"No. I didn't forget them and I never forgot you. I never could. It's complicated, so just drop it."

"Tell me why. Why didn't you visit even once? How could you stay away for so long?"

"I did come back. I came back for you!" The words pour out of my mouth, and as much as I'd like to take them back, I can't.

Kit looks at me, halting her words for a second, as if she's replaying what I just said in her head to understand it correctly. "You came back?"

I never meant to tell her. Never thought I would. Lifting my other leg onto the hood of the car, I cross my ankles and lean back on my palms. "Carter called and told me when you were admitted to the hospital. I wasn't supposed to be here. I was never supposed to come back, but I had to see you. I needed to know you were okay."

When the only sound is another rumble of thunder, followed by a crack of lightning, I look at her. It's then that she finally says, "You came to see me?"

I nod my head. "I did." I'll never forget seeing her lying in that bed with tubes all over her body.

"Kit-Kat, I'm here. Gonna need you to wake up now."

I take her cold hand in mine, hoping for any sign of life. She's so pale, so fragile, but still so perfect.

"I haven't had enough time with you. Please, come back to us."

Nothing. Her still body just lies there like a shell protecting her soul. Not a blink, not a squeeze. She's in there, though. I can feel it.

"Excuse me, sir," someone says from behind me, but I ignore her.

"Please, Kit. I'm begging you," I choke the words out as a tear threatens to break free.

"Sir. Visiting hours are over and we don't have you logged as a guest."

How did we get here? To this point of separation? I knew the girl lying lifeless in front of me—sometimes I think I knew her better than anyone—now I'm not so sure.

"You need to leave, sir."

"Would you give me a damn minute?" I shout, much louder than I planned. Getting to my feet, I squeeze Kit's hand in mine and lean over her body. My lips press to her forehead and in that instant, hope returns.

"She just squeezed my hand!" I look down at her delicate fingers in my palm. "She squeezed my hand. I think she's waking up." Her eyes begin to open, but I'm ushered away by the nurse.

"You need to leave. Now."

"So, I just left. Never told anyone I was there, not even Carter. An hour later, on my ride back to Colorado, he called and said you woke up and were getting that device implanted and were put on a transplant list."

"Why didn't you tell anyone?" Kit sniffles, wiping the tears from her cheeks.

"You wouldn't understand." I turn my head, looking at the pile of scrap metal stacked to the left.

Chills ride up my arm when Kit takes my hand in hers. "Hey." When I don't respond, she gives me a subtle pull. "Look at me, Ryker." I draw in a deep breath and turn to face her. "You can tell me anything."

"Not this time, Kit-Kat." I jerk my hand away and jump off the hood of the car.

Not this time.

CHAPTER
TWENTY-THREE
KIT

Something big happened. It had to have for him to be this closed off. Ryker has never been one to be secretive. In the past, he's always beat himself up over absolutely nothing, but I can tell this time is different. I don't want to press because, deep down, I'm not sure if I even want to know. We're all entitled to our secrets, and this one seems pretty important to him.

"Well, that conversation went south fast." I sweep the tears from my cheeks. "But I need to thank you."

His eyes snap to mine, eyebrows knitted. "For what?"

"Coming to see me. I know it must have been a tough choice to make if you promised yourself you'd never come back. So thank you. I don't remember it, but now that I know, you're probably the reason I woke up."

"Nah." He sweeps the air with his hand. "You're a tough girl. You were waking up regardless."

I shrug my shoulders. "Maybe. But maybe not."

I might not have any recollection of Ryker being there, but if anyone could have pulled me away from the brink of death, it's him. That first kiss to my cheek at fourteen years old almost killed me. I spent years searching for that same feeling—that high. I dove into everything headfirst, never coming up for air. That kiss on the hospital bed, that one must have brought me back to life.

Without a doubt in my mind, I know Ryker is my sole purpose for existing. I wanted to hate him when he left. Wanted to stay angry when he returned. But truth be told, my heart will remain beating for him and him alone.

Warmth consumes me, and this moment feels too powerful to control. I throw my arms around him, squeezing. "I'm so glad you're back, Ry."

I don't say it as the girl who's in love with him. I say those words as a friend who has missed him like crazy.

"Glad to be back, Kit-Kat. And I'm sorry for all the vagueness and secrecy. I know it makes things a little weird."

"Yeah. That's just because you are weird. A big weirdo."

He flings an arm around my shoulders and pulls my head to his chest, rubbing his knuckles on top of my head. "You love me, though. I saw proof."

"Oh my God. Shut up!" I smack his chest, giggling. "You're never going to let me live that down, are you?"

His eyes peer down at me, soft and inviting. "How about a new dare—or a promise, rather?"

"I'm listening."

"I'll forget what I saw in your journal, if you forgive me for looking in the first place."

I pull my head away from his chest, look into his eyes and say, "Maybe I don't want you to forget."

He quirks a brow, a smile threatening his lips. "Good, because I don't think I ever will."

"You were right. This is fun." I'm half-teasing, half-serious because, the truth is, there's no place I'd rather be.

Ryker looks out at the rain and I follow his line of sight. "There's something about the sound of rain on a tin roof. Knowing we're safe under here but still in the storm's eye. I dunno. Maybe it's just me."

He looks my way, and I shake my head. "No, I get what you're saying. It's the little things, right?"

"Exactly." He snaps his fingers before resting a hand on my leg. "The little things with the right person makes all the difference." His eyes dart down to his hand resting on my leg and his fingers caress my skin. "I mean, there was no loud music or body grinding, but I'm hoping that tonight will be one of those sappy stories you write about in that journal of yours."

Giddiness washes over me, butterflies fluttering through my stomach. The urge to kiss him is strong, and when his eyes dart to my mouth, I wet my lips.

"Do it," I challenge him. His eyes float back to mine, quizzical and lust-filled. "Don't overthink it. Just kiss me, Ry."

He leans in while I do the same, closing the distance between us, but the resistance is strong on his end. His breaths fan my face and the anticipation is almost more than I can handle.

When his lips graze mine, I take the leap and place my hand on the back of his head, pulling him closer.

"I'm going to hell for this," he says, before his mouth crushes mine.

My head tilts to the side, noses brushing, as we give this kiss everything we've got. My body tingles with need. A hunger only he can satisfy—but one I fear he won't.

His tongue slips between my lips, and I assault it with my own. Ryker places his hand on my upper thigh, and I cover it with mine, slowly bringing it up farther and farther. I'm desperate for him, willing to risk rejection for the slightest chance he wants me just as badly as I want him.

I mutter intent-laced words into his mouth, "I dared you to stop overthinking everything."

A low grumble climbs up his throat, and the next thing I know, I'm on my back on the hood of the car, Ryker's body cloaking mine.

My legs spread apart as he slinks between them, resting his

erection hard against my crotch. His hand slithers up, squeezing my leg, and he's close—so close.

Our kiss deepens with intensity, so much so I feel like I could combust at any moment. I'm not sure if it's possible to orgasm without physical touch, but I'm damn close. I can feel my panties soaking under my shorts, my pussy dripping with desire.

In a featherlike motion, I trail my fingers down his bare arm, feeling goosebumps erupt on his skin. I keep going until I'm near his waist, then I lift the corner of his shirt and graze his stomach. Meddling with the waistband of his pants, my fingers dip lower and lower, until my hand is stuffed down his boxers. The tips of my fingers brush over the head of his cock and my entire body throbs.

Ryker shifts himself on top of me, and for a moment, I think he's going to stop. Instead, his mouth moves to my neck. My eyes close, and even with the sounds of the storm around us, all I can hear are his labored breaths. Over the fresh rain and wet grass, all I smell is his skin.

I push my hand down farther, needing to feel more of him. My fingers wrap around the shallow end of his dick and a moan passes through his lips.

"Fuck, Kit," he murmurs, moving the lower half of his body with my motions as I stroke him.

A loud boom of thunder startles me and he must've noticed because he retreats. His body lets up, creating space between us, and I curse internally.

No. Don't stop this.

I lose my hold on him, my hand slipping back out of his pants when he climbs off the side of the car. I'm ready to lash out and tell him to quit playing games with my body, when he extends a hand to me.

I look at it, confused. "What are you doing?"

"Come with me."

I hesitate for a moment, then place my hand in his, and he

helps me off the car. I've got no idea what we're doing, but it's been proven that our ideas of fun are very different.

We walk back into the garage, the sound of the rain still hammering the building. Ryker reaches into the pocket of his jeans and pulls out his keys, then unlocks a door. I've been to this garage a few times in the past, so I know it leads to the upstairs apartment his granddad used to live in.

With my hand still in his, he opens the door and gestures for me to go first. I drop his hand and walk up the stairs, while he follows closely behind.

Once we're in the apartment, I fold my hands together, unsure where to go or what to do. Fortunately, Ryker takes the initiative and leads me into a small bedroom.

It's definitely an old place, and I can tell by the smell that his granddad smoked. Doesn't matter, though, I'd follow Ryker to the pits of hell if it meant one more minute with him.

Ryker kicks the door closed behind him and the next thing I know, I'm being hoisted up in his arms. My legs wrap around his waist and his mouth presses to my collarbone.

"Fuck, Kit. You have no idea how bad I want you."

My head falls back as I take in the feel of his lips all over my body. "I'm yours, Ry. All yours."

I'm carried over to the bed and dropped onto my back. Before he can turn and run away, I remove his jacket and lift my damp shirt over my head and toss them to the floor. My breathing becomes heavy, panting almost.

"Goddamn," he croons, eyeing my cleavage peeping out of my bra. "You're so beautiful."

I part my legs, inviting him in with my hands pressed to the mattress behind me.

On his knees, Ryker climbs until his body is hovering over mine, and I drop to my back.

There's no way in hell I'm letting him get away this time. My body burns with torment. He peers over at me, as if he's assessing the situation. Likely battling inner demons that tell him to walk away. Before he can overthink it, I wrap my hands around his head and pull his mouth to mine. That's all it takes for us to get back to where we were on the hood of the car.

I'm not above begging. Deep down, I always knew he would be my first. Even if he can't be my last, this one time belongs to him. "Fuck me. Please."

A low rumble climbs up his vocal chords, vibrating against my mouth. I spread my legs farther, letting him drop between them. His erection digs into my thigh and everything inside me throbs with an aching need.

Ryker peppers my neck with kisses, working his way down to my chest. He pulls down my bra cup and trails his lips subtly over the skin before sucking and kissing.

My hips rise, grinding myself against him, while his hand smooths down my side.

His head lifts, eyes burning into mine. "Are you sure you want this, Kit?"

I nod, not needing any time to answer. "More than anything."

Ryker tears his shirt off and tosses it to the floor. My hands press to his chest, gliding down his rigid abs and stopping at the button of his jeans. I watch him as I unclasp it and slide down his zipper.

His chest heaves while I internally scream at him, *do not fight it.*

And he doesn't. Ryker lifts, pushes his pants down along with his boxers, all while watching my eyes. His cock springs free and I swallow hard at the sight.

A smile plays at my lips and I raise my brows with a smirk.

He undresses me next. First my shorts and panties, then he reaches behind me and unclasps my bra.

I've never felt more vulnerable in my life, lying here completely naked.

I've also never felt more alive.

CHAPTER
TWENTY-FOUR
RYKER

Her body is a masterpiece. One I want to devour and lock in my memory for the rest of my life. Never forgetting a single blemish or scar.

I can tell she's nervous. Trembling hands and a quivering lip. I drop my body on hers, feeling the smoothness of her skin pressed against mine.

My hand moves downward, skating across her stomach until I'm cupping her bare crotch. A bit of a surprise from the muff I always imagined in my head.

I slide one finger up her slit, feeling proof of her desire for me. I could ask her again if she's sure, but I know the answer. Kit wants this just as bad as I do. I tried fighting it, but it's a battle I always knew I'd lose.

One finger slides inside, and her legs go slack, dropping to the sides. She's so fucking tight, and I can't help but feel selfish for what I'm doing.

I drop my forehead to hers, pressing firmly as I slide my finger in and out. Her hips rise and fall, and when I know that she's not in pain, I add another finger, loosening her up for what's coming next. I don't wanna hurt her. I *never* want to hurt her.

My lips press softly to hers, and I whisper, "You okay?"

Wrapping her arms around my neck, she nods.

I push deeper and move faster. Twisting and turning. "You're so wet, baby." I kiss her hard, a moan tearing through her parted lips.

Pulling my fingers out, I slide down a bit. She whimpers, already missing my fingers inside her.

I'm prepared with my cock lined at her entrance, but I battle the voices in my head, telling me not to do it. My forehead rests against hers, eyes wide open. "Tell me to stop, Kit."

With her forehead pressed to mine, she shakes her head. "Never."

I slide in slow, giving her just the tip, while watching her reaction for any sign of pain.

"I'm okay. I promise," she says, trying to pacify my apprehension. Grabbing my face, she pulls my mouth to hers. "Just fuck me, Ryker."

Her hips rise, willing me to give her more, so I do. I push slowly until I'm fully seated inside her.

My movements halt for a second, letting her get used to the feeling before I thrust in a slow, rhythmic motion.

This moment is everything I dreamt about since returning to Oakley Shores. Being with her, feeling her envelop my cock. So fucking warm, so tight, and all mine. She's always been mine. Even when neither of us would admit it.

My lips trail down her jawline, to her neck, and then back up. Darting my tongue out, I sweep it across her bottom lip before sliding it in her mouth.

I'm moving at a steady pace when her hands clamp down on my shoulders, fingertips pinching the skin. I can feel her legs lock around me, and she whimpers, a sound of pleasure, not pain. I move faster when she rolls her hips, meeting me thrust for thrust.

"I think I'm gonna…"

I break the kiss and lift my body off hers, wanting to watch as I carry her to the height of her orgasm. Warm breath expels from her open mouth. Her eyes flutter, nails piercing the skin of my shoulders.

Biting down on my bottom lip, I pick up my pace. Her body twitches, back arched.

"Kit…" I exhale her name in a raspy breath.

God, it feels so good inside her. I swear, her pussy was molded just for me. No one will ever break that mold. The thought alone makes me possessive. I thrust harder in a punishing manner. My cock fills to the brink of explosion. Body tingling with zaps of electricity.

She shrills in pleasure, breath held while her pussy clenches.

"Fuck," I grunt, chest heaving, heart racing.

Once I'm sure she came, I pull out quickly, shooting all over her stomach. I stroke my cock a few times, milking every last drop.

Lifting my eyes, I look at Kit—more beautiful than ever. I lean over her stomach, taking care not to make more of a mess, and I kiss her lips. "Still okay?"

"Perfect," she hums into my mouth. "Ry?" I look at her with questioning eyes. "I really do love you."

My heart quivers in my chest. I wanna scream from the rooftops that I love her, too. I wanna tell her over and over again until she's tired of hearing it and then I still wanna say it more. Because I do. I do love Kit. Not just as a friend, the way I did when we were kids. I'm in love with this girl. So why won't the words come out? Why am I still overthinking every move I make with her?

I dare you to stop overthinking everything with us.

A dare is a dare, and I never lose.

I kiss her again, choking on my words as they come out, "I…I love you, too, Kit-Kat."

CHAPTER
TWENTY-FIVE
RYKER

"Good morning," I say to Kit as she joins me in the kitchen, wearing clothing that I deem acceptable: a pair of black leggings, white high-top Chucks, and a cutoff Cougars tee shirt that *almost* reaches the hem of her pants. I set a plate of pancakes on the center island. I know she won't eat them, but I have to at least try.

"Breakfast? For me?" She claps her hands to her chest with a cheesy grin. "You're really taking this babysitter gig seriously, aren't you?"

With raised brow, I round the counter to where she stands. "Actually, I've failed miserably. In fact," I wrap my arms around her waist from behind, chin resting on her shoulder, "I think I might be getting fired."

She's quiet for a minute. I spin her around to face me, so I can get a better read on her vibe this morning. "What's wrong?" I ask when I notice her pursed lips and droopy eyes.

"You don't have to do this, you know that, right?"

"Breakfast is the most important meal of the day. Eat."

"I'm not talking about breakfast." She looks down at the small space between us. "I'm talking about this. I'm not one of those girls who is going to insist we plan a future together after a night of sex."

"A night of sex?" I wince. "Is that what that was?"

"Was it more?" she asks, bluntly.

"I mean, I did tell you I love you. Sure as hell felt like more to me."

"You've told me you loved me before." She grins, mocking my voice. *"Love ya, girl. You know I love you, Kit-Kat."*

Her impersonation of me is laughable. "That was different. *We're* different."

"Oh yeah? In what way?"

It's obvious she's grasping for answers, and I wish I had some to give. "I dunno. All those years ago, you were Carter's little sister and now…you're you."

"And I'm still Carter's little sister."

"Baby," I say, looking into her eyes, "I'm aware there are gonna be repercussions. I don't know what happens next, but last night wasn't just about sex. I wouldn't have let things go as far as they did if I didn't want more with you."

Her lips curl up in a smile and I'm put at ease. I was really hoping this wasn't heading toward another argument.

"That's all I wanted to hear."

I press my lips to hers, feeling every emotion all over again.

"So," I begin, ready to hash out the plans for the day, "you've got a doctor's appointment after school, then I was thinking maybe you could come with me to my mom's for dinner."

"Whoa. Dinner with the family already? Don't you think we should talk to Carter about all this first?"

"As friends. We'll work out the kinks later. Right now, let's just focus on us and no one else."

"I like that idea."

"Good," I squeeze her hips, and she squirms, "now you just need to dump your homecoming date."

Her movements stop and her shoulders drop. "Ry, you know I can't do that. I already told the guy yes."

"Yeah, but that was before…"

"Look at me," she says, pinching my cheeks like I'm a toddler. "Asher means nothing to me. Not anymore."

I blow out a heavy sigh. "Fine. We'll talk about that later. Right now, you need to eat so we can get you to school." I kiss her forehead lightly before pushing the plate of pancakes in her direction.

CHAPTER
TWENTY-SIX
RYKER

I'm parked in front of the school when I spot Kit about twenty feet away. She's chatting with her friend, Margo, and a couple of other girls. Someone says something that has Kit doubled over laughing. The clock on the dash says 3:18, and it's a twenty-minute drive to her doctor's office.

Impatiently, I drum my fingers on the steering wheel to the beat of "Head Up" by The Score. My attention is averted when I spot that fucker Asher and his friends. He whispers something in one of their ears, pats the guy's chest, then makes his way toward Kit. Shifting in my seat, my back steels as I watch intently.

Margo tips her head, looking over Kit's shoulder as Asher appears in their little circle.

"Keep walking, fucker," I mutter under my breath.

Only, he doesn't. He saunters to Kit's side, placing a hand around her waist, and my knuckles clench the steering wheel.

Kit grips the strap of her backpack with one hand then rubs her earlobe. I know that gesture. He's making her uncomfortable.

Who the hell does this guy think he is?

Fuck this bullshit. He needs to learn to keep his hands to himself.

I swing open my door—truck still running, music still blasting—and slam the door shut behind me. It closes with a thud that grabs the attention of a couple of students nearby, but not loud enough for Asher to notice.

With heavy steps against the concrete path, I walk straight toward them.

Kit lifts her head and notices me first. A look of indignation on her face.

"Kit," I call out, still ten feet away, "let's go."

She says something to Asher and tries to move past him, but he steps in front of her, blocking her path.

I pick up my pace, flexing my fingers as I walk. My feet don't stop until I'm grabbing Asher's backpack and spinning him around like he's a limp doll.

"What the fuck?" he seethes. "You got a fucking problem, loser?"

"Yeah, I do." I shove my hands to his chest, causing him to stumble back a few steps.

His mouth clamps shut, nostrils flared. "You're gonna regret that."

Kit latches onto my bicep and attempts to defuse the situation. "Ryker, stop it. Let's just go."

With taut shoulders, I step toward him while Kit still tugs at my arm. "Oh yeah. Make me regret it, *kid*."

"What the hell is your problem, man?"

"You. You're my problem. Stay the hell away from her."

He laughs sarcastically, only fueling the fire inside me as I bump my chest to his. "Kit's a big girl now. I think she can make that decision for herself."

A few more guys join in, standing by Asher's side, ready to take action if necessary.

"Please, Ryker. Let's just go." Kit tugs at my arm again.

I take in a few unfulfilled breaths, exhaling as soon as the air hits my lungs. "Stay the fuck away from her or you'll be the one regretting it." I hiss the threat with a sharp finger to his chest.

Kit keeps pulling, and this time, I allow her to take the lead.

"Stupid fucking kids," I grumble as we walk toward my truck.

Once we're away from the crowd, Kit smacks my arm. "Those *kids* are the same age as me. What the hell is the matter with you?"

"He had his hands all over you. Why the fuck didn't you walk away from him?"

She jerks open the door and tosses her bag in. "Because I'm not a total bitch."

Once she's in the seat, I close the door for her and as I'm rounding the truck, I hear Asher holler, "She's still in high school, asshole." Then he says, "Someone likes 'em young."

"Just get in the damn truck," Kit snaps with her head out the passenger window.

I get in and slam the door shut before I do something stupid like break that fucker's nose and end up in county jail. I'm looking straight ahead, back to white-knuckling the steering wheel. "There's no way in hell you're going to the dance with that moron."

Kit turns the volume down on the stereo and shifts in her seat, tucking one leg under the other. "Since when do you get to tell me what to do?"

"He's a grade-A douchebag. Why do you even wanna go with him?"

"Well, Ry. It's not like I have a ton of options unless I wanna skip the dance altogether, because there's no way in hell I'm going solo. I'm doing this for Kaylee. We made a promise to each other."

"A promise?" I huff, still fuming. "What kind of promise?"

"That we'd only go if we both had dates. If I don't go, she won't either."

"So let her out of the deal. Problem solved."

I shift the truck into drive and pull out of the parking space and into a parade of cars trying to exit.

"I know what I'm doing, so just don't worry about it. As for you, you can't just attack people like that."

"I don't like him touching you. Hell, I don't even like him looking at you."

"I can handle Asher Collins."

"Yeah, I can tell," I mumble.

I look over at her, and she rolls her eyes at the passenger window while rolling it up.

It's a quiet drive to her doctor's office, and when we approach, I finally say, "I'm sorry," before pulling into a parking space and killing the engine.

She looks at me with a fractured smile, pauses for a minute, then gives in to my pout. "I forgive you, but you really need to learn to control that temper of yours."

My hand rests on her leg, giving it a gentle squeeze. "I'll try to get it under control. Just seeing other guys gawk at you makes me crazy. Always has."

"I can relate. I feel the same way when I see you with Ava."

"Ava?" I laugh because it's comical. "Much like you can't stand Asher, I can't stand Ava. She's the same stuck-up girl she's always been. Not to mention, she's dating some college football player who's headed to the big leagues."

"Wait, what?" she sputters. "I seriously thought you were into her. You've been hanging out with her and you went upstairs with her to her room at the party…"

My expression twists. "I never went to Ava's room. A group of us went upstairs on the balcony to smoke a bowl."

"Wow," she palms her forehead, "I feel like a dumbass. It's just that Ava is so beautiful, and I assumed you wanted her back."

"Her beauty is only skin-deep. You, on the other hand," I sweep a strand of hair behind her ear, "are fucking stunning, inside and out."

Her cheeks blush like they always do when she's given a compliment. "Stop."

"Never." I click the latch of her seatbelt. "Come on, red face, let's get that ticker checked out."

"Actually," she slaps a hand over mine before I can unbuckle myself, "it'll be boring. Just some routine tests and me begging for my license back. Honestly, I'd rather do it alone. The last thing you wanna hear about is how broken my body is."

My neck cranes, nose scrunched. She's crazy for talking like that. "You are not broken, Kit-Kat. You're just bruised. We all are."

"If only that were true," she whispers before shifting her tone. "Go across the street, get a coffee, and I'll try and rush things as much as I can in there."

"All right," I say, knowing that she wants privacy for this appointment. "Text me if you need me."

Her fingers teeter with the handle before she turns and says, "Thank you."

My forehead creases with confusion. "For what?"

"Everything." She opens the door and steps out, closing it behind her.

I watch as she makes her way up to the building, hoping and praying she gets nothing but good news today.

After grabbing a coffee and smoking a cigarette, I take a call from Carter, who was checking in on things. Apparently, he was able to get out of a couple meetings and is coming home Friday night, while his dad will be sticking around for one more day.

Kit emerges from behind the office's double doors and her expression slays me.

Oh shit.

She looks pissed. She looks really fucking pissed.

Stomping her way to the truck, she tears open the door and gets in, shutting it with a bang.

I start up the engine, giving her a second to cool off before I ask questions. Better yet, I should probably wait and let her start the conversation. I'm sure she's got a lot to say.

We're out of the parking lot and on the highway when I cave. "You okay?"

She shakes her head no, repeatedly, breathing heavily out her nose. "No. I am not okay."

"You wanna talk about it?"

The next thing I know, she's bawling. I rub her head, then slide down to her neck and massage the tense muscle there. "Kit-Kat, what happened?" When she doesn't respond, I pull over to the side of the road. "Hey. Talk to me."

With her face in her palms, she just shakes her head no. "Just drive. Please."

I get us back to the house, mentally prepared for her to be down all night. My guess is, he denied her, her license. I'm sure she's not in the mood to go to dinner now and I hate to leave her like this, but I've gotta do this for Ezra and my mom.

We're sitting in the truck, engulfed in silence. Kit's been staring blankly at the windshield for the last five minutes. Instead of getting out, I stay here in case she needs me.

"You're wrong," she finally says, taking me by surprise.

"Huh?"

She turns her head, her sad eyes on mine. "You're wrong. I'm not just bruised. I am broken, and if you ask Dr. Hans, he'll tell you the same thing."

"Baby—"

"Don't." She holds up a hand. "Please don't pity me. I know you mean well, but I'm fine. I was fine yesterday. I'm fine today. And I'll be fine tomorrow." Her shoulders rise, then fall. "It is what it is. I won't let any of this stop me. What's the point of living if you can't do it to the fullest, right?"

"Right..." I don't even know what to say, because I have no idea what went down in that office. I can only assume this is regarding her license.

Kit brushes away her tears aggressively, plasters on a fake smile, and says, "We should go in and get ready for dinner at your mom's."

"You don't have to go if you're not feeling up to it."

"No. I want to. Like I said, I'm not letting anything stop me. I've got bad news before and I've been just fine."

I nod in response, unsure of what else to do.

CHAPTER
TWENTY-SEVEN
KIT

WE'RE LEAVING IN THIRTY MINUTES, AND I CAN BARELY MUSTER THE courage to get out of this bed. Ryker has been giving me space in the short time we've been home, and I'm grateful for that. One of the many things I love about him is that he doesn't push when I don't feel like talking. It's the same reason I've allowed him the secrecy of his own inner demons. Some things we just don't like to share.

I know I'm damaged goods. I'm not the dented can of soup on the shelf with the label chipping away. No. I'm the shiny apple, all waxed up to perfection and ready to sell. The one you bite into and realize it's rotten. I don't wear my scars; I hide them.

Kaylee's name flashes on the screen of my phone as it vibrates. As much as I want to just pretend I didn't see it, and wallow in self-pity, I miss her a lot and need to hear her voice.

"Hey, girl," I say with forced enthusiasm.

"Guess whaaaat, bitch? I'm coming home tomorrow night!"

"Wow, that was fast."

"Don't sound so excited."

"Of course I'm excited. I've missed you."

"Miss you, too. So the trip wasn't a total drag. No hot cousins, but there was this girl who's the same age as me and we managed to sneak off and go to a college party. I got smashed but had a blast."

"That's really great, Kay. I'm glad you had fun." As much as I want to hear all about her trip and the fun she had, I'm just not in the mood for her over-the-top positivity. I'd rather sulk for the next thirty minutes, then put this appointment behind me and pretend like it never existed—much like I've done with all my other ones.

"What's wrong, babe? You sound down. It's him, isn't it?"

Picking at my nails, I prop the phone between my chin and my shoulder. "Just a long day. I'll fill you in on everything when you get home."

"Hell yes, you will, because I'm coming to stay with you tomorrow night. We're gonna need a solid eight hours of catch-up time."

"Sounds like a plan."

"And you sound like you need a full day's sleep, sourpuss. I'll let you get back to what you were doing…or who you were doing. Love ya, girl."

I spit out a laugh. "Love you, too."

I end the call and pull myself together. Tonight isn't about me; it's about Ryker. It's been years since he spent time with his family, and I'm not about to drag him down into my pit of despair.

Rolling off the bed, I drag my feet to my closet and yank down a cream-colored knit sweater. I pair it with some blue jeans and slip-on sandals, and call it good.

Before I leave my room, I glance at myself in the mirror and force a smile on my face.

See, it's easy. No one will even know I'm heartbroken with a smile like this.

When I walk into the living room, Ryker jumps up from his spot on the couch and tucks his phone in the front pocket of his distressed black jeans. He's looking pretty sharp in a short-sleeved white polo. The tips of his hair are glistening from the shower he just took, and I can smell the intoxicating scent of his cologne from across the room—pine tar and sandalwood.

"Look okay?" I slap my hands to my sides, awaiting his reaction.

Ryker eats the space between us and presses his lips to mine. *God, he smells good.* "You look beautiful."

My stomach does a little flip and I feel dizzy under his spell. "You look pretty good yourself." I'm not used to seeing him spiffed up. His typical fashion is garbage band tee shirts and holey jeans—which are still intact—and his leather jacket. It's obvious tonight is important to him, and I'm not about to be the reason it goes to shit.

"Ready?" He takes my hand, leading me toward the door, and I nod in response.

It's a short drive to Ryker's old place on the other side of town. We pull up to the trailer and it's just as I remember it. I didn't come here often, but I visited once with Carter. After that night, I swore I'd never come back because his dad was all doped up and erratic.

Ryker's mom is the complete opposite of his dad and one of the sweetest ladies I've ever met. She works at The Soap Box and puts in endless hours for her and her boys—well, boy. I suppose Ryker doesn't count since he's been away for two years and is an adult now.

As sad as it was when Mr. Dawson passed away, I can't help but feel like it was a relief for this family. I don't know the horrid details, because a good part of it was left out of the news. I never asked questions, but I do know he was shot—my guess is in a drug deal gone bad—and put on life support, which was shut off a couple months later.

Carter didn't attend the funeral, so naturally, I didn't either.

I look over at the driver's seat and notice Ryker's unease. "What's wrong?" I ask him.

He looks at me, lifts the corner of his lip in a smile, and turns the key in the ignition. "Nothing. Let's go eat."

We're walking up to the trailer, side by side, and I'm trying to remember that we're here as friends. I'm not his girlfriend, having dinner with his family. I'm the high school girl he's staying with to help out a friend.

Ryker opens the rickety tin door and I'm taken by surprise when he knocks. After all, this was his home.

The door swings open, and we're greeted by his mom. "What in the world are you knocking for? This is your home, too." It's like she read my mind.

Mrs. Dawson pulls Ryker in for a hug and it looks warm and inviting. Makes me wonder what a hug from my own mom would feel like.

I brush that thought away quickly. It's best for me not to wonder what could have been.

The next thing I know, I'm wrapped up in her arms and experiencing that feeling for myself. It *is* warm and it *does* feel safe. As I suspected a mother's hug would feel.

"You have grown up so fast, Kit, and just as beautiful as ever."

"Thank you, Mrs. Dawson."

"Goodness, call me Ann, please."

She steps back, observing her son with a sparkle in her eye that makes it obvious how much she loves and misses him.

With a smile plastered on my face, I follow behind Ryker, who's talking with his mom about the shop.

Ryker stops, hesitating in front of the small kitchen. I look down and notice his hands shaking. He rubs them together, trying to stop the unwanted movements. I almost reach for him but stop myself when I remember how odd that would be.

Ann must've noticed his unease because she's staring at him with a look of distress.

"Is everything okay?" I ask, wondering what I'm missing here.

Ann snaps out of it and smiles widely. "Everything is perfect.

I'm so happy to have my boys together again. Ezra," she calls out, "Ryker and Kit are here."

Turning quickly, Ann goes into the kitchen and slides on an oven mitt.

"Is there anything I can help with?" I ask her as she opens the oven door.

"Thank you, sweetie, but I've got this. You two have a seat."

Ryker is still standing in the same spot, void of expression. "Do you wanna sit down?"

He pulls out a chair, gesturing for me to sit, then takes the one beside me.

I lean into his space, shoulders brushing, and whisper, "What's wrong?"

Before he can answer, Ezra emerges. "What's up, brother?" Ezra asks, patting Ryker's shoulder as he walks behind him.

The air shifts when Ryker smiles, rubs his stomach, and says, "Just ready for some of Ma's homemade cooking. It's been too long."

"Much too long," Ann says, setting a dish of lasagna over a couple of pot holders on the table.

We eat dinner and I can't shake the feeling that something is going on with this family. It could be the loss of Mr. Dawson; after all, the last time Ryker was home, his father was still alive. It makes sense it would be uncomfortable for him.

Once our plates are empty, I help Ann clear the table. The boys are on the couch in the living room, talking football, so I use this opportunity to thank Ann.

"Everything was delicious. Thank you so much for having me."

She squeezes an arm around my shoulders and says, "I'm glad you could be here," then resumes stacking the dishes in the sink. "I hope my son has been cordial while he's been house-sitting for your family."

"Oh, yes." I chuckle. "He's been great."

"I bet your brother is happy to have him back in town, even if

Carter is away for a short time. Those two were always attached at the hip." She drops a rag in the sink and looks past me. "So many memories with those boys. Not always good ones." She laughs.

"Yeah. They were a handful when they were younger."

"Still are. I just wish Ryker lived closer, so he could plant some roots here and rebuild some of the relationships he lost when he left."

With a bottle of dish soap in my hand, ready to squirt it on a rag, I stop for a moment. "Mrs. Dawson, err…Ann, can I ask you something?"

"Of course, sweetie."

It may be an invasion of the privacy I've given Ryker, but my curiosity gets the best of me. "Why did Ryker leave Oakley Shores?"

Ann freezes, eyes locked on a dirtied dish that once held our dinner. There's a long breath of silence between us before she responds. "At that time, it was the best thing he could do. Ryker needed to go somewhere he could thrive, and he couldn't do that here."

I know he left right after the incident with the tire slashing, but I don't know what happened after that or why he left so quickly. I also don't want to pry too much. There's just so many empty pages in his story. "Do you think he could thrive here now?" I don't say, n*ow that his dad is not in the picture*, but it's exactly what I'm thinking. The entire town knows how cruel that man was.

With a lift of her head, she looks out into the living room, where Ryker and Ezra are now wrestling on the floor. "I really do. I think he's come a long way."

Her words make me smile because I couldn't agree more.

I pick up the glass pan, ready to set it in the sink, but the dish slips out of my slippery fingers. I try to catch it in time, but it falls right to the floor with a loud thud. "Oh no. I'm so sorry."

I reach down to pick up the pan, but Ann grabs it instead. Fortunately, it didn't break.

When I straighten up, I notice Ryker on his feet and panic-stricken.

"No. No. No," he repeats over and over again, clenching the sides of his head and pacing the living room floor.

"Ryker, are you okay?" I ask. His eyes shoot to mine, and I can see the heaving of his chest from here. "Are you okay?" I ask again. It's like he's staring straight through me and on the verge of a mental breakdown.

The next thing I know, he's out the front door.

I look at Ann, then Ezra, who are both wearing expressions of horror.

"I…I should go check on him. Thank you for dinner, Ann," I say as I make my way to the door. "It was wonderful."

I find Ryker with his back pressed to the driver's door of his truck, a cigarette pinched between his lips.

"Hey," I say, walking steadfast toward him with soap suds still on my hands.

He doesn't say anything, just draws in a drag of his cigarette and exhales a cloud of smoke.

"Ry." I place a calming hand on his arm.

He twitches, then drops his cigarette to the ground, stubbing it with the toe of his boot. "Let's go."

When I think he means back inside, he proves me wrong by opening the door of his truck. I don't argue. I just get in and keep my mouth shut until he's ready to talk.

CHAPTER
TWENTY-EIGHT
RYKER

Knew it was a bad idea, but I went anyway. I thought with Kit there I might forget what took place the last time I was in that trailer.

I should have never gone back there. Should have never come back to Oakley Shores.

Glancing over at Kit, I catch her sitting there with her hands folded in her lap. She has no idea who the monster is sitting next to her. I try to forget. I try so fucking hard to pretend that everything is okay.

It was all going so well, only feeling the slightest bit of apprehension when a flashback invaded my mind, but I got past it. I convinced myself it was safe to come back to this town—to my old home—that I could move back to Oakley Shores and do this living thing like a normal person. Talking with Ezra, eating Ma's home-cooked food—it was like we were a family again.

Only…one of the members of our family was missing, and it's all my fault.

It was the night I strutted up to that wretched motel with a knife in my pocket. It wasn't premeditated, but in my head, I justified what I was doing. Thought I was giving Mom a night free of verbal and physical abuse by keeping that bastard away. It was only supposed to be one night. Who knew one night would turn into forever?

Dad comes storming in the door, staggering with dilated pupils. Mom immediately steps in front of me, but I can tell she's scared.

With a stern finger pointed at me, he pushes her to the side. "You done fucked up, boy."

"Leave him alone, Donny. He made a mistake and he'll pay for them."

Dad's attention shifts from me to Mom. "Shut your damn mouth, you stupid bitch. He slit my fucking tires. And you're damn right he'll pay for them."

I step forward, owning up to what I did. "I'll work extra hours. I will pay for them. But don't you ever talk to my mom like that again."

Dad sways to the left, bumping into the end table and knocking over a lamp. "Now look what you fucking did. You fuck everything up. Nothing but a worthless piece of shit."

"Stop it!" Mom shouts, purposely stealing his attention.

"I've got this, Mom. Just stay out of it." The last thing I want is for her to get on his bad side because of my mistake.

"You've got this?" Dad laughs. "You ain't got a damn thing. Never have and never will."

"Ryker, go to your room and let me and your dad talk about this."

"I thought I told you to shut the fuck up." Dad raises an open palm and slaps Mom right across the face.

Before she can even grasp what just happened, I charge at him. Low at the waist. My arms wrap around him and I take him straight down into the coffee table. It splits in two, slivers of wood cutting into my arm, but I pay them little attention.

"Ryker, no! Stop this, you two," Mom cries out, attempting to pull me off him.

Cocking my fist, I crash my knuckles into his face repeatedly. Dad tries to fight back, but he's too fucked up to overpower me.

"Stop! Please." Mom howls and curses, trying to stop this, but there's no stopping it.

My thoughts elude me.

He's hit her for the last time.

As I make contact with his face for the last time, two hands wrap around my shoulders, pulling me off of him and throwing me onto my back on the floor.

"What in the world are you doing, Ryker?" Ezra asks, snapping me out of my trance. My adrenaline rush fades and the realization of what I've done hits me full force.

"He hit her," I choke out. "Slapped her right across the face."

Tears stream down Mom's panic-stricken face. "What have you done? I told you to go to your room, Ryker. Both of you, go."

I look over at Dad, who's now sitting on his ass in the center of the broken table, arms perched on either side of him. His jaw tics, teeth grinding. "Do what your mom said, boy. Or I'll put you in there myself."

"Come on," Ezra says, helping me up from behind, "let's just go."

I glare at Dad, and say with unspoken words, if you touch her again, you're a dead man.

Against my better judgment, I do as Mom asked.

Ezra ends up coming into my room because he's scared, and I don't argue it. I'm pretty scared myself.

"One of these days, he's gonna get what's coming to him," I say to Ezra.

One of these days.

A screeching howl has me off my bed and out my door in two seconds flat.

It's Mom.

"What the hell did you do?"

She's on the floor, blood running down her nose. Pushing her hands to the floor, she tries to get up but only cries out louder from the pain.

"Ma," I hurry to her side, "are you okay?"

A glance over her shoulder, and I see Dad, in the kitchen, tipping back a bottle of whiskey without a care in the world.

"Stay here," I tell her, still eyeing the monster in our kitchen.

"Go back to your room," Mom whispers.

No. Not this time.

I get up and walk steadfast down the short hall, passing right by my room. Once I'm in my parents' room, I go straight to the bed and lift the corner of the mattress. There it is: a black Glock 19. Shiny and new.

Without a second thought, I swipe it up, taking no care to hide it as I walk out of the room.

Ezra's standing in the hall sobbing, so I stick the gun behind my back. "Go in your room." *I give him a push until he's inside, then I slam the door shut.*

When I reenter the living room, Mom's still on the floor while Dad stands over her, forcing whiskey down her throat and practically choking her. When she doesn't oblige, he smacks her hard against the face.

"Hey, fucker," *I deadpan.*

Dad spins around, still barely holding his body upright.

"I thought your mom told you to get your ass to bed."

I flip the safety off on the gun and his eyes dart to the weapon in my hand.

Dad laughs, loud and menacing. "You've got no fucking balls. Go to bed, shithead."

"No. It's time for you to go to bed."

"Ryker." *Mom shakes her head, begging and pleading through tears as she tries to crawl across the floor to me. Dad notices what she's doing and gives her a kick to the stomach.*

"Got balls now?" *he asks.*

I raise my trembling hands, overlapped fingers clenched around the grip of the gun.

"It appears not." *He kicks her again, and she screeches a sound that I won't soon forget.*

My finger hovers over the trigger. I swallow hard as Dad starts taking steps toward me. If I don't do it to him, one day, he'll do it to her.

Pop.

"Ryker, please talk to me," Kit says.

I glance at her. She's shaking frantically, tears riding down her cheeks.

Why are we here? Why the hell are we parked under the motel sign?

"What happened?" My voice cracks. "How did we get here?"

"You turned into the parking lot, stopped the truck, and zoned out five minutes ago. Please tell me what the hell is going on."

I don't remember that. The last thing I remember is turning onto the highway.

"You're scaring me, Ry."

I drink her in. Beautiful and innocent Kit. A girl with the weight of the world on her own shoulders, who's always trying to lighten the load for everyone else. But who lightens her load? Who takes care of her?

She doesn't deserve this. I don't deserve her.

"I…umm. I don't know what happened. That trailer…my mom, Ezra." I shake my head, trying to collect my thoughts. "We shouldn't have gone there."

"Why? Why, Ryker?"

My eyes lift to hers, tears pricking the corners of my eyes and my throat burning. "She deserved a better life."

"Who, dammit?"

"My mom. You."

"You're not making any sense. Tell me what you're talking about right now or I'm calling your mom." She holds her phone out in front of her, fingers hovering over the screen.

"Now, Ryker!"

There's a beat of silence, though it's so loud, I can barely think.

Kit keeps talking as I scramble words in my head to try and form a sentence, but all that comes out is the truth. "I killed him. I killed my dad."

Her phone falls to her lap, and she sinks into the seat, likely trying to get away from me. I'm surprised she hasn't opened the truck door and taken off running. She should. I'm no good for her.

"I thought…I thought a drug dealer killed your dad."

Now that the truth is out, there's no going back. It's time to tell her everything. How I called the cops to turn myself in, and when they came, my mom told them she did it—that she shot my dad in self-defense after he pulled a gun on her.

I tried to give them the truth that night. Tried to tell them she was lying and it was me, but she insisted on taking the fall. Sheriff Meyers knew it was a lie, but she gave her statement, and he accepted it under one undisclosed condition—I leave town until the case was closed.

He knew, Mom knew, and even I knew that if I stayed, I would fight to have my truth told. I couldn't let her go down for something I did. But he promised she would be okay, given my dad's reputation and history of domestic violence.

So I left that night while my dad was ushered away in an ambulance and taken into surgery, only to be put on life support until after the case was officially closed. Once it was, my mom took him off and he died seconds later. Everything was kept quiet, thanks to the sheriff.

Mom was arrested after the shooting and released on bail until her hearing. She was found not guilty of murder and they declared it self-defense. Even the sheriff gave a statement at the trial. I have no idea why the guy helped us, but he did, and for that I'm grateful.

I could've come back. Probably should have. But he didn't just die that night, part of me did too. I took a life. Doesn't matter that it was a no-good one. It was still a life. The image of his face as he fell to the ground lives in my head, day in and day out. I sought counseling, considered ending my own life as penance, and eventually, I just had to convince myself that I did what I had to do to protect my family, even if it meant I had to stay away to protect them.

After seeing Ezra and my mom so happy today, I've got no regrets. They're thriving, and one day, I might be able to do the same. Until then, I'll carry my baggage and grief on my own.

CHAPTER
TWENTY-NINE
KIT

I'M STANDING ON MY FRONT PORCH, WAITING FOR KAYLEE TO GET here. She comes home today and we have so much catching up to do. I'm not sure I'm ready to tell her about Ryker and me, mostly because I don't even know what's going on with us, but I do have to tell her about Asher and my agreement to go to the dance with him. Then I have to tell her that I'm backing out.

I just can't go to the dance as his date. It doesn't feel right, and these days, I'm all about doing what makes me happy. Life's too short not to. If only I could convince Ryker of that.

Yesterday, I got the answers I so desperately needed. Now I know that Ryker never left because he wanted to. Everything fell apart the night he slashed those tires and he didn't know how to put his life back together with the constant reminders of this town.

I don't judge him. What he did doesn't hurt me, and it changes nothing between us. Yeah, Ryker killed a man. But *he's* the one who did it in self-defense. He protected himself and he protected his mom and Ezra. It's Ryker that I hurt for. He's carried this trauma all on his own for the past two years.

It all makes sense now. Why he left, why he stayed away, and why he still wants to leave. My burdens are heavy, but I'm not the only person in the world carrying them around.

I'm sick. But I'm here. My heart still beats. And I intend to live.

Ryker, however, feels like he doesn't deserve to because he took that opportunity away from someone else.

"Biotch!" Kaylee squeals, running down my driveway in a pair of red-and-black plaid heels with a backpack flung over her shoulder.

"Slow down, girl. You're gonna fall."

I meet her halfway, and we embrace in a hug. It's only been a few days, but it feels like an eternity without her.

"I'm so glad you're back."

"Me too. Now let's get inside so you can fill me in on your houseguest."

I look at her bag, noticing it's completely stuffed. "What do you have in there?"

"My clothes, silly. I'm staying the night."

◆

Kaylee and I laid in bed talking for hours about anything and everything—except for Ryker and me sleeping together. She's still certain I'm setting myself up for heartbreak.

Now she's sound asleep and I'm lying here restless and all I can think about is Ryker.

Who is just down the hall.

I look over at Kaylee, who's snoring lightly with her lips parted. She's out and not waking up anytime soon. I'll be back before the sun rises, and she won't even know I left.

Flinging the blanket off me, I get out of bed. Dizziness ensues from getting up so quickly, and I have to pause for a second before leaving the room.

I tiptoe down the hall in just a tee shirt that happens to be

Ryker's and a pair of boy shorts. Ryker's door is cracked open, so I push it gently and see him lying there, wide awake.

"What are you doing here?" he asks, lifting the corner of the blanket, inviting me in.

I crack a smile and cross the room, sliding right under the blanket and into his arms. God, it feels so perfect being tangled under this blanket with him. Warmth radiates through me and there's no place I'd rather be. Turning on my side, I face him while his hand rests on my lower back. "I missed you."

Leaning forward, he presses his lips to mine tenderly. "I missed you, too."

There's a sadness in his voice that I wish I could wash away. I hate that he's hurting. "Have you slept at all?"

"Not yet. I was getting there."

"I'm sorry."

"Don't be. I'd rather lie awake with you than sleep anyways."

I nuzzle my face up to his bare chest and all the worries of the world fall away.

"I take it Kaylee's asleep?" he asks, his breath parting my hair.

"Yep. The trip home must've really worn her out because Kaylee never falls asleep before midnight."

"It's midnight already?"

"Almost."

"Damn, baby. You need to get some sleep. You've got school tomorrow."

"Actually," I say, "I was thinking I'd skip. Our week has already been cut short now that Carter is coming back a day early, and I really wanna make the most of it."

"Hard to believe our week together is almost over."

"It went too fast. But, we've come a long way."

"I'd say," he chuckles, "you went from hating me to this in a matter of days."

"And you went from pushing me away to pulling me in." I lift my eyes to his. "I'm so glad you stopped overthinking us."

"Well," he begins, "when Ryker Dawson is given a dare, he follows through."

I laugh. "Oh, is that what this is? You winning?"

"I won three years ago when I saw the look in your eyes when we almost kissed. That was the moment I knew I was in trouble."

"And in that same moment, I knew I had to have you."

"Then I left."

"Doesn't matter. You're here now. The question is, where do we go from here?"

Ryker takes in a deep breath, exhaling slowly. "Hell, Kit. I don't even know."

"Me either. I just know I'm not ready to lose you."

His lips press to mine, and he mutters, "I can't lose you unless you wanna get lost."

"Touché." I giggle.

I'm pulled closer, but it still doesn't feel like enough. Our mouths and our tongues curl together. Hearts beating against one another's chest.

"Mmm," Ryker hums into my mouth. "You're killing me, baby."

I lift my knee, rubbing it against his erect cock. "Oh yeah? Why's that?"

His hand reaches down, cupping my crotch. "This. You."

"Then I guess there's only one thing we can do." I grab his hand and push it down my shorts with my legs parted. "Live."

I don't even have to use persuasion this time. Ryker rubs his fingers against my sex, sending heat throughout my body.

One finger slides in and immediately begins pulsing inside me.

"Is this what you want?" he asks.

"Yes."

"Tell me, baby. Tell me what you want."

Humiliation be damned, I say the words, "I want you to fuck me again."

"Hmm," he grumbles into the crease of my neck. "I can probably do that. But first, I wanna look into your eyes while you come."

He definitely has a way with words. Words I never knew could turn me on so much.

Ryker pushes himself up. Kneeling over me, he peels back the blanket and his hand leaves my shorts. My pussy throbs, already missing his touch.

Still watching me with flirtatious eyes, he tugs my shorts down until I'm free of them. "Sit up," he demands, and my God, I like his commanding tone.

I do as I'm told and he removes my shirt, exposing my bare breasts.

Leaning down, Ryker sucks the bud of my nipple in his mouth. It puckers on impact and tingles spread from his mouth downward. Swirling his tongue around, he continues to suck.

His fingers crawl up my inner thigh, and I lean back on my hands, separating my legs for him.

"So sexy, baby."

No one has ever called me baby before him and I love it. It makes me feel like I belong to him.

Long fingers sweep up my slit and begin massaging my sensitive nub. I bite down on my bottom lip, flexing my lower half and forcing pressure.

When my eyes dart to my left, I notice his cock stretching the fabric of his boxer briefs. I reach over and tug them down until they're resting around his thighs. His cock springs free—long and girthy with purple veins. I take it in my hand, barely able to wrap my fingers all the way around it. As I begin stroking his length, he dips two fingers inside me.

The urge to take him in my mouth is strong. Even if I don't know what I'm doing and might mess up, I guide his length toward me. I start with my tongue, licking his undershaft.

With a guttural growl, he pushes deeper inside me. "Oh God." My breath hitches. Sweeping my tongue over his slick head, I swipe up a bead of salty pre-cum, then suck on the head of his cock. He thrusts forward, giving my mouth half of his length while his fingers still go strong, like they're working muscles of their own.

He uses his free hand to rub feverish circles around my clit with his index finger, and I'm damn near ready to explode.

I take in more of his length, letting his head hit the back of my throat. Sliding in and out of my mouth, I stroke the lower half. My mouth pools with saliva, and I use it as lube, letting it coat his cock.

"Fuck, baby. You keep that up and I'll be coming down your throat."

His words give me a boost of confidence, so I pick up my pace, sucking him harder and deeper.

"But we need to get you off first."

I like the way he thinks.

Ryker pulls back and moves down until his face is nuzzled between my legs.

My body writhes with excitement, and I'm curious to see how this feels. Everything we've done is new to me and I want to continue to experience all these firsts with Ryker.

His broad shoulders flex as he wraps his arms under my legs, bringing both hands to my sex and parting my lips.

A breath of air hits my sex and it casts shivers over my skin. The tip of his tongue circles my clit and my body jolts.

I'm not going to last long. I already feel like I'm going to combust.

His eyes peer up at me and I can feel his gaze burn into mine. I love the way he looks settled between my thighs. His abrasive tongue trails up and down, still watching me as he licks me from clit to cunt. I grab a fistful of his hair, weaving it between my fingers, and I tug.

He stops for a beat. "You taste better than I could have ever imagined."

My lips twitch with a smile, and I shove his face back where it belongs, feeling like a sex fiend in need of a fix.

Flexing the muscle of his tongue, he pushes it inside me and swirls it around before working my clit again.

My ass lifts off the bed and I force pressure from my hold on his hair. I want more. I need more.

It all happens so fast. The forcible sweeps of his tongue, his fingers drumming inside me. In and out, up and down. My head falls back, mouth open, and foreign sounds escape me. I'm hit hard with an insatiable need for release, ready to combust. It's so intense, so heart-pounding.

"Fuck," I cry out as I ride his face.

"Look at me," Ryker says. "I told you I wanna see your face when you come."

My head lifts, and I look into his eyes, watching his tongue spear my pussy and his fingers work my core.

Dizziness ensues and my heart is galloping in my chest. My God, it's so fast.

My walls clench around his fingers, squeezing them tightly as I reach my orgasm. I ride it out with a deep breath, then drop my head back on the pillow.

With his arms still wrapped beneath my legs, he lifts them up and gets on his knees. Before I can even catch a breath, he's filling me up again, this time with his cock.

One thrust. Two thrusts. Three. Over and over, he pounds my pussy. I watch his face, his attention locked on me.

I feel him stretching me until he fits perfectly. He's so deep inside me that I can feel the bulge in my stomach. There's a bite of pain, but it's nothing like the first time.

I watch intently as the rigid chords of his arms flex with each lunge.

"Baby..." He grunts. "I'm gonna come all over your tits."

That dirty mouth of his—once again, I find myself on the brink of explosion.

My hands stretch out, gripping the sheet on either side of me. I'm full-on panting as he pounds into me, each time hitting a spot inside me that sets my body on fire.

An audible moan climbs up my throat, spilling into the air around us. Just as I release, Ryker pulls out and shoots his cum all over my body. I lift my head, watching as the milky beads coat my breasts.

"Holy shit," he exhales violently, dropping on his side next to me.

Something jolts inside me, taking me by surprise, and I shoot into a sitting position.

"What's wrong?"

I clap a hand over my chest, suddenly feeling faint. "Nothing. I think my ICD just kicked in." I laugh, brushing it off as no big deal. "We're making it work overtime."

He sits up with me, an alarmed look on his face. "You're okay, though?"

"Yeah." I nod. "I'm perfect."

Kissing my lips, he hums. "Yes, you are."

When he leans over the bed to grab something, I lie back down, still feeling dizzy. I'm sure it's just my blood pressure dropping, which is nothing new; it's always running low.

Ryker comes back up with a tee shirt and begins wiping the mess on my stomach that has since dribbled down my side.

Once I'm all cleaned up, he throws the shirt across the room and drops down beside me and pulls my body flush to his. "Can this night just last forever?"

I'm tangled up in his arms, wishing for the same, when I roll to my side, feeling like it's time to confess something.

"There's something I need to tell you."

"Okay. You can tell me anything. You know that."

I do. I trust Ryker more than I've ever trusted anyone in my entire life. Even after he left and took a piece of me with him. He came back, though, and he reclaimed the part of me that always belonged to him.

"I haven't been honest with you. Hell, I haven't been honest with myself."

He props his head up on his hand and peers over at me. "What are you talking about?"

I lick my quivering lips, tears ready to explode from my eyes because saying it out loud will make it all the more real. For so long, I pretended—pretended I was okay, pretended that this Band-Aid inside me had fixed everything. The truth is, I'm not okay.

"I'm sick, Ry."

"Kit-Kat, you're okay now."

I shake my head against the pillow and look at him. "No. No, I'm not."

He drops his hands and rests his head on the pillow beside mine, staring into my eyes. "I don't like when you worry like this. Tell me what's wrong?"

The look of concern on his face has me regretting I even said anything. The last thing I want is to worry him. "Forget it." I shake my head, a forced smile on my lips. "You're right. I'm okay. Get some sleep and we'll talk tomorrow." I curl closer and snuggle up to his warm body.

Ryker falls asleep almost immediately. I, however, lie there facing the truth—I'm not getting any better.

CHAPTER
THIRTY

KIT

"H I, KIT. HOW ARE YOU FEELING TODAY?" DR. HANS ASKED, HAND *reaching for mine.*

I return the gesture and shake his hand, hating when he starts appointments like that. As if today would be the only day I'm feeling indifferent. "I feel great, thank you." *Sugarcoating everything I say in this appointment is necessary if I want to leave here with driving privileges.*

I just want to get this over with. I've already done the routine tests with Erica, the nurse. Echo, EKG, vitals. I'm well aware that he's reviewed everything, and now I am just waiting impatiently for him to give me the good news that I can drive again.

"Happy to hear." *He squeezes one of my ankles, then the other. Likely checking the blood flow.* "You've got a bit of swelling."

I've noticed. But I don't say anything in response to his finding.

He slides his stool back over to the rolling desk and flips open his laptop.

It's silent. Far too silent, and my entire body is shaking with anticipation. "Dr. Hans, can we just cut to the chase. Am I getting my license back or not?" *I hate to be so blunt, but the wait is slowly killing me.*

When he closes his laptop, drops his shoulders, and looks at me with a sorrowful expression, rage climbs up my throat.

I'm beyond crying at this point in my life. I've wallowed in self-pity, beat myself down, contemplated reduction in medical bills by just stopping my heart myself. Then five little words gave me the fight I needed—enjoy all the little things.

"Did you talk to your dad after our visit last month, Kit?"

"No," I say, point-blankly, "I'm eighteen years old and I don't want this burden on him or Carter."

His tongue clicks on the roof of his mouth. "Yes, I remember you saying that, on more than one occasion."

I can feel myself getting angry. "And I'll say it again because no matter what your tests say, I feel great. In fact, I feel better than I ever have."

"I'm glad you're not symptomatic, Kit. But as I've said at your last three appointments, your heart is getting weaker. Due to the increased size and damage to the mitral—"

"Please, stop. I've heard this all before. I just want to know if I'm getting my license back."

"No, Kit." His head shakes slowly, and those movements alone shift the air, sucking it right out of my lungs. "You won't be getting your license back today."

"How much…" My voice cracks, and I clear my throat. "How much longer?"

"You're on the transplant list, and while it's a long shot, given your circumstances, it could be a while."

My hands slap to my thighs as my legs dangle over the exam table I'm sitting on. "So never?"

"Putting you on the road would be a danger to yourself and others."

I shake my head, not wanting to believe the words I'm hearing.

"Kit, please consider adding your dad back on your authorized list. I'd really like to speak with him."

My eyes snap to him. "Why? What do you need to tell him that you haven't already told me?"

"I don't think you understand the severity of your condition."

A sarcastic laugh erupts from my vocal cords. "Severity?" I drop my feet to the floor. "If it were that severe," I air quote severe, "I'd be moved *to the top of the transplant list. Besides, I've got the implant. I'll be fine."*

"The implant only—"

"I said, I'll be fine."

I cross the room, and he knows I'm leaving. It's not the first time I've stormed out.

"Do you have your pager on you?"

"My dad has it," I huff in a single breath. He didn't trust me to pay attention to it, and for once, I agreed.

I need to get out of here before I completely break down. I know it's not Dr. Hans's fault, but I can't sit here and listen to him tell me how broken I am when I just put myself back together. I won't do it.

I tear open the door and leave the room, finding the nearest restroom. Once I'm inside, I crumble. I break. I fall apart.

Then I pull myself back together, because that's what needs to be done in order to convince everyone I'm okay.

"Kit."

"Kit…"

"Katherine Levine!"

I blink my eyes open, still wrapped in Ryker's arms. His breaths skim my neck, and I'm grateful he's still asleep.

"Kit…"

A glance over at the door tells me we're not alone. I wince when I see Kaylee standing there in her pajamas, arms crossed over her chest and a lecherous stare pinned on me.

I crack a wry smile and lift the side of the blanket, showing her the top of my cleavage, so she knows I can't get up until she leaves.

With flaring nostrils, she spins around and pads out the door, not bothering to shut it. Now that I think of it, I'm not sure it was even closed last night. It's very possible Kaylee heard everything.

I gently lift Ryker's arm to stir out of his hold, but he only tightens it and pulls me closer.

"Go back to sleep," he mumbles, eyes still pinched shut, but a smile spread across his face.

"We've been caught," I whisper.

That grabs his attention. He shifts, lifting his chest off the bed. "By whom?"

"Don't worry, it's just Kaylee. Still…I've got some explaining to do."

"Shit, Kit." He runs his fingers through his messy hair. "How do you explain this? We haven't even talked about what we're gonna do."

"I know. Maybe it's time to have that talk real quick."

Ryker and I haven't discussed a future or even wanting one together. One minute we were warding off temptation, and in one night, we dove in headfirst, never coming up for air. I've tried not to think too much into it, but the thought of losing Ryker all over again pains me. I just can't imagine a life without him in it.

He's deep in thought when I ask, "What do you want?"

His head shakes as he stares pensively at the ceiling. "I want you. Selfishly, I want you. But there are other people involved and…"

"Carter?"

He nods. "And your dad. I mean, what will they think of me? I can't lose my second family."

"And I wouldn't want you to. Carter will come around eventually. Once he sees what we have, I really think he'll give us his blessing."

Ryker's head drops down on the pillow. "Fuck, Kit. I don't know what to do."

My head rests on his chest, and we lie there for a minute, lost in our own thoughts.

I don't want to hurt Carter. It's the last thing I want. But I don't want to lose Ryker, either.

"Let's just keep things quiet for a bit. I'm still in town for a while. Haven't even decided what I plan to do with the shop. Hell, maybe I won't leave, after all."

My head springs up, a smile playing on my lips. "You're thinking about staying?"

"Maybe. After our talk about why I left, I felt this huge weight lifted off my shoulders. I mean, Oakley Shores has always been home, and it'd be nice to return to my roots. It'll take some time to get in a good headspace," his head turns to face me, "but with you by my side, I think I can do it."

I kiss his beautiful lips with giddiness swirling in my stomach. "I'll be there every step of the way."

"That's what I'm hoping. Now we just gotta see who else wants to be there."

"Everything will work out. It always does." My head rests back on his chest and we lie there, talking like old friends for what feels like hours, but it's only a fraction of an hour.

Twenty minutes later, I'm back in my pajamas and doing the walk of shame toward Kaylee in the kitchen. I'm trying hard to hide the smile on my face, but it's damn near impossible when I'm this happy.

She's sitting on a barstool in front of the center island with her fingers laced in the handle of a coffee mug. "Well, who do we have here?"

I press my lips together firmly and walk over to the sliding glass doors that lead to the patio. "Looks like it's gonna be a beautiful day."

"You're not seriously mentioning the weather right now."

I spin around, trying really hard not to smile when I see the scorned look on her face. "All right," I throw up my hands, "out with it. Say what you wanna say."

"Me?" She pushes the stool back and gets to her feet. "You're the one who's got something to say. What in the world did I just walk in on?"

"Do I really have to explain that?"

"Umm. Yes."

"Okay. A lot happened while you were gone." My tone is casual, and Kaylee counters my downplay of the situation.

"I was gone for four days. Four fucking days. And you end up in bed with the guy you swore off."

I wince. "What can I say, I lied."

"Yes. You did lie, and now you're going to sit your ass down and tell me the whole damn truth." She returns to her seat and pats the one beside her.

"What time is it? Shouldn't you be at school?"

"It's eight o'clock in the morning and we should both be at school. However, when I woke up, you were gone. And now we're skipping and you're going to tell me how the hell this happened."

With an audible sigh, but a never-faltering smile, I sit down and tell her everything.

Well, not everything. I leave out the part where he killed his dad and where my doctor insists I'm dying. Because who wants to hear that depressing shit. Instead, I tell her all the good stuff. Like how alive I feel when I'm with Ryker. And how he feels the same way. After all these years, I now know that my feelings are reciprocated. I tell her I love him. And I tell her that he loves me, too.

By the time I finish, Kaylee is on the verge of tears. "I want this."

"You want what?" I laugh.

"A love story like that." She pulls me in for a hug, almost knocking me off my stool. "If he makes you happy then, God dammit, be happy. No one deserves it more than you."

"Thanks, Kay. He really does."

The rest of the day is spent binge-watching *The Vampire Diaries* and eating our weight in food while Ryker handles business at the shop. He hasn't said the words, but I think he's staying, and I am over the moon, in the clouds, so damn excited. My future is bleak, but no matter what's in store for me, I have no doubt he'll be part of it.

CHAPTER
THIRTY-ONE
RYKER

It's Friday night and Kit's at her away game. I stayed behind to throw together a last-minute party to welcome Carter home. We weren't expecting a large crowd, but it seems word travels fast and people are already showing up.

Unfortunately, I think Carter's gonna beat the Cougar crowd, and Kit won't be here when he arrives. Fortunately, we've got all night.

I'm stacking cups on the round glass table on the porch, wishing Kit and I had more time. This week flew by and we barely skimmed the surface of our impending relationship. If that's even what it is. We haven't made anything official, but I know there's no one else I wanna be with. When I'm with her, I dread the time we have to spend apart. When we're apart, I'm missing her like crazy.

With the front door locked and instructions that the inside is off-limits, people begin coming around to the backyard. Jaxon, a friend of mine and Carter's from high school, got a nice-sized fire going in the firepit. Leon, another old friend, was able to get his hands on three kegs from some guys in Alcove.

Carter's name flashes on the screen of my phone on the table. "What's up, man?"

"Driver just picked me up. I'm headed back. Wanna ride over to Peamont and catch the second half of the game? I feel like an ass for missing two in a row."

"Nah. Kit understands. I've got something better planned. Just get your ass home."

"Oh shit. I'm worried now." He laughs. "Be there in about twenty."

We end the call, and I crank up the volume on the Bluetooth speaker, so we can get this party started.

Stacy and Ava show up, along with Ava's boyfriend. When I talked to Ava earlier, she asked if it was cool, and I said hell yeah. In fact, I encouraged it. Once Kit sees Ava with her new man, she'll see that there is nothing going on between Ava and me.

"Shotgun for old times' sake?" Leon asks, handing me a can of beer.

It's been a while since I've drank. For over a year, I didn't have a single drop, then once I started getting my shit together, I'd have a drink here and there. I'm not as good as I wanna be, but I'm better than I was, so I think a couple of drinks tonight are merited.

"Sure. Why the hell not."

"Hell yeah," Leon hoots, laying the can on the table and puncturing it with a pocketknife. He repeats the process for himself, and we start at the same time.

With my thumb over the hole, I bring it to my mouth and release it. My head tilts back and the beer slides down my throat, nice and smooth.

"Woooo," I howl, ready for another.

This time I opt for keg beer, filling the cup to the brim and sipping it slowly, so I don't get too fucked up tonight.

I look around and notice the yard has filled up. I sure as hell hope Carter gets here before too many people arrive because this isn't even my fucking house.

With my beer in hand, I make my way to the front yard, ready to greet him when he pulls in. A few others join me and we're standing in the driveway, shooting the shit, when a black car comes rolling down the road.

"That's him."

It might seem ridiculous to go to these lengths for a guy who's only been gone for six days, but back in the day, we always looked for any excuse to throw a party.

The car comes to a stop and I wish I could see his fucking face. The road is lined with cars and it's obvious this ain't no neighborhood cookout.

When the back door swings open, he emerges with a smirk on his face. "What the fuck is this?" The door closes, and he walks around to the open trunk and grabs his suitcase.

"Surprise," we all say, sounding like a bunch of overly excited teenagers.

"Six days. I was gone six fucking days." He laughs, dragging the rolling suitcase behind him.

"Six days too long, baby." I pull him in for a hug and pat his back.

"Now you've got me feeling like an ass for not throwing you a bash after being gone for two years."

He takes turns saying hi to everyone. Most of the people here are ones he sees on a regular basis. A few are in town visiting, like Ava and Stacy, but for the most part, they're all locals.

"Nah. You know I'm not a fan of attention." I hand him an unopened can of beer.

"Neither the fuck am I."

We all make our way to the backyard and Carter drops his luggage on the porch. I grab us a couple chairs and we kick back and relax around the fire.

"So, how was the trip?"

"A pain in my ass. I'm telling ya, man, I'm not cut out for this shit."

"Then why do it?"

"Because it's something to do until I graduate college. Two more years."

I tip back my cup of beer, swallowing it down, and ask, "Then what?"

"I dunno. I was thinking I might do a little traveling before I decide. A road trip across the U.S. What do you say?"

I bring my cup to my chest, neck craned. "Me?"

"Yeah, you. You're my best fucking friend. You think I'm gonna do this without you?"

Damn. I don't like the feeling settling in my stomach. It's a mixture of guilt laced with regret. Although, it's not enough to stop what's already been started.

"Maybe. I guess I'll have to see what the future has in store for me when the time comes. Who knows, I could be living down the road running Dawson Auto Repair."

"No shit?"

I shrug a shoulder and take another drink. "Maybe."

"Well, I think that's a good plan. Your family's here. I'm here. Kit's here." He drops his empty can to the ground beside him. "Speaking of, how's my little sis doing? You two good now?"

Oh, we're good all right. Since you've left, I've explored her body and locked her taste and scent in my memory. "She's good. I don't think she got the news she wanted from her doctor, but she's in good spirits."

"Aww hell. She didn't get her driving privileges back?"

I shake my head. "Nope."

"Fuck. She's probably crushed. She never talks to me or my dad about her appointments and likes to play it off like everything's fine, but I know she was expecting good news, and I can't imagine how let down she is."

"Yeah. It's tough. I can't imagine being told I can't drive, let alone having to live with a condition like that. She's all right, though. Claims she feels better than ever."

Carter side-eyes me as he cracks open another beer. "Yeah, she'll feed you that bullshit for breakfast, but it's just that…bullshit." He takes a sip, then rests the can on his knee. "She's not as healthy as she wants you to believe she is."

"Kit's fine. A happy, normal teenager with a heart condition that's under control."

He raises a brow. "I see she's got to you, too."

I quickly change the subject from Kit to football. The more I talk about her, the more guilt gnaws at me. The more we discuss her condition, the more defensive I get.

It's nice catching up with Carter, and doing so has made me realize how much I've missed out on.

The sun has set and the Cougar crowd, also known as the football players, cheerleaders, and guests, start piling in.

I glance over my shoulder from my seat around the fire and I see her. I'm feeling the effects of the five beers I've drunk and my self-control is not very controllable right now. Especially when Kit's standing there in her cheer uniform, laughing with a group of her friends from school. She doesn't know I'm watching, but fuck *am* I watching. It's like everyone has disappeared and she's all I see—my girl.

Kit's eyes slide to mine and she lifts a smile, then resumes engaging in whatever conversation is being had.

It's not until I see Asher Collins walk up beside her and set a hand on her hip that I push my chair back and stop giving her the space I intended to. She steps to the left, trying to get away, but the fucker just moves right along with her.

My chair tips over, but I don't bother picking it up. With an open beer in one hand and a closed one in the other, I walk steadfast toward her, ignoring everyone I pass by.

She catches me in her peripheral and glances from Asher to me before her happy-go-lucky expression drops.

Her head shakes no, while I bite down the urge to put this fucker in his place. Before I can make it to her, she's already walking toward me—Asher watching her every move.

"Hey, baby," I say, not even attempting to keep my voice down. "Why don't you go find your brother and welcome him home while I have a word with your *friend*?"

She looks at my full hands, taking note of the beer in both. "Are you drunk?"

"No." Lifting a brow, she tries to read me. "I'm not. Just a little buzzed."

"Well, stay away from Asher. I don't want any trouble tonight. Besides, Carter's here now and we have to ease him into this. I was thinking that we should give it a few days."

"I couldn't agree more, baby." I lean down and whisper in her ear, "But right now, all I wanna do is take you in that empty house and fuck you."

"Play nice and I might make that happen."

I growl in her ear. "You're fucking killing me, baby."

She chuckles the most beautiful sound. "You keep saying that, but you're still here."

"That's because you're here. Wherever you are is exactly where I'll be."

"You are drunk."

"Drunk on you."

She laughs again and takes a step back, so I straighten myself up. "I love you." Her voice is a whisper in the wind, but I hear it loud and clear.

"I love you and everything about you." I flip one of her braids. "Even these cute things. What are they called?"

"Those would be pigtails."

"Mmm," I wink, "I wanna pull those pigtails later while I'm fucking you from behind."

Her cheeks blush, and it's cute as hell. But she really takes me by surprise when she says, "Looking forward to it." She turns and walks away, leaving me with blue balls and a racing pulse.

Fuck. I just wanna be near her, but we have to be patient.

I can do this.

Two hours later and another beer in, plus three bottles of water, I can't do this anymore.

I spot Kit walking into the house while Carter's filling a cup at the keg, and I use this opportunity to make my move.

Bypassing crowds of people, I make a beeline right for the open sliding doors on the porch. "Kit-Kat," I whisper-yell.

I hear a door shut down the hall and follow the sound, staggering and bumping my side into the wall.

I might be drunker than I thought I was.

A beam of light shines from the bathroom door beside her room, and I knock my knuckles to it. "Kit. You in there?"

The sound of running water stops. "Ryker, is that you?"

I turn the handle, and to my surprise, it's not locked. When I push the door open, I see Kit at the sink drying her hands. "Thought I might find you here." I slide between the cracked door and the frame and close it behind me.

A smile plays on her lips. She's still wearing that sexy cheer uniform, and as much as I love it, I wanna peel it off her layer by layer.

"You shouldn't be in here. What if Carter comes looking for you?"

I step up behind her, looking at her reflection in the mirror. "It'll be worth it." My fingers sweep her hair to one side, and I lean forward, pressing my lips to her neck. Her body shivers. "I've missed you."

Kit rests her head back on my collarbone. "Missed you, too. It's hard to believe our time has come to an end."

"It hasn't ended yet." I sweep my fingers under the sleeveless strap of her top and tug it down while peppering her shoulder with kisses. "In fact, the night has just begun."

She spins around and rests her arms over my shoulders. "We should go back out there before someone comes looking for us."

I resume sucking on her neck and hum, "No one's looking for us." Pulling her in for a searing kiss, she becomes putty in my hands.

My hips flex outward, feeling my rock-hard dick press against her hip. "I need you, baby." I part her lips with my tongue, invading her mouth, and she welcomes it. Our heads tilt, and I cradle her face in my hands.

"I need you, too," she purrs, and the sound creates a hunger inside me. An appetite only she can appease.

I tear into her like she's prey. Ridding her off her top, unclasping her bra and letting it fall to our feet. Kit unbuttons my jeans and slides them down until they're pooled around my ankles. "Turn around," I tell her, and she does.

With a flip of her skirt, I expose her ass and the thin fabric of her thong that rests between her cheeks. I brush my fingers over the smooth skin, then squeeze the meaty flesh.

My hands move to her sides. "So damn beautiful." Fingers pinching her hips, I watch her in the mirror as I pull her thong to the side and slide my dick inside her wet pussy.

I move nice and slow, feeding her inch by inch until I'm fully enveloped by her tight walls.

"Fuck, baby. You feel so good."

Kit grips the vanity tighter, her eyes locked on mine in the mirror. Her mouth falls open, and she groans, "Faster."

Giving her what she wants, I pick up my pace, pounding her from behind while massaging her tits in my palms. I glance down and watch as her cheeks slap and jiggle against my pelvic bone. I twist and turn, slide and dig, filling her completely.

It's like her pussy was molded just for me. No one else. The effects of the alcohol have my mind and body feeling every ounce of emotion, and I pour it all into this moment. "You like that, baby?"

Her response is a silent nod, so I grab one of her pigtails and tug back slightly. "No one else touches this pussy but me, right?"

"Never," she says in an audible breath.

"Mine," I growl as I fuck her harder and faster.

My cock begins to fill up with a dire need of release, so I reach my arm beneath her, pressing my fingers to her clit, and rub feverishly. "Come for me, Kit."

"Ugh." She moans and pants, spreading her legs farther apart while silently begging for more. I rub faster, thrust deeper, and when her stomach contracts and she squeezes my cock, I pull out and watch as my cum coats her ass. Just as I do, her arousal drips into the palm of my hand.

"Fuck, Kit. I think we need to sneak off more often."

She chuckles as she reaches for a hand towel hooked on the wall and tosses it over her shoulder. "Good thing the night is young."

I clean her up and drop the towel to the floor, then flip her skirt back down.

As I'm reaching down for my jeans, the bathroom door flies open. Giggles coming from the intruders scatter until it's completely quiet. Kit and I both freeze. So do the two people on the other side—Carter and Stacy.

I quickly pull my pants up.

"What the fuck is this?!" Carter howls, chest heaving while mine does the same.

Kit stands there stunned and exposed. "It's not what it looks like." I step in front of her, hiding her naked body from her brother.

"Really? Because it looks to me like my best fucking friend and my sister were just…"

"I'm sorry, Carter. I'm so fucking sorry." The words spill from my mouth because, no matter what excuse or lie we feed him, we've been caught.

"Get your fucking shirt on," he demands of Kit. "Go back to the party, Stacy."

I bend down and grab her shirt and bra in one swoop and hold them behind my back for her.

Stacy hesitates, looking from me to Kit, before turning around and padding her feet down the hall.

"I trusted you," Carter seethes, eyes deadlocked on mine. "I fucking trusted you. She's my sister. My little fucking sister."

I know what's coming before it happens, but I don't stop him. I don't fight it, nor move as his fist meets my jaw. My head swings to the left, and I bite down hard on my bottom lip.

Kit messes with her bra and shirt with shaky hands. "Carter, please stop. I can explain."

"I deserve that," I say.

Carter punches me again, this time, blood spilling from my mouth and splattering around us. Red drops dribble down the beige vanity, and I turn my head to look at him again, prepared to take the beating I so deserve.

Jutting a finger at me, he fumes, "You're dead to me."

His attention turns to Kit, who's now fully clothed. "And you…you're fucking unbelievable."

Kit grabs a clean towel and hands it to me with downcast eyes. "Thanks," I say in a hushed tone.

I watch Kit as tears fall down her face, and as much as I want to console her and scream at the top of my lungs that I love her and it'll be okay—I can't.

Instead, I stand there quietly and let this play out the way that it has to, dabbing the blood on my mouth with the towel Kit handed me.

With clenched fists at his sides, Carter breathes fire. "Get out," he gnashes. When I step forward, ready to say something, anything, he raises his voice. "Get the fuck out!"

"Carter, please let us explain," Kit begins, "Ryker and I—"

"Ryker and you, what? Are in love? Have been fucking behind my back all week?"

He looks at me, and my lack of voice only riles him up more. He laughs, though it's void of humor. "You son of a bitch." He lunges at me, wrapping his arms around my waist, my head hitting the wall on the way down.

"Stop! Please!" Kit cries and shouts, and the next thing I know, between blows to my face, we're broken apart. It all happens so fast and the minutes that pass feel like seconds. The next thing I know, the bathroom fills with people, and my adrenaline is pumping so fast that I can't make out their blurry faces.

Someone helps me to my feet and I know I have to go. I have to leave this house—him and her.

I push through the crowd in the small space, stopping in front of a sobbing Kit, who's now being consoled by Kaylee. "I'm sorry," I say before making my exit.

I'm so fucking sorry.

CHAPTER
THIRTY-TWO
RYKER

Eighteen missed calls.

Eleven voice messages.

Thirteen text messages.

All from Kit.

All unread and ignored.

Temptation bites on my insides. Chewing and clawing its way to the surface. My finger hovers over the green phone on my screen when her name appears again. I could press it and hear her voice in seconds. I could tell her how sorry I am for getting caught and how sorry I'm not for what started between us.

I could tell her how it's always been her. How it will *always* be her.

Time runs out.

Nineteen missed calls.

Which is exactly how many times I've tried to call Carter.

I clutch my phone, holding it tight like I've done for the past three days.

That's how long it's been. Three days since I last saw her when Carter caught us in the bathroom in a compromising position. There wasn't a possibility of lying our way out of that one. Her being naked from the waist up, me tugging up my jeans. No. He knew what was going on as soon as that door flung open.

The doorbell buzzes from downstairs. Kit's at school, so I know it's not her. Chances are, Buck needs some help in the shop.

Dragging my ass out of bed, I walk downstairs in just a pair of black nylon shorts. I comb my fingers through my greasy hair before pulling the door open.

"Mom?"

"Good morning, son." Her eyes drag up and down my body. "I hate to say it, but you look like complete shit."

I laugh. "Gee. Thanks." My arm presses to the door, making room for her to come in.

We get up to the apartment and she looks around the small space, taking it all in. "He'd be glad you're staying here."

"Yeah. I guess."

Her hands slap to her sides and she cocks a brow. "So, I hear you're staying?"

I walk over to the kitchen sink that's loaded with dirty dishes. Grabbing a glass that I used for water yesterday, I rinse it off and fill it back up. "That was the plan."

"Was?"

I tip the glass back and take down half the water. "I don't know what I'm doing anymore." I thought I could move back and face my past with Kit by my side. With her, I feel invincible. It's not a front or a show I put on for others. It's as if I can withstand anything life throws at me because she makes me feel accepted. Now that I don't have her or Carter, I'm not so sure I can stay.

"Talked to Buck. He mentioned that you wanted him to work full-time beside you. Even said you talked about fixing up this place with the money you got from the Chevelle. Still can't believe you sold the car."

"Had to make the sacrifice for the future of the shop." I hate what I had to do. It was so much more than just a car. It was necessary, though.

I finish off my water and drop the glass in the sink. It hits harder than I expected, cracking in half. My hands press to either side of the sink and I hang my head.

"Ryker," Mom scurries to my side with a perplexed look on her face. "What has gotten into you? Is this about—"

"No!" I blurt out. "This isn't about him. Not everything is about that bastard." The words explode from my vocal cords, which wasn't my intent. "I'm sorry, Mom. It's just been a rough couple days."

She wraps an arm around me and rests her head on my shoulder. It feels nice. "We used to be so close. Talk to me, son."

"I don't know what to say. I screwed everything up like I always do and now I have to live with what I've done."

Mom lifts her head from my shoulder, looking at me. "This is about Kit, isn't it?"

I'm taken aback by her question. She shouldn't know that. "What makes you say that?"

"You came to the trailer. I thought for sure you'd cancel plans or have us meet you somewhere else, but you didn't. You came with her. She's the one who got you through it, isn't she?"

"I'd hardly say I got through it. One loud noise and I was fleeing." She's right, though. I don't think I could have even made that step through the doorway had it not been for Kit.

"Look at me, Ryker." She grabs my shoulders and turns me to face her. My beautiful, innocent but strong mom. A woman who never tells a lie and can read right through mine. My eyes drag up and I'm forced to look at her and hear what she has to say. "I've said it a hundred times and I'm going to say it again. You did what you had to do. Had you not, one of us might have been on the other end of that barrel. It's time to let go of the past, son. You have a chance to be the man you've always wanted to be. Find him and let him live and come home."

"I am home."

"No, you're not." She shakes her head. "You're stuck between here and there. Come home, Ryker."

I know she doesn't mean home as in the place where her and Ezra live. She means this town. My home.

A lump lodges in my throat and it hurts. It really fucking hurts. "Everything's such a mess. I lost him, Ma. I lost her, too."

"Who? Who did you lose?"

"Carter and Kit."

"No, Ryker. You could never lose them. They are a part of you. Just because someone is absent doesn't mean they are lost."

My chin drops to my chest, eyes closed. "He'll never let me love her like I want to."

"Kit?"

I nod, letting the tears slide down my cheeks. It's rare that I cry. Even when I saw my dad's lifeless body on the floor, blood painting the carpet, I never shed a tear.

"Love doesn't ask for permission, Ryker. It takes a path of its own and it's your choice to follow it or leave it behind. But no matter which way you go, it always finds a way to follow *you*."

"Stupid love," I choke out.

Mom chuckles. "It is stupid. But it's worth it. If you love her, show him how much. Eventually, Carter will have to make his own choices, but they're his to make."

"If only it were that easy." I suck in the snot ready to drip from my nose. "You don't know how close he and Kit are. Even if he ever did forgive me for what we did, he'll never approve of us being together."

"Well, no matter what you decide, I'm always here for you, son. You never have to fight your battles alone, even though you're as stubborn as your granddad and do so anyway."

"Thanks, Ma."

The heart-to-heart was tortuous but, surprisingly, I'm feeling a little more optimistic. Mom sticks around and insists on making me a hearty lunch of grilled cheese, tomato soup, and orange juice. I scarf it down, not realizing how hungry I actually was.

We talk a little more about Carter and Kit. She fills me in on

Ezra and how helpful he's been. She also tells me that he needs me, and I promise to make an effort to rebuild our relationship.

In the end, I've made the choice to stay. I'm tired of hiding. I can be miserable anywhere, might as well have the company of my family while I wallow in my own self-pity.

Once Mom leaves, I pace the living room with my phone in my hand and Kit's name pulled up on the screen, repeating the words my mom said. *Love doesn't ask for permission.*

She hasn't called in over an hour and, of course, my head goes to all the wrong places. Why isn't she calling? Is she hurt? Sick? Is she giving up on me already? But the truth is, she's in class, and I'm just being a dumbass overthinking everything.

I know she won't answer, but I need to leave a message, just to tell her how sorry I am. She also needs to know that my feelings for her aren't going anywhere…and neither am I.

Just fucking do it, chicken shit.

Without another thought, I press Call.

It rings. And rings. And rings.

"Hey, it's Kit. I can't get to my phone right now but leave a message and I'll call you back…maybe."

Beep.

I open my mouth to speak, but nothing comes out.

Say something, dumbass.

The words get lodged in my throat and all that comes out is air.

Nothing I say will suffice.

I can tell her how much I love her, but then what?

I can say I'm sorry, but am I?

Am I sorry for what happened between us or am I sorry we got caught like we did?

I end the call abruptly, not a single word spoken.

Instead, I start at the beginning. There's something I need to do before I can face Kit.

I snatch a dirty shirt off the floor, pull it over my head, and step into a pair of old tennis shoes with the backs pushed down.

With my keys, phone, and wallet in hand, I jog down the stairs and out the door into the shop.

"Taking off, boss?" Buck asks.

"Boss, huh? I like the sound of that." I check him with a pat on the shoulder as I pass by. "Be back later and I'll give you a hand pulling that engine."

Before he can respond, I'm out the garage door and jumping in the seat of my truck.

Ten minutes later, I'm pulling down the Levines' driveway and parking in front of the open garage, behind Carter's car.

I fling my door open and get out, but as I'm shutting it, Carter steps out of the mudroom and into the garage. He stops, glares at me, then begins walking to his car.

"Hey," I say, "can we talk for a minute?" I stride over to his side when he pulls open the driver's side door of his car.

"Yeah. We can talk about how you need to move your truck so I can get out."

"Come on, man. Just give me a chance to explain."

In a swift motion, he slams his car door shut and steps up to me, nose to nose. "Talk about what? How you've been screwing my sister behind my back?"

"It's not like that."

"Then what's it like, Ryker? Huh?" He steps closer, and I step back. "You gonna give me some lame excuse about how your pants fell down while she was changing her shirt? Save it. Kit already told me everything."

My eyebrows hit my forehead. "She did?"

"Yeah, she did. Also tried convincing me that she loved you. But you know what I told her?" He steps into the lost space again and this time, instead of backing up, my feet stay planted to the cement floor of the garage. "Told her she can't possibly love a snake like you."

"Well, you might see me as a snake in the grass, but this wasn't a spontaneous thing. So if you think I took advantage of her or used her for a quick lay, you're wrong."

His fist meets my face so fast that I don't even have a chance to try and dodge it. This time, unlike in the bathroom, fire burns inside me. "You don't wanna do this, man," I bark out as he tries to tackle me to the ground.

I swoop a leg behind him and swing through his legs, guiding him down to the ground so he doesn't fall and bust his head on the cement. He pulls on my shirt, cursing and wailing, but I take hold of his wrists and hold his hands in place over his head. Carter knows I'm stronger. He also knows I won't knock his ass out because he's like a brother to me. I don't expect the same level of respect from him, not right now.

"Get the fuck off me!"

"Not until you hear me out."

"I'll fucking kill you, Ryker," he seethes. "You better let me go right now."

"I know she's your sister, but you should know more than anyone, I'd never hurt her. I love her…and love doesn't ask for permission."

His legs kick, and he tries to break loose. "You have hurt her. You already broke her fucking heart by starting something with her in the first place."

"We can fix it. She can be happy if you'll let her."

"Never. You stay the fuck away from her. I mean it, Ryker. You go near her again and I'll destroy you."

"Do it then. Without her, I'm useless anyways. So you wanna destroy me? Go ahead. Give it your best shot."

"Let me up and I will. Come on, you coward, let me go and fight like a man."

"I don't wanna hurt you, Carter. You're my best fucking friend. Like a brother to me."

"Was. Was your best friend. Now, you're nothing to me. As good as dead. The scum your father always said you were."

"Wow." I nod, shoulders slack, and my hold on him loosens. "All right." I let go of him and get to my feet. My arms fly out to my sides. "Go ahead and destroy me. Knock me down, stomp on me, and dig me into the ground. I'm scum anyways."

I didn't think he'd actually do it, but when his knuckles collide with my already swollen cheek, I have to say I'm pretty shocked.

"Don't ever show your face here again."

"I second that." The voice has me looking over my shoulder where Mr. Levine is standing. "Stay the hell away from my daughter, Dawson."

I swallow hard and nod. Because what else can I do?

Carter gets in his car, revs his engine and begins to back up. Slamming on his brakes, then repeating the action.

I've got no choice but to get in my truck and leave.

In a matter of seconds, two hearts collided, not knowing it would create an explosion around them that took out everything they love.

One.

By.

One.

CHAPTER
THIRTY-THREE
KIT

"You all set?" Carter asks when I walk into the living room. He closes his laptop, sets it on the coffee table, and stands.

"Yeah," I tell him in another one-word sentence. I haven't spoken to him much, even when he barks in my ear all day long that this is for the best. After I poured my heart out to him and told him I've been in love with Ryker since I was fourteen years old, he looked me in the eye and had the audacity to tell me I don't know what love is. That what I feel is infatuation over a guy who should have been off-limits. He proceeded to tell me he's not mad at me because Ryker took advantage of me by using his authority over me while staying in our house.

Bullshit. It's complete and utter bullshit. For one, Ryker had zero authority over me. I am an adult. Two, Carter and my dad will never see me as an adult because they still treat me like a child.

Their reasoning: I behave like one.

So what if I stopped sharing my health records with them when I turned eighteen? It's my body and my health. I still take my meds and I'm doing just fine.

I fling my duffel bag over my shoulder, not looking forward to the ride to the football field because *he* has to drive me.

"Kit. Please just let this go. I don't like fighting with you."

I look him straight in the eye, lips pressed in a thin line. "Do I look like I'm fighting? Am I attacking you and punching you in the face over and over again until your blood splatters all over? No. I wouldn't do that to someone I care about."

"If you're referring to my fight with Ryker—"

"Fights," I correct him. "Two fights."

"How did you know—"

"Before you ask, no, Ryker didn't tell me because he still won't talk to me, thanks to you. Dad did."

"Good. I'm glad he's heeding my advice and leaving you alone."

My head shakes as I spin around to face him, on the brink of another meltdown. "You're loving this, aren't you? Feeling like you have this power and control over me?"

"I don't feel like I have any power or control. In fact, I feel anything but powerful. My best fucking friend snuck behind my back with my sister, who also happens to be one of my best friends. If anything, I feel power*less*, not to mention, betrayed."

"Of course. Because this is all about you. Poor Carter wasn't in on the secret. And what would you have done if we came to you and told you we had feelings for each other we wanted to pursue?"

He's silent for a tick. Shrugging his shoulders, he says, "I don't know. I guess we'll never know."

"You're right, we won't. Please just take me to the field."

I walk out the door, Carter trailing behind me.

No amount of pain felt before touches this. Not only have I lost Ryker, but I've lost my brother, too. The difference, Carter is pulling himself out of my life instead of being pushed.

God, I just miss Ryker so much. It hurts so fucking bad. I have moments where I get distracted and forget about him and what happened, then in the blink of an eye, it hits me. Smack-dab in the chest. The heaviness is suffocating.

If I could do it all again, I wouldn't think twice. I'd run away with him. Move to Colorado and keep our love a secret—only for us to see and feel. Then no one could touch it.

If only.

I can't help the tears that fall, once again. I can't control them anymore.

"Kit," Carter says.

I sweep my fingers across my eyes, air catching in my throat.

"Kit," he says again, tepidly, "please don't cry."

"I love him, Carter." I choke on the words, and my voice cracks through sniffles and tears. "I can barely breathe without him."

"You just need time."

"No!" I shout. "Every minute away from him is agony. I don't want time! What I want is to go back to the day before you returned and make time stand still. Don't you get it?" He says nothing, so I sink down in the seat. "Of course you don't. You've never been in love."

He shifts into reverse and begins backing out of the driveway. I'm completely taken by surprise when he says, "You really love him?"

Those four words are like music to my ears. All week I've heard Carter telling me how I *should* feel or what I *need* to do. For the first time in days, he's asking *me* what *I* feel.

"I really do."

"But it's Ryker. The guy who bribed you with candy and gave you noogies in our blanket forts."

"The candy was never a bribe. Turns out, he just liked to make me happy. As for the noogies," I feel myself smile for the first time in a while, "I kinda liked 'em."

I always sought out those weird acts of attention from Ryker.

"He didn't force you into anything? It was one hundred percent your decision?"

"He didn't force me. If anything, I forced him. He resisted. Thought about your feelings every step of the way."

"So what? You want a relationship with him? And what

happens when this thing between you two ends and your heart's completely broken?"

"Doesn't matter. It's not whole without him. I'd gladly give it to him to break if it meant more time together."

"See," Carter exhales profoundly, "this is what I'm talking about. You don't think rationally, Kit. Life is not a fairy tale. You can't jump in the water for someone who weighs you down. You'll drown, sis."

"I'm already drowning. Sometimes I wish I could just stay under the water and never come up for air."

"Don't talk like that. This world needs you. Which is exactly why you need to start taking better care of yourself. Speaking of, I know you had a doctor's appointment a couple days ago. Ryker told me it didn't go as planned."

I'm not sure if we're still talking about Ryker, but it sure feels like this conversation is headed down a path I don't wanna take.

"That's not important. We're talking about me and Ryker right now."

We pull up to the curb and Carter shuts his car off. "What did the doctor say?"

"I said I don't want to talk about it."

"Just tell me—"

"I'm still sick, Carter." My voice rises with each word. "My heart is still broken! Is that what you want to hear? Does that answer your question?"

"I just—"

"I've gotta go." I swing the door open and step out, slamming it shut behind me and not giving Carter a second look.

If he makes me choose between him and the man I love, I choose me. I will always choose me. And without Ryker, I am not myself.

"One cheer?" I ask in a puppy dog pout with my hands folded together in a plea.

"One," Coach Lynn says sternly, but with one corner of her lip tugged up.

I jog out to the track and jump in the back line.

"More power to the hour, more bounce to the ounce. We're the mighty Cougars and we'll knock you out."

We repeat the cheer three times, and I notice Coach Lynn engaging in a conversation with the assistant football coach, so I stay put. One more won't hurt.

We're about to begin when the Cougars get a touchdown. Asher's standing on the sideline and runs over, grabs me by the waist, hooting and hollering with everyone else. He spins me around, making me feel dizzy, but I'm caught up in the moment of excitement and laugh through it.

Just as Asher sets me down, I look over to the standing crowd and see Ryker. My eyes lock on his as he draws in a drag of a cigarette. The school cop, Gordy, is beside him, saying something sternly.

"You can't smoke in here," I think he said.

The next thing I know, I'm getting swooped up again by Asher, who's celebrating the extra point kick along with the entire stadium of guests. He spins me around again, and each time my eyes pass Ryker's, they catch his.

"Put me down. I need to talk to him," I holler, though my words are masked by the chants coming from every person in attendance. Every person aside from me and Ryker.

Once I'm back on my feet, I'm feeling pretty off-balance. I try to walk toward him, staggering a bit, but it doesn't stop me.

My eyes catch the smoldering look on his face. He takes another hit of his cigarette, pinches it between his fingers, and flicks it before he's pulled to the exit by Gordy.

I cup my hands around my mouth and shout, "Ryker!"

"Kit," Coach Lynn calls, curling a pointed finger right at me.

My unsteady legs from being spun around turn to jelly, and I tip slightly to the right. Coach Lynn reaches out and catches me. "Are you okay, honey?"

"Yeah. I'm fine. One of the football players got a little too excited and swung me around." I laugh it off, hoping she doesn't make this something it's not.

"Why don't you have a seat and put your legs up. Your ankles are pretty swollen."

I nod, not caring to argue with her because she's right. My ankles are swollen.

By the end of the game, I'm feeling much better. Coach Lynn made me drink my weight in water and my head has finally stopped spinning. Note to self: if someone picks you up, headbutt them if they start spinning.

Kaylee comes skipping to my side, adorned with a smile so big I can barely see her eyes. "All right, chica. It's party time."

"Actually…" I look up at her as I retie my shoe on the bench.

"Nope. You need this more than anyone. Besides, you have to break the news to Asher that you're bailing on him twenty hours prior to the dance.

She's right—I am. After careful deliberation, I decided not to go. I never wanted to go as Asher's date anyways. I only said yes because I had tequila swimming through my veins and I saw Ryker with Ava. Now I have to tell Asher that he's welcome to take one of the many girls who grovel at his feet. Do I feel bad for my short notice? A little bit. Does it change my mind? No.

"Fine. One hour, tops. I really wanna swing by Ryker's and try and talk to him again."

He's still ignoring me, but I'm never giving up. I've been trying to call him nonstop and now it just goes to voicemail, leading me to believe he's shut his phone off altogether. He was here tonight, though. He came to watch the game—or maybe me. That is until that idiot Asher picked me up. I could tell by the look on his face he was affected. I don't see it as a bad thing, though. The way I see it, it means he still cares.

Kaylee and I go straight to the party from the game. It's tradition that all the players and cheerleaders go in uniform to celebrate homecoming so, fortunately, we don't have to stop at home.

We're walking through the parking lot and everyone is piling into shared vehicles so they don't have to drive home from the party after drinking. Logan pats the bed of a truck, and I don't even know whose it is. "Hop on it, sexy ladies. There's room for everyone."

I look at Kaylee, who shrugs, before flinging her body over the side—cheer panties on display—and dropping down on her ass beside Damon.

"Come on, Kit. Don't be shy," Logan says. Beside him are Liza and Carly. I look around and notice that Micah is not here. Poor guy is probably still heartbroken over his breakup with Carly.

Giving in, I respond with a smirk and hop in the same way Kaylee did.

We're leaving her car behind, but, chances are, she's staying with Damon, and I'll just catch a ride with the Sober Squad again.

Logan throws an arm over my shoulder with a koozie holding a beer in the other hand. "You know, it really is a shame that you're going with Asher to the dance. We could've had a good time."

"Actually, Kit's not even going to the dance," Kaylee spits out, and my head snaps to her.

"Kaylee," I mouth through clenched teeth.

"Ooops. My bad." She covers her mouth.

"Wa…wa…wait," Logan sputters, "you're not going to the dance now? What about my boy, Asher?"

She just had to open her big mouth. I know Kaylee is the queen of gossip, but usually I'm not the dish.

"It's a last-minute decision. I'm not in a good headspace. He'd be better off going with someone else."

"Well, you coulda given him a little notice," Damon says. "The dance is tomorrow."

"At least she didn't wait until tomorrow," Kaylee chimes in, trying to atone for her fuck-up.

I know I look like a total bitch, but I don't even care.

"So this is final? You're not going to the dance with Asher?" Liza asks, and as much as I'd like to just ignore the bitch, because it's not her business, I nod in response while biting down on my thumbnail.

I despise unwanted attention.

Liza begins whispering something in Carly's ear as she types into her phone, but her eyes are on me the entire time. There's a devious look on her face that irks me.

We're following behind a train of cars with people hanging out windows and standing up through moonroofs with their music blasting.

I breathe a sigh of relief when we make it to Asher's house. Not because we're here, but because we didn't get pulled over for this parade of minors, who are already drinking.

Everyone piles out, and Logan offers his hand, helping me step down. We all give Logan shit because he's such a goofball, but the truth is, he's one of the sweetest and funniest guys in our school. I really wish I would have just told Asher to fuck off and gone with him to the dance instead. I might still be going if that were the case.

Kaylee and Damon are holding hands and whispering sexual innuendos in each other's ears, so I use this opportunity to find Asher. Like a Band-Aid. Quick and painless.

After searching for a good twenty minutes, I find him in his kitchen, taking shots with a group of girls. Good. Maybe one of them can be his date and I won't feel like such a bitch for dumping him.

"Asher," I say, tapping him on the shoulder, "can we talk for a minute?"

His head twists and his expression goes sour. Eyebrows dipped into a deep V, he says, "I think we should." He downs another shot, mumbles something to the girls about not going anywhere, then grabs my hand and pulls me out of the kitchen and away from the crowd.

"Look. I'm really sorry that I have to—"

"Shh." He presses his fingers to my lips. "Not yet."

Weird, but okay.

We keep walking until we're upstairs, then we continue down the hall to his room. "Is this really necessary? What I have to say will literally take thirty seconds."

"Oh, it is necessary." He turns the handle to the door and pushes it open. I walk inside, and it's dark. Fortunately, light from the hall shines inside. That is until Asher closes the door.

I slap my hand around on the wall in search of a light switch, but before I can find it, Asher puts his hand over mine. "You think you're hot shit, don't you?"

My neck cranes. "Excuse me?"

"Asking you to that dance was a favor to you, not me, and you think that one day prior you can dump me and try to make me the laughing stock of the school?"

I'm not sure how he knows I was even…

Liza. Of course.

"Look, Asher. I am so sorry. There's just so much going on in my life."

"Shut up!"

He squeezes my hand so hard that I can feel the bones of my fingers grind. "Stop it. That hurts." I try to pull away, but he only strengthens his hold.

"For years, I watched you watching me. I turned a blind eye because I'm not into bitches who are no fun. You can't even run in gym class. Probably can't even ride a cock."

My stomach churns with bile. Is this really happening right now? "Let me go, asshole." I jerk my hand away, and this time, it frees from his clutches.

But when I go to grab the handle of the door, I'm shoved backward. Losing my footing, I fall hard onto my ass.

"What the hell?"

I go to get up, but I'm pushed right back down.

My heart begins racing and the pitch-black room spins, even when I can't see a thing.

I can feel his presence lingering over me, and it's confirmed when he drops down, straddling my lap. "You're nothing but an entitled cunt."

"What are you doing?" I begin to panic. "Get off me."

"Tell me, Kit. Does this make your heart feel like it's gonna explode again? I mean, all it took was me looking at you last time."

"Get off me!"

I don't bother telling him my heart didn't explode and what happened had nothing to do with him. I save my breath and fight like hell as he lifts my skirt up and grinds his cock on me through his game pants.

Warm breath hits my ear, and he whispers, "You wanna know a secret?"

"No, I want you to get the hell off me." My legs flail, hips bucking, doing everything I can to get out from underneath him, but he's too strong. His hold on my hands that are pinned over my head is too tight.

"I didn't wanna take your maimed ass to the dance anyways."

"Good! Now let me go so you can go find another date."

His hand trails up my inner thigh, fingers teetering with my panties.

"I hope I didn't give you too big of a head because I'm about to deflate it. "It was a bet. And because of you, I lost."

A bet?

I stop moving. Stop trying to fight him off as I listen to what he has to say.

"Yeah, that's right. Liza bet me the homecoming crown that I couldn't get you to go as my date. And now, because you decided to be a selfish bitch, I have to turn down the crown as king tomorrow when it's offered to me. You see what the fuck you've done? I mean, what will my parents say when I do that? What will the student body think?"

His fingers dip beneath my panties and I take in a ragged breath. "Please stop."

"I know one thing, if I lose that crown, I'm taking something else in return."

Something strange happens to my body. Instead of my normal rapid heart rate, it feels faint—absent. Like I don't have a heartbeat at all.

CHAPTER
THIRTY-FOUR
RYKER

I know she's here. Unfortunately, I can't find my fucking phone, so I can't call her.

"Hey," I grab a guy by the back of his shirt, "gimme your phone."

Without a fight, he reaches into his pocket and hands it to me. I tap in her number quickly and it starts ringing. Five rings later, I'm sent to voicemail, so I end the call and hand it back to him.

"Thanks, man. Have you seen Kit Levine around by any chance?"

"Uh no. Sorry."

I tip my chin and keep walking, asking everyone I pass if they've seen her.

Finally, progress is made.

"She went upstairs with Asher about fifteen minutes. Lucky girl."

My heart jumps into my throat and I push through about three dozen people to get to the staircase. Skipping over two steps at a time, I fly up them.

I don't know what room is his, so I knock on them all, pushing each one open.

"Kit," I say each time I look into an empty room.

I come to another and knock, and this one's locked. I knock my knuckles to the door brashly. "Kit, are you in there?"

There's some shuffling and mumbles, but I can't make out anything. "Kit," I say again, now pounding on the door.

Still nothing.

I step back, turn to my side, and slam my body against the door. Over and over again, until it busts open.

First, I see her. Second, I see him.

Asher steps aside, chest puffed out like he's ready to fight. And fight he will.

"You okay?" I ask a sobbing Kit, who's sitting on the floor adjusting her cheer outfit.

She shakes her head no.

"What the fuck did you do to her?" I lunge at Asher, taking him straight down to the floor. "If you touched her, I swear to fucking God I will kill you."

I raise my fist to punch him, but before I make contact, I hear Kit.

"I don't feel good, Ryker."

"This isn't over." I jump off him and I'm back at her side. "What's wrong, baby?"

"I…I don't know."

"Okay. Take a deep breath. You're gonna be all right. I'm here and I'm not going anywhere. Just look at me. Focus on me."

Her body trembles in my arms as her beautiful eyes hold tight to mine.

"We need to get you to the hospital." Any other person could sit this one out and take a minute to collect themselves. Kit isn't any other person. She's got a heart condition that requires immediate care when shit like this happens.

To my surprise, she nods in agreement before her body goes limp. Panic ensues. "Kit! Stay with me. Keep your eyes open. Look at me, baby."

Scooping her in my arms, I cradle her like a baby and rush her out. Knowing that I'll be back for that fucker who did this to her.

CHAPTER
THIRTY-FIVE
KIT

"There you are," Ryker says, brushing his fingers across my cheek. "Way to scare the shit out of me."

My smile pushes the tubes in my nose that are feeding me oxygen. "I'm sorry."

"Don't you dare apologize. If anything, that asshole Asher needs to apologize, but I won't even let him near you to get the chance."

I'm not sure what happened, but once again, Ryker saved me. Just like the first time when he woke me from my coma and I didn't even know it.

"Am I going to be okay?"

"Yeah, baby. The doctor said your blood pressure and oxygen dropped, but it's moving in the right direction."

"My phone?" I begin patting at the mattress and lifting the sheet. "I need to text Kaylee and let her know I'm all right."

"Right here." Ryker hands it to me.

I send Kaylee a quick text, letting her know I'm fine and got a ride home. She's probably three sheets to the wind and won't read it for hours.

Dr. Hans steps around the curtain. "Good evening, Kit."

I shift in my bed uncomfortably. The last thing I want is for Dr.

Hans to give me a lecture while Ryker is sitting right beside me. "Wha…what are you doing here?"

"I happened to be in the hospital for an emergency surgery when I heard one of my patients was brought in. Heard you had quite the night?"

"Yeah," I say, ready to jump to my own defense, "but it was just my blood pressure. I'm okay now."

I want to ask him to have the nurse take the oxygen off and start up my paperwork, so I can go home—with Ryker.

"We ran some tests and your BNP levels are elevated more so than they've been in the past. The nurse will be in soon to get you hooked up with the EKG and I'd also like to get another echocardiogram while you're here. At this point, I think it's best you stay a few nights, so we can monitor your—"

"No," I gasp, "I'm not staying. I wanna go home."

"Just listen to him, Kit. He knows what he's talking about."

"No," I say again. "I know my body and I'm fine. I'd like to leave. It was a panic attack from a tense situation. I'm okay now."

Dr. Hans continues, as if he was never even interrupted, "We'd like to monitor you so we can adjust your medications accordingly. You're okay this time, but next time, you might not be so lucky. It's important to get you on the right regimen."

I look at Ryker, and it's obvious in his expression that he's stunned. "What's he talking about?"

"Nothing. He's just doing his job. I'm okay. I promise."

I just want to go home. I hate hospitals—the smell, the awful feeling in the pit of my stomach, the impending death of patients. It's depressing, and staying even one night makes me feel like I'm going to vomit. "Can I just make an appointment to talk in your office next week?"

"I can't make the decision for you, but I highly recommend you stay here for at least twenty-four hours. For your own sake."

"I'll call the office Monday morning."

Dr. Hans tips his chin. "Okay then. We'll talk soon. Until then,

I will be calling in a prescription to reduce the water weight and swelling."

"Okay. Thank you."

Ryker holds a disturbed look on his face. "I'm okay," I tell him.

I need him to believe I'm okay because, if he doesn't, I can't either.

CHAPTER THIRTY-SIX
RYKER

Kit has made it a point not to call her dad or Carter, and so far, I've obliged. It's been three hours, and it's only a matter of time before they find out she's here and I'd prefer they don't hear it in passing from someone at the party.

I asked the cardiologist so many questions, but I wasn't given one single answer. Instead, I made Kit tell me. I'm not sure I got the whole truth, but three months ago, Dr. Hans was straight forward with her and said if she kept ignoring her condition, she was risking her life.

Thank God, I found her in Asher's room, or this might be another thing swept under the table and ignored. Now that I know, I plan to do everything in my power to keep her healthy.

"Excuse me," the nurse says, "I've got Kit's discharge papers."

"She's going home?"

The nurse shrugs a shoulder with a raised eyebrow. "She wants to leave and we can't force her to stay."

"Take me home," Kit says through a bated breath with one eye open. "I wanna leave."

I take the papers from the nurse and hand them to Kit as she scoots into a sitting position. She scribbles her name on one that states the hospital and doctors aren't responsible for anything that happens when she leaves, then hands it back to the nurse.

Twenty minutes later, we're in an Uber headed to her place.

I place a hand on her shaky leg, wanting to ask what I walked in on in Asher's room, but I'm not sure it's the right time. So I start with, "Do you wanna talk about it?"

"Well," she begins, "apparently Asher Collins had zero interest in me, thank God."

She's still gazing out the car window when I look at her. "What makes you say that? The guy's been manhandling you all week."

"It was all for show." She exhales a heavy breath and looks at me. "Turns out, him asking me to the dance was just a bet. Spoiler alert, he lost."

The expression on my face says all I need to say. *I'll fucking kill him. With my bare hands. I'll strangle the life right out of him.*

"Yep," she continues, "when I tried to tell him I wasn't going to the dance, he took me to his room and proceeded to feel me up while belittling me. That's when the anxiety attack came on."

I clench my fists, jaw locked tight. *He's a dead man.* I try to hold it together for Kit's sake. She's been through a lot tonight, but there's no way in hell that fucker is getting away with this.

"It's over now. Asher will get what's coming to him."

She shakes her head. "Nah. Just leave it alone. Last thing I want is attention on me, especially when it comes to Asher Collins."

"You can't seriously be considering letting him get away with this."

"I am. Because I really don't care. I got out unscathed, and eventually karma will handle the rest."

I don't ask about the game when he swept her into his arms. I don't even mention it. I know Kit has no interest in that guy, and if he's ever a problem again, I'll handle it myself.

We pull into Kit's driveway, and she takes care of paying the driver on the app on her phone since I still can't find mine.

As we're walking up the driveway, I take her hand in mine and stop her. "I should probably get going. I don't think it's a good idea for me to come inside."

Her lips tip into a frown. "What? No. I want you here. We still have so much to talk about."

"We've got tomorrow and every day after that."

"Please, Ry. I don't wanna be alone."

"Where's Carter?"

"On some business trip in Harbor City."

"Your dad?"

"Well, he's here, but he's probably working in his office."

Staring over her shoulder, I look at the place that was home all of last week and one I wish I could say still felt like it. Truth is, I feel like a stranger more than I ever have and I'm only standing in the driveway.

I do want to make sure she's okay tonight. After everything I heard from the cardiologist, I think Kit and I have a lot more to talk about than just us.

"Okay. Go to your room and I'll be there in a minute."

I press a chaste kiss to her cheek, and she narrows her eyes. "But I thought…"

"I'm coming. I'll stay until you're asleep."

Kit goes inside and I walk around the side of the house and into the backyard. It only takes a second for me to get to her bedroom window. It's best this way. If her dad sees me coming in, he'll likely pitch a fit and Kit doesn't need the added stress right now.

Déjà vu hits me all at once. It's been years since I've been at this window. This time, I'll be greeted with the grown-up version of Carter's little sister, who once had a mouth full of metal and pimples on her face.

Once her light comes on, I tap the window gently.

And there she is. The girl I loved then and the woman I'm in love with now.

Kit slides the window up, with the little strength she has, and offers me her hand. I can't help but laugh that she thinks she can actually pull me through this window.

"What?" she asks, innocence in her tone.

"Step to the side, Girl Scout. I've got this."

With my palms on the ledge, I push myself up and fling my legs over until I'm in her room—standing this time.

"I'm impressed. Usually your landing isn't so graceful."

"Crazy how things change, isn't it?" I tackle her around the waist and fall onto the bed, my body cloaking hers.

Our lips brush. "Get some sleep. You need it."

Dopey eyes peer up at me. "Stay with me?"

"Until you're asleep. The last thing I need to do is piss off your old man any more than I already have.

She obliges and curls around me.

I roll to my side and slip my arm under her head, pulling her close until she's resting on my chest. She doesn't even get a chance to change out of her cheer uniform before she falls asleep. Next thing I know, my tired eyes are closing, too.

CHAPTER
THIRTY-SEVEN
CARTER

"I DON'T FEEL GOOD, CARTER. MY TUMMY IS ANGRY."

"I know, Kit. You just need rest. How about if I warm you up some magic soup that will make it all better."

Her eyes widen with wonder. "You have magic soup?"

"Of course I do. Big brothers have a secret recipe for magic soup that makes everything feel better."

"Okay." She nods, her rosy cheeks lifted by the smile on her face. "I'll eat some of your magic soup."

When she's not looking, I open a can of chicken noodle soup and dump it into a ceramic bowl and stick it in the microwave.

"What are you doing, sweetie?" Gail asks as she joins me in the kitchen.

"Kit's not feeling good. I'm making her some soup."

Gail wraps an arm around my head and pulls me close to her. "You are the best big brother in the world, Carter Levine. Always looking out for your sister."

"It's my job. I'll always make sure Kit's safe and happy."

She ate that soup, and I kept her trust. Kit's always hung on my every word. At least, she did. Somewhere between then and now, she grew a voice of her own and boy does she use it. I'm glad she has because she'll need it as she continues into adulthood.

I just want her to be happy and safe. Deep down, I think I knew that she would end up with Ryker. He's always been so good to her. Like a second big brother. He'd never hurt her in the ways I've convinced myself he would. I guess part of me is being selfish because he's my best friend and she's my sister. I feel betrayed. Left out and abandoned.

But it doesn't have to be like that. Nothing has to change.

She's still Kit and he's still Ryker, and me, well, I'm still the overprotective brother who wants to shield her from pain. I love them both, more than anything, and I don't want to be the person standing in the way of their happiness. I want to stand by their sides and cheer them on. She's not a little kid anymore and it's time to let her go. Even if it means she'll run into the arms of my best friend.

It's eight o'clock in the morning, and I'm sure Ryker's ass is still in bed, but it's worth a shot.

Since I bailed on a meeting during mine and Dad's trip to New York, I was forced to sit through an eight-hour seminar in Harbor City, which is a three-hour drive. Sheer exhaustion from listening to a lecture last night on profit margins had me in a hotel room the minute I got out of the place. Now I'm heading home.

"Hey, Siri. Call Ryker."

"Calling Ryker. Is this correct?"

"Yes."

Dammit. Straight to voicemail.

I leave him a message, a lengthy one at that, and end the call.

Flipping my blinker, I turn left, headed home.

Now that I've had this change in my mindset, I need to tell him.

I can't wait to see the look on his face when I tell him I agree with what he said—love doesn't need permission.

CHAPTER
THIRTY-EIGHT
KIT

Knock. Knock.
"Kit."
Knock. Knock. Knock.
"Kit."
Pound. Pound. Pound.

The sound of my bedroom door flying open and the wisp of wind on my face has me blinking an eye open. I immediately see Dad standing in the doorway with a pissed-off expression. "What the hell is Ryker doing in your bed?"

My hand shakes Ryker's chest, trying to wake him. "Ryker, wake up."

His lips smack together; his eyes open, then they *really* open, and he's on his feet in two seconds flat, and I can see his heart thudding through the fabric of his shirt.

"I'm sorry, sir. I brought Kit home last night and planned on—"

"Save it," Dad seethes as he crosses the room with heavy steps. "Get your shit and get out. Kit, we need to go."

"Go? Where?" My voice is almost breathless, probably because my brain is still fuzzy as I try to catch up with what's going on.

Ryker snatches his keys off my nightstand, and I blurt out, "Wait. Don't go."

"We have to go, Kit. Now."

"Go where?" I lash out. "It's nine o'clock in the morning.

Ryker looks down at his feet, awaiting instruction, or approval. But right now, I just want him to stay.

"We got the page, Kit. You have a match."

My entire body breaks out in chills. "I got a match?"

"We won't have any details until we get to the hospital, so we need to go. Now."

"Wait," Ryker cuts in, "are you…are you saying that Kit's getting a new heart?"

"That's exactly what he's saying. But I'm not sure I'm ready."

Dad careens toward my side and sits down on the bed. "What are you talking about? Of course you're ready. This new heart will give you many years to live a full life of happiness. College, marriage, babies."

I look over at Ryker, who appears to be in a state of shock. Just yesterday, he found out how sick I really am, and now he's hearing my heart will be replaced.

Ryker steps forward and voices his opinion. "Do it, Kit. It's a gift you can't refuse."

This is too sudden. Dr. Hans and everyone else said it could be years, if ever. He said I'm a status-six patient on the registry, which means I'm low priority. He always made it sound like I wasn't critical—or not *as* critical as other patients on the donor list.

I'm scared. Every limb on my body trembles with fear of the unknown.

"What if…what if I don't survive the transplant? What if my body rejects the heart?" I begin sobbing uncontrollably.

"We can assess our options at the hospital, but we need to go now." Dad offers me a hand, but all I can focus on is Ryker.

"Come with us. Please."

Ryker shares a glance with my dad, who nods his head, and a

sense of relief washes over me. There's no way I could even consider doing this without him there.

"Pack a bag and meet me downstairs in twenty minutes. You've been instructed to have no food or drink." Dad pulls me in for a hug, and I lose it in his arms. "It's going to be okay, Kit. This is a good thing."

He steps back, gives me a tipped smile, then leaves my room. As he goes to close the door, he steals a glance at Ryker, before pushing it all the way open.

The minute he's out of sight, Ryker sits down on the bed, and I fall apart in his arms, the same way I did Dad's. "I'm so scared."

"I know you are, baby. But like your dad said, this is a good thing."

"If my body were to be healthy, it wouldn't need a major part replaced. I told you, Ry. I'm broken and weak."

"No," he disputes, "you're neither of those things. You're one of the strongest girls I know. We all have weaknesses beneath the surface. But your broken parts are the other half to mine, so I need you to do this. For us."

We were given twenty minutes, so I use every last second letting Ryker hold me, while I'm still me. Because in the not-so-distant future, the heart that fell in love with him will be ash and a new one will take its place.

CHAPTER
THIRTY-NINE
RYKER

After Kit's dad demanded I stay in the waiting room, she threw a fit and insisted I come with her. She's stubborn as hell and I need her to use that trait while she recovers from surgery.

I walk in her room and see her hooked up to a bunch of different monitors. Lab techs have come and gone. Doctors have been in and out, and it feels like a scene straight out of *Grey's Anatomy*. I've masked my own worries and held it together the best I can, but the truth is, I'm scared to death.

All this chaos of preparation, and she's still on the fence about the transplant.

"I don't think I can do it. I'm so damn scared, Ry."

There's a knock at the door before Kit's cardiologist, Dr. Hans, steps into the room. He doesn't seem concerned in the least. In fact, he's much too mellow, given the situation.

"And we meet again," he says, smiling broadly as if our worlds aren't about to change. How can he be so calm and collected at a time like this? Doesn't he know that the girl I love is putting her life at risk, just to have more time on this earth?

Of course he does. This is his job. He knows exactly what he's doing, and I need to trust in that.

"You know," Dr. Hans continues, "when we got you registered on the list last year and met with your transplant team, in the back of my head I thought, she'll never get the call. A young girl full of life with a heart that just can't keep up. But we did it because there is always a chance. You, Kit, are very lucky. This is a rarity and now I will say what's on my mind. Don't pass it up because, chances are, you won't get this opportunity again."

"But what if my body rejects the heart? What if I don't survive the procedure?" She asks all the questions and voices each and every concern she had back at her house.

Dr. Hans does a good job of informing her of the risks, but an even better job of telling her why it's worth it. In the end, even I'm convinced.

"So. Are we doing this?" He asks the question still lingering around us.

Kit looks at me, searching for the answer, but I can't make the choice for her. Instead, I reach into the inside pocket of my jacket, bypassing a lighter and grabbing a candy bar. I pull it out, peel her fingers back, and set the candy bar in her palm. "Do it. I dare you."

Even in this time of complete and utter hell, she manages a smile. Her hand squeezes the candy bar as she is forced to make a life-or-death decision. One that has a time limit. One that can pass her by if she doesn't answer immediately.

"Dare accepted," she says with a glint of adoration on her face before turning to Dr. Hans. "Let's do this."

I swipe the tears from her cheek and lean forward, pressing my lips to her forehead. "That's my girl."

"Okay," Dr. Hans smiles widely. "We have to take you to run some tests." He looks at Mr. Levine. "We'll notify you once we have the go-ahead and you'll get to see her before she goes into surgery."

I lean down and whisper, "Don't think of this as a big thing. Think of it as one of those little things that eventually becomes something huge."

She nods her head against my lips pressed to her forehead. "I love you."

"I love you, too."

Suddenly, papers are shoved at her, and with shaky hands, she signs her life away. It all happens so fast. The next thing I know, she's being pulled away with my hand still holding hers. We're being pulled farther and farther apart, until our fingers slip, and all she's holding is the candy bar I gave her. "I love you," I tell her.

"I love you, too."

Once she's gone, I lose it. My back hits the wall, my face in my hands, and I cry like a fucking baby. I've never been the religious type, but I beg and I plead with God to get her through this.

A hand on my shoulder has my head shooting up, and I see Kit's dad. "Thank you," he says, sincerely.

"For what?"

"Convincing her. Had you not, she wouldn't have done it. Kit thinks she's got all the time in the world. Now, thanks to you, she's got more time."

"But what if…" I can't even say it.

He shakes his head. "We're not going to think like that. Now, could you do me a favor and call Carter? I haven't even had a chance to let him know what's going on."

"Yeah. Yeah, of course."

Mr. Levine tips his head in an unspoken, *thanks*, then leaves the room.

Since I don't have my cell phone and I've had no luck tracking it down, I use the bedside phone.

I take a minute to clear my head before making the call, reminding myself that Kit is in good hands and she's gonna pull through this.

Lifting the phone, I tap in Carter's number, and after a few rings, I get his voicemail.

"Hey. I know I'm the last person you wanna hear from, but please call your dad. It's about Kit… I miss you, man."

I shake my head, warding off the tears as my emotions resurface.

An hour later and there are still no updates. I'm getting really fucking antsy and the four cups of coffee I've had aren't helping in the least. Well, they're keeping me awake, but certainly not calming my nerves.

I'm at the coffee station, filling my fifth cup, when I see Mr. Levine pacing behind a row of empty chairs, talking on his phone. He wipes his hand across his forehead and ends the call, but then stares at the phone for a minute.

I continue to watch him as I stir the sugar into my coffee, then drop my stick in the trash. "Everything all right?" I ask, now standing six feet in front of him.

He lifts his head from his phone and gives me a perplexed look. I can tell he's as tired as I am, and I'm tempted to offer him my coffee. "I'm not sure. That was Sheriff Meyers. Said he needed to talk to me immediately. I told him I couldn't leave the hospital because Kit is heading into surgery. He's on his way here."

"What could the sheriff possibly want that's so important?"

Mr. Levine stuffs his phone in the pocket of his gray slacks and clasps his hands behind his back. "I don't know, Ryker. Maybe you could tell me."

"Me?" I clap a hand to my chest. "I didn't do anything. I've walked the straight and narrow since I've been back in town." Well, aside from sleeping with his daughter, threatening a high school punk countless times, and drinking as a minor. But that's all harmless shit.

"I suppose we'll just have to wait and see." He moves past me and heads for the coffee station on the back wall.

We could be here for hours, so I decide to make myself comfortable on a chair in front of the television. The late morning news is on, but the sound is muted. It looks like some gruesome footage of a deadly crash. Next up, women who kill their lovers.

Okay, then. I slap my hands to my legs. I've had enough of this depressing shit. I get back on my feet, wishing I had my damn phone, so I could try Carter again.

After pacing the room a few dozen times, passing by a vending machine, a woman consoling a crying baby, and a dripping sink, I decide to go on the hunt for a phone.

I could go out to the reception area and ask to use the phone there and try Carter again, and call Kaylee to let her know what's going on.

Screw it. I'll just suck it up and ask Mr. Levine to use his phone again. Who knows, maybe he's reached Carter by now.

Instead of turning to do another lap around the room, I walk out the open door. Stopping in the doorway, I look left then right.

Where'd he go?

I spot one of the nurses at the station, who was doing vitals on Kit before she went for her testing.

"Excuse me," I say, grabbing her attention. She lifts her head from the computer screen. "Have you seen the man I was with earlier, Kit Levine's dad?"

"I believe he's with his son."

Oh, thank God. Carter's here.

"Do you know where they went?"

"Room 121, but I believe it's family only at this time."

Kit's back from her tests and no one fucking told me. Dammit. What if I miss seeing her before she goes into surgery?

I tap the desk and say, "Thanks," before walking briskly down the hall to Room 121.

Family only, my ass. No one is going to stop me from seeing her before she goes under. She's scared to death right now and I need to be there to comfort her.

I don't even knock on the door, out of worry someone will tell me I can't come in. As soon as it opens, my heart sinks.

My mouth opens to speak, but the words don't come out.

Mr. Levine looks over his shoulder. His eyes brimmed with tears and his skin ghostly white. "Ryker." He takes three steps and throws himself into my arms like a child in need of comforting.

His sobs drown out the thoughts in my head and my arms stay planted at my sides. My entire body is frozen solid.

"What...what the hell happened?" I swallow hard, trying to ask the dozens of questions going through my head. *Why is Carter lying in that bed? Why is he so bloody and bruised? Why are there tubes shoved down his throat?*

Why?

Why?

Why?

"He was in an accident."

An accident? My skin turns to ice—frozen, numb. My thoughts elude me, but I manage to say, "He's gonna be okay, though, right?" *What the hell am I thinking?* Of course he's not okay. I can see with my own eyes that he is definitely not okay.

He doesn't even have to say the words. I already know.

His head shakes slowly while his entire body trembles.

"No. No!" I raise my voice. "This can't be happening."

Mr. Levine tries to hold himself together while I completely let myself go.

"Fuck!" I fist my hair. I gasp for air. I cry and I fall to my knees on the floor of this hospital room. After a few minutes of internally begging for this to be a nightmare, I lift my head and see him wipe his shaky fingers across his damp eyes. "He's gone, Ryker. They're just keeping him alive because he's a registered donor."

"What?" My head doesn't stop shaking no.

No.

No.

No.

My eyes shoot wide open. "Wait. Does that mean...the heart that Kit's getting prepped to receive?"

"They won't say much except that he was a registered donor. It has to be for Kit. Carter registered as a donor with her named as the recipient of his heart, should anything ever happen to him. That must be why we're all here."

Some people come into the room—three, four of them. I don't get a good look. Don't even care. I can't think. I can't speak.

I just listen.

"Have you made a decision?" a lady in a dress suit asks with a clipboard in her hand.

"You're sure there's nothing you can do?" Mr. Levine looks over at his lifeless son, and I follow his train of sight.

"I'm sorry, sir. He's gone. We can keep him on the ventilator, but it's only prolonging the inevitable."

Mr. Levine breaks down. Dropping into a chair, face in his hands. I take a step toward him and place a hand on his back, trying to hold it together, because I might be losing my best friend, but he's losing his son.

Moments pass before he lifts his head and looks at me. "We need to do this." He nods. "It's what Carter would want."

I push down the lump in my throat and manage to say, "I agree."

Mr. Levine goes over some things with the other people in the room while I go over to Carter's bedside.

"Fuck, man. Why?" I lift his hand, his broken, bloodied hand. "This isn't fucking fair."

Dammit. Let me trade places with him. Let him live. Take me instead and give Kit my fucking heart. If only it were that easy.

"We never got to fix this shit between us. I didn't get to tell you I fucking love you, man." Tears skate down my cheeks, dropping onto my hand that's squeezing his.

"He knows." I look to my left and see Mr. Levine. The room has emptied and it's just us. "He knows we all loved him."

We both stand there looking at Carter. Staring at this beautiful young man whose life was taken too soon. Everything is suddenly put into perspective. They say life is short, but you never know how short it really is.

"We can't tell her yet," he finally says, after long minutes of silence.

I look at him with questioning eyes, and he continues, "Kit. We can't tell her until after the transplant. She'll be mad, but she'll be alive, and that's all that matters."

"I think that's a good plan. As much as I hate the secrecy, it's far too much for her to handle right now. Kit's stubborn and we can't risk her rejecting the heart, thinking that Carter is being taken off life support just so she can have it."

A nurse comes in the room, joined by the chaplain, who asks if he can pray with us before the machines are shut off.

With me on one side, Mr. Levine on the other, we hold tight to Carter's hands while the chaplain lays his hand on Carter's chest.

"God, thank you for being with us in this time of need. We admit we do not know why things happen the way they do, but we trust in your plan. We know you are walking with Carter right now. Please be with Carter's family and grant them strength for the days ahead. We trust in you. In Jesus's name, we pray. Amen."

"Amen."

I've never been a religious person, but I felt that prayer deep inside me. Almost as if it offered a sense of peace.

We're asked to leave the room for a few minutes, and when we return, Carter is no longer hooked up to any monitors. There are no more tubes in him. He's just lying there. Peaceful. Still.

Mr. Levine and I reclaim our spots on either side of the bed, and we watch and wait.

Only a couple minutes later, he's gone.

I squeeze his hand, lean down, and whisper, "Thank you for being the best fucking friend in the world. And thank you for the gift you've given Kit."

As much as I don't want to leave, I have to. Mr. Levine needs his own time to say goodbye to his son.

I'm standing outside the room, barely keeping it together. Long, torturous minutes pass that feel like hours. Then the door opens and I pull myself together and console the man who just lost his son.

We stand there, holding each other up in front of the hospital door, with Carter on the other side. Eventually, a team of people force us away, and we're notified that we can see Kit again.

She's in a different room this time, on a different floor, so we take the elevator up.

We reach Kit's room and Mr. Levine pushes it open, steps aside, and lets me enter first. As soon as the door opens, I see her beautiful face.

A smile parts her lips while her dad and I make every attempt to hide our emotions. None of this feels real. Not a damn thing.

"I guess it's time," she says.

"Yeah, baby. It's time. And you're gonna do great. We'll be here waiting for you when you wake up."

Her dad kisses her forehead and tells her how proud of her he is for being so strong, then steps back. I do the same, telling her I love her.

Then, it's go time.

CHAPTER FORTY
RYKER

"You know sitting on your ass, starving yourself isn't doing anyone any good."

I lift my tired eyes and see Coach. My body reacts, and I jump to my feet and pull him in for a hug.

He's this big, burly beast who has a way of making the worries of the world disappear, only to bring them front and center again and remind us why things have to get worse before they get better.

This time, I'm not so sure that analogy will work. That things will get better.

"I'm sorry to hear about Carter." His words cut deep because hearing them out loud make this nightmare all the more real.

I don't say anything; I just close my eyes and let him pat my back in that fatherly way he always did when I was in high school.

"He's not going far. His heart will continue to beat inside his sister."

Gerald contacted someone who confirmed that it was, in fact, Carter's heart that was donated. I still can't wrap my head around it all.

I know Coach's words are supposed to make me feel better,

but right now, it just makes everything worse. Maybe because it's true and I don't want to face the truth. Not yet. Right now, I'd just like to pretend he's out there, making his way to us.

We separate and sit down on a couple chairs in the waiting room.

"Any word on Kit yet?" he asks.

"Nothing. I wish they'd give an update or something."

"Kit Levine is one hell of a girl. She'll pull through this and be just fine."

I quirk a brow. "Didn't know you knew her well."

"I didn't. Just through Carter. He'd talk about her often. I remember the time he told me she stole his car after her license was taken away, just so she could go to Tasty Dip and get an ice cream cone."

A smile draws on my face. "Sounds like Kit."

"She's gonna need you. Together, you two will always be connected through Carter. Lean on her and let her lean on you."

Coach doesn't know anything about Kit and me—that I'm aware of—yet, he's talking like he's reading a page right out of our book.

My mouth opens to speak, but it quickly clamps shut when Mr. Levine says, "I got an alert. She's out of surgery."

I stand up, ready to go to her, even though I know damn well I won't be seeing her for a while. She'll have to go into recovery for a couple hours and wake up. "Any news on how she's doing?"

"I imagine the doctor will come in soon with an update." Until then, we sit and wait.

And we wait.

Mom comes by and offers her condolences. She hugs me and I lose it all over again. Then I go back to being numb while we wait some more.

The minutes pass slowly.

Those minutes turn into an hour.

That hour turns into another.

Finally, Dr. Hans comes in.

His eyes immediately find Mr. Levine's, but I join his side to hear everything he has to say.

"She did good."

Thank God. I breathe a sigh of relief, and some of the tension in my body dissipates.

"We didn't encounter any complications. So far her body has accepted the new heart—"

"So far?" I cut him off. "What's that mean?"

"Well, rejection can happen at any point, which is why she'll be on immunosuppressants for the duration of her life, as well as some other vital medications. Now, I'm sure you're both aware that we're dealing with a strong-willed girl here."

Mr. Levine and I share a glance. "We're well aware," he says.

"There's a support group, Hands on Hearts, on the third floor of the hospital that meets weekly, and it'd be beneficial for Kit's support system to attend. You'll learn ways to help her through the road ahead."

"I'll be there," I blurt out, warranting a surprised look from Mr. Levine.

"Me, too," he says, and I'm also surprised, given his heavy work schedule. Maybe that'll change now that his entire life has been flipped upside down. Kit's all he's got left in this world.

Dr. Hans continues to go over some information about the transplant and Kit's stay in the hospital. It looks like she'll be here for at least a couple weeks, and that's assuming no complications arise.

He leaves to go grab info on the support group, and I drop down in a chair out of sheer exhaustion. None of this even feels real.

"You know," Mr. Levine begins, taking the seat beside me. The hollowness of his eyes shows his age and the bags under them prove he's just as worn out, if not more, than I am. "You don't have to go to that group. I can take care—"

"I want to." I straighten my back in the seat, hands planted on my upper legs. "I wanna do everything I can to help her."

"If this is about you feeling some sort of obligation since Kit got Carter's heart, then you're freed from it."

"No." I shake my head in disbelief at his words. "This isn't about the heart or Carter; this is about my heart and where it lies with Kit. I love her, Mr. Levine. Always have and always will."

There's a long beat of silence before he asks, "Why do you call me Mr. Levine? I've known you since you were, what, seven years old? Why not call me Gerald?"

That's an odd question, given the situation. Regardless, I answer it. "Respect, I guess." I shrug a shoulder. "And to be honest, you've always intimidated me, so it felt safer to call you Mr. Levine."

"Seems Kit wants you around for a while, so how about if we start over with Gerald." His hand slaps over mine, patting it a couple times, before he stands.

My head's been in a fog all day, so it's very possible I'm misconstruing what he said, but to me, it sounds like acceptance.

"Kit's going to be in recovery for a while. I have to leave and take care of a couple things. Call me immediately if anything changes."

"Yeah. Of course."

When he leaves, someone else comes in—or runs, rather.

"Oh my God, Ryker. Where is she? How is she?" Kaylee is a mess. Tear-stained cheeks, puffy eyes, even her hair is matted. And she's still wearing her cheer uniform from the game last night.

"She's okay. Transplant was a success and she's heading into recovery."

"Thank God." She sobs, throwing herself into my arms and soaking the sleeve of my shirt, infusing it with the scent of tequila from last night's festivities. "I heard about Carter. I'm shattered. It doesn't even feel real."

"Tell me about it."

Kaylee takes a step back and wipes the back of her hand across her nose. "Does she know?"

I shake my head slowly. "Not yet."

More time passes, and somehow, I manage to drift off to sleep in the waiting room chair. Kaylee has done the same. She hasn't left since she got here.

Gerald returns, and just as he does, we're told that Kit is on the sixth floor in the ICU and can have visitors now.

Without a single wasted second, we all head up.

We're in the elevator when Gerald reaches into his pocket and pulls out a phone—my phone. "Found this in the garage when I went home. You musta dropped it during your quarrel with Carter. Battery's dead, so it needs a charge."

My quarrel with Carter. The last time I saw him and a memory that will forever be etched in my mind. He died hating me, and that is something I will carry with me for the rest of my life.

We get to Kit's room, and she's sound asleep. All three of us surround her bed and watch her as if she's this rare life-form. Every sound she makes has us springing to our feet. Every movement has us anxiously waiting to see those beautiful blue eyes.

We decided not to tell her about Carter—not yet. Kit's body has been through so much trauma today and it's best to keep her as calm as possible. Until then, we just pretend. And I'm okay with that, because pretending sounds pretty damn good to me.

CHAPTER
FORTY-ONE
KIT

Where am I?

What happened?

My head turns left, then right, as I try to focus my eyes on my surroundings.

I'm in a hospital.

I lift my arm, seeing the tubes in it. Then the other. More tubes.

My fingers fidget with my face and I find more running into my nose.

I'm in the hospital.

That's right. I had surgery.

I pat at my chest, but a hand over mine stops me. "Careful, baby. You've got some hefty staples there."

"Ryker." My voice is hoarse and my throat feels like I've swallowed sandpaper. I wrap my fingers around his, holding tight. "You're here."

"Of course I'm here. I wouldn't be anywhere else."

"My dad?"

"He's here, too."

"Carter?"

"He wants to be. But, he's not here yet, Kit-Kat."

My shoulders hunch in disappointment. "He must be busy with school or work."

It's no secret that my dad has spent the majority of my life working—for good reason, since he's the sole provider and an only parent—and now it seems Carter is following in his footsteps. Part of me is angry that he's not here on one of the most crucial days of my life.

Dad steps forward. "Ryker, do you mind giving me a minute alone with my daughter?"

"Sure." Ryker squeezes my hand. "I'll be right outside the door."

Ryker leaves and Dad takes a seat on the edge of the bed. With a downcast gaze, he takes both of my hands in one of his. "I'm proud of you, Kit." I can clearly see that this is painful for him. His Adam's apple bobs in his throat and he chokes back tears.

"Hey. I'm okay, Dad."

He nods, eyes set on our clasped hands. "I know." He swallows hard, sniffles, and tightens his hold on me. "Things are gonna change, Kit. The long hours at work, the frequent traveling. It's gonna change."

"Where is this coming from, Dad? I'm fine. I promise."

Was there a device implanted inside of me that allows people to read my mind, because I swear it's like he heard my internal thoughts right before Ryker left.

"You always say that."

"Because it's true. I don't want you worrying about me."

His eyes lift to mine. "It's my job to worry about you, and you have to let me in, honey. I can't help you if you don't let me."

It hurts to hear him talk like this. Sure, I've kept him in the dark about a few of my health issues, but it's because I didn't want to see him like this. Sitting here in anguish because of his worry over me. I don't want that burden on anyone I love.

"You have to let me in because this new heart needs to be taken care of. No more pretending. No more secrets. Can you do that for me, Kit?"

I spent an entire three months researching heart transplants once I was registered on the list. I know that it's not as simple as just getting a healthy heart. It requires care and consideration in everything I do. Dad's right. No more pretending. If I do this right, I can live a normal, healthy life. It might not be as long as I'd like, but it beats the alternative with my old, broken heart.

"Yeah, Dad," I say. "I can do that."

His lips press to my forehead. "We'll do it together. Me, you, and Ryker."

"And Carter."

His lips freeze on my forehead. "And Carter."

"Wait a minute," I spit out. "Did you just say *Ryker*?"

Last thing I knew, Carter and my dad were anti-Ryker. They were entirely against us being together and ready to kick Ryker right out of our lives.

"I did. I stood back and I watched the way he was with you. Saw the way your presence lit up his eyes. The concern for your safety. He loves you."

"I love him, too, Dad."

My heart—my new heart—jumps a beat. There's warmth in it. A feeling of contentment. Almost like it was always meant to be mine. I can't wait to find out who it came from, so I can meet their family and thank them for this gift of life.

The next thing I know, the heavy moment passes between us and the door is flying open. "Kit. Oh, Kit." Kaylee hurries to my side, arms spread wide. As she comes in for a hug, Dad gets up just in time. Tears slide down her cheeks as she wraps her arms around me.

I squeal a little from a sudden pain in my chest, and she jumps back. "Did I hurt you? Shit, Kit. I'm sorry." Her hands claps over her mouth and she turns to my dad. "Sorry for the language, Mr. Levine."

Dad chuckles. "It's all right, Kaylee. I'll give you two a minute."

Ryker

While I was waiting for Kit and her dad to have their time together, I managed to snag a charger from one of the nurses to plug my phone in.

As it was charging, Kaylee emerged, and I had to remind her that we're waiting to break the news about Carter. She understood, and she's in with her now.

I'm back at the nurses' station and my phone is charged enough to make a quick call to my mom to see if she and Ezra want to come by and have lunch in the hospital cafeteria tomorrow. This whole traumatic experience has taught me that life is too short to miss out on time with the people you love. I've already missed so much, but it ends now. My next step is to rebuild my relationship with my little brother and be the man in his life that he needs—the man I never had.

Everything still hurts. Nothing feels real. I'm almost positive my body has turned numb to avoid going into shock. But I'm grateful Kit's going to be okay.

I unplug my phone, thank the nurse, and walk over to the waiting area. Dropping down in a chair, I see Gerald come out of Kit's room. "Kaylee must be with her?"

"Yep. If anyone can lift her spirits, it's that girl. She's a firecracker."

I chuckle. "Yeah, she is."

I'm looking at my phone when I see that I have a voicemail from Carter.

Timestamp: 8:02 AM.

Today.

My entire body shivers.

Gerald woke us up at nine o'clock. Carter must've called right before the accident, at which point, they saw he was a donor and immediately contacted the family he was signed up to give his heart to—*his* family.

"Mr....err...Gerald." I wave him over, without lifting my eyes from my phone.

"Everything okay?"

I look up. "Carter called me." My voice shakes then cracks, and a lump lodges in my throat. "He called right before the accident."

His forehead wrinkles and his voice is feeble. "What did he say?"

"I haven't listened to it."

With a trembling finger, I press Play and put the message on speakerphone, fully prepared for it to be another lashing or threat to stay away from his sister.

"Hey, man."

Those first two words immediately cause my chest to cave in and I know listening to this will likely be one of the hardest things I've ever had to do in my life. Even more painful than taking a life. Second to what's coming when we tell Kit she lost her brother.

"Listen, I know we've had a really shitty week and I've said a lot of cruel things." He clears his throat. "But I've done a lot of thinking and self-reflecting on this trip. I'm sorry, Ryker. Sorry for the way I reacted, sorry for the things I said. I'm sorry I called you scum because you're anything but. You're tough as nails and as soft as a fucking teddy bear. Really just depends on the day and the situation." He laughs, and I find myself smiling in response to that sound. "The truth is, I look up to you. You've got a lot of the strengths that I lack, and one of them is your ability to see the best in people." There's an audible sigh before he continues, "She loves you, man. I see it now. Everything over the past thirteen years suddenly makes sense. You didn't come into my life for me; I was always just the stepping stone so you could get to the love of yours. Now, I'm not saying this means we're done being best fucking friends, because you're my ride or die."

I pause the message and take a minute. With my head hung

low, I fist my eyeballs, rubbing away the tears. I can't even look at Gerald.

A second later, once I've pulled myself together as much as I can, I tap Play again.

"Soulmates come in many different shapes and sizes, and I think your lucky ass was destined for two—me and her. So don't go making me a third wheel. We're no longer a duo but a trio. Look, I'm headed home, and I think we should talk about this face-to-face, knuckles down this time. I love you, brother." He laughs again. "Crazy, huh? One day you might actually be my brother. Don't go getting any ideas, though. We're still young and still have too much trouble to get into before getting the old ball and chain. Anyways, I'll talk to you soon."

The voicemail ends and I come unglued.

CHAPTER
FORTY-TWO

RYKER

Minutes turn to hours.

Hours turn to days.

Days filled with card games and small talk. Movies and ice cream cones. Laughter and tears, hugs and kisses. Visitors come and go. We moved floors, and she's out of the ICU, which is one step closer to her coming home.

And now…it's time to tell her.

You can only put someone off for so long before they become suspicious. It's been four days since Kit's transplant. Four days that we've lived in this world without Carter.

Carrying this pain and keeping this secret has been nothing short of torture for all of us.

Kit asks about him every day. She's tried calling him, left him more voicemails and text messages than I can count. Her dad told her he had to take a trip to the mountains and has no cell service, which is genius, but he's really fucking lucky Kit bought it because it's a little far-fetched. Regardless of what story he gave her, it would have been a lie either way.

A heavy, earth-shattering, life-altering lie.

"Carly and Micah came to see me earlier today," she says, laying down a red five card on the UNO deck.

"Oh yeah? How'd that go?"

"Really good, actually. They brought flowers and said the entire school now knows Asher is trash and apologized for any part they ever took in his antics. Apparently, at the dance, he accepted the crown that he was supposed to turn down from his loss in that stupid bet he had with Liza. Liza proceeded to tell the entire student body he assaulted an unnamed senior classmate."

My blood pumps to a boiling rage just thinking about what that fucker did to her. "Still don't think it's enough."

"It is for me. Like I said, karma will find him."

Gerald walks in the room, along with Kaylee, and our conversation ends abruptly.

We all talked and decided telling Kit about Carter would be best if she had her biggest support system at her side.

"UNO," Kit exclaims, slapping her second to last card on the bedside tray.

"Dammit." I draw and draw, until I finally have a card.

"Winner." She slams her last card down and dances with her shoulders.

"Hey, Kay. Wanna get your butt kicked at UNO? I'm on a roll."

"Yeah, babe. In a few, 'kay?"

"Okayyyy." Kit's eyes dance from person to person. "Why the glum expressions? Is this like an intervention or something? I swear I haven't asked the nurse to up my morphine all day."

God, I love her, and I hate what this is going to do to her.

Gerald lifts a smile and careens toward her bed. "Kit, there is something I…we have to tell you."

Her expression immediately drops to one of concern. "Is it the heart? Is my body—"

"No, honey." Gerald shakes his head. "Your heart is healthy. It's Carter."

Fuck. I can't do this. I turn around, fighting like hell not to break down. I can't look at her. I can't survive the pain she's about to feel.

"What's wrong with Carter?"

Kaylee shuffles over to the other side of the bed, while I'm over here being a coward.

Pull it together, Ryker. She needs you.

I turn back around and stand beside Kaylee, my hand rests on Kit's leg.

"He's gone, honey. Carter was…" Gerald's voice cracks and breaks, "he was killed in a car accident."

Fuuuuuuck!

It's silent. Too silent. I finally look at her face and my heart shatters into tiny pieces.

"You're lying." Her words are angry and accusatory. "Quit lying," she shouts.

Say something. Anything. "It's true, baby." The words just fall from my mouth and I barely recognize my own voice.

"He's gone?"

Gerald nods and I squeeze Kit's leg while Kaylee holds her hand tightly.

"His heart," Gerald begins, "his heart is still beating…inside you."

Kit jerks her hands away from her dad and her best friend and claps them over her chest. "I got his heart?" Her voice shifts and crackles. "But that was days ago."

"We all wanted to make sure you were strong enough to take the news," Kaylee says with a softness to her tone.

Then Kit loses it. Just like we all have done silently every day since Carter left us.

The sound of her harrowing cries slice through me with the tenacity of a serrated blade. I'd prefer the knife because it would be less painful than what I'm witnessing right now.

"Noooooo!"

I can't take it. I can't take it anymore. What I do is selfish, but I worm my way between her and Kaylee and I wrap my arms around Kit and I hold her for what feels like an eternity. I hold her while she screams, begs, and cries.

Time passes. I'm not sure how much, but it was long enough for Kit to cry herself to sleep. So I stay there and I watch her. I wait until she's ready to cry again because, when that time comes, I'll be the strength she needs to get through this battlefield.

CHAPTER
FORTY-THREE
RYKER

THREE WEEKS LATER

"This should be the last one," Buck says as he drops down the last box on my apartment floor. "Place is looking pretty damn good. Your granddad would be proud."

"Eh, I don't know about that. I can almost hear him screaming in my head, telling me to leave the original countertops and quit messing with his shit."

Buck snaps a finger. "Sounds just like that crazy bastard. Hey." His tone shifts, and he waves a hand over his shoulder as he turns around. "Why don't you come down to the shop for a minute? There's something I wanna show ya. I think you'll like it."

My eyebrows cave in a sideways glance. "Okay."

I follow Buck downstairs, feeling like I'm being set up or something, but I keep following him out the back door, without asking any questions.

Then I see it.

The Chevelle.

"No fucking way." My hands fly to my face and my chest tightens. "How? I sold this car."

"A couple calls and a few bucks, and we were able to bring her home where she belongs."

My legs go weak, so I press my back against the brick wall of the shop. "We?"

"This wasn't my doing. Gerald Levine came in last week for an oil change and we got to talking about you. The conversation ended with the Chevelle and how you sold it to keep the place afloat and fix up the apartment. He gave me a blank check to get it back."

I run my hands down my face, staring at the car in complete disbelief. My gaze slides to Buck, and I cock a brow. "Gerald did that?"

He nods.

"Wow. I…I don't even know what to say. Thank you, I guess. This is the best surprise…ever."

"Thought maybe you and your brother could work on it together. Ya know, give him some of those memories you had."

"Absolutely." I'm still in shock. All this time, I thought Gerald hated me, but this selfless gesture leads me to believe otherwise. Looks like I'll be giving him a great big thanks—even if it won't suffice.

I pull Buck in for a hug and we talk about the repairs needed on the car before I head back to my apartment.

Buck is more than just a mechanic in the shop. He's family. And we've now brought in a couple other guys to give us a hand part-time, who I'm hopeful will grow into being a part of the Dawson family as well. Leon, my buddy from high school, is one of them. Leon is also the one who helped me rough up Asher Collins while dishing out threats in the form of my fists. Needless to say, he won't bother Kit anymore.

Once Kit's settled and we start our new normal, I'll be working alongside Buck, as well as starting up the sales part of Dawson Auto Repair and Dealership.

I never wanted to be a mechanic, but sometimes things don't work out the way we planned. However, it's no excuse to stop chasing your dreams—even the ones that find you at three o'clock in the afternoon at a ring shop where you're trying to barter a deal. Turns out, I've got the gift of persuasion.

I stand in the middle of my small living space and look around, feeling pretty damn proud of myself, even if Granddad is rolling over in his grave with the changes to his place. It's a modern look. White walls, refinished, original hardwood. Everything is new and everything is clean.

"Shit." I glance down at my phone and see that it's almost time for Kit to get released. I can't wait for her to see the place. The majority of my time has been spent at the hospital while any spare time has been here.

I grab my keys off the counter and send Gerald a quick text, letting him know I'm on my way. We decided to save an argument on who she'll ride with and just ride together. We've butted heads a few times over Kit and her care, but for the most part, we've both been accommodating. It's a small step in the right direction. Obviously, Kit will be staying with her dad and I'll be living in my apartment, but I do plan to be there often while she continues to recover. Gerald also made it clear he won't be finding me in Kit's bed early in the morning. I can respect that. His house, his rules.

I make it to the house in record time and Gerald is already sitting in the driver's seat of his running truck. "About time," he says before my ass even hits the seat.

"Sorry. Got caught up with the renovations."

"How's that going for ya?"

"Good. Pretty much done, aside from replacing a couple windows."

"I remember drinking beer on the roof of that old building in high school with your uncle Greg." The corners of his eyes crinkle with his smile. "I'll have to stop by and see the place sometime."

"Yeah. Yeah, that would be nice." I'm surprised that he's even considering stopping by, then again, I shouldn't be. He did buy back my car for me. "Saw the Chevelle today. I don't know what to say. Thanks is hardly enough."

He doesn't look at me, just keeps his eyes on the road. "Thanks *is* enough."

A man of few words but somehow, they are always enough. "I'm gonna pay you back—"

"It's not even an option. Just promise me you'll take good care of my girl and we're even."

"Absolutely."

Gerald turns the radio up a bit and we make the rest of the drive in silence.

By the time we get to the hospital, Kit's already in a wheelchair, waiting at the doors with her team of doctors. They hug and bid her farewell, while I take the copious amounts of balloons, flowers, and stuffed animals and lug them to the back seat of the truck.

Gerald opens the door and gets Kit in the front seat and I take the back.

"How's it feel to be a free bird?" Gerald asks.

"Ugh," she blows out a heavy breath, "you have no idea how good it feels to be out of that place. I mean, the staff is great, but I felt like I was slowly losing my mind in there."

Gerald reaches over and squeezes the back of her neck. "I'm glad you're coming home. The place is too quiet without you."

There's a strained silence that has us all feeling a hint of sadness.

"So tomorrow's the celebration of life?" Kit asks, breaking said silence.

"Yeah. Just a nice get-together in the backyard. It's what Carter would have wanted. He always said he didn't want some sappy funeral where people cry. He preferred an event that brought people together to smile. Gail and some of her friends from church are handling all the food. Ryker put out an event on Facebook."

Kit twists her head to look at me. "You? Facebook?"

I throw up my hands. "What can I say? Someone told me I needed to get with the times."

She reaches her left hand back and I shift forward, so I can hold it in mine. "Next up. Instagram." She smirks. "But yes, I think that sounds like exactly what Carter would want."

This moment, her hand in mine, is an opportunity. I've already told Gerald about the ring and swore up and down that it's not a proposal; it's just a promise. After a couple hard glares and a few dozen questions, he finally said it would make Kit happy.

With her hand in mine, I reach into the pocket of my leather jacket and fumble with the ring box until the ring is out. Kit's none the wiser as I slide it on her finger. Once I push it down, she notices.

Pulling her hand back, she squeals. "What is this?"

Gerald shifts into park in the garage, not even realizing we were here already. "I'll be inside." He winks at Kit, and I see it as him offering his approval. "Holler if you need a hand getting out."

I open the back door and meet Kit at hers. I take her hands in mine, looking down at the ring before gazing into her big, blue eyes. "This is a promise. A promise to love you and cherish you, and a promise that one day, when we're ready, I'll replace it with a new ring. It's also a dare."

"A dare, huh?"

"Yep. I dare you to accept it and promise me forever because, without you, forever doesn't exist."

She looks at me in awe. One little look that makes me feel like the luckiest man alive. It's the same one I give her every time I walk into a room. "Well, I accept your dare and I raise you a double dare."

"This is new. I'll bite."

"I dare you to kiss me."

I bite the corner of my lip before leaning in and pressing my mouth to hers. "Dare accepted."

CHAPTER
FORTY-FOUR
KIT

The hospital therapist I've been seeing told me it could be therapeutic to write a letter to Carter, telling him how I feel.

I flip open my journal and a bunch of sticky notes and pictures fall to the floor. Ignoring them, I grab a pen and sit on the edge of my bed.

Dear Carter,

The dust has settled, and the house is quiet. Family from all over came to celebrate your life with us. Practically the entire town was here. You were so loved. You *are* so loved.

I miss you.

I miss your voice, your smile, your laugh. Even that nasty look you'd give me when I did something you'd disagree with. I miss the way you'd give me a double take to make sure I was dressed appropriately before I walked out the front door.

Nothing feels real without you here. The days go by and I'm still stuck on the last conversation we had in your car on the way to school. I begged for you to understand. I cried for your approval. More than anything, I wanted you to tell me loving Ryker was okay and that he could love me back. When you didn't, I slammed the door, and I shut you out. I was fully prepared to choose him over you and Dad if it came to it. I hate myself for making that choice before I even had to. I should have known you'd never make me choose.

I've listened to the voicemail you left Ryker at least three dozen times. I have it saved on my phone just so I can hear your voice, but it kills me a little more each time I hear it. Because that message was proof that all you needed was time to come to terms with mine and Ryker's relationship.

I'm so sorry I lied to you. If only I'd told you sooner that I was falling for Ryker, then you would have had the time you needed and our last conversation might have been a positive one. Instead, it haunts me and I fear it always will.

You gave me a selfless gift, Carter. One that will prolong my life and give me so many years to fill it with memories and love. You're forever a part of me and I promise you I will take care of your heart—and Ryker will, too.

Every step I take, every mile I walk, every corner I turn—you're with me. Sometimes my heart does a brief flutter and I like to think it's you. I smile in response, place my hand over my heart, and whisper, "I love you, too."

I do. You were the best big brother. Made me soup when I was sick, lent a shoulder when I was sad. When Mom stepped out and Dad had to work, you stepped in. You took care of me when you didn't have to. Now it's my turn to take care of you. Ryker said you wanted to travel, and now you will. We're going to spend an entire year going to all the places I know you'd love to visit. I'm going to fill this heart with the best memories for us.

I won't let you down, big brother.

I love you always, Kit

EPILOGUE
RYKER

Five years later.

There will come a point where my life with Kit is cut short. When that time comes, I'll beg and plead for them to take my heart because, without her, mine will be broken anyways. Selfishly, I want to keep her forever, even when I've been more than fortunate to have this sliver of time in her life. She's my past and my present, and I'm lucky enough to have her in my future. My entire world is wrapped up in that beautiful girl with her hand resting on our unborn son. Tomorrow isn't promised, but we always have today. No matter how far she travels when she leaves this earth, our love will never go far.

Kit looks over, catching my stare, and a smile parts her lips. "What are you doing home so early?"

I unbutton my left sleeve and roll it up, then the other, as I cross the room. "Cut out early to take my beautiful wife to dinner." I lean forward and press my lips to her forehead.

"Out for dinner? I thought you and Ezra were working on the Chevelle tonight?"

It's been a good bonding experience, working on the old car with my brother. He's married now, too, and attending community college locally, while giving a hand at the shop. During his free time, we've been rebuilding the engine in the Chevelle. It's taken more time than we planned, but life doesn't care about our plans.

"We are. Later. First, we're celebrating."

"What's the special occasion?"

I slouch down beside her, grinning. "As if you don't know. You've only texted me at least ten times today, beaming with excitement."

"I know." She smirks. "I just want to hear you say it."

"I'm taking you to dinner to celebrate the publishing of your first book."

"Ahhh," she squeals, "can you believe it?"

"Most definitely. I never doubted you for a second."

Four years ago when we were traveling across the country on a road trip, Kit pulled out her journal and started writing entries about grief and loss. It started as something therapeutic for her, and even me, but eventually, it became something for everyone else experiencing the same issues. Every night she returned to it and little by little, she finished. Last year, it was picked up by a publishing house. Today, it's finally been published.

Kit jolts, her hand still on her stomach. "He just kicked!" Grabbing my hand, she places it beneath hers.

My fingers tap as I try to grab baby Carter's attention.

I wait anxiously to feel that small movement for the first time.

A bump to my hand has my heart sprinting.

"Did you feel that?" She beams with excitement.

I look up at Kit, all smiles. "Yeah, baby. I felt it."

That little kick coming from the little life growing inside my wife's body beneath my best friend's heart is proof that the little things aren't to be missed. Whether it's a moment in time, a memory etched in your mind, or a candy bar before bed. One day, they all become the big things.

Hold them tight. Never let them go. Because one day, even the big things will fade to just a memory.

The end.

Thank you for reading!
I hope you enjoyed Kit and Ryker's story.
If you like the forbidden trope, check out Devil Heir: A stepsibling romance.

ACKNOWLEDGMENTS

Thank you, readers for taking the time to read All The Little Things. I hope you enjoyed Ryker and Kit's story. I want to give a big thank you to everyone who helped me along the way. My alpha reader, Amanda and my beta readers, Erica, Brittni and Kerri. Candi Kane PR, thank you for all you've done to help me promote and get the word out. My amazing PA, Carolina for all you do. Thanks to Rebecca at Rebecca's Fairest Reviews and Editing for another amazing edit and proofread, as well as Rumi for proofreading. To my street team, the Rebel Readers, I love you all so much and I'm so grateful for all you do. Thanks to Cassie at Opulent Swag and Designs for this gorgeous cover! And to all my Ramblers, thanks for being on this journey with me. xoxo-Rachel

ALSO BY RACHEL LEIGH

Bastards of Boulder Cove

Book One: Savage Games

Book Two: Vicious Lies

Book Three: Twisted Secrets

Wicked Boys of BCU (Coming March 2023)

Book One: We Will Reign

Book Two: You Will Bow

Book Three: They Will Fall

Redwood Rebels Series

Book One: Striker

Book Two: Heathen

Book Three: Vandal

Book Four: Reaper

Redwood High Series

Book One: Like Gravity

Book Two: Like You

Book Three: Like Hate

Fallen Kingdom Duet

His Hollow Heart & Her Broken Pieces

Black Heart Duet

Four & Five

Standalones

Guarded

Ruthless Rookie

Devil Heir

All The Little Things

Claim your FREE copy of Her Undoing!

ABOUT THE AUTHOR

Rachel Leigh is a USA Today bestselling author of new adult and contemporary romance with a twist. You can expect bad boys, strong heroines, and an HEA.

Rachel lives in leggings, overuses emojis, and survives on books and coffee. Writing is her passion. Her goal is to take readers on an adventure with her words, while showing them that even on the darkest days, love conquers all.

www.rachelleighauthor.com
Rachel's Ramblers Readers Group

Printed in Great Britain
by Amazon